T0373522

THE BROKEN SPEAR

A NOVEL ABOUT VICTIM VICTORY

JACOB M. VAN ZYL

WESTBOW
PRESS
A DIVISION OF THOMAS NELSON

All scripture quotations, unless otherwise indicated, are taken from the New King James Version®. Copyright © 1982 by Thomas Nelson, Inc. Used by permission. All rights reserved.
Scripture quotations marked (NIV) are taken from the Holy Bible, New International Version®, NIV®. Copyright © 1973, 1978, 1984 by Biblica, Inc.™ Used by permission of Zondervan. All rights reserved worldwide. www.zondervan.com

WestBow Press books may be ordered through booksellers or by contacting:

WestBow Press
A Division of Thomas Nelson
1663 Liberty Drive
Bloomington, IN 47403
www.westbowpress.com
1-(866) 928-1240

ISBN: 978-1-4497-1008-8 (sc)
ISBN: 978-1-4497-1009-5 (e)

Library of Congress Control Number: 2010942171

Printed in the United States of America

WestBow Press rev. date: 1/7/2011

~~~~~~~~~~~

⁷ The LORD of hosts *is* with us;
The God of Jacob *is* our refuge.
⁹ He makes wars cease to the end of the earth;
He breaks the bow and cuts the spear in two;
He burns the chariot in the fire.[1]

~~~~~~~~~~~

---

1   Psalm 46:7, 9

CHAPTER 1

To life! With this toast, a persecuted nation celebrates the wonder of life, gratefully remembering their survival of numerous genocide attempts.

Man and beast exert themselves to survive—by fight, flight, or submission. Respecting the pecking order prevents conflict in and among species. If not, lethal fights for dominance occur. Man's inconsistent rules about self-defense confuse those in mortal danger. As a result, surviving in violent circumstances has been a dreadful yet intriguing challenge for people of every time and place.

The Roman era was a violent time. In the first century, forty-eight miles west of Athens, Corinth guards a land-bridge between two gulfs. The Gulf of Corinth stretches to the west and the Saronic Gulf to the east of the isthmus that joins the Peloponnesus to mainland Greece, determining Corinth's lucrative socio-economic activities and lifestyle.

In the spring of every third year, the year before and after the Olympics, Corinth hosts the Isthmian Games on the southeast corner of the isthmus, honoring Poseidon, god of the sea, for bringing the trade ships to Corinth.

Boys regularly see athletes practicing on the sports fields or competing in the stadium. Youngsters revere the champions they observe more than the gods they can't see. From early childhood, the amazing feats of their heroes have been imprinted on their minds and hearts. In their play, they mimic those they adore.

After school, small peer groups gather at open ground, developing their skills by testing their speed and strength against each other. Gradually, they come to know their fortes, sorting themselves into long distance runners, sprinters, wrestlers, jumpers, archers, or discus and javelin throwers.

In the time of Caesar Caligula, about AD 38, a group of five boys are seriously working on their javelin abilities. Among them are two lads—Jason, a lean nine-year-old with curly black hair and soft black eyes, and Krato, a sturdy eleven-year-old with short black hair and intense yellow eyes. Being the oldest and toughest, Krato bosses the others.

Jason's dad builds wagons for carrying goods between Corinth's west and east harbors, one on each side of the isthmus. Krato's dad has a security business, providing safe passage for the wagons between the harbors. Jason wants to become a wagon builder like his dad. Krato aspires to surpass his father by becoming an officer in the Roman army.

This group of boys has something in common: They are gifted with special sensitivity and coordination for hurling the javelin and discus farther than others in their age group. By friendly competition, they spur each other on to greater excellence.

"Come on, pumpkin-heads, try harder! See if you can beat me," Krato incites his "soldiers," who acknowledge his superior skills, but silently detest his controlling manner.

Two of them try again, hurling their spears—made of straight tree shoots—as hard as they can. The javelins land a few paces short of Krato's. Then it's Jason's turn. Though he is lean and not as beefy as Krato, Jason shows excellent coordination and smoothness of motion. He has a deep-seated desire to beat Krato, shutting up his big mouth and ending his teasing and name-calling.

The complexion of Jason and his dad is slightly darker than that of the average Greek. Rumor has it that many generations ago, an Ethiopian chief married an Egyptian girl and became part of Jason's bloodline, with fourteen other great-great grandparents. Krato uses this gossip to tease Jason about his bronze tan, calling him a slave.

"Now let's see what the African slave can do," Krato taunts, hoping to unsettle Jason, whose distances have been creeping up on Krato's lead. Actually, Krato likes Jason, but Jason is too meek for Krato's taste. By teasing Jason, stirring up his anger and assertiveness, Krato tries to make a man of him. Krato never could have guessed the eventual outcome of his efforts.

"Don't hold it that way, stupid," Krato corrects his junior, helping Jason to alter his grip on the javelin and the position of his arm. "Turn your upper-body this way, idiot. Stretch your arm back full length, then hurl with your arm while twisting your upper-body swiftly in the direction of the throw; it adds power to your arm," Krato instructs his junior pedantically, showing how it's done.

Before he throws, Jason first practices the movement Krato has demonstrated. Jason is eager to learn Krato's secrets in order to beat him some day. When Jason makes the throw, he immediately feels there is more power in his movements. His javelin hits the ground only one pace behind Krato's mark.

"Well, I'll be damned—you almost equaled me," Krato reacts, amazed and unsettled by Jason's sudden success. "Good shot, slave-boy, good shot! See, you will improve if you listen to your master. Now don't get big-headed, sucker, I haven't put in my best yet," Krato adds, giving Jason a soft kick in the butt.

Jason reacts by making an ugly face, sticking out his tongue at Krato. In a tit-for-tat exchange, Krato shoves Jason at the shoulder. Jason staggers backwards, pulling faces again.

Krato ends the exchange by giving Jason a backhand swipe on the cheek. Ouch! It hurts—skin and ego. Jason is subdued, boiling with anger on the inside.

"Don't you get hard-ass with me, slave-boy, you will be sorry for it," Krato warns in a bossy voice, his face only a few inches from Jason's.

Jason wants to grab Krato, wrestle him to the ground, and punch him in the face. However, Jason knows that he is still too light for the husky Krato. Jason lacks the courage and confidence to take on the bully. He fears he will lose the fight, and that it will only increase Kato's teasing and derogatory remarks. So Jason swallows his pride, endures the injustice, and waits, with suppressed anger, for the day he can turn the tables.

Jason has mixed feelings now about his success with the javelin. He feels good to have come so close to Krato's effort, giving his opponent a pretty good scare. Jason cannot help but smile with satisfaction. However, he hates owing his improvement to Krato, the arrogant pest he hates and who once again has humiliated him in presence of his friends. Beating Krato with the javelin gradually becomes an obsession for Jason.

After they have recorded their best distances for the day, they proceed with target practice. Krato cuts a cross on a huge leave of a prickly pear cactus. They take turns hurling their spears at the target from a fifteen-pace distance. As lion cubs develop their predator skills by play-fighting each other, these boys are unknowingly perfecting techniques that may help them survive life-threatening situations later in their lives.

When the son touches the sea in the west, they know it's time to return home for supper—mom's orders.

"One day, Krato," Jason vows by himself as he lingers home, "one day...when we're grown up...there will be a day of reckoning."

The survival of the fittest is sometimes thwarted by the sheer tenacity of the underdog. It happens when Jason is bullied and humiliated by his pugnacious rival. It will not be a quick fix, though, rather a long trek.

*

While his mother is still preparing supper, Jason pays a visit to his grandpa, Hermes, who lives in a separate backyard room. As usual, the sixty-eight-year-old man, with silvery medium-length hair and beard, is working outside his room on his hobby of sculpting marble statuettes.

"Hi, Grandpa," Jason greets, without his usual gusto.

A quick glance from Hermes confirms that something is bothering his grandson. He knows he will have to draw it out of him with patience, wisdom, and understanding.

"Wow, Grandpa! You've made great progress on the warrior!" Jason strokes his hand lovingly over the polished area of the statuette. He can see that the polishing is really bringing the eighteen-inch figure to life. The intense determination and action of the warrior show in his attacking posture, bulging muscles, and facial expression.

"How was your afternoon?" Hermes inquires, focusing attentively on the statuette.

When Jason does not shower him immediately with all of the adventures he and his playmates have had, Hermes is even more convinced of a lurking problem.

"How did you do with the new javelin we cut a few days ago? Did it wobble?" Hermes plans to move gradually from things to people.

"No, it was great—I almost beat that jerk!"

"A-hum..." Hermes knows he's getting warmer.

"By playing submissive, as you told me, Grandpa, I got Krato to share some of his javelin secrets with me," Jason begins to open up with a glow of satisfaction in his eyes.

"You did, hey?" Hermes shows a little of his suppressed excitement, glad that his advice helped his grandson.

"So, what was the big secret?" Hermes probes.

"The movement of my arm and the movement of my upper-body must go together. As my arm shoots forward, I must twist my body swiftly in the same direction, giving more power and speed to the javelin," Jason says, showing what he means.

"Well, that looks like good advice. Did it work?" Hermes rests his hands on the statuette. He looks at Jason with keen interest and a faint smile.

"Oh yes! I practiced the movement a few times before throwing—just to get the feeling, you know. When I threw, I could feel I had more power. My javelin landed only one pace short of Krato's. I wish you could've seen his face!" Jason relishes his success with a crow of laughter.

"Yes, I guess you shook him up pretty well. He realized you're blowing on his neck," Hermes remarks, hoping Jason will proceed with the rest of the story.

"Then everything went wrong." Jason's face falls. He frowns as he plays with a piece of marble. He does not want to be a crybaby, but this darned thing is so deep and painful; he will not be able to get it out without letting out the feelings, too. Jason puts his forehead on his arm resting on the workbench. His anger and hurt blend into tears. He starts sobbing. His grandpa is the only person with whom he can share this dark secret of his life. They have talked about it before.

"He began to call me names again," Jason squeaks, sniffling. "He said I'm just a slave from Africa. He kicked me in the butt, and said I must know my place as a slave. I hate him! I hate him!" Jason hisses, banging the piece of marble on the desk.

"What an asshole!" Hermes blurts. He usually moderates his language in his grandson's presence.

Jason laughs through his tears, concurring, "Yes, he is, he is!"

"I hope you punched him on the nose!"

"I wish I could," Jason says, wiping his tears, "That's the problem, Grandpa; I'm two years younger, and he is stronger. I know I will lose the fight and then things will only get worse."

"So you just had to swallow the humiliation, hey?"

"I stuck out my tongue at him," Jason chuckles, "He got mad and shoved me. I did it again, and he slapped me. Oh, how I wish I could beat the bully!"

"Patience, my son, patience!" Hermes knows the abscess has been opened. The time has come to put some balm on the wound.

"Great victories are won by years of good preparation, my son," Hermes comforts him. "Just a few years from now, in your early twenties, the two-year difference will fall away. Believe me! It now looks far off, but if you focus on your development instead of brooding on revenge, time will pass quickly. Don't allow this fellow to mess up your life."

Hermes talks slowly, resembling a wise old prophet at the Oracle of Delphi, allowing every sentence to sink in. Jason listens attentively. He knows his grandpa. When he shares his wisdom, it is best to shut up and listen.

"You have done the right thing today, Jason. I'm proud of you. That's what discerns a real man from a bar-fighter. A real man can control his fear and anger while he patiently waits for a better opportunity. The best choice is seldom a perfect choice. Often we have to choose the best among imperfect options. Even in the heat of battle, the real man keeps his cool. Then he can use his weapons and abilities to the best. When panic or anger overcomes the warrior, his enemy will also overcome him."

Jason connects his grandfather's words about war with the figure of the warrior he is working on.

"Did you fight in a war, Grandpa?" Jason wonders, watching the tender care his grandpa bestows on the statuette.

Maybe this figure represents a moment in his grandpa's life. Maybe the warrior is his grandpa.

Hermes resumes his polishing on the statuette. After a while he says, sighing, "Yes, I did." Jason senses that it is a sensitive issue his grandpa would rather avoid.

"Did you kill some of the enemy?" The boy's innocent dark eyes search the face of his grandfather for the truth of his past. Jason's straight question suddenly jolts the old man back in time, back to his moment of truth about life and death. He stops polishing. He stares far away into the distant past.

"I had to," he admits softly.

"Did you feel guilty, Grandpa?" Jason wonders.

After another moment of silent pondering, Hermes tries to shed light on a dark side of human conduct: the reality of war and the key to survival.

"In war, you don't have a choice: It is either kill or be killed. If you don't get him first, he will get you. I suppose it is the same in the arena...or when one is attacked by robbers. Those guys mean business. It's not a game."

He turns, looks straight at Jason, and emphasizes in serious tone, "My son, I hope you never get into such a situation, but if you ever do, defend your life to the best of your ability. Never give up your right to LIVE—not for one moment!"

Riveting the nails, he continues, "That's what our commander told us the night before the battle. It saved my life the next day. I had my doubts about war and violence. If I went into battle half-heartedly, I would have been killed within a few minutes."

Jason senses that his grandpa is sharing something near to his heart with him, wisdom that has been polished over the years—like the statuette he is working on.

"The commander also gave us a piece of his mind I will never forget. He said, 'You have only one life; so, protect it with all your might. Don't allow anybody to rob you of your one precious life. Prevent the enemy from doing so, even if he is killed in the process. In war, you have to kill the enemy so that you and your comrades can live. That's the simple logic of war.' Yes, that's what the commander told us. I guess those words stuck with me because they saved my life. I'm glad I can pass them on today. Maybe you'll need them in future."

Jason is impressed by his grandfather's seriousness, sharing something that has been buried deep in his soul for many years.

"Supper is ready!" Jason's mother calls. That's an order they always obey immediately, spurred by their rumbling tummies.

"Thanks, Grandpa, I feel much better," Jason remarks.

"You're welcome. Don't worry too much about that sucker. Focus on your development. Eat your food; keep practicing. Good planning and hard work will bring you out on top," Hermes concludes his lesson.

Jason decides to eat all the food his mother puts on his plate from now on, and help move heavy stuff at his dad's workshop so that he can become stronger than Krato. He is ready and willing to make sustained inputs to achieve his goal—moving from victim to victor.

As the years slowly roll by, the repeated confrontations between Jason and Krato reinforce Jason's resolve to shake off the dominance of his archrival. Defeating Krato becomes a life-goal for Jason, a dream he has to make reality to regain his self-respect. In his imagination, Jason envisages a grand revenge. He can see and hear the applause of the crowd when his javelin lands two...no, ten paces ahead of Krato's best.

*

Twelve years later, Jason is a sturdy twenty-one year old, working in his dad's workshop where wagons are built and serviced. He and a few workmen are heating the iron band of a wagon wheel in a circle of glowing charcoal in the backyard of the workshop.

This age-old method makes iron bands fit tightly on spoke wooden wheels. The band—slightly smaller than the wheel—is expanded by heat, put on the wheel, and quickly cooled by water to make it contract, bracing the wheel.

Two workmen assist Jason. They love and respect their six-foot-six-inch broad-shouldered supervisor who became their friend. Jason has a soft spot for underdogs. He knows the feeling.

Perforated earthen pipes surround the coal circle. With bellows, the men blow air through the pipes to flare up the charcoal, heating the hoop to red-hot condition.

While the hoop is being heated, the wooden wheel is soaked in water to prevent damage to the wood when the hot band is placed around it. When the hoop is ready, the men lay the wheel flat on the ground, lift the hoop with iron hooks, and carry it to the wheel. It takes quick and precise cooperation to put the hoop on the wheel correctly, hammer it into place, and douse it with water before the hot iron damages the rim.

Jason and his helpers prepare the next hoop in the same manner. The procedure is jeopardized by a dangerous slip. Short-tempered by his hangover, Jason shouts at the helpers to hurry. In his haste, he stumbles over a brick on the ground. The hoop tilts, and the others panic and let go as well, jumping away from the falling band. Sparks and curses fly. They quickly pick up the band with the hooks and proceed with the risky operation.

Jason's dad approaches, wiping his strong, hard hands on a dirty cloth.

"Jason," Philip says softly but sternly, gesturing with his head, "please, come over here for a moment."

Jason knows his dad. Such a sidebar usually spells trouble. He leaves the pouring of water on the hoop to the workers and joins his dad at the workbench.

"Son, you could have hurt yourself or the men badly with such carelessness—remember you work with searing hot iron! That's not how I taught you!"

Philip does not look at Jason, but keeps filing a piece of iron. It's painful to scold the apple of his eye. Jason knows he was wrong. There's no point in defending himself against his dad's better judgment.

"Sorry, Dad," he mutters with a frown. He shakes his head and explains, "This damn hangover is killing me."

"That's no excuse!"

"I know, Dad, I know, I know, I know! I'm sorry."

In a soft but stern voice, Philip hammers in his advice, staccato style.

"You have to cut down, Jason. Don't throw your young life to the dogs. Break company with that scum. Go out with good friends. Enjoy life in moderation. Trust me. I was young, too. I've tried both ways. Drunkenness has no rewards—only penalties."

In the best of times, Philip finds it hard to express his affection for his only son. Jason suspects his dad's advice may arise from protective love. He assumes his dad cares about him. He says it in many non-verbal ways, but never in words.

For a moment, Jason glances from the side at Philip's stern face and pepper-gray hair. He loves his no-nonsense "old man." Though Philip is only forty-seven, the fine wrinkles around his eyes and mouth testify to the toughness of his vocation.

"Son, if you go on like this, that centurion will crush you into the dust at the next games. We don't want that, do we?"

This remark makes the hair on Jason's neck stand up.

Philip's straight and honest reprimand hits Jason's recent poor self-esteem as well as his secret plans of revenge. He is proud of his dad, and he wants this feeling to be mutual. Sadly, his recent decline has eroded their relationship.

"Yes, Dad, you're right," he confesses, adding with determination, "I must and I will." He does not respond to Philip's reference to the centurion. That topic is too sensitive to discuss. Jason wishes he could have had the same open relationship with his dad that he had with his grandpa, who passed away two years ago.

"I'm proud of you, Jason. Please, don't spoil my joy."

It's the first time Philip has said something so positive to him. A warm, good feeling fills Jason's heart.

Philip has hammered the nail deep enough. He will not rub salt into the wounds any more. He changes his tone.

"I suggest you go home and freshen up," he says casually. Jason knows it's a command in disguise.

"Come back this afternoon when you feel better."

With that, Jason is dismissed. Actually, with his headache, he is immensely grateful for the break, though embarrassed about his blunder.

"Thanks, Dad," he whispers. He turns around and leaves. Blushing, he winks at the workmen who try to suppress their giggles. He hates to be sent home, like an unruly child to his room. He has to admit—he deserves it.

This is the first time this has happened, and it's going to be the last, Jason solemnly vows by himself. He wants to please his dad—and the two girls he likes a lot.

Why do I burden myself with drinking? he wonders. *It's my worst enemy!*

*

On his way to the public baths, he picks up clean clothes at home. He gives his mother, Irene, a quick kiss on the cheek, scoots off, and says, "Don't ask questions!"

With a knowing smile, she can only say, "Take care!" before he's out by the door. She is not surprised he was no good at work. He came in so late last night, falling over a chair, probably half-drunk. She's concerned about her little boy who plunged into young-adult problems too soon. Her seventeen-year-old daughter, Helena, still stays in line.

Jason loiters listlessly along a back street of Corinth, half aware of a few people coming and going. The sun hangs high above Acrocorinth, the mountain south of the city. It is a hot day in late summer. Jason feels sweaty.

He can only vaguely recall who was with him last night at the Seaman's Inn. A few scenes flash through his mind. *I probably made a fool of myself again.*

He wants to become the discus and javelin champion at the Isthmian Games, yet sometimes he knowingly abuses his athletic body. This inconsistency puzzles and haunts him. He has promised himself many times not to go overboard again, just to fail miserably after a few good weeks. Deep inside, he begins to realize: *I'm trying to prove my manhood in a stupid way.*

He was crowned discus and javelin victor in the under-twenty division at the last games. "But look at me now!" he whispers. Since his grandpa passed away, Jason has lost his focus. He knows his grandpa would not have approved of his present lifestyle. His bad feelings about himself nudge him in the right direction—learning from his mistakes.

The back street bars and brothels he passes are desolate now. In daylight, they appear dirty and repulsive to Jason. Flies crawl over spots in the street where guys vomited or urinated last night. The sour odor of spilled wine mingles with the rotten stench of old garbage. The business of these joints soars from evening till the early morning hours in the dim light of oil lamps, when the inebriate customers, including himself, are less fastidious.

Thanks to its strategic location, Corinth prospers from both east-west sea trade and north-south land trade. Corinth's nightlife caters to the pleasures of the workers, supervisors, and owners of Corinth's lucrative transport and shipping industry. His dad's wagon business depends on this weird economy.

The sea route around the Peloponnesus peninsula is hazardous. Most seafarers choose to unload their cargo at Cenchrea or Lechaion (Corinth's east and west harbors, named after the sons of Poseidon), transport the goods by wagon from one harbor to the other eight miles away, and load it on another ship to proceed to the destination. After unloading their cargo, smaller boats are hauled by trolley over the four mile wide isthmus, using the Diolkos, a narrow stone-paved road.

Sadly, Corinth's hard work and good money spawns indulgence and excess. Taverns and brothels increased and flourish. The city's immoral ways have become proverbial. Even in other parts of the Roman Empire, a person with a wild lifestyle is labeled a "Corinthian." Jason cannot understand why he sometimes enjoys and sometimes hates being part of this unhealthy lifestyle.

*

With wandering thoughts, Jason has loitered closer to the city center with its shops and people.

Suddenly, he stops in his tracks. For a moment, he considers disappearing into an alley, but it's too late. She has seen him, waved, and called his name.

"Damn it!" he whispers, "I don't want her to see me in this condition."

Tabitha is a handsome, innocent, seventeen-year-old Jewish girl. She and Jason's sister Helena are friends. The better acquainted Jason has become with Tabitha, the more he likes her. Her dad has a front-line shop at the downtown shopping square, also called *agora* by Greeks and *forum* by Romans.

"Hi, Tabitha!" He returns her greeting with a sheepish grin. He doesn't want her to know of his bad side. She comes from a religious family.

"Pardon my looks. I'm on my way to the baths," he tries to excuse his appearance.

They stroll together. She ignores his uneasiness and continues the conversation with her usual bubbly spontaneity. Though self-conscious and shy, she's focused on her plan.

"My dad asked me to invite you to our Sabbath supper. Will you come? Please?" she asks sweetly, with a blush on her cheeks and a twinkle in her eyes. She hides the real reason for the invitation.

Jason stops, turns to her, and looks into those large, innocent, smiling brown eyes, set in her beautiful almond-shaped face. Her dark brown hair is bound up, with two long locks draping down behind her ears. Jason notices her maturing curves beneath her attire. He enjoys her youthful beauty while he considers her invitation.

He regains confidence, takes her hands in his, and says with his best smile, "Now who can decline an invitation coming from such a pretty face?"

"So your answer is 'yes'?" she giggles with excitement.

"Of course!"

He likes her and would like to hold her, but hesitates.

"I wish I could give you a hug, young lady, but look at me!" he blurts. He's still in his dirty work clothes. There are black marks on his chin and arms.

"This one is not dirt; it's your trademark," she says lovingly, touching the small brown birthmark on his left upper arm.

He smiles, appreciating her friendship. She's not like his other female friends. Something in him wants to treat her like a lady, though she's still a teenager.

"Thanks for accepting my invitation! You won't be sorry," she coos, with relief and excitement.

"I know," he responds, chuckling, "your meals don't give me a hangover."

She cannot hide her excitement, "My sisters will be green with envy when you sit next to me at the table!"

Jason can see that she cherishes the thrill of the moment. Tabitha's inner goodness is radiated by her friendly face. Her waggish laughter accompanied by a cute, pleated nose bridge steals his heart. In times of trouble, he turns to her for comfort.

They stroll on, chatting about the coming visit. She promises Jason there will be a surprise for him.

After they have walked and talked for a while, Jason excuses himself and turns off in the direction of the baths.

"See you Friday night!" they said together, waving.

*

Jason decides that Tabitha must never see him with one of his wild girlfriends. He knows she adores him, and he wants to keep it that way. From his side, he places her on a pedestal. In his eyes, she's pure.

Part of him enjoys the wild parties, drinking, and easy girls; part of him longs for better things, things that do not give remorse the next day, things personified by Tabitha.

He proceeds on his way to the public baths.

"Maybe a quick dip will pick me up," he decides. "I'll feel better when I look better."

After he has washed himself in a cubicle, he dives into the large pool and swims a few lengths. The cool water cleanses his skin and relaxes his body and soul.

He leans with his back against the side of the pool, stretching his long, strong arms sideways on the rim like the wings of a soaring eagle. His body floats. He closes his eyes and rests the back of his head on the edge of the pool. His feelings soar as his thoughts linger with Tabitha, his innocent little turtle dove.

She really does something good to me, he dreams on. *Dad spurs me to a better life, but Tabitha inspires me! I will do it for her. I know this desire comes from the real me, the better me.* His idealism carries him away. *Will she be my bride someday?*

The consequences of this thought churn in his mind. Cultural differences are less important to young people like them than to their parents, but will her Jewish parents ever get over their hearts to give their daughter in marriage to a Greek? Though Jews of the Diaspora are more lenient toward other cultures than the ultra-orthodox of Jerusalem, it is also a fact that mixed marriages always have been taboo for Jews since the time of Moses.

Jason has lost track of time. He can't remember how long he has been daydreaming. He swims two pool lengths and pulls himself vigorously out of the water.

*

When Jason leaves the bath area, he runs into Diana, who bathed in the women's section to rid her of the mental haze caused by last night's indulgence.

They greet and hug casually. Her perfume smells great. It awakens strong sensual feelings in Jason. He wishes he could jump into bed with her right away.

Diana, a sexy twenty-year-old girl with a round face, high cheek bones, and alluring green eyes, is from a Greek family. Their many gods do not interfere much with the sexual morality of the worshipers. Sex is as natural to them as eating pork in a Greek temple. The goddess of fertility, Aphrodite, expects them to honor her with luscious feasts before she sends rain every year.

Until the Romans destroyed Corinth two hundred years ago, the Aphrodite temple on the summit of Acrocorinth housed one thousand temple prostitutes. When Julius Caesar rebuilt Corinth ninety years ago, the Aphrodite temple was not restored. Its sensual services shifted to the brothels in Corinth.

They proceed hand-in-hand along Lechaion Road in the direction of the *agora*. In Diana's company, Jason feels like a man. He gazes up to Acrocorinth. Ah, life is good!

His adoration for Tabitha and her respectable lifestyle fades into the fog of his sensual feelings for Diana. He likes both of them, for different reasons. Tabitha will be a wonderful soul mate, Diana a superb sex mate. He knows he can't have both. It is as irreconcilable as having a drunken and sober life together.

Maybe I can first enjoy Diana and then marry Tabitha, he reasons as he tries to solve the conflict in himself.

Diana's dad, Andreo, feels the burden of his transport business. His wagons creep daily between the two harbors, heavily laden with cargo from the ships.

Andreo entertains his customers—captains and traders—to keep their support. Because he does it often, he maintains moderation with food, wine, and women. His wife and two daughters often enjoy dinner and music with guests, but they don't get sexually involved with customers.

It's another story, though, when Diana parties with her friends. Jason has watched her often. She enjoys attracting admirers like moths around a candle. She uses her sex appeal to get what she wants. She does not do it haughtily, but spins her web with the soft silk of polite friendliness.

As Jason and Diana walk over the *agora* square, they notice a platoon of Roman soldiers. They have just returned from a patrol on horseback to the isthmus. The horses are wet with white sweaty patches. Apparently, the soldiers were in a hurry.

Krato is in charge. He is now a lively centurion of the Roman military stationed at Corinth. He and Diana wave to each other. Jason ignores him deliberately. At twenty-three years, and six-foot-two-inches tall, Krato has made rapid progress in the army, thanks to his iron will and muscular frame. His family, Romans originally from Sicily, is in the security business. Their guards ensure the safety of wagons between the two ports. Krato grew up with a strong sense of power.

When they get to Diana's home, she gives Jason a goodbye hug that puts him on fire. She presses her body against his. Through their thin summer clothing, he can feel her breasts, pelvis, and thighs. After a while, she moves her head backwards, eyes closed. Jason grabs the invitation. It's their first kiss. Her lips are soft and moist. She smells wonderful.

His heart bounces, his blood rushes. By the gods, this is good! He wishes it could go on for ever. He stretches the moment as long as possible.

She pushes him gently away, lures him with her green panther eyes, winks, giggles, and throws a kiss at him—a cat playing with a mouse. Knowing that he is burning with lust, she tiptoes away and disappears into the house.

Diana's teasing goodbye brought Jason close to climax. He proceeds home, numb in the loins, confused in the mind. His heart is divided. Diana pulls him one way, Tabitha to the other. He is in love with both.

*

At home, Jason rests for a while in his dark bedroom, hoping his headache will further subsides. His thoughts keep whirling around Diana and Krato. This guy has always been a thorn in his side. If he wants Diana, Krato is the one to beat.

Jason recalls his unpleasant experiences with Krato. They have been rivals since school days. Being two years older, Krato was bigger and stronger. Jason remembers with bitterness how he repeatedly suffered under his teasing and bullying. Krato called him names. Jason knows how it feels to be the underdog. He has not forgotten his vow to take revenge when he is grown.

In the past few years, Jason has shot up and become four inches taller than Krato. Jason is less brawny, but more athletic than his archrival.

As teenagers, Krato had an edge over Jason in the discus and javelin events. However, since Jason matured, he has caught up with Krato. They competed in different divisions at the last games, but checked on each other's performance. Jason's distance with the discus was better than Krato's, thanks to Jason's superior swing with a longer arm. With the javelin, though, Krato was still a few paces ahead.

In the next games, they will be in the same division. Then it will be the great showdown between men in their prime. Jason has burdened himself with the obsession to defeat Krato at the next games. It will symbolize his triumph over Krato's reign.

Both of them admire Diana. Their virile, masculine bodies crave her voluptuous femininity. They have taken turns to flirt with her, but neither of them has won the big prize yet. Diana is attracted to both of them. She enjoys them for who they are, knowing that in the long run, Jason will probably be a better husband, but right now, Krato is more fun at parties.

*

After a good lunch at home, Jason goes back to work. He feels much better now.

He enjoys talking to the workers at the factory. Once they began to open up in his presence, he has learned a lot about the lifestyle, views, and values of the lower class. He has discovered they show remarkable simple wisdom and humor about the trials and tribulations of life.

Knowing that the Isthmian Games will take place over nine months, they fish for information on his training for the event.

"That centurion guy looks tougher than ever," one ventures. "I wonder if our man will measure up." With a naughty smile, he glances sideways at Jason.

"Yes, it will be a really bad advertisement for the factory if our man bites the dust—*really* bad!" another one adds pepper to the stew.

"My training goes well. Don't worry, guys, 'our man' will come out on top," Jason retorts with confidence.

They weigh his words. Is it big talk or real guts?

"I suppose a man can't be his best if he parties every night. Booze doesn't build muscles," one expresses his doubts, giving not-so-subtle advice, too.

"Not to say anything about the girls, that taps a man's strength," another rubs salt into the wounds.

"Will you guys get off my back!" Jason exclaims. "I know I have messed up the past few months, but I have recovered my balance. I'm doing fine," Jason defends himself, amused to be lectured by his workmen.

"How long will it last? That's the question," another adds a penny to the pouch. "I have seen reforms in this place before. Just a few weeks, and the strong man is on his knees again—like this morning," he hits the nail on the head.

"Just watch me. This time it's different," Jason vows.

"Want to bet?" the same guy tries his luck.

"Sure!" Jason holds out his right hand.

"What's the bet?" another asks.

"If Jason doesn't drink till the games are done, then we will bring him one twenty-pounder fish every week for five weeks. Five fish in total. However, if he drinks during this time, he will give each of us a twenty pounder fish. Do you all agree?"

"Agree!" his mates affirm.

"Agree!" Jason says, unwavering. They shake hands.

"I can already smell that fish," one of the guys retorts.

They exchange laughs and wisecracks about this deal with the son of the boss. They are fond of Jason. Deep in their hearts, they hope he will make it. They will gladly come up with the fish if he comes out on top.

Jason welcomes the deal. He knows the men are actually trying to help him. This bet will be a stone behind his wheel, preventing the wagon from running downhill again.

Jason is trying to sort out who he really is. His inner conflicts about lifestyle, values, girls, and male self-image blur his vision and rock his boat. He wants clarity and stability, but often obstructs his own objectives. Instead of developing an inner sense of direction, he relies on friends and circumstances to guide him in making the right choices. Maybe they will, but he won't always like the outcome.

CHAPTER 2

The daily pulsing life of Corinth brings prosperity and pleasure to some, but hardship and injustice to others. Laborers, slaves, oxen, and mules bear the burden of the labor-intensive economy.

A large ship carrying grain from Egypt, wool from Laodicea, purple fabric from Thyatira, and scroll-quality hides from Pergamos—all destined for Rome—has docked in Cenchrea, Corinth's east harbor. The pier is as busy as an ant's nest. By pulleys on long levers, workers haul cargo from the lower decks and swing it onto two-wheeled barrows. Slaves push the laden barrows from the ship over wooden gangways to waiting wagons where the goods are hoisted onto the vehicles.

The oxen and mules harnessed to the wagons are used to the activity and noise and patiently wait till the command is given to depart on the next arduous trek to Lechaion, Corinth's west harbor. The smell of fresh dung mingles with the odors of sea and merchandise. The calls of gulls, the shouting of supervisors, the rolling of wheels on the ship's deck, and the squeaking of the vessel against the dock create a symphony loved by some and hated by others.

Andreo, Diana's dad, stands on a conspicuous spot, chatting with Jason, whom he invited over to discuss some new railings he wants to install on his wagons. By observing the loading, Jason can get a better idea how the railings should work.

Philip's wagon industry and Andreo's transport business are interdependent. Both have entertained the idea that a marriage between Jason and Diana will bring the two enterprises even closer together. Jason tries to meet Andreo's expectations. It may count in his favor someday.

Jason's physical needs are not against such a possibility. After Tabitha, that will be his best option. Two Greek families will integrate easier than a Greek and a Jewish family ever could. However, knowing the lifestyle of Diana's family, he realizes that he will never be able to free himself from Corinth's excesses if he and Diana marry. Their lifestyle will suck him in like a whirlpool.

Andreo's mere presence motivates his supervisors to do their job well, regulating the flow of goods to the wagons. He is a well-off man with much influence. There is many a slip between the cup and the lip. If the slaves are not closely watched, some of the goods easily disappear between ship and wagon. The endless movement of workers and barrows serves as camouflage for snatch-thieves.

Two barrows bump against each other, merchandise falls off, and the workers swear loudly at one another, creating a distraction that enables a thief to steal something from another barrow. He is detected by a supervisor, who cracks his whip on the culprit's back, forcing him to drop his loot and scoot off.

Jason decides impulsively to intercept him. As the man runs through an opening between two stacks of wool bales, Jason's huge figure suddenly blocks his way. Jason grabs the short guy by the neck and arm, lifts him up, and presses him against the bales.

"What do you think you are doing?" Jason snarls.

"Hungry! Hungry!" the fellow croaks through his choked throat. Jason realizes the man is amazingly thin and light and probably starving, another underdog. Jason mellows. He lets him go with a warning. He tells Andreo that the man got away.

Another wagon has been loaded. The goods are covered by a tarpaulin, tightly fastened to the wagon to keep thieves and rain out. When the driver barks his command, the leader at the front end of the team pulls on the rope and yells "Come!" The oxen slowly move forward, the chain tightens, and the wagon—squeaking under its load—starts to rumble forth on its iron-rimmed wheels.

Jason has the needed information on the railings. He hikes a ride with the wagon back to Corinth. He hopes he can impress Andreo with well-made railings.

Wagons travel in groups. There is strength in numbers. Four guards walk alongside each wagon, two on each side, each armed with spear and dagger to deter robbers. To motivate them not to become robbers themselves, Krato's dad pays them a handsome fee for their services. If they screw up, they will never obtain work as guard again.

The city council of Corinth has laid out the roads between the two harbors in such a way that all transport has to move through tollgates on the city's north side. Bringing the wagon trail close to the city benefits the merchants, too. After a long walk, the guards and drivers need drinks and snacks.

The wagons move from Cenchrea westward to Corinth. Having paid the toll, they proceed north to Lechaion on the Gulf of Corinth. The location of city and harbors forms a triangle. The two-mile long Lechaion Road is paved with flat stones and protected by stone walls on either side. When Roman officials visit Corinth, they enter via this road.

The wear and tear on the wagons is considerable due to heavy loads and rocky roads. Consequently, Philip has an industrious workshop. He is burdened with the building and servicing of wagons to keep Corinth's economy going.

Wheels have to be repaired occasionally and refitted with shortened iron bands. Stones on the road hammer the iron rims, gradually thinning and stretching them in the process. The circumference of the hoop increases over time until it falls off. A short section of the hoop is then cut out and a new joint forged. The shortened hoop is refitted on the wheel by the heating and cooling method described earlier.

A convoy of wagons is needed to move the cargo of one ship between the two harbors of Corinth. Often, there are several ships to be serviced on the same day. Andreo depends on Philip's quick and efficient services.

The spin-off economy of Corinth's trade route stretches far into the Peloponnesus. The teams of animals have to be fed, as do the sailors of the ships and the workers at the ports. At night, the animals are corralled and guarded, and the slaves retire to their quarters, while other workers have to find a place to sleep after they have had their fun in Corinth's nightlife.

Many people make a living by selling services and goods to those involved in the industrious commercial activities in and around Corinth. The families of Jason, Tabitha, Diana, and Krato are part of this trade metropolis.

*

Early the next morning, Jason is at the Diolkos to test a new trolley from their workshop. Philip would like to be present, but he has to oversee some urgent repair work on some of Andreo's wagons at the workshop.

Hauling boats up to fifty feet in length over the isthmus created an additional industry for the city over the past six centuries. Originally, they dragged the boats on rollers. Improved iron production enabled the use of trolleys with small iron wheels.

Jason and his dad test improvements on their vehicles occasionally. Watching how the trolleys perform on the short and long term expose their weak and strong points. Jason is an inventor. He always comes up with plans to improve their products. Philip likes Jason's creativity, and gives him leeway to test his ideas.

Ordinary wagons have large rear wheels and small front ones for a reason. The front wheels run on a straight axle that can swivel on a pivot-pin in the middle of the axle. The wagon is steered by the pole attached to the front axle. Wooden blocks on top of this axle lift the front end of the wagon, allowing the small front wheels to swivel underneath the wagon in a sharp turn.

This front wheel structure has not been used on the Diolkos trolleys. The weight of the boats as well as the flatbeds of the trolleys made front wheel steering impossible. The old trolleys have eight wheels on four axles, spreading the load. To guide the small iron wheels to stay on the pavement, two grooves (five foot apart) were chiseled out in the pavement. Wear and tear over many years gradually erodes the grooves, making them less effective. Sections of the grooved pavement have been replaced.

Improvement of iron production enabled Jason to devise a new front wheel structure that allows steering movement on two front axles. It should diminish wear on both pavement and wheels. He mounted the two front axles close together on a sub-frame with an iron disk on top. This disk swivels against a rimmed disk mounted onto the four main beams beneath the flatbed of the trolley. The disks are kept in place by the rim of the upper disk and the pivot-pin running through the center of the disks. Jason moved the rear wheels farther back so they can follow the front wheels more easily.

Jason watches the loading of a boat onto the new trolley. At the water's edge, slaves drag the boat with ropes onto the cradle of the trolley, halfway submerged in the water. The trolley is much shorter than the boat, so the bow and stern overhang the front and rear ends of the trolley.

The slaves pull in unison on ropes attached to both sides of the boat. Jason has done away with whipping taskmasters.

He proved that with good teamwork, the slaves perform their tasks better and more easily. There is no need for the cruelty of the whip. They show their gratitude through loyal service to the man who improved their work situation.

With the trolley still halfway submerged under water, the boat is secured with ropes to the cradle on the trolley. A team of twelve oxen is now harnessed to the chains bolted to the trolley's front end. The oxen slowly put their massive strength to the yokes, while the slaves on both sides maintain tension on the ropes to steady the boat. Because of the trolley's narrow base, the slaves have to maintain a delicate balance, preventing the boat from tilting. The boat-on-trolley moves forward, out of the water, and up against the incline.

Jason watches the front wheels carefully. He risks his own safety by staying close to that crucial point. The boat looms above him. Will the steering mechanism survive the massive burden? His reputation is at stake. If his invention works, his dad may be proud of him and hopefully forgive his recent blunders.

At the west side of the isthmus, the Diolkos first turns to the left, then to the right, then straight ahead to the east side of the land-bridge. To Jason's relief, the pivot system survives the strain. By fixing the pulling chain of the oxen to the front end of the trolley, not to the front axles, Jason diminished the strain on the pivot-pin. The steering pole of the front wheels is attached to the yoke of the rear oxen only.

One of the slaves on the left side of the trolley stumbles, distracting his mates. The diminished tension on their ropes causes the boat to tilt to the side where Jason is inspecting the front axle. The slaves on Jason's side shout warnings. Six of them rush forward, propping up the leaning boat with sheer body power, preventing it from crushing the man who secured their humane treatment.

The cradle has been damaged. The two slave teams on each side of the trolley cooperate to pull the boat back into an upright position, while Jason rearranges the beams of the cradle to support the boat. Cautiously, they resume hauling.

Jason accompanies the boat-on-trolley to the other side. The flat stretches of the Diolkos present no problem. The team takes three breaks on the uphill side, and one on the downhill side. The slow procession completes the journey between two high tides. The slaves maintain moderate tension on the ropes, preventing the boat from tilting again.

On the east side, all the oxen—except for the two rear ones controlling the steering pole—are unhooked. Mules in full harness are hooked up to the rear of the trolley, assisting the slaves to act as brakes. Slowly, they allow gravity to pull the trolley and boat downhill. At the water's edge, the animals are unharnessed, the boat untied from the cradle, and the boat-on-trolley pushed into the water. When the rising tide lifts the boat, the slaves pull the trolley out.

Jason inspects the trolley after its strenuous journey. The slaves help to turn the trolley on its side so that Jason can see the wheels and axles better. He can't detect any damage. His invention passed the test.

He has proven his motto again: Obstacles can be overcome by smart planning and hard work. He believes he will beat Krato eventually with the same policy.

Savoring his success, Jason sighs with relief. His recent poor self-esteem receives a realistic boost. The thought arises that his success calls for celebration.

"No-no-no!" he corrects himself, "Not with booze!"

Satisfied with the outcome of the day's experiment, he returns on horseback to the workshop. He shares the good news excitedly with his dad. Philip's brief praise and pat on the back are cherries on the cake. Jason feels great. He is climbing out of the hole he dug for himself. His negative feelings about his recent relapses are being replaced by new ambitions for the future.

*

Tabitha often helps as assistant in her dad's shop, located at the downtown *agora*. Small shops of all kinds surround a stone-paved square where farmers sell their produce twice a week in makeshift stalls.

Isaac, Tabitha's dad, is a general dealer who, like many of his fellow Jews in foreign countries, makes his living by buying and selling.

Some Jews are zealously defending Orthodox Judaism against Christians who are winning over both Jews and Gentiles, exempting Gentile converts from keeping Jewish law. Caesar Claudius has recently banned all Jews from Rome, blaming them for frequent religious unrest. Many of these banned Roman Jews came to Corinth, the first stop east of Italy. Among them are Aquila and Priscilla, a married couple who are tentmakers.

Aquila met Isaac at the synagogue situated near the south end of Lechaion Road. Aquila invited him to visit his workshop the next day to see his products. Isaac recognized the excellent quality of Aquila's workmanship. He made a deal with Aquila to sell his products in his shop.

Tabitha is not yet aware of the deal. When someone asks for tent material, she says they don't have any in stock.

"We will soon have," her father interrupts, "I expect my supplier to deliver the day after tomorrow." He does not mention that tomorrow is Sabbath.

When the customer has left, Isaac tells Tabitha about his deal with Aquila. "My child," he adds in earnest whisper, "never say 'we haven't got it,' rather say, 'we will get it.'" He likes to teach his children the tricks of the trade.

"What if the client asks for an elephant?" Tabitha reacts, amused. Her dad burst into laughter.

"Then we get it!" he retorts between his giggles.

"We haven't got room for it in this place," she counters. Together, they enjoy the humor of the imagined situation.

"We'll tie it to the *bema* over there. It will shock the judge out of his sandals when he finds an elephant in his court!" Isaac shakes with laughter when he imagines the judge's amazement. He enjoys sharing fun with Tabitha.

Later, when the setting sun draws red lines on the Gulf of Corinth, Tabitha goes home to help her mother with supper. Jason is invited, and Sabbath starts at sunset. All preparations must be finished by then. She hurries home.

*

At the barracks of the Roman military the daytime duties are coming to a close. Some of the soldiers spend their last minutes on duty by honing their spearing skills. They use an old, dead tree trunk as target.

Krato enjoys showing off his superior abilities and conveying some of his expertise to the less experienced soldiers. When they apply his advice, there is indeed a marked improvement in their accuracy. The group cheers each other on as they make progress in the last rays of the setting sun.

There is no military threat to Corinth now, so the soldiers take turns for night duty. The others are free to spend the night with family or friends. Some try out the nightlife of the city. They are cautious, though. The commander tolerates no drunkenness or unruly behavior. Some have learned the hard way that the penalty for bad behavior is severe—latrine duty for six months!

When the dismiss bugle sounds, all cheer, leave what they were doing, and run towards their quarters to get ready for the night's adventure.

Krato goes home, changes to comfortable clothes, and departs to his secret workout place in a ditch on the foot of Acrocorinth. He has burdened himself with weightlifting to improve the strength of his bulging muscles even more. His apparatus is a five-foot iron rod with a wooden bucket hanging from either end. He uses stones in the buckets to increase or decrease the weight. He has come up with several movements to give exercise to his arms, legs, and torso.

Over the past few months, his distances with the discus and javelin have improved considerably. Sweating through his arduous workout, he sometimes smiles with delight, imagining the disbelief on Jason's face when Krato beats him at the next games.

He follows up his brisk workout with a quick bath at the public pool. He feels frisky, and looks forward to his evening with Diana. She invited him to accompany her to a friend's birthday party. He is determined to beat Jason in the race for Diana, too.

*

While Krato flirts with Diana, Jason arrives at Tabitha's home. Though he has been here several times, Jason is never quite at ease in the Jewish household. They are burdened by so many rules about what one can and can't do that Jason is always walking on eggshells, fearing he may inadvertently offend his host.

Never mind the darned law, he reasons, *I'm not here to study their law but to enjoy Tabitha.*

At supper, they stand around the table. Esther, Tabitha's mom, makes a few circling movements with her hands around two candles on silver stands while she chants a song. Isaac says a Hebrew prayer, praising God for his goodness and for the Sabbath. Tabitha and her two younger sisters, Hanna and Abigail, stands motionless, gazing down, wondering what their Greek friend makes of this Jewish ceremony. Jason has learned to hold his pose. Soon, he will enjoy the delicious meal.

"So, how was your day, Jason?" Isaac asks when they are seated, trying to start conversation while Esther dishes up for everyone.

"I tested my new invention," Jason says proudly.

"Invention!" the two younger girls exclaim.

Tabitha, who knows about the project, is all ears to hear the outcome. She hopes it was a success. Jason needs it.

"I made a new trolley for transporting boats over the isthmus," Jason explains, "one that has cranking front wheels. It will make the few turns on the Diolkos easier, reducing wear and tear on the trolley and on the stone pavement. We tested it today, and it worked well."

"Mazel Tov, Jason!" Isaac rejoices with him.

"Wow!" Hanna and Abigail echo.

"I'm so glad, Jason," Tabitha says, excited, "I know how much it means to you."

"Your parents will be proud of you," Esther adds.

"Do you think the cranking mechanism will stand up to the huge weight of the boats?" Isaac inquires, interested.

"I stayed with the trolley for the whole trip over the isthmus," Jason responds, "and everything worked properly. I hope that it will show the same toughness over time."

"Yes! Yes!" Isaac affirms. "We wish you the very best with this project. We are glad we can celebrate with you."

All lift their chalices, toasting Jason's triumph.

"To life!" they chorus enthusiastically.

Jason feels accepted and supported. *These Jews are okay, I'll fit in*, he thinks.

They continue with the meal, consisting of a superb fish dish, complemented with fresh home-made bread, butter, cheese, dates, and jam. Jason has learned from Tabitha that Jews may eat fish with dairy products. Esther buys products from a Jew, assuring that everything is kosher.

After a long day, Jason is hungry. He gratefully accepts a second helping. Esther smiles with satisfaction. She knows the path to a man's heart runs through his stomach.

The dessert is fantastic. The apple cake, topped with honey syrup, is served with whipped cream. When Jason expresses his delight, Esther remarks casually, "Tabitha made it." Jason rewards her with a smile and a wink.

"That's the surprise I told you about!" Tabitha blooms.

After the meal, the three daughters clear the table and do the dishes. Isaac, Esther, and Jason move to the sitting room. The parents want to get acquainted with the suitor.

Suddenly, Isaac changes his tone and shifts attention to something that weighs heavily on his heart. He clears his throat and announces, "Jason, there's something we have to talk about."

Jason wonders if he has said or done something wrong.

As Jason's tension rises, Isaac continues, "I can see that you and Tabitha like each other. I don't know how serious it is or will become, but before it goes too far, I think it is only fair—to you and to her—that we get clarity about the religious side of such a relationship."

Esther gets so tensed up that she excuses herself. She also wants to keep the girls out of this man-to-man negotiation. It is better if there are no spectators in this face-off. She fears Jason may be scared off, robbing Tabitha of a good friend and possibly of a good husband.

"What are your views on religion, Jason?" Isaac's opening move is general and vague, allowing Jason space to formulate his own insights the way he sees fit.

Unknowingly, Isaac has put his finger on another conflict in Jason's life. Neither Greek nor Jewish religion satisfies him. He and Tabitha have discussed his search for meaning. Without hesitation, he gives his opinion on Greek mythology.

"To be frank with you, I don't care much about our Greek gods," Jason responds, to Isaac's amazement.

"To me, the stories about our gods are mere folklore, myths that try to explain the mysteries of life to inquisitive children. Five centuries ago, those stories might have satisfied people. I need something more. I am searching for a religion or a philosophy that will make more sense to me, enlighten and guide me in my current situation."

After several moments of digesting, Isaac says with relief, "I'm glad to hear that, Jason. Have you perhaps considered Tabitha's faith as an alternative?"

"Oh yes!" Jason declares with confidence. "Since Tabitha and I became close friends, I have watched your customs with interest. I have sensed that her faith means more to her than a set of rules. I can see that her trust in one God gives her power in good and bad times. I went through a bad time recently. When I almost gave up on myself, Tabitha remained hopeful. I need that kind of faith."

In the mean time, Esther and the girls entertain themselves in a bedroom with music and song. Tabitha plays on the lyre. All four join in Jewish songs, harmonizing. They hope they will have a benign effect on the tone of the conversation in the sitting room. Jason's words about Tabitha, complemented by the music and song, bring tears of thankfulness to Isaac's eyes. He is immensely grateful that his daughter's faith has made such a strong impression on this young man.

"Are you interested in taking classes at the synagogue?" Isaac tests Jason's level of interest. *Will it remain only good words, or is he prepared to do something about it?*

"I don't want to start impulsively and then quit halfway," Jason wiggles himself out of the tight corner. "I do admire Tabitha's faith, but I must tell you that the strict Jewish laws put me off—most of all, the circumcision."

"Yes, I can understand that. I had it when I was eight days old, so I can't remember it," Isaac responds, chuckling. "I assume it must be scary for an adult man."

They both enjoy the humor of Jason's fear.

Isaac tries to reassure him: "Jason, maybe you don't know that you can convert to Judaism without circumcision. Such converts are known as *God fearers*."

"Really?" Jason exclaims with relief. "That will make it much easier. I don't want my manhood to be mutilated."

"Maybe you have the wrong idea about circumcision, Jason," Isaac explains, "it's only the foreskin that is removed, not the whole thing."

"I know," retorts Jason with an uneasy grin. He leans forward and whispers so that only Isaac can hear, "I'm just afraid the rabbi's knife may slip..." Jason holds his left index finger out and signals a chopping movement with his right hand. "Swish! Just like that—gone!"

Isaac shakes his head, giggling, "For heaven's sake, Jason, we use a scalpel, not an ax!" They realize the prejudices and misunderstandings of the two cultures they represent. Their humor helps them to accept one another's goodwill and friendship.

Hearing them laughing, Esther judges that the main talk is behind them. She rejoins them, and when she sees that it's safe, she calls the girls.

They all move to the verandah. Enjoying mild wheat beer, they chat about trivialities, avoiding any conflict material. After a while, they discreetly excuse themselves one by one, leaving Jason and Tabitha alone to enjoy each other's company.

"So, what was the big talk about?" Tabitha fishes.

"Religion."

"What about religion?"

"My feelings about Judaism."

"What part of Judaism?"

"Some things I like, others not?"

"Come on, Jason, share with me! Must I pull it out of you bit by bit?" Tabitha burns with curiosity.

"Well, it concerns things that are not for girls," Jason shields.

"Oh, I see! Circumcision scares you off, hey?"

"I don't want to discuss it. It's embarrassing."

"I can understand that. Just don't make an issue of something that's of minor importance. God is the center of our faith, not circumcision. You can believe in the one true

God with your heart without receiving the mark in your flesh. As I understand it, this mark is for male Jews, descendants of Abraham."

"Thanks for that viewpoint, Tabitha, it gives me better clarity. That's what I need—perspective. I'll think it over."

Jason wants to tell her about his feelings for her, but can't find the words. Tabitha kindles tender feelings in him. Diana arouses his animal instincts.

When he walks home, he weighs the lifestyle of Diana's family against that of Tabitha's family. Joining Diana's family will be easy culturally, but morally perilous; joining Tabitha's family will be difficult culturally, but morally uplifting. His common sense knows what's best; however, his heart can't write Diana off yet.

He is bewitched by the desires of the flesh. He wants to taste Eros before Agape, lust before love.

*

In sharp contrast to the pleasures of Corinth, another drama is playing out a few hundred miles to the north.

In the muggy dungeon of Philippi's prison, two jailed Christian missionaries, Paul and Silas, sing hymns of praise in the middle of the night. Before their arrest, they were assaulted by a mob and beaten with sticks.

Paul feels compelled and burdened to bring the gospel of Christ to as many people as possible.

"Oh God, please rescue us from this hole, so that we can proceed with your work," Paul pleads. They start praising God for the expected relief by singing psalms.

As their songs resound against the walls of the austere Roman prison, the other prisoners are intrigued by this unusual phenomenon. They are used to groans and curses coming from the dungeon.

An ominous, escalating rumble suddenly sweeps over them, droning out the singing. The solid building begins to shake like a tent in a gale. Prison doors spring open. Chains fall from prisoners. As the earthquake dies down after a minute—which felt like an hour—everyone waits in silence, fearing the walls may cave in on them any moment.

The jailor who has been sleeping in the guards' room of the prison comes running in, shouting to his companion to bring light. When he sees the cell doors open, he concludes that the prisoners have escaped. Knowing his punishment will be severe, he draws his sword to commit suicide.

Paul realizes the jailor's predicament and shouts, "Don't kill yourself! No one escaped!"

The jailor investigates and sees that is true. He knows that these prisoners preached a new religion and drove an evil spirit from a slave girl the previous day—and now a miracle has happened that saved his neck. Who are these people? What strange powers do they control? Relieved from punishment, fear of the supernatural overwhelms him.

Shaken, he falls on his knees beside Paul and pleads, "How can I be saved?"

Paul's response is quick and to the point: "Believe on the Lord Jesus Christ, and you will be saved, you and your household."[2]

After the other prisoners have been locked up, the jailor takes Paul and Silas to his home adjacent to the prison, nurses their wounds, and prepares a meal for them.

While he cares for their bodies, the evangelists attend to his soul. Paul gives him a quick course in the good news of the Christian faith.

The jailor and his family open their hearts to the simple message, realizing that their paths have met in an extraordinary manner. A chain of events brought Paul to that prison on that specific night. If only one link in the chain were missing, they would not have met.

---

2   Acts 16:31

The missionaries now begin to realize the purpose of their suffering.

Paul and Silas are freed on the next day.

They leave their helpers, Luke and Timothy, in Philippi to assist the new church in that city, while they proceed to Thessalonica.

They teach in the synagogue for several weeks. Gradually, animosity builds up again. Paul is gradually driven toward Corinth by a power beyond his control.

CHAPTER 3

Jason still lives with his parents. Decent rooms for rent in Corinth are as scarce as sausage in a dog pen.

Their next door neighbor, Julia, is a single mother with a nine-year-old son, Toni. Jason is his hero. Toni likes to accompany Jason on fishing trips, hikes on Acrocorinth, and to the sports field when Jason practices with the discus and javelin. Jason feels sympathy for Toni. The boy was born out of wedlock, and on top of that, he was crippled by a severe illness. His left leg is slightly shorter, giving him a limping gait.

Because he promised Toni an outing on a hiking trail against the foot of the mountain, Jason left work early so that they would not descend in the dark. They enjoy the fresh air, attending to anything of interest to them—birds, gazelles, insects, plants, and the view over the two gulfs and the isthmus. It's breathtaking, especially before sunset.

Jason prepares Toni for realistic expectations regarding reaching the top of Acrocorinth: "Toni, we have to increase our stamina with a few hikes on the foot of the mountain before we can go to the summit."

"I cannot wait for that day when we will view the whole world from the top," Toni responds excitedly.

"Yes, you will enjoy it. The view is fantastic. But we have to be patient. If we expect too much too soon, we set ourselves up for disappointment," Jason warns.

On their way back, they follow a trail that they have not tried before. A few hundred yards from the houses on the outskirts of Corinth, the trail goes through a ditch. Unexpectedly, they come upon Krato in his secret workout place.

"Hi, Krato! What are you up to?" blurts Toni.

Jason is surprised that they know each other. He wonders what the relationship may be. Neither Julia nor Toni has ever referred to Krato's family.

To hide his embarrassment, Krato calls Toni over, "Hi Toni! Come, I want to show you something." Krato ignores Jason completely.

Krato grabs his weights (two boxes with stones, hanging from the ends of a rod) and performs a few curls, presses, and squats to impress Toni with his strength and bulging muscles. When he puts the weights down, Toni tries to lift it, but cannot even move it.

Chuckling, Krato advises, "You have to start with light weights, Toni. Your strength and muscles will gradually grow. When you are my age, you'll be just as strong."

For Jason, it's an eye-opener, a wake-up call. *So that's how he wants to beat me!* he concludes. Jason realizes that he, too, will have to use strengthening exercises to catch up with Krato's power.

"Come, Toni, we have to go home. Your mother will get worried. We're late already," Jason says, walking off without saying anything to Krato.

In his bravado, Krato just cannot resist the temptation of taunting his rising rival. "Only six months to the games, Jason!" he shouts. "This time, the Roman centurion will give the African slave a good licking!" He burst into a mocking laughter that makes Jason's blood boil. He realizes, though, that Krato is mad because they have discovered his secret workout place.

That night in his room, the inventor starts planning movements that will help him to increase his distances in discus and javelin. Jason makes the movements with which the discus and javelin is hurled, determining which muscle groups are involved. He decides that his shoulder, chest, wrist, and abdominal muscles are active in discus throw, and that his upper arm and side muscles are needed for launching the javelin.

Jason decides not to build big muscles like Krato. Those may slow him down. He is convinced that a combination of strength, speed, and technique makes a champion in these events—not power alone.

He will start with only two stones the size of his fists.

*

Diana still lives with her parents, too. They are on vacation to a Greek island. When the cat is gone, the mouse rules. Diana invited some friends, including Jason and Krato, to a party. She invited her guests as singles, ten guys and ten girls. She wants them to mingle freely and select their mates as the night progresses. She is actually testing a plan she has in mind for her own "entertainment" business.

With his usual boisterous loudness, Krato attracts a large group around him all evening. He entertains them with stories about his steer-wrestling in Spain. Jason joins a smaller group and participates in the humorous exchanges without becoming the center of attention.

He tries to get close to Diana, but she keeps moving away. She looks gorgeous in her shiny maroon outfit with its silver embroidered lace. Intermittently, she invites guests to help themselves to drinks and snacks. For her experiment to work, they have to drink well.

Knowing that the guys can't take their lusting eyes from her, Diana entices them to the hunt by showing off her assets. She occasionally shakes her shoulder-length wavy auburn hair. When she smiles, her enticing green eyes and sensual lips drive her admirers crazy. Her bulging breasts are barely covered by the low neckline of her dress. Her swinging hips, enhanced by frills and leather belt, are complemented by well-formed, long legs flashing through the slits in her silky dress.

Her eyes meet with Jason's occasionally, sometimes she even winks at him, but she never allows him to catch up with her for a personal chat.

This cat-and-mouse game continues till midnight. Most of the guests have paired off to get acquainted intimately. Jason searches casually in the garden, the verandah, and in the guest hall for Diana, but can't find her. He enters the back part of the house. The doors of four bedrooms are locked, probably occupied by half-drunken love-makers.

One door stands ajar. Jason cautiously pushes it farther. A little oil lamp inside spreads its dim light. What he sees shakes him to the core.

Diana and Krato—both half naked—stand next to the bed. They kiss passionately. Their hips are pressed together, simulating intercourse. Their mutual caresses are intimate. They undo each other's clothes. Sex seems imminent.

Jason is showered by intense feelings of pity for Diana and anger towards Krato. A cold flush rushes from his head through his body, followed by a burning sensation. His emotions scare him. Giving free reign to his feelings now may end in murder. *I must get out of here before I do something stupid,* he concludes.

He takes a deep breath, regains self-control, turns around and sneaks off—disgusted, disillusioned, and angry. How can she surrender herself to such a creep? Doesn't she know the true character of this brute?

He wishes he could save her from calamity. Doing it with violence may not have the desired effect. Attempting it in a subtle way may take time and may pull him down to her level.

Well, if this is Diana's choice—and obviously it is—then he will not contest Krato's prize. Jason silently leaves the house and goes home. Once more, he is the loser.

Damn it!

He needs the escape of sleep. He's drained. Tomorrow will be a tough day. Time will tell what to do.

*

The next day, Jason works hard in an effort to ban thoughts about the previous night from his mind. However, time and again those images creep back from his subconscious mind to confront him with his ambivalence.

As much as he despises Krato's interaction with Diana, Jason wishes he himself could have been in Krato's place last night. If Diana could surrender herself to him like that only once...

He is still in her web. He has to get her out of his mind. He tries to put Diana in a bad light to rid his mind of her luring image.

She probably has done it with many men, Jason tells himself. *Maybe she's just a common whore, tempting men into her clutches like a spider. Poor old Krato just got caught before me. If I had not seen them, she might have done the same to me.*

Yes, it works. He hates Diana.

I'm finished with her, he decides, *I'm not going to eat Krato's leftovers.*

After work, he tries to keep busy with his new training schedule. Now he just must beat Krato in the games. He cannot allow himself to become a loser twice over. *Morbid moods and circumstances should not be used as excuses for passivity. I will stick to my motto: Smart planning and hard work will give me the victory.*

"Yes, soldier, I'm going to kick your butt!" he says out loud.

Determined, he starts with his new schedule.

Jason lies on his back on a small bench, holding the two stones in his hands, his arms stretched out sideways. He moves his straight arms upward in a wide swing until the stones click above his chest. That is more or less the trajectory of his arm when hurling the discus. He repeats the movement twenty times, putting as much force as he can into it. When done, his shoulders and chest muscles are swollen. The plan works. With short rests in between, he repeats the set of twenty movements for a second and third time. His muscles feel pumped up.

While resting, the thought occurs to him that by losing Diana, he is free to win Tabitha. Had he won Diana, he would have lost Tabitha.

So actually, I'm the winner, and Krato the loser, he concludes, feeling much better about himself. He proceeds with his training, invigorated.

He tries a second exercise that may strengthen the muscles involved in the javelin throw. While lying on his back on the bench, holding the two stones, he stretches his arms in the direction his head is pointing. He moves his arms up till the stones are above his face. He repeats the movement twenty times, forcefully. After short rests, he repeats the twenty movements a second and a third time.

The discus and the javelin are thrown with a sudden twist of the upper body. Therefore, Jason's third exercise is for the front and sides of his abdomen. He hooks his feet under the wooden garden bench, bends his knees halfway, and does twenty sit-ups, turning his torso alternately left and right when in a sitting position. His abdomen muscles start to hurt before the count of twenty.

The next morning, he is amazed that the muscles he exercised the night before are quite stiff and sore. He thought his hard work at the wagon factory as well as his practice with the discus and javelin provided sufficient exercise to keep him fit.

He continues with his new program every evening for the next week, alternating his stone workout with his discus and javelin practice on the sports field. At the end of the week, he can feel there is new vitality in his movements, resulting in better distances with the discus and javelin.

Another idea is taking shape in Jason's inventive mind. The traditional way of throwing the discus is to stand at the back of the circle, take two steps forward, and then hurl the discus with a swing of the arm and a twist of the body. If he could swirl around before releasing the discus, it should give him extra momentum and distance. He practices the movement in his bedroom. He wants to keep his idea a secret.

Jason realizes he actually owes his new training methods indirectly to Krato. If he and Toni had not found Krato in his secret den that evening, he would still have lived in a fool's paradise. This stroke of luck was not accomplished by his philosophy of good planning and hard work. From where did it come—from fate, gods, or God?

Whatever the case may be, Jason figures he doesn't have to thank Krato, who tried to hide his secret. Furthermore, he has copied neither Krato's equipment nor his exercises. He is not riding on Krato's back. With that, he puts the matter to rest.

*

A few days later, Jason has an unexpected encounter with Diana. He thought he got her out of his system, but being close to her re-awakens his suppressed affection.

Returning from the baths, Jason passes Diana's home. She probably saw him going to the baths and waited for his return—a dangerous ambush.

"Hi, Jason!" She sounds as inviting as ever. She comes to him in the street. She wears a thin casual dress that accentuates her breasts, middle, and hips. Jason is not sure if he hates or loves her. He cannot tell her that he spied on her and Krato.

He greets her as casually as he can, "Hi, Diana, how are you doing?"

She does not answer, but asks, "Can we go for a walk?"

"Sure! I guess you have something to tell me," he fishes, hoping she will open up the issue.

Though he loathes her intimacy with Krato the other night, he cannot help to feel attracted to her. Her looks, voice, perfume, and skin radiates a presence Jason craves. Despite a warning voice inside him, he enjoys her company intensely. He decides to experiment for a while.

They walk to the ancient temple of Apollo near the *agora*. The shops have closed. Though in disrepair, the massive pillars of the temple are still impressive. They frame the mountain perfectly in the pink hue of the setting sun.

"You disappeared from my party without saying goodbye," she cast out the bait.

"I searched for you but could not find you."

"I was occupied for a while. Usually you don't quit early. Why did you leave so soon? I noticed you didn't drink. Did you become bored? " she fishes.

"I had a tough day ahead of me. I needed sleep."

Then Diana gives him an unexpected shock: "I saw you from the corner of my eye at the door of my bedroom. I wanted to make you jealous. Krato agreed to play the prank on you. That's why we left the door ajar. I tried to drive you crazy."

Jason is suddenly speechless. *What is the truth? If she was teasing me, how far would this woman go to entice men? What is the vile pleasure she derives from sexual temptation without going through with it? What drives her behavior? If she's lying, well, then she's really cheap, coming up with such poor excuses, thinking I'm a dumb fool.*

"I know what I saw, Diana. I don't think you were only playing games."

Dusk surrounds them. They are the only ones left among the pillars of the Apollo temple. She stops and stands close to him, putting her hands on his shoulders, looking up to his face. Their bodies touch, but she does not entice him like the other day.

"Jason, we are both Greek. We know our culture's view on sex. I'm not a virgin, and I doubt that you are. However, I'm very picky with whom I go to bed. I esteem you highly. I know we are strongly attracted to each other, but I don't want to hurt you or to get hurt myself. When we go to bed, it must be different—the beginning of a true, permanent relationship. Do you understand what I mean?"

Diana's serious talk takes Jason by surprise. He softens, savoring her subtle promise. His body wants Diana, his soul wants Tabitha. He is torn in two. *Can I believe Diana? Or is she playing her old games again—enticing my appetite and then pushing me away?*

He has Diana at his feet now. *Should I pass up the opportunity? Why not enjoy her while I can?* He puts his arms around her. He ignores the little voice warning him not to play with fire. *Just once*, he promises himself. She surrenders to his embrace. He smells her fragrance, feels her body, tastes her lips. He enjoys her bewitching femininity. He wants to be one with her. They press their bodies together as they indulge in a long and passionate kiss.

Diana rests her head on Jason's chest. His chin touches her hair. She smells beautiful. To be close to her is heaven.

"I have found my Apollo in the temple of Apollo," she whispers, arms around his waist.

They slowly walk back to her house, hand-in-hand. Their body language demonstrates their new relationship, so they don't discuss it. They feel at peace. They have found each other. They look forward to becoming one in the flesh.

"When you beat Krato at the games, we will celebrate it in bed together," Diana promises.

After a short goodbye kiss, he walks home. He tries to suppress it, but deep down in his heart of hearts there is a nasty feeling of guilt because of Tabitha. *I have dropped the girl I love differently and more deeply.*

*

There are several Aphrodite festivities through the year. The great one has arrived, consisting of parades, orchestras, marches, and floats decorated with beautiful girls in glittering dresses and ostrich feathers. The floats are pulled by muscular young men.

Krato leads a platoon in their shiny copper harnesses and red-plumed helmets, accompanied by their military band with drums and trumpets.

Diana is on one of the floats. They will depart from the *agora* and proceed along the main streets of Corinth. Jason watches from the sidewalk, not far from Isaac's shop. Tabitha sees him, joins him, and hooks her arm into his.

Diana waves at them when her float passes. The contrast hits Jason like a hammer to the chest: His Greek goddess of sex on the float, versus his plain Jewish girlfriend at his side—two people he loves, two religions he can't accept. *Why is life so complicated? Why can't the choices be clear and simple? Why is it so hard to decide what one really wants?*

Jason knows from previous experience that the feast will gain momentum as the day progresses. In late afternoon, they will light the fires to produce charcoal for barbecuing whole sheep, geese, and piglets. After sunset, the eating and drinking will start, mixed with dancing and flirting. To safeguard his bet with his workmen—staying sober till after the games— Jason decides to avoid the festivities. He gets carried away too easily by the spirit of the crowd.

At midnight, in the flickering light of torches, the feast reaches its climax with the Aphrodite ritual. By then, the crowd has drunk well, the senses are dulled, and the consciences lulled.

Since the temple and temple-prostitutes of Aphrodite no longer exist, the pretty girls of the floats act as priestesses for the goddess of love and fertility. They perform sensual dances with the young men who pulled the floats. Eventually, the dancers go into tents to honor the goddess with sex, beseeching her to send rain for the crops.

Diana makes a grave mistake.

*

Jason judges that Toni is not yet ready to climb Acrocorinth to the summit. Even on their short hikes, Toni's handicapped leg hurts. He probably will never be able to climb to the top.

"Toni, I have an idea. While we proceed with our hikes on the foot of the mountain, increasing our fitness, we go by horse-cart to the top just to satisfy our curiosity," Jason suggests. "There is a winding road ascending the mountain from the other side. What do you think?"

"Wonderful!" Toni rejoices. "I thought I would never see the top because of my weak leg, but now I will! Yippee!"

It is a long and slow trek. The incline is steep. The horses go at a walking pace and often have to rest. After several hours, they reach the top. They unharness and walk the two horses to cool them down. Toni feels great to lead one of the horses. Jason enjoys it to build up Toni's self-esteem. They tie the horses to the cart and refresh them with the water and feed they brought along.

Now they can attend to the views they came for. They have to walk quite a distance before they reach the rim from where they can see the whole area.

It is a beautiful clear day, no haze.

They let their eyes glide over the scene, from Cenchrea on the Saronic Gulf, to the isthmus, and to Lechaion on the Gulf of Corinth. Cautiously, they move a little closer to the edge to look down on Corinth at the foot of the mountain.

They point out landmarks as they recognize them from the strange new angle, a bird's eye view.

"There is the forum!" Toni shouts, "And there is the temple of Apollo, and the theater!"

"Yes, and just to the right I can see Lechaion Road, the baths, and Peirene Fountain," Jason adds. After a while, they identify Philip's factory and guess where their homes are. From their high vantage point, the wagons moving between Corinth and its harbors look like ants. After an hour of viewing, they return to the cart for drinks and snacks. They enjoy their picnic while scanning the lesser-known terrain on the other side of Acrocorinth. Toni is surprised to see that there are several parallel mountain ranges to the south, running from east to west, and fading into lighter blue haze as the distance increases.

Jason enjoys treating Toni to worthwhile experiences. Toni is like a little brother to him. Jason encourages the boy to enjoy life to the fullest despite his handicap.

Toni's speckled face and brown eyes beam with joy. This day will remain an unforgettable peak in his young life.

They start their descent with several hours of sun left. Downhill is easier on the horses. They brake the cart with their full harnesses that are attached to the crossbar and pole of the cart. With an hour's sun left, they arrive in town. They care for the horses and then walk home.

Toni's mother greets them with relief and a string of questions, "How was the trip? Did you reach the top? Could you see anything?"

While Toni is still describing their trip and views with zest, his mother suddenly interrupts him, "Before I forget: Krato was here and brought you something."

"What? What?" Toni shouts, excited.

His mother gives him a little statue of a javelin-thrower carved from wood. The thrower is caught in action as he leans back with an outstretched arm just before he releases all his power to the throw of the javelin.

"Wow! Has Krato carved it himself?" Toni inquires with admiration.

"Yes, he said so," his mother responds.

Jason is puzzled, but refrains from asking questions. *What is the relationship between Toni and Krato? Why is this brute interested in a handicapped child?* Jason finds it hard to believe Krato's actions are driven by compassion.

After adoring the sculpture for Toni's sake, Jason excuses himself, picks up some clean clothing at home, and leaves for the baths. He has a strange premonition that Krato is busy with something sinister.

If he harms Toni, I will break his neck, Jason vows. *Krato and I are opposites—how can Toni love both of us?* Jason is puzzled and worried.

*

Things take a turn for the worse a week after the feast. Knowing Jason goes for a bath every evening, Diana waits for him outside the baths. She looks worried.

"What's wrong with my goddess?" he asks, concerned.

What she tells him makes him sick at heart.

In short sentences, she briefs him about the tragic turn of events. Carried away by the spirit of the Aphrodite feast, compounded by too much wine, she fulfilled her role as a priestess of Aphrodite to the letter. She had sex with a guy at the climax of the feast.

"Now I have an infection! The physician told me that it is one of the virulent venereal diseases," she says, bursting into tears, devastated and burdened by the diagnosis.

Jason is completely dumbfounded. He holds the sobbing Diana. He feels her pain. He searches for words to comfort her, but feels powerless. Then anger boils up in him toward the guy who got his beloved Diana into this mess.

"Who did this to you?" Jason inquires softly, steel in his voice. Recalling the sexy embrace between Diana and Krato, Jason suspects Krato of this crime. Jason does not even think about the possibility that Krato may suspect him to be the guilty one. Their mutual unfounded suspicions further inflame their sick relationship.

Diana senses right away the male need for reprisal in Jason's tone and demeanor.

"I won't tell you. Revenge won't cure me. I need understanding and treatment."

"You can be treated for it, right?" he asks.

"There is a cure, but I have to go to Rome for the lengthy treatment," Diana adds. "It is expensive; fortunately, my dad can afford it. He persuaded an old customer, the captain of a fast ship, to sail directly to Rome to get me there as soon as possible. Dad offered the captain enough money to change his plans pretty quickly. We depart tomorrow. This is goodbye." Diana leans against Jason, resting the side of her head on his chest.

"It's terrible, but it's not the end of the world, my dearest Diana. I will always love you—no matter what!"

"Thank you, Jason. I need your friendship now more than ever," she whispers through the tears.

In silent empathy they walk home, hand-in-hand.

Then a thought strikes Jason and he blurts, "If we went to bed before the feast, this might have been avoided."

"Oh Jason, don't plunge yourself into undeserved guilt. What happened, happened. I'm to blame. I often used my sex appeal as weapon to get my way—now I've cut myself with my own sword."

"Don't beat yourself up, Diana. Get the treatment, get cured, come back healthy. That's the important thing now.

Don't look back, look forward now, look forward to our happy reunion. Let's live for that day."

He tries to sound upbeat, but they both know that it will never be the same. People avoid men or women who have had a venereal disease.

After a tender hug and kiss, they say goodbye, not knowing what else fate will throw into their way.

Jason goes home, avoiding everyone. He sits in the dark garden all by himself, wondering about this shocking event. He feels burdened by Diana's plight.

Jason wonders whether Tabitha's God infected Diana to lead him towards Tabitha. What kind of God would use such mean methods? Then Tabitha's God is not better than the Greek gods who manipulated people with mean interventions. He feels as if he is a helpless victim.

Devastated by Diana's crisis, he has lost his appetite for the games completely. He already has lost the big prize.

*

A week later, Toni inspires Jason to resume training. They enjoy their activities on the sports field. Jason made a small light discus and javelin for Toni. Jason shows him the finer secrets of these sports. Toni is excited when he increases his distances. After throwing the discus and javelin, they walk together, pick them up, and repeat the throw in the opposite direction.

Toni wants to handle the real stuff Jason works with. He stands at the far end, marks where Jason's discus and javelin lands, and throws the heavy discus and javelin back as far as he can. Jason meets him halfway.

Before Jason throws, he urges Toni to stand at least twenty paces farther than Jason's best distance, watching the trajectory of the discus and javelin carefully.

"We don't want you to get hurt by one of these, do we?" he warns the boy repeatedly. Toni makes sure he waits at a safe distance.

When Jason has made a good throw he measures the distance in paces. After more than two months of sobriety and extra training with his stones, Jason feels stronger than ever. He warms up well. An injury at this point will take him out of the games. Even without straining him to the utmost, he has registered several throws that exceed his previous records by five paces. Knowing that Krato is also training hard, Jason can't allow himself to become complacent. He has to drive himself till the games are over.

Tabitha wants to see him more often. He asks her for patience—the games will be history soon. She admonishes him not to make an idol of his sports. She wants to discuss spiritual matters with him, but all he can think about is physical glory.

"Later! Later!" is all she hears from him. He cannot share with her his obsession to beat Krato. She will not understand that he has a score to settle. The only civilized way he can beat Krato up for all the bad things Krato has done to him is to humiliate him on the sports field. He feels guilty about his motive of revenge, though. *If this is sin, may the gods forgive me,* he says to himself.

*

Krato is not resting on his laurels. As he has been adding more stones to his weights, he has been adding muscle to his body. Lately, he looks more like a wrestler than an athlete. He has not neglected his practice with the discus and javelin, either. He wants to keep his muscles flexible.

Krato got permission from the commander to exercise for a few hours per day on the large parade grounds of the military. This concession was made to all military staff representing the army in the upcoming games.

A few of Krato's friends spur him on by telling him of his opponent's success.

"I put on civilian clothes last week and watched the athletes at the city's sports field. Your opponent measured his best efforts in paces. He hurled the discus fifty-two paces, and the javelin seventy-six paces. Have you measured your best?"

"Let's do it!" Krato wants a comparison before the games.

He draws a line from where he throws. His friends stand where the discus and javelin land. They put up markers at his best distances for three tries. Krato paces the distances himself. He stretches his paces a little to make a conservative estimate. With the discus, he is two paces short on Jason's best. With the javelin, he is only one pace ahead of Jason.

"It's going to be a close call," one of the guys sums up the situation. "Too close for comfort."

"Only two weeks left," ponders another.

"Thanks, guys! You've helped a lot," Krato remarks. He is determined to put in everything for the next twelve days, and then he will rest his body to accumulate energy for the final showdown. He has been bragging about his superior strength at parties and practice sessions. If he loses to Jason, he will never hear the end of it. Ridicule is the one thing Krato has never learned to handle. It just must not happen.

*

In contrast with Jason and Krato's physical competition, Paul is engaged in a spiritual battle with the enemies of Christ. When they threaten Paul's host in Thessalonica, he and Silas flee by night to Berea. The Jews receive them cordially, allowing them to start a Bible study class in their synagogue.

After a few weeks, Timothy joins them in Berea. To their displeasure, the adversaries of Thessalonica follow them to Berea and incite opposition to their teachings. Animosity from some Jews forces Paul to Athens. He leaves Silas in Berea and sends Timothy back to Thessalonica to assist the young churches.

Paul wonders why God allows people to drive him from place to place. Is God spurring him on to a specific goal?

In Athens, Paul wanders around by himself in the city, concerned about the new churches he planted and had to leave in a hurry. The numerous statues of Greek gods in the city add to his frustration.

He discusses his views with some philosophers in the *agora*. They invite him to address them at the Areopagus, a rocky outcrop next to the Acropolis with its magnificent Parthenon temple. When he tells them that the Savior he follows rose from the dead, they find this idea ridiculous and discard it right away. Only a few accept his message.

He proceeds to Corinth, 48 miles west of Athens. From the intellectual and sophisticated Athenians, Paul moves to the commercial and carnal Corinthians.

In the middle of the first century, Paul of Tarsus arrives with the holy gospel at one of the most sinful cities in the Roman Empire.

An intriguing interaction of cultures—Roman, Greek, Jewish, and Christian—represented by people of flesh and blood, is unfolding. They will make their choices and moves amid the formidable forces of their time.

CHAPTER 4

The two weeks passed too soon for both Jason and Krato. They would have preferred more time to prepare. Their distances have not increased in the last week. They have reached their peaks.

Jason stops exercising two days before the games, but he continues with loosening-up and stretching exercises. The last thing he wants is a torn muscle or ligament on the day of the competition.

The day before the games he receives a little note from Isaac. Toni delivers it.

Isaac writes, "Jason, please come and see Tabitha. She is in tears since early morning. She doesn't say what's wrong, only that she must see you urgently."

In view of the games, Philip has given Jason the day off. He goes directly to Isaac's shop. Tabitha waits for him. He can see that she has been crying. They walk to the nearby temple of Apollo. At ten o'clock, there are no visitors to the temple. Jason can't help but to recall the day he and Diana had their long kiss here.

He and Tabitha stroll slowly among the massive pillars. She tells him about the terrible nightmare she had.

"I saw you covered in blood. It was so terribly real. Blood trickled from the corner of your mouth. Your eyes glazed over. You were dying!"

Jason holds the sobbing, sniffling Tabitha.

"It's okay, honey. It's just a nasty old dream. Don't torture yourself about a silly nightmare."

It does not comfort her.

"It happened twice!" she reiterates. "After the second one, I could not sleep. I felt it was a warning, an omen. Oh Jason, please be very careful tomorrow. I don't want something bad happening to you."

"Okay, okay, I will be extremely cautious, I promise!"

He holds her against him. He often wanted to kiss her, but could not muster the courage. Now he experiences again that divine feeling of genuine, caring love. His body enjoys the erotic stir; his soul is filled with compassion. She looks up to him with her beautiful brown eyes. He bends his head over to meet her lips. She closes her eyes, ready to enjoy what she has been hoping for a long time.

The kiss begins tenderly. They feel the fizz of blood rushing through their veins to their reproductive organs—nature's way to prepare them for mating.

Tabitha doesn't know what exactly is happening in her body and soul, only that it is indescribably pleasant—the highest joy she has ever tasted.

They break for a moment and look into each other eyes, realizing they are being submerged into new and wonderful feelings for each other. Yes, it's real! It is happening!

Jason is almost a foot taller than Tabitha. He lifts her onto the stone rim running around the temple floor. "Ah, that's better!" he says, resuming kissing with more surrender until it grows into an engulfing passion. They feel the erotic impulses of their bodies mingle with the agape of their souls—

the awakening of true love in young hearts. Jason knows this feeling is far above the lust he felt for Diana.

When they stop to catch their breath, Jason is sure of his love for her. He puts his cheek against hers and whispers in her ear, "My dearest Tabitha, I love you, I love you."

She whispers back, "Oh Jason, I have been loving you for a long time already. Haven't you noticed?"

"I knew we liked each other, but I was not sure of love. I was blind. I have been chasing after the wind. Now I know I want to be with you forever." Jason has a wonderful peace inside him. He has found a jewel of great value.

She wanted to warn him about her premonition. Instead, she broke through to his inner self. Her fear is gone. Now she knows: Her nasty dream actually told her how much she cares about him.

*

Jason and Tabitha's families go by horse carriage to the games a few miles from Corinth. The terrain of the Isthmian Games is southeast of the Diolkos, near the temple of Poseidon, god of the sea. This event is popular with the Athenians too, as this locality is closer to them than any of the other major Greek athletic events. Even more important—they can come in great numbers by boat, eliminating an arduous journey by foot or horse carriage. What better way to honor Poseidon than to come by sea? They are brought by wagons from Cenchrea to the games.

After the sacrifice at the temple, people stream to the stadia to the east of the temple. The old stadium starts at the temple, its far end meeting the new stadium in a T-formation. The 600 foot running course of the new stadium is flanked by seat-covered embankments on each side of the running track. The length of a stadium has become the unit to measure long distances. Corinth is 422 stadia from Athens.

The myth of Apollo's discus killing his friend Hyacinth made the organizers decide to have the discus and javelin events take place at the old stadium, where spectators can keep a safe distance from the deadly discus and javelin.

After Corinth's destruction by the Romans, the embankments of the old stadium have been eroded for two hundred years. When the Romans began rebuilding Corinth ninety years ago, a new stadium was laid out. The old one was left as it was—an open space with a slight depression in the middle.

Although the Romans have been influenced by some aspects of Greek culture, the culture of the conqueror has been rubbing off on Greeks, as well. Competitors at the great Roman events like chariot races and gladiator fights are not nude, so women can share in the excitement. Eventually, this tradition spread to Roman colonies. The former nude competition of men at the Isthmian Games, barring women from attending, eventually was replaced by a more civilized approach. Now that the bottoms of the athletes are covered by light shorts, women are welcome too, adorning the occasion with their elegant presence.

Snacks and drinks are sold at temporary stalls outside the stadia. The joyful music of a band as well as the colorful attire and noisy interaction of spectators give a carnival atmosphere to the great occasion. Excited anticipation fills the air.

For Jason, this occasion is not about honoring Poseidon, but about the showdown between him and Krato. He does not ask for help from his gods or from Tabitha's God. He wants to beat Krato with his own hard-earned fitness. He has fantasized about this day since Krato teased him as a child. Today Jason wants to throw off Krato's dominance.

Jason, Krato, and their fellow competitors are warming up for the discus event. Some have come from hundreds of miles away. All are in top form, hoping to win honors for themselves and for their cities.

Athletes draw a number from a box to determine in what order they will compete. Krato is four numbers ahead of Jason.

Jason warms up gradually, swinging his arms, twisting his torso to the left and right, and stretching his leg and arm muscles. Eventually the competitor before him goes into the ring. Jason will be next.

Jason's devout supporters stay near the circle from where the discus is thrown. Toni assisted Jason in his training for months. He completely identifies with Jason. He is united with his hero. Toni can hardly contain himself. Over-tensed, he bounces up and down, occasionally pressing down on his pubis, fearing he may pee in his pants. Toni's mother puts her arm reassuringly around his shoulders, trying to calm him down.

Tabitha and her family stand together, the two young ones clinging in tense anticipation to their parents' arms. Tabitha walks up and down, not knowing what to do with her trembling hands. She folds her arms, wrings her hands, puts them behind her back, and fiddles with her hair, but nowhere do they feel at rest.

Philip and Andreo chat casually, trying their best to look at ease. Andreo is pleased with the new railings Jason and Philip have made for his wagons. He wants to show his gratitude by supporting Jason today.

Near them, the workmen who made the bet with Jason chat and laugh anxiously. Never was there a betting team so glad that they had lost a bet. They now eagerly wait to see if their plan will bear fruit.

Jason's number is called. All competitors use the same twelve-inch bronze discus, to prevent an unfair advantage. He takes the discus and shifts it around in his hand until his fingers feel comfortable with it.

To reduce drag, the disk must spin and travel horizontally as fast as possible without wobbling. The height of the trajectory, as well as the angle of the disk's upward tilt, impacts the distance.

Jason steps into the circle. He swings his arm and upper body back and forth three times. Then he spins around quickly like a top. His torso, arm, wrist, and fingers release the discus with perfect coordination, power, and speed.

The discus climbs fast and smoothly like a gull on a breeze. Jason's eyes follow it—the angle and height is right. The crowd cheers. Some competitors whistle in disbelief. The discus glides to the ground and makes its mark seven paces ahead of Krato's, who has been the leader so far. Jason smiles with inner satisfaction. He waves at his supporters who cheer him on, waving their arms above their heads.

The other competitors are amazed at Jason's technique. They jump two steps forward before they throw; Jason spins around. Three of them launch a complaint with the judges against Jason's technique. After only a minute, the judges rule unanimously in Jason's favor. The rules do not prescribe technique. The rules stipulate that the thrower may only use his body to propel the discus, and he must stay in the circle until the discus has landed.

Krato walks over to Jason to congratulate him on his impressive throw. Krato shakes his head in disbelief, and says, "That was absolutely brilliant, Jason! Take my hand!"

They shake hands. Jason is baffled. This is totally unlike Krato. Maybe he is more of a man than Jason thought, or maybe Krato is delighted as long as Corinth wins. There is another possibility: Krato may be sending the subtle message: *I will grant you the discus crown, if you grant me the javelin crown.*

In the second round, nobody comes near Jason's mark, so he holds back, putting the discus down three paces short of his first effort. In the last round, Krato mobilizes all his power and lands the discus next to Jason's marker. It is his personal best distance ever. Krato knows he has taken Jason by surprise.

Krato hopes Jason will fumble his throw in his over-eagerness to win.

Knowing that he has to improve on his best shot to win, Jason goes full out with his third effort. He performs the movement so fast and flawless that the crowd and the competitors burst into spontaneous applause even before the discus lands. He adds another four paces to his best distance.

The other competitors congratulate Jason. The judges crown him with a pine wreath. Tabitha runs up to him, rewarding him with a hug and a kiss on the cheek.

With his small hands, Toni shakes Jason's big hand, looks up at him with admiration, and loudly shouts, "We won! We won! We won!"

Jason goes down on one knee to look Toni in the eye. With his hands on Toni's upper arms, he says warmly, "Yes, Toni, WE did it! You helped me to do it!"

Proudly, Toni throws his arms around Jason's neck, crowing out, "My hero! My hero!"

*

It's lunch break. Competition will resume over about two hours. Several events have been completed in the main stadium. Winners bask in their fame. The many losers lick their wounds, fabricating excuses for their failure. Spectators discuss the events of the morning eagerly, reliving nail-biting moments.

Jason and his friends get themselves a snack. Though hungry, Jason eats only a little. He can't throw the javelin on a full stomach. Tabitha is still so tense that her appetite is gone. She forces herself to eat a few bites. She won't relax till they are all safely home. Her nightmare still bothers her, though she tries to brush it off as totally unfounded.

The guys who do well in the discus and javelin can proceed to sprint, long-jump, and wrestling, and so compete in the five-item event called the pentathlon. Those who specialize in one or two of these events do not have to enroll in the pentathlon.

The noon break goes by too slowly. Jason and Tabitha hope the javelin event will start promptly. When it is announced at long last, Jason joins the other competitors. This time Krato is number five, and Jason number eight.

The javelin throwers are allowed to use a leather thong that enables them to grab the javelin firmly at its balance point. It improves direction and distance—better for both throwers and spectators. The main rules are that the thrower must not step over the line, and the javelin must land on its front point.

The javelin is Krato's forte. After all, it is one of the main weapons of a Roman soldier. He carefully shifts his right hand back and forth as he holds the javelin at shoulder height, trying to find the sweet spot in the javelin for a long throw and a perfect landing.

He walks backwards from the line, measuring off nine paces. For a few moments he concentrates, preparing his whole body for the quick succession of powerful movements ahead. He moves forward quickly and stretches his arm backwards, javelin in line with his arm. With good footwork he maintains momentum, hurling the javelin at a perfect angle with the forceful thrust of his muscular upper body and arm.

The javelin lands point first about fifteen paces ahead of his nearest rival. Krato knows it was an excellent throw, and enjoys the applause of the crowd and other competitors.

Jason knows he will have to deliver his best to beat Krato's magnificent throw. He takes a few deep breaths. If he gets tensed up, he will not be able to do his best. He swings his arms in circles to relax his muscles.

The two guys who came after Krato do not pose a threat to the gloating centurion. Jason takes the javelin and gets the balance point. He secures a good hold with the thong. He walks about twelve paces back, takes only a few seconds to get ready, speeds forward, throws his torso and arm backwards for a moment, and releases all that muscle tension onto the javelin.

His speed is good, but his angle is a little low. Before the javelin runs out of speed, it hits the ground, point first. His mark is about five paces short of Krato's.

Philip casually approaches his son.

"It's an excellent throw, Jason, only a little too low. Just relax. Next time, lift your angle and you will overshoot him easily with ten paces. Just keep your cool."

Jason forces a little smile, "Okay, Dad, cross your fingers."

Krato saves energy with his second effort and does not reach his first mark. Jason gets a better angle with his second try and lands his javelin next to Krato's marker. Now, they are equal.

That will shake him up, Jason thinks by himself.

Indeed it has. Krato realizes that he has to improve on his first magnificent throw. He tenses himself up with a now-or-never attitude. He takes longer to prepare himself emotionally and physically. He tries to mobilize as much energy as possible. He storms forward with so much vigor that he can't stop himself before the line. Though this throw is three paces better than his first, the throw is disqualified because he stepped over the line.

Jason now realizes that he can beat Krato if he can only add two paces to his last throw. He practices his steps while the two guys before him do their throws. He tells himself over and over not to make the same mistake as Krato, stepping over the line with too much speed.

The crowd knows his throw will determine the outcome of this competition. Tension and excitement increase. The two lines of spectators move a little closer in a pincher formation in order to see well. They know Jason throws accurately.

Toni and his mother stand with Krato at the far end of the spectator lineup. They don't want to miss a thing. They want to see exactly where Jason's javelin lands.

Krato is nervous. He knows Jason can surpass him if Jason gets everything right. He crosses his fingers. Maybe it will help.

Toni sees Jason walk back to prepare for his final approach. Toni begins to bounce again, his anxiety beyond his control. His mother focuses on Jason.

Jason takes a few fast steps forward, leans back with his arm and torso, and lifts his left leg high just before he hurls the javelin, planting his left foot firmly on the ground to stop himself before the line. Simultaneously, he hurls his body and arm forward with a powerful twist of his upper-body. He puts in all the strength he has accumulated over the past year. The thrust is so powerful that he lands on his hands just before the line.

Jason feels in his arm that it's a good throw. For the first part of the trajectory, the javelin shoots forth like an arrow from a bow. It climbs and climbs. The angle is right. As it slows down, it hangs in the sky, then descends, front point down.

When Jason drops his gaze to the field to see where the javelin will land, he freezes in horror as Toni hobbles onto the field, right into the path of the javelin!

In his practice, Jason has thrown his javelin many times in Toni's direction. Toni always stood back far enough and kept his eyes on the javelin. Now Toni thinks he is a safe distance from the landing spot. His mother and Krato yell to him to look out. They start running after him.

Toni takes his eyes from the descending projectile.

The javelin hits Toni in the chest, ripping through his thin body, pinning him to the ground.

The crowd utters a momentous roar.

Women scream, shocked by the gruesome accident.

Toni's mother buries her face in her hands and falls to her knees, groaning: "No! No! No!"

Within a second, Krato is with Toni. He plucks the spear from Toni's chest, kneels beside him, and lifts the small body against himself, mumbling, "Toni, my dear Toni."

Jason and Tabitha elbow their way through the shocked but curious crowd. When they reach Toni, his chest is covered in blood.

Jason's big frame shakes like a reed in the wind. Tears roll over his cheeks as he kneels beside Krato and Toni. All he gets out is: "Toni! Toni! What happened?"

Tabitha sees her nightmare becoming reality before her eyes. Blood trickles from the corner of Toni's mouth. His eyes glaze over.

She knows Jason will never get over this. Something in Jason is dying with Toni. That's what her dream means. The shock and pain of the tragedy are too much for her. She feels nauseous and dizzy. Fearing she may faint, she sinks to her knees, whispering, "Oh, God! Why? Why this? Why now?" She feels Jason's pain, but she can't help him. Their world is crumbling.

Isaac puts his arm around her. He helps her to her feet and leads her off.

With tears in his eyes, Krato looks at Jason, and mutters, "He's my little brother... my little half-brother."

It is as if a merciless boxer gives Jason a second knock-out blow to the head.

"Your...your brother? How?" Jason stammers.

The first-aid people arrive with a stretcher. They rush Toni to the field hospital for injured athletes. Upon arrival, the boy is declared dead by the physician.

The crowd disperses, replaying in their minds what they saw, debating the facts, and trying to imagine what would have happened if this or that were different.

Isaac and his family wait at a short distance. He holds Tabitha, who is in shock, burdened by the possible negative consequences.

Jason and Krato stand alone, gazing over the Saronic Gulf without seeing any of its beauty.

"My dad had this son with this girl. He has been paying her well to keep silent." Krato's voice is hoarse and broken.

Then, Krato's attitude hardens. He picks up the javelin and angrily breaks the handle over his knee. He throws the broken spear down at Jason's feet, adding firmly, "I will break you like that spear! You killed my brother, slave-boy, so I have to kill you. That's the unwritten law in my family."

"But it was an accident, Krato. You saw it. Toni was like a little brother to me, too. I would defend him with my life!" Jason is totally disconcerted by Krato's unreasonable stance. He is probably overreacting in his shock.

Krato continues like a real man-hunter, his yellow lion eyes showing no mercy, "It doesn't matter. I have to kill you, slave! If you have not tried so hard to beat me...If your throw was only two paces shorter...Toni would still be alive. Your ravenous greed killed my little brother, so I will kill you! And what is more, you humiliated me today before the crowd. I will never forgive you for that!" His words are drenched in raw hate.

After a few moments of tense silence, Krato continues, softly but firmly, "I will give you a fair chance. I give you two days from the funeral to remove yourself from Corinth. Never stop looking over your shoulder, Jason. Sooner or later, I will find you."

"You can't be serious," Jason objects, alarmed.

"You know me, Jason. I'm as hard as rock. Don't be fooled by my tears for Toni. I mean what I said. It's deadly serious!"

Jason has received his third knock-out blow of the day. Instead of throwing off the Krato burden, it has increased tenfold. Jason has looked forward to this day of triumph over Krato for many years. His record throw brought grief, not jubilation. Instead of the joy of freedom, he tastes the pain of loss and persecution.

Jason is not crowned as the winner. People do not want to remember this awesome throw with such awful results; however, no spectator will be able to forget it, either.

Jason shakes his head slowly in disbelief as he walks over to Isaac and Tabitha.

They assure him of their condolences and support. Isaac suspects that Jason may take responsibility for Toni's death. He offers some balm for Jason's wounds: "We understand your grief, Jason. We're deeply sorry. However, I plead with you— for your sake and for Tabitha's sake—please, don't aggravate your grief with self-blame. You could not have prevented this tragedy. I was nearby. I could see the javelin and the boy. He started running when you made your throw. It was completely out of your hands."

Jason is so drained emotionally that he can't reason about accountability. With heavy hearts, they silently move towards the waiting horse carriages to go home.

His dream of victory ended in a gruesome nightmare.

CHAPTER 5

Jason feels like a zombie tonight. He is only vaguely aware of the people around him. His emotions have been so overburdened by the tragedy that he feels numb. His senses and nerves have shut down to protect him from further shock.

Deep inside, his heart bleeds for Toni and his mother. Julia must be devastated. What can he say to her? In the presence of death, words are hollow. However, he must see her soon. If she allows him to, he could hold her. His family and friends surround him with love and support, but he can't really take it in.

"Be strong, my son," Philip urges in staccato style, "You've done nothing wrong. It was an accident out of your control. Don't torture yourself with guilt-feelings. Look the world in the face. Be proud of who you are. Act like a man. We stand with you."

"Yes, Jason, we love you," his mother adds with teary eyes. "We won't abandon you. You're not alone in this. Your family and friends are all behind you."

His sister Helena sits next to him on the couch and rests her head against his shoulder. Supporting the words of her dad and mom, she puts her hand on Jason's.

Someone knocks at the front door and lets herself in. Tabitha appears in the doorway. She greets Philip and Irene with a respectful nod. Her words are few.

"My parents sent me. Is there anything we can help with? Please, no matter how big or small, we want to do something."

"Your presence already means a lot, Tabitha," Irene reassures her. "Come and have a seat. Maybe you can get through to Jason. He seems to be in a trance."

Helena vacates her seat with Jason, gesturing that Tabitha should take it. Jason stands up, takes Tabitha's hand, and lets her sit down. When he takes his seat next to her, they make eye contact for a moment. There are no smiles; the atmosphere is somber.

Irene offers drinks, but everyone declines. Then they excuse themselves one by one and leave Jason with Tabitha. They need time alone. Maybe her faith can disinfect his wound. She puts her hand on his and rests her head against his shoulder. He is glad she came over. Her closeness is a balm to his aching heart, though the reality of Toni's death can't be changed.

She wants to shoulder his burden with him, but doesn't know how. She prays for God's guidance. The right words at the right time have healing power.

Before she can say anything, he dryly remarks, "I've received a death threat."

Her body jerks upright. She turns toward him, her eyes on fire, brow frowned.

Bewildered, she asks, "From whom?"

"Krato."

"Why?"

"Toni was his half-brother. Please, don't tell anyone, not even your parents. It will only make things worse. Krato's dad had this child with Julia. It's a big secret. We have been her neighbors for nine years, and even we didn't know."

"But why on earth...It was an accident!" Tabitha objects, eyes closed, hands on her cheeks, trying to get clarity in this mental fog.

"He said my obsession to beat him killed Toni. There is some truth in it, you know ...If my javelin landed only two paces short..."

For a moment, Tabitha forgets about Jason's emotional pain. She turns towards him, grabs him with one hand on the chest and the other on the shoulder, trying to shake his big frame.

"Listen to me, Jason Ben Philip!" she hisses through clenched teeth, determined to wake him up from his false assumption. "Don't do that to yourself! Don't allow groundless guilt to destroy your life! Don't make the load of your loss unbearable! Accept reality for what it is—an accident you could not have prevented."

"Okay, okay!" he reacts with a smile, surprised at her fervent attack on a false assumption. "I'm just trying to review what happened. That's what Krato said, and I have to find the right answer that will satisfy me in the long run."

"Can't you see he's the devil in disguise? Listen to God, not to the devil!" she fires her cannons. She is firm with Jason because she does not want to see him suffer unnecessarily. He must be freed from needless guilt.

"Don't talk to me about God or gods," Jason retorts bitterly, "Where were they at that critical moment? A light breeze would have pushed the javelin away from Toni."

"Jason, why do you want to put blame on someone? It will not undo what happened. Blaming yourself, God, or somebody is a futile game. It will not heal your wound, only make it worse. Oh, I wish I can get you to someone who can help you see this horrible thing in perspective."

She feels desperate, against a stone wall. Then, a thought suddenly strikes her.

"Jason, I know you don't have much confidence in Greek, Roman, or Jewish religion. However, a Christian missionary, Paul of Tarsus, arrived here a week or so ago. Crispus, Aquila, and Stephanas are quite impressed by his insight into scripture. We heard that Paul will teach in the synagogue next Sabbath. Will you please come and hear him? My whole family is going!"

"Just another wise guy who thinks he can solve the problems of the world by a secret formula," Jason remarks skeptically.

"Please, Jason, don't be stubborn, don't reject water when you're dying of thirst," Tabitha pleads. "Just give it a try, will you?"

"Okay, Tabitha, I'll come to please you," he agrees half-heartedly.

They sit silently for a while, searching for solutions.

"The sun has set. I have to go now," Tabitha softly announces.

"I'll walk you home," he insists.

On the way, they don't talk, but walk hand-in-hand. They say goodbye with a short hug and kiss. She got him out of his trance. He can feel and think again.

Tabitha prays that God will give the right message to Paul, a message that will help her beloved Jason to prevail over the severe blow that life has dealt him without a clear purpose.

Jason is too drained to brood on the tragedy any more. At home, he falls asleep from pure emotional exhaustion.

*

His raw nerves do not allow him to sleep in. Before sunrise, he is wide awake. He decides to go for a walk on a trail on the foot of the mountain. He wants to absorb the beautiful vistas. Maybe it will help him to get perspective.

The uphill climb accelerates his heartbeat and breathing. The exercise and cool breeze makes him frisky. He feels like himself again. He and Toni walked here a few weeks ago. It is as if Toni is with him. His body may have died, but his spirit will forever be alive.

"Hi, Toni!" Jason says aloud. "I'm terribly sorry about the accident. When I saw you, the javelin was already descending. I could do nothing to stop it. You were such a joy to me! I'm sure you are happy where you are. Thank you for being such a wonderful friend. I will miss you a lot. When I walk here, I will always feel your presence. Toni, as you helped me to win at the games, please help me to come over this terrible loss."

Jason feels as if a massive burden has been lifted from him. He couldn't say goodbye to Toni when he died. It happened so fast! However, now that he has told Toni how he feels, Jason is relieved and lifted out of the dark pit.

He sits down and lets his gaze glide over the panorama below him. Despite birth and death, Mother Nature proceeds undeterred. The isthmus between the two gulfs is still the same. Acrocorinth still guards over the age-old scenery. As people change from baby to adult to senior, they still maintain the same identity. Toni's death has hurt him deeply, and yet the wound will heal, leaving only a scar. His dad is right—he has to be himself and face the world.

Jason decides not to run from Krato. *Maybe he too will heal over time, realizing that his threats were immature and unbecoming.*

Jason descends with new perspective and courage. He still believes in his motto of good planning and hard work. However, what has happened to him and his friends lately makes him realize that he does not have full control over life. There are things that come to a person like a bolt from the blue. That's why Tabitha has an unwavering faith in her God's provision for her. Jason knows he needs that.

*

At the burial that afternoon, Jason stands with his family. Tabitha is at his side. Krato and his family stand with Julia. Jason can't face Julia. His javelin killed her son, though the throw was perfectly safe. How will Julia react? Her sorrow must be much worse than his.

After the ceremony, Julia walks over to Jason.

He freezes. *How can I express my regret? What will her attitude be?*

Julia speaks slowly, sniffling between sentences: "Jason, I want to thank you from my heart...for the time you spent with Toni. Every time he went with you somewhere...he was so excited...before and after the outing. He couldn't stop talking about it. You were his hero. Thank you for bringing so much joy into his life...and mine."

Amazed and relieved, Jason puts his arms around her.

She weeps softly with her head on his chest.

A tear trickles down Jason's cheek. He cannot utter a word, completely choked up. His body language speaks for itself, confirming solidarity with Julia in her pain.

"Never blame yourself for his death," Julia continues, now more composed. "You took part in a competition. Your throw was completely safe. Toni was with me. I saw how excited he was. I should have held him. However, I'm not going to blame myself. What happened was completely unexpected and unforeseen. Jason, you will always remind me of Toni's happiest days. Please, keep on visiting me."

Julia looks up in his face, her hands on his upper arms.

Jason nods, "Okay."

"Thank you!" she says warmly.

Then she walks off with Krato. Jason is amazed at the difference in attitude between Julia and Krato. The burdened can choose how to react to their burdens.

Julia's words and attitude brought immense relief for Jason. He believes her. If he reminds her of Toni's good days, he will visit her occasionally. That's the least he can do to compensate in a small way for her immeasurable loss.

He always has had empathy for people who suffer. He heard that Christians accentuate love toward others. Tabitha is right—he should hear the Christian missionary. Maybe they have something in common.

*

Synagogues outside Israel do not have all the scrolls of the Bible. They exchange scrolls with each other to ensure that their entire holy book is read over time. Copies of their Bible are made by hand. These copies are subjected to extremely high standards in order to qualify as authentic copies, making them scarce and precious.

On the Sabbath, as Tabitha has assumed, Paul is invited by Crispus, the ruler of the synagogue, to read and explain scripture. He hands Paul the scroll of the Psalms. It is a copy of a Greek translation made in Alexandria about hundred years ago to accommodate Hellenistic Jews and Greek proselytes who can't understand Hebrew.

Paul reads the second, sixteenth, and twenty-second Psalms. All three refer to the Messiah.

Paul closes the scroll, bows, and touches the scroll with his lips, praying in his heart that God may anoint his lips to explain scripture according to God's will. He thanks the leadership and audience for the honor they have bestowed upon him by their willingness to hear his message.

Jason accepted Tabitha's invitation to the meeting. Apart from hearing Paul, he wants to see Tabitha, too. Men and women in the synagogue are separated by lattice. Tabitha and Jason take seats near the lattice so that they can eye each other occasionally.

Paul starts his exposition by pointing to the fact that Jews have been expecting the Messiah, the Anointed One, for twenty centuries since the time of the patriarchs. God promised Abraham that in his seed (singular), all nations would be blessed. A thousand years after Abraham, King David made many references to the Messiah in his Psalms.

"Some of these I have read to you from the scroll today," Paul remarks, preparing the audience for bridging the gap between past and present.

Jason turns his head slowly and searches for Tabitha through the lattice. They make eye contact. He winks at her. She blushes and looks down. Distracted by their youthful hearts, they listen only with one ear to Paul, a Christian Jew.

Paul continues his teaching by reminding his listeners of what happened in Israel about twenty years ago.

"At that time, a young rabbi, Jesus of Nazareth, attracted large crowds with his remarkable healing and teaching. I was a student in Jerusalem at that time, but I did not make an effort to hear him, because our leaders in Jerusalem were against him. I studied under Gamaliel, and I did not want to offend my Pharisee teacher," Paul explains.

He proceeds to summarize the historic events about Jesus. He was eventually condemned by the Jewish Council for declaring himself the Son of God. They convinced the Roman governor, Pontius Pilate, that Jesus was a dangerous imposter who advocated himself as the king of the Jews. To appease the Jews, Pilate granted their request and sentenced Jesus of Nazareth to death by crucifixion.

"His followers claimed that he had risen from the dead on the third day," Paul adds, "a claim I found preposterous. When this new sect started to gain more and more followers, I organized a campaign against them. I just could not allow them to continue ripping our nation and faith apart."

Jason has heard stories about these Christians. To listen to someone who personally lived through those events got Jason's attention. He senses that Paul is heading for a dramatic turn around. *Paul is a Christian now. How did it happen?*

Paul gives an overview of how he persecuted Christians. He even went to Damascus to round up some more of them. He describes the vision he had at noon near that city. In a blinding light, he saw a divine person who reprimanded him for persecuting Christians. It was the shock of his life when this person identified himself as Jesus Christ.

The synagogue is deadly silent now. Everybody waits for what happened next. Paul's personal testimony has grabbed their attention.

Paul goes on to tell them of his complete change of heart. "For three days after seeing that bright light, I was blind. In the darkness, I began to see another light—the light of scripture. I knew sacred Hebrew scripture well. As I reviewed the well-known passages in my mind, they got new meaning as I understood them from a new perspective.

"Psalm 22 was literally fulfilled when Jesus was crucified. He quoted the first verse on the cross: 'My God, My God, why have You forsaken Me?'[3] The mocking by his enemies, the piercing of his hands and feet, his physical suffering, his thirst, and the dividing of his clothes—all this happened to Jesus precisely as prophesied in Psalm 22.

"Brothers, King David said in Psalm 16 that God will not allow his Holy One to see decay in the grave. This Holy One was not David, for he died and his body decomposed. However, if Jesus rose from the dead—as affirmed by the vision I had—then the prophecy of King David was fulfilled in Jesus," Paul concludes.

"Therefore, brothers, I urge you to study the scriptures with renewed fervor and discover how the prophecies about the Messiah were fulfilled in Jesus of Nazareth. You do not have to decide right away. Ponder and discuss scripture from this perspective with an open mind. Ask God to guide your thoughts, and he will show you the way.

---

3   Psalm 22:1

"Brothers, I know that the idea of a crucified Messiah is hard to accept. I know we all expected a victorious king. We failed to notice that there are two series of messianic prophecies, some referring to his first coming in humility to die as our supreme Passover lamb, the others referring to his second coming in glory as the King of kings and the Lord of lords. Because of his suffering in our place, Jesus invited the burdened to come to him, to exchange their heavy loads for his light yoke, finding rest for their souls."

This last sentence is balm for Jason's wounds. *Yes, I need rest for my soul.*

Paul leaves the cathedra and takes his seat. The silence continues. Everybody is weighing the evidence presented. After a while, Crispus rises, and encourages everyone to think about Paul's message, and to discuss it calmly.

"Brother Paul plans to stay in Corinth for some time. He assured me that he will welcome any questions and discussion. So, we have ample time to make up our minds."

After a short prayer and a song, Crispus adjourns the meeting.

Then people start talking, first in whispers, then louder as their excitement for or against the message grows. Any boredom or stagnancy that might have existed in this group has been put on fire by Paul's simple message.

Some are excited and some disturbed by the possibility that their Messiah had come and they had missed him.

Jason and Tabitha find each other among the buzzing crowd outside the building. They move away and chat beneath a tree.

"What do you think?" Tabitha tests the ground.

"Well, Paul seems serious about the matter," Jason replies, cautiously. "I suppose people should examine the prophecies and decide for themselves."

"My dad is conservative about traditional Jewish beliefs. He will not shift his position easily," Tabitha concludes with some sadness in her voice.

Jason gets the message: *If I become a Christian, my chances to marry Tabitha would be diminished even further. Isaac is not in favor of his daughter marrying a Greek. However, a Greek can still become a Jewish proselyte, a step a Christian will never take.*

Jason does not respond to the idea that others want to control his choices. Actually, he detests such a notion.

"Maybe we should leave the matter in the hands of the elders. They have the knowledge to make the best decision," Jason concludes, to get himself out of the difficult situation.

They change the subject and discuss everyday matters. After a few minutes, Tabitha and Jason join her dad and mom on way home. Isaac invites him for lunch.

Isaac asks them not to discuss Paul. "This is serious business. It needs careful consideration. If Paul is right, we have to change our whole way of thinking. If he is wrong, then we have to define our viewpoint carefully on solid scriptural grounds."

Jason gets the impression that Paul's hailing of Jesus as the Messiah will stir up a lot of controversy. However, he is glad the meal will not be spoiled by religious speculations. They chat cheerfully and enjoy a hearty meal.

After lunch, Jason and Tabitha enjoy each other's company for an hour or so before he returns to his dad's workshop. There is no Sabbath for Greeks.

*

When he enters the workshop, one of the workmen shouts, "Boys!" All immediately leave what they were doing and walk over to Jason. They want to express their condolences to Jason, but struggle to find words for what they feel.

"We just want to tell you we are sorry about what happened. We know you and the little guy were close. When he came here, he had only eyes for you. We think about you and hope you will get over it in time," the appointed spokesman recites his speech.

"Thank you, guys, I appreciate your sympathy," Jason responds, uneasy.

To get them out of the sad atmosphere, one of the guys says more cheerfully, "And we want to shake your hand for winning the bet and the competition!" Their somber faces change to smiles as they all shake Jason's hand.

"Thank you, thank you," Jason responds as he shakes their hands one by one. Then he asks with a frown, "So where's the fish?" They grin uneasily. The spokesman explains, "It will come, it will come. Just be patient. We first wanted to see how you feel. Now that we see you're okay, the fish will come."

They disperse to resume their work. They feel relieved that Jason has regained his balance. They care a lot about their boss-friend whom they have watched growing up to a handsome, sturdy, young man.

*

Jason kept his promise not to drink before the games. He has not seen his old drinking buddies in months. A month or so after the tragic accident, he decides to visit an old drinking hole and see who shows up. He needs a break. He puts himself in harm's way unnecessarily.

Three hours after sunset, the regular customers have had quite a few spots. Their jokes and laughter are becoming noisier. When Jason shows up, they are overjoyed and order him a large beer. They lift their mugs and drink to his health. Jason feels accepted by the old club.

He is determined to drink slowly and moderately. He knows his weakness for fermented drinks.

After he has been hanging out with the boys for about an hour, Krato and a few friends in civic dress enter the tavern.

"Uh oh, the skunk has entered," one of Jason's buddies remarks softly. They are well aware of the feud between Jason and Krato. They don't know yet about Krato's death-threat.

They ignore the soldiers and carry on with their chats. The soldiers are outnumbered and should not make trouble.

When Jason goes to the counter for a fill-up, Krato joins him. They stand with their backs to the tables. Krato speaks softly but firmly.

"Jason, I just want to let you know that I have not changed my mind. If you have thought that I would soften over time, you're dead wrong. The only two places where I can kill you legally are in war or in the arena. Both are unlikely to happen. So I have to plan it cautiously. I will choose the circumstances well. It must look like an accident. I don't want to be executed for executing you."

The bartender is filling their mugs. He is near enough to overhear the conversation. He is not amazed by further developments.

Jason stands at Krato's right side. Boiling with anger inside, Jason turns slightly towards Krato, looks him sharply in the eye, and says in soft but caustic tone, "As far as I'm concerned, you can go to hell, barbaric brute!"

Krato starts giggling, "At last you got it out, Jason! All the years I have taunted you, you always kept silent and walked away. I hoped you would someday act like a man. And now you have! Is there something else you would like to tell me?"

Jason's right arm, not seen by Krato, is bent halfway, his hand fisted.

"Yes! This!" Jason's short right hook hits Krato's chin like a sledgehammer. The simultaneous swing of his body and arm, a movement he performed thousands of times with the discus, mobilized so much force that Krato staggers and lands on his back on the nearest table, completely lights-out.

Jason's and Krato's pals jump to their feet and quickly surround the two. One of Krato's buddies feels his pulse.

"He's okay." He takes the flowers from a vase and shoots the water into Krato's face. Krato comes by with a grunt, shakes his head and asks, "What, what happened?"

"You got kicked by a mule," his buddy says. All burst into laughter. Krato's pals take him to their table. He is still dizzy and unstable on his feet. Jason and his group return to their table, too.

A brawl has been prevented because of the small number of the soldiers, and because of their aversion to six months of latrine duty. Jason's group knows the soldiers will sooner or later come back in sufficient numbers, both to win the bar fight and to give sufficient evidence to the commander that they were attacked and had no other choice but to defend themselves.

After another round, Jason and his friends leave together. As they walk out, Krato and his pals lift their daggers above their heads and give a bone-chilling war-cry in unison.

Jason gets the message: From now, on he will face a gang. He realizes he will have to go away. Despite his vicious retaliation, he is still the underdog. His anger has aggravated the animosity between him and Krato to the point of kill or be killed. The childish rivalry between boys has escalated to a major problem. The game has become deadly serious. He humiliated Krato in presence of his pals—an unforgivable sin.

Jason is not a killer. To diffuse the volatile situation, he would rather withdraw. He will wait out the storm in a safe harbor. He hopes Tabitha and his family will understand. He takes this burden of exile on himself to prevent bloodshed.

*

The next week, just before closing time, Jason calls on Tabitha at their shop. He is unsure how to introduce her to his plan. They are in love, so she has to know. His departure to an unknown destiny may hurt her, but it may hurt her even more if he disappears without telling her the reason.

When Isaac starts to lock up doors and windows, Jason and Tabitha walk over the forum, proceed through the arched entrance, go down the steps to Lechaion Road, and turn off to the Peirene Fountain. According to a myth, Peirene shed so many tears over her son's death that her tears turned into this fountain, a source of comfort for the grieving and thirsty.

The marble arches form an idyllic picture in the soft pink evening light. The sound of dripping water muffles voices. It's the ideal place to share secrets without being overheard. Tabitha wonders why Jason has brought her here. Jason searches for words to break the bad news of separation to her without causing her too much distress.

They sit down on a stone bench. He puts his arm around her shoulders, takes a deep breath, and forces the words through a choked throat.

"Tabitha, I have to tell you something...something rather sad."

She looks up, searching with her brown eyes for answers in his serious face. A bad feeling of pending doom engulfs her. Her fighting spirit wants to take the bull by the horns and face this thing right away.

"Okay, Jason, bring it on! Don't torture me any longer—out with it!"

"Tabitha...I have to leave for a while. Actually, I have to flee to an unknown destination for an indefinite period of time. My life is in danger. I think it's real and imminent."

"Krato?" she asks with a worried frown.

"Even worse—Krato's gang."

"A gang? How come?"

Jason briefs her about the event at the tavern a week ago when he had the altercation with Krato.

"When he repeated his death threat, I lost my temper and knocked him down. When I left the tavern, he and his friends gave a war-cry with lifted daggers. Last night on my way home, Krato and his gang cornered me in an alley with drawn daggers. The sound of approaching, marching soldiers on night patrol saved my life."

Jason sighs deeply and muses, "When it was only Krato and me, I could handle it. Now he is turning the whole regiment against me. When one of them stabs me, the others will cover for him. Laying a charge in court to prevent it will be futile. It's impossible to prove their deadly conspiracy in court. It will be my word against his. Guess whose side the judge will take? I've considered the pros and cons of fight or flight carefully. In a no-win situation like this, I think it's best to flee and live to fight another day. My grandpa said that the best choice is seldom a perfect choice. We often have to choose from various imperfect options."

Tabitha is silent. Her mind searches for a solution. When she finds none, she tries to anticipate the consequences.

"How can we maintain contact without exposing your whereabouts to Krato?" she wonders.

Jason has planned his movements thoroughly.

"Making contact with each other will be virtually impossible. Someone may convey information innocently to someone else, spreading the rumor from one person to the next, until it eventually reaches Krato and his gang. To make contact will be extremely risky," he concludes.

Only one option remains for Tabitha's love: "I'll go with you, Jason!"

He ponders the possibility. Though it may still his yearning too, it will make things much more difficult, especially if he has to make a quick move on short notice.

"Tabitha, I may sometimes have to flee into mountains, wilderness, or desert. I don't want to drag you through such hardships. When I'm on my own, I can take temporary tribulations like a man. I will hate myself if I do it to you."

She had not thought about such extreme exposures. She may become pregnant, too. She does not want to slow him down and put both their lives in jeopardy.

"I can see your point. It will be terrible, nonetheless. My heart will bleed for you everyday. When will this ordeal start?" Her lower lip starts trembling. A tear trickles over her cheek. Jason reads the pain in her eyes.

"As soon as possible. I have to slip away unnoticed, change ships often, leave a zigzag trail that is hard to follow, and hope I can settle in a remote place. As soon as I can contact you in a safe and secret way, I'll do it."

"Before you leave, I hope you can attend synagogue on Sabbath. Maybe God will have an important message for us for the trials ahead." Tabitha tries to buy time.

"I'll come," he promises. "In any case, I'll say goodbye before I leave."

They sit speechless for several minutes, struggling with their bewildered thoughts and anticipated hardships. Tabitha feels as if her sadness may turn her into a fountain of tears too, like Peirene. Dusk is creeping over the city, like the dark cloud that has moved over their young lives.

"It's getting dark. We have to go," Jason remarks somberly.

They are the only ones left at Peirene. Jason enfolds her with his love. They kiss long and tenderly. The deeper they sink into love, the harder they make this separation on themselves.

*

For several weeks, Paul has been talking to Jews and Gentiles in Corinth about the gospel. Various leaders of the Jewish community have asked Crispus to give Paul another opportunity to explain to them why he thinks Jesus of Nazareth is the Messiah. Paul gladly accepted the invitation. Jason and Tabitha attend the meeting as agreed.

When Crispus calls on Paul to speak, Paul thanks him for the honor and privilege. Paul reads from a Greek translation of the Isaiah scroll:

> [3] He was despised and rejected by men,
>> a man of sorrows, and familiar with suffering.
>
> Like one from whom men hide their faces
>> he was despised, and we esteemed him not.
>
> [4] Surely he took up our infirmities
>> and carried our sorrows,
>
> yet we considered him stricken by God,
>> smitten by him, and afflicted.
>
> [5] But he was pierced for our transgressions,
>> he was crushed for our iniquities;
>
> the punishment that brought us peace was upon him,
>> and by his wounds we are healed.
>
> [6] We all, like sheep, have gone astray,
>> each of us has turned to his own way;
>
> and the LORD has laid on him
>> the iniquity of us all.[4]

After touching the scroll with his lips, Paul elaborates on the suffering "Servant of the Lord" depicted by Isaiah.

"Brothers, like you, I was brought up with the view that the scripture I've read points to the suffering of Israel."

Paul proceeds, waving his index finger next to his head to draw special attention, "However, when we read it with an open mind, it is clear that a single person, not a nation, is described here. Furthermore, it's not just any suffering person, but a person on whom the sins of the world have been laid.

"Listen again to these words, 'HE was pierced for OUR transgressions, HE was crushed for OUR iniquities; the

---

4 Is. 53:3-6 NIV

punishment that brought US peace was upon HIM, and by HIS wounds WE are healed.'"[5]

Paul's emphasis makes it clear to Jason that one person carried the sins of many others. *He* and *us* cannot both point to Israel.

Jason can relate to the suffering of the Messiah. His own suffering because of Toni's death and Krato's threats helps him to feel empathy for Jesus, who was falsely accused and illegally executed.

Paul explains, "Brothers, when our father Abraham and his son Isaac ascended Mount Moriah, the boy asked where the lamb for the sacrifice was. Abraham answered that God himself would provide the lamb. That was a prophecy about the Messiah, the Lamb of God. Just as God provided a substitute for Isaac that day, so he provided a substitute for us. The ram died so Isaac could live; Jesus died so we may live.

"The Messiah is the Lamb of God who took our sins onto himself so that we can be reconciled to God. That is the essence of the good news, the living water, I bring to you today," Paul emphasizes.

He continues, "God's plan of salvation is the fruit of his love, not of our good works. Our observance of the law is imperfect. Who of us dare say that he or she keeps the law perfectly? We cannot save ourselves by the law—we need a Savior. Jesus paid for our failures so that we can receive eternal life by grace, not by works. We accept this grace by faith. We then do God's will by the power of the Holy Spirit to show our gratitude, not to earn salvation. The Ten Command-ments start with salvation already received: 'I am the LORD your God, who brought you out of the land of Egypt, out of the house of bondage.'"[6]

Then Paul makes a statement that will eventually unlock the door for many in the synagogue, "Brothers, accepting Jesus

---

5   Is. 53:5 (Emphasis by Author)
6   Ex. 20:2

as the Messiah is not a mere intellectual insight, but a surrender of the heart. Then the miracle happens, the scales fall from our eyes, and we begin to see everything in a new light."

Paul adds a few sentences on the spur of the moment. He did not plan to say it—maybe God gave it to him for the sake of Jason and Tabitha.

"Brothers, since the Lamb of God gave his life for sinners twenty years ago, many Jews and Gentiles have accepted him as their personal Savior. Today, groups of Christians meet every week all over the known world—from Ethiopia, Alexandria, and Cyrene in the south, to Philippi and Thessalonica in the north; from Jerusalem and Antioch in the east, to Rome in the west. Those of you who eventually accept Jesus will not be isolated. You will belong to a large family. May you do good deeds wherever you go. Whether Joseph was forced into the role of slave, prisoner, or governor, he had a positive influence on others. Whatever happens to you, remember: All things work together for good to those who love God.[7] Amen."

Paul's excitement about the new life in Christ rubs off on Jason. He can tell that, for Paul, it is a practical reality that empowers him. Jason senses that this faith is exactly what he needs, but he hesitates to decide right now. He resists the Spirit, but this Counselor will not relent.

*

He hopes that Tabitha and her family will accept Paul's message, too. If all of them become Christians, all his problems with the Jewish faith will fall away. He will have to wait and see.

When talking to Tabitha outside the synagogue, Isaac joins them and invites Jason for supper that evening.

"I think it's time that we start discussing Paul's message," he adds, and walks on. Jason burns with curiosity the whole day.

---

7   Rom. 8:28

Jews are not allowed to do any cooking on the Sabbath. However, after sunset when the Sabbath is over, they can prepare a meal. The main dish is fish grilled over charcoal, supplemented by bread, butter, cheese, jam, curds, and dried dates and figs. For Jason's good appetite, it's a delicious meal.

During the meal, Isaac kicks off by asking everyone to give their honest opinion about the possibility that Jesus is the Messiah.

Esther glances at the others around the table. When nobody volunteers, she says, "From the passages Paul read, it seems a possibility we should at least consider."

"I agree, Mother," Tabitha immediately responds. "There are so many descriptions of the Messiah that are applicable to Jesus that it can't be a mere coincidence. We cannot just ignore it."

Jason rejoices in his heart about Tabitha's positive stance. He tries not to show anything on his face. Will Isaac concur?

"What about you, Jason?" Isaac catches him by surprise.

"Well, at the moment I'm an outsider to Jewish and Christian faith, even to Greek mythology. I know too little about your holy scrolls to judge whether their picture of the Messiah corresponds with Jesus of Nazareth. However, what struck me is that Paul has something that I lack. I wish I could attain a faith or a conviction that can empower and direct me as Paul's faith does for him."

"Yes, I could see it on his face, he seems so inspired by his faith," Hanna adds.

"I wish I could know more about Jesus," says Abigail.

Isaac finishes his chewing. He's thinking, weighing.

"It looks as if you are all very positive about Paul's message."

After chewing another bite of bread and cheese he concludes, "I'm glad we all feel the same."

"Oh!" Esther and the girls utter sighs of relief. For Jason, it's a pleasant surprise. He smiles from ear-to-ear.

"However," Isaac continues with a serious face, "we have to consider the practical implications of our decisions well before we make any moves. We serve both Jews and Greeks with our business. We can lose many customers if we choose wrongly. It concerns our bread and butter, our house and clothes. We can lose everything, just like that!" Isaac concludes, snapping his fingers.

"Should we put material things before spiritual things?" Tabitha challenges her dad's standpoint.

"That's not what your father meant," Esther explains, "he just warns us that religious choices may have severe practical consequences; therefore, we should not act impetuously."

"Thank you, Mother," Isaac says, laying his hand on Esther's. "Let us continue to discuss these matters among ourselves, but don't give any indication to others. Jason, we would appreciate it if you don't tell anyone about our stance."

"Count me in!" Jason responds, to Isaac's relief.

Isaac and his family are considering the possibility of exchanging the heavy yoke of legalistic religion for the light yoke of salvation by grace through faith in Christ. Paradoxically, the lighter theological yoke may go with a heavier socioeconomic yoke. Isaac's business may suffer when they accept Jesus as Messiah and Savior.

Jason is glad there is no division in the family. He is also pleasantly surprised about the positive stand the family is taking. He can understand Isaac's caution. Putting food on the table is a dad's primary responsibility.

When Jason walks home, he avoids his regular route, just in case the gang tries to ambush him again.

Jason postpones a decision about Paul's message. He is so preoccupied with his plan to leave Corinth secretly that he pushes everything else out of his mind. He does not want to get confused by several major decisions at the same time. He wants to stay focused on what he sees as his primary problem.

CHAPTER 6

Jason plans to slip away from Corinth on a small boat that has been dragged over the isthmus on the Diolkos. It is farther away from Corinth, and there are fewer people than at the Lechaion and Cenchrea harbors. Spies cannot easily blend in with a crowd as they can on busy piers.

Jason hopes he can step over to another fishing boat at Athens, sail to a few Greek islands, and go from there to a harbor in Asia Minor.

He receives a short letter from Diana. Her treatment is proceeding well. All signs of the infection have disappeared. However, she has to continue treatment to ensure the disease is completely cured. She is in good spirits and looks forward to her return. Jason puts the letter in his backpack. He plans to answer it later.

His family knows about his plans and is sworn to secrecy. They understand the situation. They can't dare to say anything to anybody, lest they jeopardize Jason's safety.

Philip helped Jason negotiate with an old customer, the skipper of a fishing vessel transported over the isthmus with Jason's newest trolley. Philip supplied fifty valuable silver coins Jason can wear in a band around his waist underneath his tunic. Jason decides to keep the money for emergencies. He hopes to get employment on the ships and pay for his passage.

With his plans in place, Jason told Tabitha he would come to her house later that evening. To reduce pressure on Tabitha, Jason told Isaac and Esther he is fleeing for his life, and he will not make contact, securing his secret. They vowed to keep silent. Now they can better empathize with Tabitha and Jason, and pray for them.

Isaac and Esther retire. Jason and Tabitha can share their last closeness for...God knows how long. Every fiber in them objects to the unavoidable. They kiss and embrace repeatedly, intensifying the pain of the goodbye.

Eventually, Jason has to leave. The boat is waiting.

"Shalom, Jason! May God be with you."

"Shalom, my love! May we see each other again soon. Jason forces himself to leave. He sneaks away in the dark streets of Corinth. Conflicting emotions churn inside him: love, sadness, anger, fear, insecurity, but also determination. Though burdened by exile and uncertainty, he is ready to grab opportunities and to prevail despite the odds.

When he's gone, Tabitha falls down on her bed and buries her face in her pillow, sobbing inconsolably. *Why is life so cruel and unfair? Why must I lose Jason so shortly after I have found his love? Why has my greatest joy become my deepest sorrow? Why do I have to carry this burden of frustrated, yearning love without any news from my beloved?*

Jason goes on horseback to the east side of the isthmus. His dad will send one of the workers to fetch the horse in the morning. The skipper brings him from shore to the boat with the dinghy. Jason climbs on board with a sigh of relief. The sails are hoisted, and with the help of a soft breeze, they glide silently off into the night. The stars shine brightly, the future blanketed by a fog of uncertainty.

Many questions swirl around in Jason's head: *Why did this happen to me? Where will I end up? How will Tabitha and I cope with the yearning? Will the saying, 'out of sight out of mind,' eventually catch up with us or will absence makes the heart grow fonder? When will we see each other again? What must I do to prevent Krato from tracking me down? When will I see my country and loved ones again?*

Drained by stress, he eventually falls asleep at the stern on folded sails. When the sun rises, they enter a fishing harbor near Athens. He has to find his next boat.

He says goodbye to the skipper, and starts asking for a boat that goes north. He thus ensures that they will remember a tall guy who was heading north. The skipper of the fifth boat responds, "No, we're sailing south to Aegina, then east to Mikonos." That's what Jason actually wants.

"Can I go along?" Jason tries his luck.

"You're welcome. We need an extra hand."

Immediately the deal is done. The skipper plans to leave within an hour. Jason has time to get himself some bread rolls. He will have to make due without mom's breakfast of ham, cheese, and eggs. He wonders when he will taste that again.

Jason is used to heavy lifting in his dad's workshop. His extra power is welcomed by the crew. They move some stuff around and get the deck of the forty-foot boat in order. They depart with a light northwesterly breeze in the sails.

A few hours later, near a small island, the skipper allows them to cast out a light net to fish for lunch. They are lucky. Soon three big fish are hauled in and prepared for frying in a large pan in the galley where the crew always keeps some charcoal alive for such occasions.

Never has plain fish tasted so good to the famished Jason. After working and eating together, the crew accepts him as one of them. They chat like old friends. They stick to general stuff and don't ask personal questions.

They make a delivery at Aegina, and load some stuff for Mikonos. The wind has been picking up. When they leave Aegina, the water is quite choppy, but with the wind in their backs, they move in the same direction as the waves, smoothing out the ride. They make good progress, though they have to watch the sails and make adjustments often.

A sudden gust from a different direction slams the boom of the main sail against the back of a seaman standing near the side of the boat, knocking him overboard.

Jason looks at the men and skipper for a cue about the modus operandi in such an emergency. Immediately, they lower the sails and throw out the bow anchor. The boat swirls around, bow to the wind. Now the boat faces the waves and bobs like a cork. The anchor rope hangs straight down, indicating the anchor has not reached the seabed. The wind will gradually push them away from their mate.

They hear the cries of the man and occasionally see his arm waving, some fifty paces from the boat. They shout instructions to their mate, Alex, urging him to hang on and keep his head above water. Shouting into the wind is probably useless. Quick action is needed.

"Are you a good swimmer?" the skipper shouts through cupped hands to Jason.

"I can try!"

Jason assumes that the others are not up to the task. Maybe he can earn their loyalty this way. To sail upwind to Alex, they will have to zigzag. In the process, they may not find him. They try the rope-rescue first.

The skipper ties one end of a long thin rope around Jason's waist. Jason throws off his tunic, jumps into the wavy water, and swims at a moderate pace to the place he last saw Alex. The waves aggravate swimming against the wind. He proceeds at a steady pace to preserve energy. The slow strokes of his strong arms and the paddling of his feet pull him through the water. He keeps his head in the water and exhales slowly, taking a breath when he has broken through a wave. One guy has climbed the mast from where he can better see his mates in the water. When Jason is halfway, the man on the mast shows him the right way by shouting and gesturing.

Don't panic! Easy does it! You can do it! Jason says to himself. He realizes panic will kill them; perseverance will prevail. His old motto pushes him on—good planning and hard work will bring him out on top. A little bit of luck would also help a lot.

As the wind slowly pushes the boat away, they run out of rope. Jason feels the rope tighten on his waist; Alex is only twenty paces away. It would be suicide to untie the rope. He just doesn't have the energy left to swim back to the boat on his own—let alone help a drowning man.

"Come! Come!" Jason signals to Alex to move closer. The guy gets the message and puts in his last bit of waning strength. At the boat, the skipper realizes the problem, and ties another piece of rope to the one attached to Jason.

Jason and Alex exert themselves to reach each other. When they are only three paces apart, arms and hands stretched out in a final desperate effort, Alex disappears under the water.

"Oh, God! Let him come up one more time! Please!" Jason prays out loud.

Suddenly, a wave pushes Alex right onto Jason, as if an invisible hand has lifted him from the deep. Alex is unconscious now, making his handling easier.

Jason puts Alex's arm over the rope and signals to the crew to pull them in. The guys on the boat really do their share now and haul them in pretty fast. The pulling action helps Jason to keep head above water.

Two of the crew lean over the side of the boat, grab Alex by the arms, and hoist him into the boat. Jason grabs the side of the boat and with the help of a wave pulls his upper body over the rim. The others help him to climb in. He is exhausted.

The skipper is attending to Alex. They lay him on his belly over a barrel with his head down. The skipper applies pressure on his back. Water flows out, and air flows in. Alex starts coughing, ridding his lungs from water, and gasping in fresh air.

The men are jubilant, babbling all at once, patting Jason and Alex on the back. When the excitement subsides, the skipper guides them to get the boat on course again.

The skipper shakes Jason's hand and thanks him for his brave endeavor, "Providence put you on my boat today. Thank you for fulfilling your task."

After a while, Alex has recovered enough to come to Jason. He takes Jason's hand with both his hands, thanking him with teary eyes, "If it were not for you...the others can't swim...you saved my life...I can never repay you..."

"Yes, you can," Jason responds. "My life is also in danger. When anyone asks you about me, deny that you have seen me. This way, you can save my life."

Alex promises to show his loyalty, and to convince his buddies to do the same. Their gratitude makes them comply.

They reach Mikonos before sunset. Jason will have to find another boat from here. He helps the crew with mooring and unloading. When he says goodbye to the captain, Jason expresses his wish to remain unknown, a request the skipper gladly grants.

*

To get his next boat, Jason follows the same procedure he used near Athens, asking skippers of fishing boats whether they are going north. This time, the third one gives the answer he is looking for:

"No, we're going east tomorrow."

"Do you need an extra hand?" Jason wagers.

The skipper looks the sturdy Jason over, and likes what he sees. "Yes, we can do with a fellow like you!" They close the deal with a handshake. Jason asks permission to sleep on the boat. It suits the skipper—it gives extra security to his cargo.

Fishing boats earn extra income by transporting small cargo fast between islands, especially when fishing is not good.

When they leave Mikonos the next morning with a moderate breeze behind them, Jason learns that they will deliver and pick up at Patmos, and then proceed to Miletus on the west coast of Asia Minor. It suits Jason. At Miletus, a great port city, he may get work on a large ship that will take him far away.

Jason has learned a lot from his first trip on a fishing vessel. He knows the ropes and makes himself handy. With moderate wind, they make good progress. At a small island, they catch their lunch, and shortly afterwards enjoy fried fish and bread.

This crew is nosier. During lunch, they try to find out where he comes from, where he's heading, and why he makes the trip. Jason says he's from a small village in the Peloponnesus. He wants to see the world, and will stay where the prospects are good. His answers are vague. It makes the guys more curious—maybe this guy has something to hide.

"How was the recent Isthmian Games?" one throws a stone into the bush, hoping to scare out a rat. A shock goes through Jason. The guy has put his finger on an extremely sensitive area. He remains silent, chewing, thinking of a way out.

"Yes, tell us about that nasty accident that happened there. I've heard that a child was killed by a javelin. I wonder if the javelin thrower did it on purpose," another adds fuel to the fire.

"I heard it was an accident," Jason answers, as casually as he can. "Apparently the child ran over the field and was hit."

"Did you compete in the games?" the first guy fishes. "You have the right frame for discus or javelin."

Jason smiles and shakes his head. He wishes they will change the subject. They are sniffing too close to his secret. To his relief, they start talking about the next Olympic Games, speculating about the chances of the champions.

It disturbs Jason that the story of Toni's death has spread so far so soon. The Athenians who attended the games probably spread the dreadful news. Any hint from his side that he comes from Corinth will immediately ring a bell with people who heard about the tragedy. That would blow his cover right away.

This crew will definitely remember him. He has no leverage to persuade them to cover for him. His tracks can only be wiped out if they all drown. However, since he questions Greek mythology, it is highly unlikely that the god of the sea will intervene on his behalf.

At Miletus, Jason leaves this vessel and searches for work on larger ships. The four ports are enormous. The first day passes without any luck. That night he visits a few taverns in the harbor area, hoping to pick up a contact, but to no avail. Discouraged and exhausted, he decides to sleep in a tavern.

*

When the sun sets at Corinth the same day, Tabitha eventually has to face the feelings she desperately tried to suppress for two days by staying busy.

To please her mother, she eats two bites of bread and butter at supper. She cannot face the fish, fearing she may throw up. Seeing her daughter's distress, Esther excuses Tabitha from cleaning up. Her child must deal with her emotions.

Esther walks with Tabitha to her room, arm around Tabitha's shoulders, advising softly, "You can't keep on suppressing your feelings, darling. Don't be afraid to cry your heart out. We'll understand. We stand with you."

Tabitha enters her room and bolts the door. Now she is in her private domain, isolated from the world, alone with God and Jason. The moment she begins praying for Jason, her bottled-up emotions erupt in uncontrollable weeping. She tries to muffle her crying by pushing her face into the pillow.

When anger boils up, she hits the pillow with her fists, hissing in angry frustration, "Why? Why? Why?"

In the kitchen, her parents and sisters hold hands and intercede for Tabitha in prayer. They can faintly hear her weeping and shouting. They are one with her in her agony. Why has her joy been turned into sorrow?

After twenty minutes or so, Tabitha calms down. Having cried her heart out, she feels relieved. She surrenders herself and Jason to the Lord's care. She finds peace in God's loving-kindness. He is almighty and omniscient. He knows exactly where Jason is and what he needs. God will provide.

With her pain and concern handed over to God, she can now dare to think of her beloved Jason. She remembers their first kiss. She tries to capture every detail in her imagination— the moment she realized Jason was going to kiss her, the wonderful feeling of excited anticipation that bubbled through her body.

She recalls how she closed her eyes and waited for the miracle. Their lips touched gently, they tightened their embrace, and her heart sang, "It's happening, it's happening, don't stop..."

His huge stature and strong arms enfolded her. His manly figure and odor put her femininity on fire, merging woman-Tabitha with man-Jason. Her cup ran over. It was the fulfillment of a long cherished dream—Jason loved her!

Reliving that wonderful first moment makes the blood rush through her veins again. She has no need to fantasize about what they have not yet tasted. Re-experiencing what they have tasted is fulfilling enough right now.

*

At the same time, Jason dozes off in his tavern room. There's a knock at his door. He wakes up and waits, not sure if he's mistaken. There it is again, softly, *knock-knock-knock*. Irritated, he goes to the door.

It's a pretty girl, about sixteen, with beautiful face and curves. Jason looks her up and down in the dim light of an oil lamp in the hallway. She's in a short tunic. *Nice legs*, he thinks.

"Do you need company?" she asks, with luring eyes and a tempting smile.

She reminds him of Diana. He hesitates for a moment. He's a refugee, lonely, in a foreign place. Who will know?

"I will know!" his conscience responds—with Tabitha's voice.

With a shake of his head, he indicates that he does not require her services. To prevent quibbling, he closes and bolts the door. Back in bed, his thoughts jump to Tabitha and Diana. How different they are! The girl at the door is, like Diana, physically attractive and tempting, but her attractiveness is just superficial.

Tabitha has that other dimension that is hard to define. Her total being—face, body, personality, and faith—makes up that unique person with the character he loves and respects with all his heart.

An intense yearning for Tabitha engulfs Jason. While he had no real appetite for the sexy girl at his door, he yearns for Tabitha's physical and emotional closeness.

He wonders how she's doing. Most likely, she is engulfed in the same miserable yet wonderful yearning. He embraces his pillow as he starts kissing her in his imagination. He feels her lips, her body, and how she kisses him back. He smells her fragrance, tastes her lips, touches her skin, hears her voice, and looks into her eyes. He is amazed by how real his imagination is. His memory has stored all those impressions of the senses, mixing them with the inner feelings of love and care. In spite of the distance separating them, he experiences the whole Tabitha. He decides he will do this often.

Comforted by Tabitha's imaginary closeness, Jason dozes off into blissful sleep.

About the same time that night, these young lovers have enjoyed each other over a great distance by calling up stored memories, enhanced by lively imagination, and fanned by intense yearning.

They carry this bittersweet burden of love together.

The pain of this yearning seeks the balm of joyful memories, and yet, those joyful memories also increase the pain. In a vicious cycle, the pain and joy intensify each other until the lovers consider any possible way to reach each other, irrespective of the cost or sacrifice.

It may blind and incite them to such an extent that they may make fatal mistakes.

*

The next morning, Jason offers a short prayer to Tabitha's God. Although he does not know this God yet, he wants to know him better. He prays for guidance and protection.

Maybe, if his and Tabitha's prayers can merge...

To his utter amazement, the first captain he approaches has an opening for a deckhand. The ship is heading for Alexandria in Egypt. On top of that, he will receive usual sailor privileges.

This is great, he silently savors his luck, *I get free passage, free food, and some pocket money as well—not too bad! Thank you, God! Thanks, Tabitha!* He knows his fortune this time has not come from his own planning and hard work, but as a godsend. Tabitha's God has helped him twice recently: when rescuing a drowning man, and when desperately searching work. He feels grateful yet uneasy about this unknown God.

Egypt has an abundance of grain and vegetables, but due to an outbreak of foot-and-mouth disease months ago, they are short of livestock. This large ship is taking two decks full of cattle, sheep, and goats for breeding purposes to Alexandria, and planning to pick up a cargo of grain for Italy on the return trip.

As soon as the animals are on board, Jason knows why the captain had a problem attracting enough crew. Apart from the regular feeding of the animals and cleansing of the stalls, this ark is rather noisy and smelly. The provisions of the unknown God have some strange strings attached, that's for sure!

Though it is dirty work, there are no passengers on board. It suits Jason perfectly. The fewer people see him go to Africa, the better. Therefore, he does not complain about the stench. Like farmers, he gets used to the odor after a day or two. He can imagine what his drinking pals in Corinth would say if they could see him shoveling dung: "Can you believe it? The Isthmian Javelin and Discus Champion, the son of Corinth's master wagon builder, has become a stable cleaner." However, Jason does not feel degraded. His dad drilled him from an early age to be proud of his work, no matter how simple or common that work is. Philip stressed that glory does not lie in the type of work, but in the quality of work. Therefore, Jason does his best—even when he shovels dung.

They enjoy favorable weather till they are halfway into the Mediterranean. The wind picks up and soon they have to cope with a gale that sweeps up a high swell and white-crested waves. The wind buffets them from the northeast, making the vessel list toward the right, starboard. Fortunately, the decks have been subdivided into small stalls so that the animals cannot slide to one side of the tilting ship and make it capsize.

The captain knows they are driven off course to the west of Alexandria. However, he cannot steer more into the wind, fearing it may make the ship list even more. They hope the storm will abate before they reach the sandbanks of Africa.

As the gale increases in ferocity, sailors remove all sails except for one small one on the main mast and the jib at the bowsprit. These help to steer the boat. The jib controls the bow; the rudder controls the stern as long as the boat moves forward through the water.

At nightfall, the situation becomes perilous. The overclouded sky makes navigation by stars impossible. Wind direction gives an idea, but they don't know if the wind is gradually shifting. There are no landmarks to indicate direction.

The captain has depth readings taken every half hour by means of a fathom-line, a rope with lead at one end and with a knot every fathom (6 ft). When the sailors report that water depth is decreasing, the captain—fearing rocks or sand banks—gives the command to steer westward, parallel to the coast of Africa. They are not sure about direction; they have to guess. It is a dark moon, associated with extremely low and high tides. At low tide, hidden rocks and sand will be closer to the surface.

When first light shows in the clouds, they notice hilly country several miles away on the left, port-side. They assume it must be Africa. The gale is not letting up. If they anchor now, the ship may drag the anchors along and strand. Not having much of a choice, they continue in a westerly direction. Hopefully, the land will show them where they are and where they are going.

Suddenly, the ship shudders. It comes to a screeching halt. The keel of the boat has run onto something. Is it rock or sand? The sailors lower a weighted bucket with a rope, trying to scoop up something from the ridge. They hoist it—full of large pebbles. The ship's keel will last longer on a pebble reef than on a rocky ridge.

The waves lift the stern and push the keel further onto the reef. The waves now splash on the ship as if breaking on a rocky shore. Unless the wind dies down soon, the waves will bash the wooden ship to pieces.

Up to this point, Jason has put his trust in the experienced captain and crew. He realizes that they are now at the mercy of the wind and waves. The land is too far and the sea too rough for swimming out. The crew can put a raft together, but what about the poor animals? Jason launches an emergency prayer to the unknown God.

Realizing the full extent of the emergency, the captain orders the crew to open the loading hatches and drive the animals from the ship into the sea. In this way, some of them may reach the shore a mile off. If the animals stay on board, they will drown. The crew has trouble pushing them out through the latches. Once the first ones make the plunge, the herd instinct of the others makes them follow. Soon, most of the animals are in the water, swimming in circles, not knowing where to go.

Released from the weight of the livestock, the ship is lifted from the reef by the swells. The wind and waves pushes the doomed vessel toward the shore.

Suspecting the ship will get stuck on a reef again, the crew empties wine barrels, tying them two-by-two together with ropes, planning to use them as rafts when the ship strands again.

The bewildered animals follow the drifting ship. When the ship gets stuck again about three hundred paces from shore, the crew pushes the barrel-rafts overboard, jumps into the water, and climbs onto the rafts. The wind drives men and animals to the shore. Their drenched clothes increase the wind chill.

Approaching the shore, they are surprised to see a few people on the beach in the dim light of an overcast dawn. Jason wonders if he will become lunch in a big black pot. This is Africa! He hopes the animals will interest the locals more than cannibalism. When he planned to come to Africa, he had something else in mind.

As they come closer to the beach, Jason is relieved to see that the people wear Greek clothes. When they hear them speak Greek, they are overjoyed. They learn they have stranded near Apollonia, the harbor of Cyrene, five hundred miles west of Alexandria. Greeks colonized this area about seven centuries ago. Known as Cyrenaica, it has been under Roman control for the past century. Jason learned about this colony at school, but to him, Africa was an extremely far-off place.

Greek mythology depicts Cyrene as a nymph obsessed with hunting. Apollo fell in love with her when he watched her wrestling a lion. He carried her off to North Africa where they married. Apollo put her in charge of the city he named after her.

The hospitable inhabitants of Apollonia take care of the shivering castaways, providing fire, blankets, bread, and soup. The animals are rounded up and driven to corrals. The drowned ones will be picked up later with wagons.

Word is sent to Cyrene, an hour by horseback. Late in the afternoon, four ox-wagons from Cyrene arrive, followed by another five the next morning. They figure there may be something to salvage from the wreck.

The next day, Jason and some of the crew go by ox-wagon to Cyrene. It is a slow, monotonous, uphill journey of twelve miles. However, as the crow flies, Cyrene is only four miles from the sea. From the harbor, the wagons first go three miles west, parallel to the coast, then four miles south, up through a ravine, and then five miles southwest before they reach Cyrene below the crest of the mountain range.

Jason passes time by chatting with the driver. He wants to learn as much as he can about this area. He plans to go deep into Africa, ensuring Krato will not find him.

Jason learns by observing and listening. The limestone plateau of Cyrenaica rises from the coast in several steps, each a few miles wide. The mountain range is known as Green Mountain, thanks to its tree-covered slopes. The escarpment lifts and blocks clouds moving in from the Mediterranean Sea, causing rain to fall mostly on the northern slopes, providing adequate water to Cyrene and surrounding farms. On the south side of the range, the plateau gradually slopes down over sixty miles of rocky and sandy terrain to the Sahara. Cyrenaica sits like an emerald gem between the red-brown desert and blue sea.

Wherever Romans go, they try to create a little Rome where they can enjoy at least some of Rome's luxuries. When Jason's group eventually arrives in Cyrene, he is amazed that this city—in true Roman tradition—can also boast with its forum, baths, temples, theater, stadium, and hippodrome.

Helpful citizens volunteer to take the stranded crew as guests into their homes. Jason is invited by a certain Lucius to lodge with his family. Jason wanted to go to a far-off place. He got it.

At supper, Lucius prays over the food and ends with, "In the name of our Lord Jesus Christ, amen."

Jason can hardly believe his ears—he is lodging with Christians! If only Tabitha could know of this! Once again, Tabitha's God provided without Jason's help. He feels relieved from a terrible burden. He wonders what this new acquaintance will hold for him.

CHAPTER 7

About a third of the ship's animals drowned. They were washed ashore by the wind and waves. Such abundance of fresh meat can't be wasted, so the two towns organize big parties. As soon as possible, the drowned animals were slaughtered and salted, preserving the meat for public use.

The livestock that survived the shipwreck will be auctioned off in the coming week. Cyrene's farmers are glad to add new blood to their stock. The captain of the ship is grateful he has not lost everything.

All are invited to the feast. However, the Jews and Christians can't participate because they are barred from eating the meat of animals whose blood has not been drained properly. Lucius explains to Jason that the Jerusalem Council decided a few years ago that Gentile Christians don't have to obey Jewish laws. However, to make socialization between Jewish and Gentile Christians easier, the Council decided that Gentile Christians have to shun practices of heathen temples, such as sexual immorality, eating meat offered to idols, eating blood, and eating meat of animals that did not bleed out.

In order not to exclude Jews and Christians from the feasting, the city council has bought some of the surviving cattle and sheep from the captain, and handed them over to these minority groups to prepare them the way they see fit. A spirit of generosity and celebration fills the air, because there was no loss of human life when the ship stranded, and because of the great bonanza the community can enjoy.

As they wait for the huge portions of spit-roasted meat to cook, people barbeque smaller portions to feast on in the meantime. For young people, eating is not enough fun. When they have stilled their hunger, they start up various activities to occupy themselves and to get in touch with the opposite sex. Some engage in music and folk-dancing. Others try group games, showing off their speed and strength. A few acrobats entertain people with their stunts.

Lucius' sixteen-year-old daughter, Mary, drags Jason by hand into a circle of folk-dancers. The movements are similar to the Greek group-dancing at Corinth. He blends in easily, but because of his tall stature, the girls adore him and try to make contact. He wants to minimize public exposure for safety's sake. As soon as he gets a break, he tells Lucius that he is going home because of a headache.

*

Lucius soon sums Jason up correctly. Something is bothering the young man, but he refrains from sharing his burden. Lucius decides to invite Jason on a trip into the desert. Maybe he will eventually open up. Twice a year, Lucius travels with a camel caravan to the south to trade with the Imazighen, called Berber by the Romans. A subgroup, the Tuareg, undertakes long, arduous camel journeys over the Sahara to trade salt for commodities.

Jason gladly accepts the invitation. It takes him out of the public eye, and it gives him the opportunity to meet these mysterious desert dwellers.

Lucius warns Jason that they may be attacked by robbers on their journey through the desert. Therefore, they take four helpers along. They introduce Jason to the art of stab-spear fighting. The iron spearhead is eighteen inches long and sharpened on both edges. The five-foot handle is thick and copper-plated, protecting it against the swords and daggers of the enemy. Because the spear is about three times the length of a Roman sword, it reaches farther, giving advantage to the bearer.

First, the instructor instills the right motivation into his trainee. Jason must realize the danger is real and serious. Then he needs practice to defend his life.

With a calm and authoritative voice, the guy makes himself clear, "In a life-or-death situation, you don't get a second chance. Either you kill your opponent, or he kills you. It's not a game. You have only one life. When you lose it, it's gone forever. So, guard it with all the power and dexterity you have. Do you get the point?"

Jason nods, struck by the instructor's bluntness and tone of voice. The words sound familiar. His grandpa said something similar to him long ago. Jason realizes his soft spot for underdogs will kill him if he hesitates in the heat of battle.

He practices with his instructors. For practice, they use stab-spears without spearheads. The tips of the sticks are covered by wooly sheepskin, allowing them to touch each other's bodies without inflicting injury.

Jason has to grab the spear with both hands, about two feet apart. He can block blows with either end or with the middle. By extending one arm and retracting the other in quick succession, the enemy is battered from left and right, top and bottom. Defensive action is swiftly followed by offensive stabs aimed at the opponent's arms, legs, head, or body. The trainer demonstrates defensive and offensive moves, and then has Jason practice those motions until they become second nature. When attacked, there is no time to think about defense—he has to act instinctively.

As soon as Jason defends himself well against one, they show him how to handle more than one attacker. A forward stab with the spearhead is immediately followed by a backward knock with the blunt end of the spear handle. They decide to resume practice and rehearse strategy every evening at campfire as they go deeper into the Sahara.

Jason learns from Lucius that they have to walk long distances with the camels, especially when the animals are heavily laden, when the sand is soft, or during the hottest time of day. However, to make it easier for Jason, Lucius takes along two extra camels for them to ride on when the conditions are favorable.

At first, Jason finds the rhythmic, rocking gate of the camel exhausting, but after several hours, he gets into it. After three days, they leave the Cyrenaica Plateau and enter the emptiness of the Sahara.

Jason realizes that the real test of this trip will be perseverance amid boredom—moving his body back and forth in rhythm with the camel's strides in baking-hot sun from dawn to dusk. For Jason's untrained eyes, there is nothing to see except the wide expanse of eerie desolation, nothing to hear but an occasional grunt of a camel, nothing to enjoy but two sips of water every hour. Relentlessly, the slow procession moves on and on—hour after hour, day after day.

Lucius doesn't try to nudge Jason to share his feelings about his problems. He waits patiently for the desert to sink into Jason's soul and to open the door of his heart from the inside. The desert has a tremendous effect on the human psyche after a few days.

Some of these patient beasts of burden carry the merchandise for trading, while others carry their feed and the men's gear. Leather water-bags hang low on the shady side of the camels. Once an hour, one of the men disperses water rations in a bowl on the go.

Every scorching day is followed by a chilly night. The guards collect the droppings of the camels for the night's campfire. To preserve their body fluids, camel droppings are amazingly dry, ready for use as firewood within hours. After the regular spear practice every night, the men cook their meal, huddling close to the fire to fend off the desert chill.

They sleep in sheepskin bags with the wool on the inside. These protect them against the cold and the nasty creepy-crawlies of the desert. In the morning, beneath his sleeping bag, Jason is alarmed to find a few scorpions that were attracted by the warmth.

On the seventh day, just when Jason begins to regret his decision to accompany Lucius on the trip, they come over a sandy ridge and see some palm trees and black tents in a distance. The sun hangs low and red in the west. Jason assumes they will camp at the oasis for the night. What a relief! Man and beast can be rested and refreshed. Homesick, Jason remembers the privileges he enjoyed in Corinth.

They are warmly welcomed by Lucius' old customers, who have become his friends. Since Alexander the Great, Greek spread from Egypt to surrounding regions. This family speaks Greek quite well, though with a peculiar accent.

After Jason has been introduced to Agizul, the head of the family, sweet Berber tea is served in tiny cups. Made from a desert herb, it has a revitalizing effect on the weary. While enjoying this herbal tonic, guest and host inform each other about the well-being of their families. This lengthy protocol is part of polite behavior in this culture. There is no nosy probing. They grant each other the freedom to tell as much as they want to.

When Lucius and Agizul are done, they look in Jason's direction. He feels obligated to tell something of himself and his family. He keeps it short: "I come from Southern Greece. My father is a wagon-builder. I left home to start my own business. A storm landed me in Cyrene and with Lucius, who invited me to accompany him on this trip. So, here I am." Though Jason's self-introduction gives Lucius some new insight into his young partner, the absence of facts is conspicuous.

At supper, fresh camel milk, goat cheese, and buttered bread patties, baked on glowing charcoal, are served. The main dish is a stew called couscous, consisting of small millet rolls, goat meat pieces, and vegetables produced in the shade of the palm trees. Dried dates and figs round the meal off with something sweet.

Jason is amazed at the satisfying cuisine these people enjoy in a region that seemed lifeless to him. Over the ages, they have adapted to the harsh desert climate to make life not only livable, but quite enjoyable. Their tents are designed to diminish the daytime heat and the nighttime chill. They use the reeds at the fountain to thatch the roofs of large shady parasols fixed on four posts to survive desert storms.

Agizul warns his guests against possible danger. Despite the renowned hospitality of these desert dwellers, piracy does occur occasionally. They would never deny each other water, but some do try to improve their situation by robbing others of camels and taking their women and children as slaves.

A few days ago, a passing caravan alerted Agizul to the fact that a gang of robbers has been active in the region. He briefs them about the defense strategy in case an attack occurs. That night, they sleep with their stab-spears close to their bodies, one hand resting on the weapon. They take turns to stand watch. The movement of the stars measures the time. They relieve each other often, preventing the watch from dozing off.

*

While Jason learns survival tactics in the desert, the young church of Corinth faces its own struggles. Paul's companions, Timothy and Silas, join him in Corinth. They have assisted the new churches in Thessalonica and Berea respectively. However, they want to tell Paul about problems in those churches, and take his advice back to them.

Timothy is only eighteen years old; therefore, Paul gives him more authority by writing a letter to the church in Thessalonica. Later, he follows it up with a second one. These first letters of

Paul contain important information about the end time and the resurrection. He reminds them that Christians will suffer tribulation, and urges them to persevere in their sanctification. Paul makes copies of the letters for the church in Corinth because the information is vital for them as well.

Before Timothy and Silas joined him in Corinth, Paul helped Aquila in his tent-making industry in order to pay for his own expenses. He could only communicate with the Jews on the Sabbath. Now that his helpers are with him, they can earn an income while Paul can give more time to his mission.

With new vigor, he teaches in synagogue every day, showing from the scripture that Jesus is the Messiah.

Paul reiterates, "The Messiah's kingdom is not political, as we Jews have wrongly expected, but spiritual. Christ did not come to free Israel from Rome, but to free sinners from evil and hell. God said that the punishment for sin is death. By his death in our place, Jesus bought us free. Instead of God's wrath, we may now receive his grace, accepting it in faith. In this way," Paul emphasizes, "God's holiness and love both prevailed. His holiness could not leave sin unpunished, and his love could not leave man unsaved. By the atoning sacrifice of God's son, our sin-debt was paid, and we are reconciled with our Heavenly Father."

Eventually, the message sinks in with both Jews and Gentiles. Even Crispus, the ruler of the synagogue, accepts Christ as Messiah and Savior. It makes the conservative Jews furious; Crispus loses his job. Most Jews cannot accept Paul's suffering Messiah, and they hate to see others do so. The debates get more acrimonious by the day. When the opposing Jews begin to blaspheme Jesus, Paul decides the Jews have had their chance. From now on, he will take his message to the Gentiles.

He leaves the synagogue and moves in with Justus, who lives next door. Those Jews who consider conversion to Christianity will still see him often, enabling them to contact him whenever they want to.

However, now there is a painful split in the Jewish community. Paul is blamed for it by some, and thanked for it by others.

In this time of division among the Jews, Paul has a vision. The Lord tells him not to flinch, but to proceed boldly in Corinth, for there are still many who have to be saved. God has lifted the burden from his tired servant. Paul gladly extends his stay in Corinth to eighteen months.

Isaac finds himself sitting on the fence. He tries not to take sides. However, each side interprets Isaac's neutrality as a sign that he belongs to the opposition. Now, he is losing support on both sides. He hopes that by showing his true colors, his friends on both sides will understand his position.

He attends meetings in both the synagogue and at Justus' home. He makes his position known: He will not stop being a Jew if he becomes a Christian.

"Roman, Greek, and Jewish Christians worship together. They don't have to lay down their nationality or culture. Free men and slaves, men and women, Jews and Gentiles, they all belong to the same Christian family," he explains to his critics.

Soon Justus' house becomes too small for the growing church in Corinth. They get permission from the city council to meet in the theater. It does not bother most Corinthians that a new religious group exists in the city. They are used to the co-existence of Roman basilicas, Greek temples, and Jewish synagogues in all their major cities. Roman law allows freedom of religion—as attested to by Pantheon temples—but it does not tolerate religious unrest.

News of the new religion spreads, luring the curious and the disillusioned to the meetings, who are hoping to find answers that the existing religions in the city have not given them. When Isaac and his family attend Christian worship, he is amazed to notice many slaves and lower-class people in the audience. When Julius Caesar rebuilt Corinth a century ago, he populated it with freed slaves and retired soldiers. In one of his letters, Paul later reminded Corinthian Christians, "Not many of you were wise by human standards; not many were influential; not many were of noble birth."[8]

Isaac is glad and amused to see that the wealthy dress modestly, presumably to make the middle and lower class feel at home.

Paul does not have to defend the gospel any more against Jewish criticism. He can now feed his flock with the basic facts about Christ as well as the practical implication of Jesus' teaching, suffering, death, resurrection, and ascension for everyday Christian living.

Paul's practical messages empower Tabitha in her loneliness, worries, and yearning. Like her dad, she sees herself as a Jew interested in the Christian gospel.

Several times, Paul accepts Isaac's invitation to have supper with them. Tabitha shares her worries about Jason with Paul, and he prays with them that God will protect and guide Jason wherever he goes.

Tabitha asks Paul's guidance on a question that distresses her: "Rabbi, Psalm 37 was read in synagogue on Sabbath. It promises that if we delight ourselves in the Lord, he will give us the desires of our hearts. Why does God refuse the earnest desire of my heart to have contact with Jason? I think I do delight myself in the Lord. Where do I go wrong?"

"Tabitha, I have struggled with this question too," Paul admits. "The Lord showed me that *delight yourself in the Lord* is the key to the riddle. Delighting yourself in the Lord is the exact opposite of fretting. When we want something dearly, we often shift from persevering prayer to fretting prayer. The following verses teach us how to avoid fretting. You have to commit yourself to the Lord; trust him; rest in him; wait patiently for him; and remain thankful to him. Whenever I get impatient with the Lord, I test and correct myself with these five indicators. I can assure you, it works!"

---

8   1 Cor. 1:26 NIV

Tabitha looks down on her lap and confesses, "Yes, I can see where I went wrong. What are those five tests again? Commit, trust, rest, wait...What is the last one?"

"Thankfulness!" Isaac adds, knowing that Tabitha has not been counting her blessings lately.

"Yes, thankfulness extinguishes the fires of fretting," Paul concurs with Isaac. "When we fret, we focus on what we don't have, and then moan about it. When we are thankful, we focus on what we do have, and thank God for it. So when David repeatedly says, 'Don't fret,' he actually reiterates that we should be thankful for our blessings."

The aging missionary has provided an anchor to the restless young heart, yearning for her beloved.

*

Just before daybreak, a raid is made on Agizul's little oasis. The sand muffles the footsteps of the sneaking pirates. When the watch sounds the alarm, the robbers are already close and storm the tents. The defenders grab their spears and jump to their feet.

The marauders are in for a shocking surprise. They are unaware of the timely reinforcement that arrived the previous evening. In the dim light of the flickering campfire, Agizul sums up the situation quickly and barks his order for a counterstrike. Agizul and his two teenage sons block the path of the arsonists who want to torch the tents. Blinded by the torches, the attackers are taken by surprise by the phantoms of the night. The stab-spears of the defenders eliminate them quickly.

Lucius and three of his men rush with their stab-spears to secure the camels—their lifeline to home. Their weapons give them an advantage over their assailants, who are armed with daggers and sabres. In line with their training, they hold their spears with both hands, shield off dagger and sabre blows with the spear handles, and stab at the bodies of their opponents when an opening occurs. One by one, the enemy succumbs to the superior fighting skills of the defenders.

Jason and a guard—both armed with a stab-spear—run to the defense of the women rounded up by some of the pirates. In the twilight, the attackers suddenly face two vicious warriors, stabbing wildly at them, uttering a loud "Yah!" with every stab. Jason's training serves him well. Attacked by five robbers, they fight in different directions, stabbing with the spearhead at one and bumping a rear attacker in the tummy with the blunt end of the spear handle. The determined robbers fight viciously, breaking through the defense occasionally, grazing the skin or inflicting shallow cuts.

Jason fights as he has been trained—wounding arms and legs, knocking weapons from their hands, and piercing chests with the long spearhead. When Jason and his mate have eliminated three robbers, the other two leave their loot and flee for their camels as if the devil's blue funk burns their backsides. Jason refrains from pursuit, fearing an ambush; he does not throw his spear at them, knowing it can be used against him.

The whole commotion is over in a brisk ten minutes. Agizul cannot find the right words to thank his guests for their brave counterstrike. He is convinced that he would have been killed, the women and camels stolen, and the whole place burned down, if it was not for Providence, who sent his guests to him at the right time.

It dawns on Jason that this good timing cannot be ascribed to human cleverness. Had they arrived a day sooner or later, this family would have been enslaved or killed. Jason's trust in Tabitha's God is slowly increasing.

Jason has received a life lesson about violence and self-defense he will never forget. He is humbly grateful that he could help to save Agizul's family. He recalls Paul's words about Joseph: God used him to do good deeds wherever he went.

At sunrise, they drag the dead bodies off by camel and bury them far from the oasis so they can't pollute the water. Agizul gladly gives the camels of the deceased to Lucius. Agizul's wife and daughters put some herbal medicine on the cuts and bruises the men suffered in the fight.

*

Jason is baffled by this nerve-racking experience. For the first time in his life, he deliberately killed people, yet he doesn't feel guilty about it. He decides to discuss the experience with Lucius to hear his view on the matter.

"The kill-or-be-killed situation totally overruled my reservations about violence and killing. I felt compelled to defend my own life and the lives of my friends. How do you feel about the event?"

"I believe that when your life is threatened by attackers, you have the right to defend yourself," Lucius responds in a matter-of-fact way, adding, "When someone attacks you and tries to kill you, he gambles with his own life. If he loses his life while willfully attacking you, he has staged his own demise. That is exactly what happened this morning. We were the victims of an attack, but we turned it around and became the victors."

"That sounds logical, but is killing not against the principles of both Jews and Christians?" Jason wonders.

"The Ten Commandments say, 'You shall not murder.'[9] God does not forbid all killing, because that would prohibit the killing of pests, the slaughtering of animals, the execution of murderers, and defending your country in war," Lucius points out, showing that he has pondered the problem.

He continues, "Respect for life has limits, you know. God gave bled-out animals as food to Noah and his descendants. On two occasions, Jesus gave Peter a net full of fish meant for public consumption. I think that human need for animal products helps maintain the balance in nature. Every farmer can tell you that both under- and over-harvesting of animals are unwise. As

9   Ex. 20:13

far as humans are concerned, well, I think their numbers are kept in check by war, disease, and natural disasters."

"Is war really necessary?" Jason wonders aloud.

"It seems to me that often evil regimes can only be toppled by force. God told Joshua and David to wage war against evil nations," Lucius responds. "That included a lot of killing. God did not contradict his own law when he allowed the eating of meat, or when he ordered Israel to fight their enemies. God gave us a mind to study his word. When we compare various parts of scripture, we can make the right conclusions."

Jason throws Lucius another hot potato: "I don't know much about the Christian faith yet, but don't you think Christians should follow Christ's example by giving up their lives instead of fighting to survive?"

"You must remember who Christ was and what his mission was. He had to surrender himself on the cross to pay for our sins," Lucius explains. "Jesus could have called in legions of angels to wipe out his enemies. But then we would be without a Savior. He submitted himself to his Father's plan, he laid down his life voluntarily to open the way of salvation for sinners. I see it this way: Christ's submission to his executioners was part of his submission to his Father's plan of salvation. By his submission, Christ defeated God's main enemy, the devil. Through all of it, Christ remained the victor."

"So Christians cannot imitate Christ in all he did," Jason concludes.

"Yes, we cannot duplicate Christ's redemptive work," Lucius concurs. "He is the one and only Mediator, the unique Lamb of God. However, his followers should imitate his character in attitude, love, service, integrity, and by fighting against evil. Just as we fought the robbers with all our might, so we must fight Satan relentlessly."

"I see," Jason says, ruminating on the insight Lucius conveyed. "Thanks, Lucius, you have answered many questions in my mind today," Jason concludes. He can now look upon this unfortunate event with new perspective and understanding. One of the main stumbling blocks for Jason in becoming a Christian—self-defense—has been addressed and clarified.

His training with the guards prepared him well, both physically and emotionally. Jason now better comprehends the truth his grandpa conveyed to him long ago about war and survival. When the robbers attacked, he automatically snapped into survival mode. He realizes that in such a situation, there is no time for negotiation. If they would have tried to talk themselves out of this mess, they would have ended up dead.

Turning the other cheek was not an option. He avoided bloodshed by fleeing from Corinth, but in the present situation, flight would have been cowardice. He felt compelled to fight with deadly intent. The underdog has learned that in a life-threatening situation, he has the right to defend his God-given life. If the attacker is killed in the process, it has to be accepted as unavoidable casualty.

*

After they have cared for the animals, they enjoy a breakfast of grain porridge, goat milk, and dates.

Agizul entreats Lucius, "Please, stay till tomorrow morning, then you can teach us more today about Jesus." The old jackal knows that Lucius will never pass up such a golden opportunity.

Jason realizes that Lucius has used his excursions into the desert to spread the Christian message. Obviously, he has sown some seeds here before.

When the women have cleaned up after breakfast, Agizul invites Lucius to start with his lesson. The whole family is summoned for the occasion. The children like Lucius' teaching—it exempts them from chores till noon.

Through her mother, Agizul's fifteen-year-old daughter asks her dad if she may present a token of gratitude to the brave young man who saved her from slavery. Agizul gladly agrees.

They all sit flat on the ground. The girl kneels in front of Jason and presents to him a necklace with a green stone. There is a faint smile in her large black eyes when she whispers, "Thank you for risking your life for us…for me."

Jason thanks her and her dad and puts the necklace on. It is probably her most valuable possession. He will cherish it as a gift coming from the heart.

Agizul is touched by the gestures from both sides. He reveals something deep down in his heart. "Someday, the God of Lucius will use me to help you when you are in trouble." He looks at Jason, who listens attentively. It sounds as if Agizul is prophesying.

"This God will call me ahead of time. He knows I cannot fly like the eagle. I come slowly, by camel. Lucius' God will arrange it with good timing—just as he brought you to us at the right time. I like this Jesus-God. He is a good God. He became a man like me, so he can understand me. Inside himself, he remained God, so he can help me. I like him. I trust him. I'm glad we can learn more about him today."

In the ensuing silence, all ponder Agizul's words of wisdom and mystery. Will his words come true? How?

After a while, Agizul signals to Lucius to proceed.

Time is not a problem in this culture. Lucius proceeds at a leisurely pace, knowing—as long as the content is interesting—his audience will patiently grant him time till noon. To keep them engaged, he uses interactive teaching, giving them chances to ask questions and to make comments.

Lucius first tells them about Jesus' birth, and then explains the meaning of it: "God sent the Messiah to us to free us from sin. Other religions tell us what we must do to climb up to God. The gospel tells us that God's Savior came down to us to show us what God is really like. Jesus said, 'He who has seen Me has seen the Father.'[10] Other religions say, 'Do this and that, and you *may be saved*.' Jesus came, paid for our sins with his life, and now tells

---

10 John 14:9

us, 'Believe in me, and you *are saved* today.' This is the difference between other religions and the gospel of Jesus Christ."

Lucius proceeds with three miracles Jesus did: the healing of a leper, the feeding of the multitude, and the raising of Lazarus. He answers questions from his class.

"For Jews, a leper was untouchable. Jesus touched the leper in love. Jesus was not infected; instead the leper was healed. Christians, too, will bring healing by reaching out to sinners and untouchables."

"When Jesus fed the multitude, he demonstrated that he is the true bread from heaven. The Israelites who ate the manna from heaven got hungry again, but whoever takes Jesus, the bread of life, into their hearts will never be spiritually hungry again."

"What is manna?" one of the children asks.

Lucius summarizes the story of Israel's exodus, their hunger and thirst, and how God provided manna from heaven and water from the rock. He then proceeds with his lesson on the life of Jesus.

"Nobody can raise a person from death, but Jesus did it on three occasions: the son of the widow, the daughter of Jairus, and Lazarus, the brother of Martha and Mary. Thus, he demonstrated what he said to Martha: Whoever believes in him will live forever, though their bodies will die."

For the sake of the children and youngsters, Lucius points out that Jesus raised a son and daughter from death because he loved children and young people, and they loved him. Jesus welcomed children to interact with him, and added, that to them belongs the kingdom of God.

Lucius proceeds by telling and explaining a few parables: four kinds of soil on which the seed of the gospel falls, a prodigal son, and a rich man in hell.

"Jesus said that his words are like seeds. In the sowing process, some seeds land on the path and are picked up by the birds. Likewise, the devil snatches the word from hardened hearts. Some seeds fall on rocky places or among the weeds.

When these seeds germinate, they wither fast because the soil is shallow, or because the weeds choke it. In the same way, the worries of life can make the words of Jesus unfruitful. Fortunately, some seeds fall on good soil and bring forth a rich harvest. What do you think that means?"

Agizul's eleven-year-old son, fascinated by Lucius' stories, says spontaneously, "The good soil is the good heart! The seeds of Jesus will grow and make me do good things."

"That's right. You have listened well!" Lucius exclaims with a teacher's satisfaction.

Realizing the sun is climbing, Lucius proceeds, "Now I want to tell you a parable of Jesus that is very dear to me, because I see myself in it. It is the story of the lost son. He demanded his inheritance while his dad was still living. He sold all of it and left with a fat wallet for a far-off land. He spent all his money, entertaining bad friends. When he went broke, a famine swept over the land. His former friends abandoned him. He got work on a hog farm. He was so hungry that he wished he could eat with the pigs. Then, he suddenly got insight into himself. He realized that his father's servants were far better off than he was. He decided to swallow his pride, return to his father, confess his sins, and ask for work as a servant. He put his idea into practice. He went back just as he was—dirty, lean, and in rags. When he was still a long way off, his father recognized him, ran to him, embraced him, and welcomed him home, providing new clothes and a feast to celebrate his son's return. What do you think is the lesson of this story?"

Agizul's daughter, who gave the necklace to Jason, answers softly, tears in her eyes, "It is the story of a sinner, like me."

"Yes! Yes! And like me...like all of us!" Lucius affirms with enthusiasm. He continues, "The Father yearns for our return. Wouldn't it be sad if we stay with the pigs, wanting to return... but not really doing it?" Glancing at Jason, Lucius emphasizes: "Wouldn't it be sad if we take a very long time from the pigsty to the Father's house?"

Jason's knowledge about the life of Jesus is limited. He finds Lucius' teaching illuminating. He realizes that he, too, is a lost son, somewhere between the pigsty and the Father's house. He is on his way, but has not yet arrived.

In a serious tone, Lucius proceeds with the parable of the rich man and the beggar: "If we postpone our decision to accept Jesus as our Savior, we may end up where the rich man did. In this life, the rich man lived in luxury without compassion for the beggar or his brothers. When he finds himself in hell after his death, seeing the beggar in heaven, he begs for a drop of water, and wants to send a warning to his brothers. Both requests were denied. If one rejects or ignores God's word in this life, you will not get a second chance in the life hereafter," Lucius rivets the nail.

At this point, Agizul suggests a tea break, allowing the lesson to sink in. After they have stretched their legs, they enjoy a refreshing cup of Berber tea. Lucius lifts his cup in celebration of their survival and in thankfulness for eternal life made possible by Christ: "To life!"

"To life!" the others concur.

*

Lucius concludes with Jesus' death, resurrection, ascension, and the conversion of thousands in Jerusalem on Pentecost.

Lucius points out that Jesus paid our debt of sin by dying in our place: "He died so we may live. Every meal points to this event: Plants and animals died to sustain us with food. You have seen it many times—you slaughter animals regularly and prepare the meat for meals."

"But Jesus did not stay dead," Lucius continues. "Jesus conquered death by rising from the tomb. Like a kernel of wheat, he was put into the soil so that a new plant, the church, may sprout and produce may seeds. He ascended to heaven to intercede for us at the right hand of the Father. In our deepest calamities and in our highest achievements, he is praying for us."

"The good news gets even better," Lucius emphasizes. "Jesus will come again to resurrect believers and unbelievers, to renew heaven and earth, to defeat all his enemies, and to start the eternal wedding feast with the church, which he calls his bride."

"I was in Jerusalem at that time to worship as a faithful Jew," Lucius continues. "I was one of those three thousand brought in on Pentecost. The Holy Spirit opened my mind in a moment. I saw scripture in a new light." With a twinkle in his eye, he glances at Jason, adding, "However, with some people, God takes a longer route."

Lucius proceeds, "I stayed on in Israel for a while to help with the expansion of the church. I met the apostles and other leaders such as Barnabas. I returned to Cyrene and planted a church there. When I heard that the church was spreading northward from Jerusalem, I went there to help. We were extremely blessed in Antioch. Many Gentiles accepted Jesus as their Savior. It was there in Antioch that the followers of Christ were first called 'Christians,' a name we carry with pride and devotion.

"Barnabas persuaded Saul of Tarsus to come and help us. Simeon Niger, who had carried the cross of Christ to Calvary, was with us, too.[11] While we were praying and fasting, the Holy Spirit told us to send Saul and Barnabas on a missionary journey. Though persecuted, they had a successful trip through Cyprus and Asia Minor. After their return, we went to Jerusalem to settle the question of whether Gentile Christians have to observe Jewish law.

"After that, I returned to Cyrene. I've heard that Saul, now known as Paul, went on another missionary journey. I wonder how he's doing. His health was giving him trouble."

"He's okay. I listened to him in Corinth," Jason blurts. He got so carried away by Lucius' enthusiasm that he spontaneously gives the desired information, forgetting about his secrecy.

"You heard Paul?!" Lucius asks, thrilled.

"Yes, on two occasions."

---

11 Acts 13:1

"Is he well? Who are his travel companions? How did people respond?" Lucius strings the questions together.

Jason gives the information in a matter-of-fact way.

It's time for the women to start working on lunch. Lucius' time has run out. He is delighted, though, knowing it was a fruitful morning. He and his students have learned a lot from one another.

*

Gallio becomes proconsul of Achaia. He is stationed in Corinth, the capital of the province. The Jews opposed to Paul's mission decide to test Gallio's resolve by dragging Paul to the bema, an eight-foot high stone platform at the *agora*, used for announcing decrees and hearing petitions. They accuse Paul of provoking unrest by teaching a new religion. Before Paul can start with his defense, Gallio throws the case out. He sees his task as applying Roman law, not mediating in religious disputes.

When he commands the soldiers to drive the agitated Jews off, the Greeks see it as an opportunity to vent their anger on the Jews. They grab Sosthenes, the new ruler of the synagogue, assaulting him right there at the Bema. Gallio turns a blind eye.[12] The Jewish opposition to Paul has been silenced.

Paul can now continue with even more dedication with his mission of winning people for Christ, and educating the church in their faith and its practical implications.

Eventually, Paul thinks that his task in Corinth is done. He says goodbye to his diverse Corinthian flock, consisting of rich and poor from Greek, Roman, Jewish, and far-off cultures. Paul departs with Aquila and Priscilla from Cenchrea to Ephesus. Though the congregation realizes that Paul has to bring the gospel to people elsewhere too, they will miss the spiritual food he has been preparing for them. Tabitha loses a firm anchor.

---

12 Acts 18:12-17

While Aquila and Priscilla proceed in Ephesus with church planting, Paul visits Jerusalem, Antioch, and the churches he planted on his first journey.

In this period, a Christian Jew named Apollos,[13] a fiery preacher from Alexandria, visits Ephesus. Aquila and Priscilla lead him to a deeper understanding of Christ and the Holy Spirit. He proceeds to Corinth, where he convinces many Jews from scripture that Jesus is the Messiah.

Isaac gladly welcomes many of his former Jewish friends into the church. Unfortunately, Apollos' popularity in the Corinth church causes schisms. Some adore Apollos, while others support Paul, Peter, or Jesus.[14] Paul later explains to the church in Corinth that he and Apollos each made their unique contribution: "I planted the seed, Apollos watered it, but God made it grow."

When Isaac invites Apollos to break bread with them, Tabitha finds Apollos' description of Alexandria fascinating. The city was founded by Alexander the Great three centuries ago. Like Corinth, Alexandria connects two harbors, one on the sea and one on Lake Maryut, making the city a prosperous trade link between Egypt and other countries around the Mediterranean Sea.

Many thinkers and artisans have flocked there. While many Roman and Greek cities cater to the lower drives of mankind, Alexandria is still speaking to the higher intellectual functions of the human race. Apollos sees the colossal lighthouse and library of Alexandria as symbols of the light and knowledge the city radiates to the rest of the world. Tabitha wishes she could visit this famous city.

After Paul's visit to the churches he planted on his first journey, he returns to Ephesus, where he eventually stays about three years. In that time, he has to deal with problems in the church of Corinth. He writes several letters, he sends Timothy

13 Acts 18:24-28
14 1 Cor. 1:12

and Titus to them, and he makes a short visit to Corinth himself.

*

Diana continues with her devious schemes. Having almost completed her treatment in Rome, she feels healthy and energetic. She decides to test her ideas about erotic entertainment for the wealthy.

During her stay, she has made a number of friends. She invites them as singles to a party, leaving the rest to Mother Nature. She hopes they will pair off and enjoy the intimacy of such a blind date. If it works, next time she can charge a small fee, telling them it's to cover costs. Gradually, she may gather a group of excellent hostesses who can cater to wealthy men. Once they're hooked, price is not an issue.

After several months, her hostess business has picked up so much speed that she cannot keep pace with demand. She trains her workers in the fine art of luring conversation and enticing body language—Diana's forte.

Her theory is that men want more than a quick orgasm. Their hunter instincts must be satisfied, too. When they have to use their charms to conquer the girl gradually, they experience an ego boost as well as physical satisfaction. While they are engaged in the hunt, they discover and enjoy the emotional qualities of the girl, a companion who satisfies a deeper need of which they were not even aware.

This refined form of erotic/social enjoyment is especially popular with the sophisticated rich. Diana compares lower and higher class pleasures with cheap food and wine on the one hand, and superb cuisine and wine on the other. The first two fill the belly; the latter two refresh the soul.

Doing so well, she writes to her dad that she has begun a small business and wants to try it out for a year or so. Andreo is proud that his daughter has put up a business in Rome. He is unaware of its nature, and wishes her well.

Because of the infection she had, Diana is too scared to expose herself to strangers again. The girls working for her do it out of their own free will, and they love the excellent pay. Therefore, Diana convinces herself not to feel guilty making money from the risk those girls are taking.

Brushing shoulders with the rich eventually brings her into contact with a few senators. Now she is in big business. Maybe the new emperor, Caesar Nero, will eventually hear of her services.

*

Though Jason suspected that Krato checked on him while he was still in Corinth, he actually overestimated Krato's spying system. Once a week, Krato and his gang visited a few taverns with the intent to corner and harass Jason. After several fruitless searches, they confronted one of Philip's workers after work. With a dagger on his throat, they forced him to admit that Jason had left several weeks ago. He could tell them nothing more. Krato believed the guy—Jason wouldn't have told anyone where he was going.

With a gloating smile, Krato enjoys the fact that he succeeded in chasing Jason from his hometown, scaring him off to a life of exile in a foreign country, most likely less comfortable than the one he had in Corinth.

Krato is not in a hurry to find Jason. As long as he suffers somewhere, it gives Krato enough satisfaction. The world is small, and Roman soldiers are everywhere. Jason's sturdy, tall figure stands out like a sore thumb. Eventually, the news as to where Jason is hiding will surface.

*

Tabitha has become hypersensitive to Roman soldiers. They drove her beloved Jason away. *I will never forgive them. Never!*

She's coping better. She accepts that for the time being, she will hear nothing of Jason. He cannot dare to send word. When her longing devours her, she no longer suppresses her feelings, but lets them out by crying, talking to Jason's sister Helena, and by unloading her baggage at the throne of grace. She makes sure she's not fretting by testing herself with the indicators Paul provided.

Sometimes Tabitha tries to channel her yearning into music. She improvises a melody on her lyre, gradually adding a painful yet hopeful song:

> "Young hearts yearning,
> heartache burning,
> inward turning,
> loss of meaning.
> After finding
> joy of loving,
> ripped apart
> —bleeding heart.
> Young hearts hoping,
> earnest praying,
> new dawn breaking,
> never failing."

Once a week, she treats herself to a special imagination game, reliving one of her special moments with Jason. When she recalls what happened, she tries to activate all her senses. Blended with the love in her heart, it feels as if Jason is with her. She can smell him, feel him, touch him, hear him, and see him. Though it soothes the pain, it also intensifies the longing. She uses the technique sparingly, knowing she will drive herself crazy if she does it too often.

A recurring thought, born from desperation, is taking shape in her mind. Instead of sitting passively and hoping for the best, she considers visiting a few places abroad in the hope she will get lucky and pick up Jason's trail. She will have to convince her dad to let her go. It bothers her, though, that if it was that easy, Krato could do the same. He may even have her followed, hoping she may lead him to Jason.

*

Lucius and Jason visit two other oases in the desert, about a three days' trek from each other. They come to a deep well in the middle of nowhere. The well is so deep they have to use camel power to draw water. A rope runs over a pulley on top of the well. One end of the rope is attached to the leather bucket, the other end to the camel. They reflect sunlight into the pit with a copper mirror to see if the bucket is submerged. Then, someone walks the camel seventy paces away, pulling the bucket out via the pulley. Camels and men take turns to spread the burden.

Jason realizes how privileged Corinth is to have fresh spring water, flowing down to them from Acrocorinth, accumulating at the Peirene fountain in the center of the town. Here in the desert, it is hard work to get one bucketful of brackish water to the surface.

Paul compared the gospel to living water. That, too, is on the doorstep of some, and hard to get for others. Jason feels guilty that he did not accept the water of life in Corinth. Now he has to hear the gospel again in the middle of a desert. Is God trying to get his attention, to get through his thick skull? Though he is attracted to Jesus and his salvation, Jason is hesitant to make a full commitment. He fears he may fail to achieve the expected devotion. He does not want to be a slothful Christian.

With the same slow rhythm with which they ventured out into the desert, they now return, looking forward to a bath and clean clothes. Jason's Sahara experience convinced him that desert life is not for him.

Lucius has done well in both teaching and business. Thanks to their help against the pirates, Agizul and his family is now more receptive to the gospel. Lucius traded goods for camels that will bring him a handy profit.

At long last, they arrive home safely. Having been without the niceties of civilization for a month, Jason relishes the small things he took for granted in the past.

Lucius' daughter, Mary, looks more attractive than before. Both she and Jason are now more responsive to each other, make more eye contact, and share smiles more often.

Jason wants to enjoy Mary without giving her false hopes. He wants to stay loyal to Tabitha. He convinces himself that he can stay true to Tabitha while enjoying Mary's company. Only Tabitha can completely fulfill the needs of his body and soul.

Will I be able to withstand the temptation in the long run? Jason wonders.

CHAPTER 8

Since Cyrenians accepted Christ as their Savior at the first Christian Pentecost in Jerusalem, and brought the gospel to their hometown, the church in Cyrene has grown to several hundred members. They congregate in the amphitheater on Sunday evenings. Jason has accompanied Lucius to church after their return from the desert.

Jason has befriended a number of guys and girls in his peer group. They sometimes gather on their own for discussions and fun. He has inquired about employment, but positions are scarce. Jewish artisans have flocked to Alexandria, and the overflow has come to Cyrene. Protectionism also plays a role, as Cyrenians' first priority is to supply work for their own young people. As an outsider, Jason needs nothing less than a miracle.

Unable to sit idle, he wanders through the city of Cyrene, weighing the pros and cons of various options while sightseeing. He admires the large mosaic covered pavement of the *agora*, he adores the impressive architecture of the Zeus, Apollo, and Demeter temples, and he enjoys the views of the Mediterranean Sea from vantage points on the mountain. Across that sea his beloved Tabitha, parents, and homeland await his return.

Jason is no longer inspired by the pagan religion he grew up with, nor is he empowered by the Christian faith he has been introduced to, but to which he has not yet made any commitment. He is suspended in uncertainty between two worldviews. He needs the courage of Cyrene and Samson to overpower a lion and the determination of Hercules and Moses to prevail over insurmountable obstacles.

One night he decides to pray to the God he wants to meet—the God of Tabitha, Paul, and Lucius: "Oh God, like the lost son, I'm somewhere between the pigsty and the Father's house. I know I have not arrived yet, but I'm on my way to you. Please, help me to persevere and stay the course. Lord, you know my situation: I had to flee to this foreign place. I need to earn a living. Please, open a door for me. Show me the way. Amen."

A strange peace of mind, an inexplicable trust in this unknown God, envelops him. He dozes off into a refreshing sleep. The next morning, a plan takes shape in his mind. He realizes it will be wise sticking to what he knows and does best—building wagons. If he were to start on a completely new skill, it would take him years of hard work and poor pay before he would be qualified.

Familiar with Corinth's location between two harbors, and the transport business associated with that, Jason realizes that Cyrene's location twelve miles from its harbor offers the same opportunities.

At the moment, a few dozen private wagon owners compete with each other to convey goods between harbor and city for either import or export. This system promotes selfish competition, small profits, and thus poor services.

Jason puts his inventive mind to work. If some of the wagon owners can be convinced to pool their resources, they can prevent duplication, bring down operating costs, and use increased profits to improve the quality of their service. However, bringing these economic rivals together looks highly unlikely.

He discusses the matter with Lucius, who right away sees the sense of his idea. Lucius knows some of the wagon owners, and thinks he can act as mediator.

"Jason, I have an idea," Lucius says, as his face lights up. "Let me introduce you to a few wagon owners who are also cooperative members of the church. I will invite them to a barbeque here at home, you can explain your vision, and then we can hear what they think of the idea."

Jason is delighted. He waits excitedly for the barbeque a few days later. He prays for a breakthrough.

Enjoying wheat beer around the fire, Lucius tells his guests that Jason and his dad were involved in Corinth's lucrative transport industry, and that Jason has some interesting ideas that may be applicable to Cyrene.

Jason draws a map on the ground with a stick, explaining to the men the geographical location of Corinth between its two harbors on each side of the isthmus, how the wagons transport the cargo from harbor to harbor, and how many people make a living from that system. One of the men had been to Corinth and confirms Jason's picture of the situation.

"We have almost the same situation here in Cyrene," Jason continues. "Imports have to be transported from Apollonia to Cyrene, and exports have to go the opposite way. News about ships arriving in Apollonia takes time to reach Cyrene, and then it takes more time to go with wagons from here to Apollonia. Because of the lack of coordination, empty wagons sometimes go from here to the harbor, and sometimes wagons return with half-loads. Knowing the Corinth system, I can help you to pool resources, minimize duplication, decrease cost, increase coordination and efficiency, and thereby make the whole industry more profitable and cost-effective. The public will like quicker service."

Jason realizes he is taking a chance by sharing his vision with the men. They can easily implement his idea without making him a partner. He hopes their Christian values will make them refrain from such a mean trick.

The four men—all in their forties—like Jason's idea and wonder why they have not thought of it themselves. By pooling their wagons and resources, they can increase their number of wagons for busy times, and at times of low activity, they can save cost by using fewer wagons instead of making the arduous round trip to Apollonia with half-full wagons.

The more they share ideas, the more enthusiastic they become. They welcome Jason as partner. He will be in charge of service coordination, as well as the building and servicing of wagons. The wagon owners will share responsibilities regarding contracting, transport, and bookkeeping. They will meet every morning before starting time to coordinate their tasks for the day.

Jason is ecstatic about the opportunity that opened up. He is absolutely sure his prayer was heard by Tabitha's God. In his room that night he kneels and thanks the One who has provided for him, though he still does not know him personally. Showered by God's goodness, he feels guilty, knowing he does not deserve it. Slowly but surely, he is beginning to comprehend the essence of God's grace.

Though they sealed the deal with only a handshake and trust in each other's integrity, they gradually realize that for tax and inheritance purposes, they need to put the deal into writing. A lawyer friend of Lucius helps them drawing up the contract. They name the company Cyrene Transport.

They pay a messenger in Apollonia to obtain from the captain of incoming ships information about imports to Cyrene, space available for exports from Cyrene, and the ship's next ports of call. The messenger has to deliver that info on horseback to Cyrene Transport, thus expediting transport both ways between Cyrene and Apollonia. Ten wagons and their drivers are stationed at Apollonia so that they can start loading shortly after a ship's arrival. The greater speed and efficiency of deliveries are popular with businesses and the public. Cyrene Transport becomes the service of choice.

Jason throws himself into the work he knows so well. At the end of the first month, his first wagon is rolled out of the shed. His partners are excited about several sensible improvements Jason has incorporated into the wagon, features their old wagons lack, such as railings to protect goods against thieves, and a more efficient braking system.

As Jason's apprentices improve their skills, the building process accelerates. After only three months, five new wagons have been added to the fleet. Now the old ones can be serviced and refurbished, improving their functioning and longevity.

When some of the other wagon owners see how the business of the new company waxes and how their own wanes, they want to join Cyrene Transport.

Jason persuades the company to take the other wagon owners in as contract workers in order to avoid a large and divisive management. He also suggests that all their workers receive a small percentage of the profits—when the business flourishes, they win; when it suffers, they lose. Thus, they are involved in the success of the business.

Some wagon owners found their own company, but struggle to maintain unity and efficiency. They are hindered by greed.

Within six months, Cyrene Transport has contracted most of the wagon owners. Only a few stubborn hardliners stay independent.

The company pays its owners a salary, and keeps money in the business for improvement, development, and possible downturns. Jason has a good income. He rents a room in Lucius' backyard. Surrounded by friends, he saves up for the future.

Jason is not conspicuous in the organization. He works with the guys who service and build wagons. Though Apollonia is the point of Africa nearest to Greece, the chances that news of his whereabouts may reach Corinth is small. By sea, it is about four hundred miles from Apollonia to Corinth.

*

After another year, Cyrene Transport is functioning according to plan. They have enough new wagons, the old ones have been refurbished, and Jason's partners run the business smoothly.

Jason has saved up well. His partners encourage him to go on vacation to Egypt. They feel he deserves it.

"Take your time. Egypt is a vast country. We'll keep the business running, don't worry," they advise.

Jason likes the idea. He always wondered what the real Africa is like, not the desert one—the jungle one. Ever since his grandpa told him that one of their ancestors came from the heart of Africa, he has entertained the idea to go there, have a look for himself, and explore this part of his roots.

Jason hikes a ride to Alexandria on a fishing vessel. This city sits on a strip of land between the Mediterranean Sea and Lake Maryut. The harbor on either side of the city, on the sea and on the lake, reminds Jason of Corinth's two harbors on either side of the isthmus.

Along the lake shore, Jason searches for a Nile boat, a felucca, that has brought goods from the upper Nile, and is about to return there.

After a long search, Jason finds a skipper named Faki, who has brought caged lions to Alexandria for use in Roman arenas. He is not in a hurry to start the return trip. Jason learns from him that the cataracts of the Nile, from Aswan to Khartoum, are easier to navigate from June to September when the Nile is flooded. Those who want to sail to the southern parts of Sudan have to plan their trips accordingly.

Faki uses the time between Nile floods to earn a living by transporting goods on the Nile with his felucca. It is still two months before the water of the Nile will rise.

Jason persuades Faki to start now so they can visit the historic sites along the way. It gives the skipper a bright idea. Instead of embarking on the long way home with an empty boat, he can earn some extra money by taking tourists as far as Aswan, about six hundred miles to the south. Navigating the cataracts from Aswan to Khartoum is not for tourists. Even for adventurers, it is a daunting task.

Jason helps Faki by finding people who want to travel south on the Nile. After two days, they sail off with twelve passengers via Lake Maryut and the Alexandrian channel to the western branch of the Nile flowing through the delta.

Because eateries are few and far between along the Nile, Faki uses part of the passengers' fees to purchase non-perishable food, such as dried fruits, grains, and flour. The boat has a small stove for baking bread and frying fish caught from the river.

South of the delta, the Giza pyramids and the city of Memphis come into view on the west bank. Here, the Nile is still one broad river before it splits into several branches running through the delta.

The Egyptian guide informs them that the great pyramids are named after three pharaohs: Khufu, Khafre, and Menkaure. These pyramids are located in this order in a straight line running to the south-west.

Gazing up at the great pyramids, Jason tries to figure out how people who lived two and a half millennia ago managed to get those massive blocks of stone one upon the other, layer by layer, till they reached the apex 481 foot high. It is rightly recognized as one of the Seven Wonders of the World.

Yet, what purpose did the pyramids serve? They are only massive tombs, memorials of death, pointing to the passing over to life hereafter. Apparently, the afterlife became more important to these pharaohs than this life. They dedicated their entire lives and burdened thousands of workers to the building of these massive mausoleums.

Jason decides that he would rather make the best of this life, believing that is the best preparation for the next.

The nearby mysterious Sphinx lies east of the Khafre Pyramid. The guide tells them that the human head and lion body of the Sphinx resemble a pharaoh. The ancient Egyptians worshiped the sun gods Ra and Aten, as well as the river god Hapi; therefore, the Sphinx faces the rising sun and the flowing river. Sun and water are two essentials for life. Jason finds the Judæan/Christian viewpoint more acceptable that sun and water are part of God's creation, not part of God.

On the next leg of the Nile journey, Jason enjoys the scenes along the broad, slow river. The Nile is still low. Faki has to navigate carefully to avoid sandbanks. Scenes vary as they proceed. Beyond the papyrus at the water's edge, he often notices farther-off date palms, green fields, and mud houses on the banks. The Nile brings life to Egypt. Its whole population lives from the river and close to it.

Farmers draw water from the Nile with shadufs, consisting of a leather bucket fixed to a long counter-weighted wooden lever swiveling on a vertical pole. Because the water level is low now, one shaduf passes the water on to the next one on a higher level. Sometimes there are three or more in a row, one above the other. At the top, this water flows off in channels to refresh plants and animals.

Jason wonders if massive shadufs were used to hoist the pyramid blocks from one level to the next. Long cedar beams could have been imported by sea and river from nearby Phoenicia.

The River Nile is the major transport route of Egypt. Many feluccas of all sizes navigate up and down the river with the help of one or two sails and a steering oar at the stern. They transport people and goods.

Further south Faki and his passengers visit the ancient city of Thebes. On the East Bank—the sunrise side—they visit the enormous temples of Karnak and Luxor with their colossal pillars, arches, statues, obelisks, and carved murals.

The two temples are linked by a two-mile long avenue flanked by sphinxes. Carving hundreds of these figures must have taken sculptors a considerable time. Successive pharaohs added to the complex. The ancient Egyptians took their religion seriously.

On the West Bank—the sunset side—is the city's cemetery, including the Valley of the Kings and the Valley of the Queens, where many pharaohs and their queens were buried. Jason is again baffled by the ancient Egyptians' preoccupation with death and afterlife. Somehow, they must have realized that there is life after death. It dawns on Jason that their religion was actually a cry for a savior. He is fortunate to have heard of the Savior, and yet, he hesitates to take the crucial step.

Jason weighs and compares the religions he has already encountered: Egyptian (3,000 years old), Jewish (2,000 years old), Greek (1,200 years old), Roman (400 years old), and Christian (20 years old). The older ones do not satisfy him; the youngest has not been proven yet.

*

While Jason wrestles in Egypt with one of the oldest religions, Tabitha watches the growing pains of the youngest one in Corinth.

The Corinth church exists in a wicked environment. Many of them find it hard to be in the world but not of the world. They become contaminated by surrounding standards, views, and customs. Until recently, these customs were normal parts of their lives; now, they are seen as sinful.

Paul's first letter to Corinthian Christians, written from Ephesus, gives a peek into the struggles of this early church. In the first part of his letter, Paul reprimands them for wrong attitudes, and guides them in the right direction.

They have split up into arrogant cliques, despising each other, and idolizing a specific leader such as Paul, Apollos, Peter, or Christ. By comparing the church to a field and building, Paul shows them that God uses the gifts of every leader to make a unique contribution to the common good of the church. Paul planted, Apollos watered; Paul laid the foundation, others built on it. However, without God's blessing, the efforts of the various leaders would be in vain. God should receive the glory, not the leaders.

Likewise, they should not glorify human wisdom, because unconverted people don't understand the simple wisdom of the gospel. Consequently, Christians should not take their disputes to worldly courts, but to the wise in the church who can discern spiritual matters.

Those who are guilty of immoral behavior have to be disciplined firmly, but lovingly. Paul also answers their questions regarding marriage, celibacy, eating practices, socializing with non-believers, the role of women in worship, the Lord's supper, love-meals, gifts of the Spirit, and the resurrection.

Though Paul is dealing with the problems of a specific church, his answers have universal application. Eventually, all the letters of Paul will be copied and circulated to all churches.

Though Paul advocates celibacy for the unmarried, he encourages those with strong sexual needs to marry and so avoid temptations. He advises that married couples should not withhold marriage rights from each other for long, lest they give in to temptation. A Christian should look for a mate among Christians. However, the Christian who is already married to a non-Christian should not seek divorce if the non-Christian spouse does not ask for divorce.

Paul's explanation of the varied gifts of believers who are united by love—the most important gift of all—will probably be cherished for ages. His explanation of what love is, and what it is not, should become a classic:

⁴ Love is patient, love is kind. It does not envy, it does not boast, it is not proud. ⁵ It is not rude, it is not self-seeking, it is not easily angered, it keeps no record of wrongs. ⁶ Love does not delight in evil but rejoices with the truth. ⁷ It always protects, always trusts, always hopes, always perseveres. ⁸ Love never fails.[15]

Tabitha yearns for the moment she can share Paul's ideas about love and marriage with Jason. Yes, she will rub it in, "It is better to marry than to burn *with passion*."[16]

Paul's teaching on the resurrection in this letter reveals a completely different view on the afterlife from the one Jason encounters in Egypt. The Christian view is simple, clear, and focused on a Savior who walked on earth with his disciples. Their Friend is also their Mediator who prepares a place for them in the Father's house. The views of the ancient Egyptians were clouded in a fog of mystic uncertainty, and controlled by vague and scary forces of the dark underworld.

Paul's exposition of the resurrection[17] will remain a major source of reference for present and future Christians.

The church in Corinth is discovering that their acceptance of Christ as their personal Savior has a ripple effect on the rest of their lives. They cannot be followers of Jesus in name only—they have to follow him in practice, too. He must be Lord of every square inch of their lives.

It takes four letters (of which two are lost) and three visits (by Timothy, Paul, and Titus, respectively) to persuade the congregation to get their church in order.

The problems in the Corinth church exasperate Isaac's family. Seeking relief, they visit the synagogue occasionally, but the legalistic messages of Judaism do not satisfy their grace-tuned souls any more.

---

15 1 Cor. 13:4-8a NIV
16 1 Cor. 7:9
17 1 Cor. 15

During the same time, Paul has a fruitful ministry in Ephesus. His students visit the surrounding area and plant churches in the whole region. Many healing miracles take place, and many renounce their magic practices.

*

All passengers, except Jason, disembark at Aswan and return with another felucca to Alexandria. Faki waits in Aswan, at the first cataract, for the Nile to rise. Thanks to the early rainy season, they can depart in the middle of May.

About 180 miles southwest of Aswan, they visit the temples Ramses II hewed into the sandstone cliffs of the Nile's West Bank. Both are guarded by colossal statues of the pharaoh and his queen. The figures are half-covered in sand carried by winds from the Sahara. Situated near Egypt's southern border, these massive figures were probably meant to scare off invaders coming from the south on boats.

From Aswan to Khartoum, in the huge S-bend of the Nile, the river is dominated by six rapids, called cataracts. The northward flow of the river here turns southwest for 180 miles. Though Aswan and Khartoum are only 600 miles apart as the crow flies, the S-bend doubles the distance by felucca.

In Northern Sudan, the sand of the Sahara lies west of the river, while agricultural land lies to the east. The sand the wind blows into the Nile is washed down to the sea, causing sandbanks in the river.

Now that the river is swollen, Faki can navigate the cataracts. At some places, the flow of the water between the rocks and islets are so fast that the boat has to be hauled upstream with ropes. Locals living on the banks make a living from this service.

When they eventually pass Khartoum, where the Blue Nile and White Nile merge, they proceed south with the White Nile. They soon leave the sand of the Sahara behind and enter greener areas. The trees gradually increase. Finally, they reach the bush country of Southern Sudan.

Faki stops at a small village and introduces Jason to his brother, Bari, who traps lions for Rome's arenas. Faki is going farther south to his family. He urges Jason to stay with Bari until he returns in three months, depending on how long the rains last.

These bush dwellers don't understand Greek. Jason has to start learning key words from them for the most common things and actions. He writes the words—with Greek spelling—on a piece of papyrus-paper and repeats them many times.

Within a week, he has learned about a hundred words. By using the key words with some gesturing, he can convey questions and ideas. By listening to Bari, who talks slowly for Jason's sake, he picks up phrases, too, such as "good day," "my name is Jason," "what's your name," "I'm hungry/thirsty," "what are you doing?" and, "where are we going now?"

Before Bari takes Jason with him into the bush, he first gives him some training. He shows him a number of hand signals that he will use to indicate what they will do, or what Jason must do. The hearing of animals is extremely sensitive, so Bari can't talk to Jason when they are close to animals. He will signal.

When he tests Jason's spearing skills, he is surprised at Jason's accuracy and force. He can tell Jason has had a lot of practice.

With a stick, Bari draws two lions on the ground. One lion is seen from the side, and one from the front. He shows Jason that to kill a lion from the side, he must aim his spear at the ribs behind the shoulder. If the lion is running, he must aim his spear two paces ahead of the lion. When a lion comes straight at him, he must aim for the point where the lion's neck meets its chest. That is where the air-pipe enters its body. Through that soft spot, the spear can penetrate the lion's heart.

Lions are powerful animals, especially the males. They sometimes break free from the cages made of straight branches. When that happens, Jason must know how to defend himself against a vicious lion.

Bari takes Jason on a buck hunt so he can hone his skills on running targets. When the rainy season starts, many animals migrate south, avoiding swamped areas. The place where herds cross a river is the best place for an ambush. Predators know that too, so one has to stay alert for lions (on the banks) and crocodiles (in the river).

"Woe is you when you are caught between the two," Bari warns. "Then hope there's a tree with no leopard in it."

Though Jason finds this pessimistic worse-case scenario amusing, he knows that if it actually happens, it will be no laughing matter.

They sneak up to a point where antelope cross a tributary of the Nile. Some white-eared kob, antelope the size and color of impala, are congregating on the other side of the river. The water is orange-brown, colored by the silt it picks up from the banks when flooding.

Bari and Jason hide behind bushes.

Eventually the numbers of kob have grown enough, urging them to attempt the crossing en masse. Bari allows the first ones to pass. As soon as the stream of animals flows, their herd instinct forces them onward, despite the danger on the other side. Other spear-hunters appear one-by-one from the trees. Some of them enter the water and spear animals in the water. Jason thinks it gives them unfair advantage.

Despite the hunters in the water, kob now come running from the water and up the bank on both sides of Bari and Jason. Bari gives the go-ahead-signal to Jason.

From a kneeling position, only eight paces from a running buck, he aims one pace ahead of the buck and hurls his spear. He hits the huge dark-brown ram in the ribs behind the shoulder-blade. The animal slides over the ground as it drops dead in its tracks.

When the herd has passed, Bari removes the intestines of the buck to diminish weight for carrying. He keeps the liver, which is a delicacy. He cuts a straight branch from a tree with his *panga*, and binds the hoofs of the buck to the branch. They shoulder the burden, one at each tip of the pole.

They have to rest every hundred paces or so. It feels as if the buck becomes heavier the farther they go.

They are shocked to a halt when a lioness growls close by in thick underbrush. They quickly drop the buck and prepare for the charge, one spear in the right hand, ready to throw, and an extra one in the left hand. Bari signals to Jason to move a few paces away.

Snarling viciously, a lioness suddenly charges from the bushes toward Bari. He and Jason hurl their spears. Bari's spear hits the lioness on the chest but does not enter. Jason's spear, coming from the side, glides through her short ribs.

The lioness plows through the dirt. Bari jumps aside. The wounded animal bends her head backwards, desperately trying to bite the thing that tortures her ribs. In those few seconds, Bari thrusts his second spear through the soft spot below her neck, while Jason's second spear hits her behind the shoulder. In her death convulsions, she makes a vain attempt to get her enemy. Then she collapses and lies still.

With pounding hearts, they relive and analyze what happened in the previous ten seconds. Bari's first throw for the soft spot below the neck was too low. His spear hit the thick muscle and bone on her chest. Jason's first spear hit the lioness in the center of her body, so it pierced her lungs, but not her heart. Bari could have been killed. The lioness' snapping at the spear in her side gave them a brief second chance to stop the ferocious predator.

Bari bows to Jason, "I owe you my life. You are a good hunter. God brought you to us at the right time."

Jason's heart is still beating at top speed. Facing a charging lioness shakes up the bravest hunter. He knows it was pure luck, or rather pure grace, as Tabitha would say. Even in the face of death, the burdened has a choice: fight and live, or cringe and die. Once again, God used him to do a Joseph's deed in a far-off place.

He and Bari put their right hands on each other's left shoulders, confirming their brotherly covenant.

Then they hear another lion sound: the calling of a cub. He is coming out to see where his mom is. The cub is about six weeks old; it shows no fear.

It comes to Jason, rubs his body against his legs and starts sucking on his finger. The cub looks thin and famished. It has a peculiar spot of black hair above its right eye. Jason and the cub immediately take to each other.

"Hi, Spotty! Are you hungry? We'll get you some food soon," Jason says, stroking the cute little fellow.

They examine the lioness. She is rather lean. Her lower jaw is broken. Apparently, she suffered a kick by the powerful hind hoof of a zebra. Being unable to hunt, she could not deliver milk or meat to her cub. They stared death by starvation in the face, so she tried to scare Jason and Bari off to claim their quarry.

The cub is famished. Jason slices small pieces from the buck's liver and gives it to Spotty. He gobbles it down and asks for more. After his hunger is stilled, they move on. When they pick up the buck and resume their tough walk home, Spotty follows Jason, meowing in bass tones.

"Wow, wow!" he seems to be saying, complaining about the long walk. Jason carries it when it tires. It puts its forepaws on Jason's shoulder and rests its head on its paws, apparently quite content to be with a human being.

At Bari's home, he skins and salts the buck. Jason feeds the cub a mixture of porridge and goat milk from a bowl. He first dips his fingers into the milk and then allows Spotty to lick the milk from his fingers. Jason moves his fingers closer to the milk until Spotty starts to lick the milk-mix directly from the bowl.

Associating Jason with food, stroking, play, and a specific scent imprints on Spotty's brain as an experience it will never forget. It absorbs these stimuli, day-by-day, for four months. It shadows Jason wherever he goes, probably accepting him as his mother.

Bari watches the growing bond between Jason and Spotty. Shaking his head, he warns, "You make trouble for yourself." Bari knows from earlier experience that cubs very soon become lions.

"When such a pet becomes dangerous, you have to put it down. It will break your heart to kill your friend."

*

Bari is satisfied that Jason can hit a moving target with a spear. Now they can try to trap a lion. First, they have to locate the right lion. For the arena, a lion with a full mane is worth twice as much as a lioness, because of its impressive, majestic appearance.

Jason is intrigued by the small signs Bari notices while tracking. He reads the ground and the vegetation like a book: a faint footprint, a broken stem of grass, some hair on a twig, and scent-marking on tree trunks—all these signs tell Bari when the lion passed and where he was heading.

As they track the lion, Bari shares with Jason his knowledge of the other animals they see on their way. Birds and monkeys detect danger first from their high pitches in the trees and give alarm calls. That alerts prey animals; therefore, most predators hunt at night. Cheetah hunt by day because they prefer open terrain (without the alarm calls of monkeys and birds) and because the competition—lion, leopard, and hyena—sleeps then.

Most animals smell or hear danger before they can see it; therefore, the hunter has to stay downwind from the prey. To curtail their odor, Bari and Jason rub their bodies with dry animal dung. To deter flies and mosquitoes, they also rub their skin with the crushed leaves of a medicinal herb. Applying these tricks, Bari brings Jason in proximity of dangerous animals like elephant, rhino, and buffalo. Being so close to these giants makes excitement and fear rush through Jason's veins.

"When these animals have little ones with them, it is advisable to keep your distance, because they are very protective of their young and defend them viciously," Bari advises. "You never know when the wind may suddenly change direction and reveal your presence."

Bari points out to Jason that apes, lions, elephants, and zebras form long-term family groups. They show their bonding with one another regularly by mutual grooming and calling. Lions are the only big cats that live in family groups, which include mature males. Lions use playing, head-rubbing, paws, and tongues to show mutual affection.

Elephants push small trees over to get to the succulent bark and twigs, thus clearing patches to become savannah for grazers. Jason is amazed at the abundance of herd animals like zebra, wildebeest, buffalo, and kob. They provide sustenance to carnivores, including man. Bari and Jason see prey animals grazing near a feasting lion pride—as if they know that one of them has given its life so that the rest may graze in peace for a while. In the food chain, life and death are intertwined. It reminds Jason of Lucius' message to Agizul's family: Plants and animals die to feed us physically. Likewise, Jesus died so that sinners may live spiritually.

Eventually, the hunters come on fresh lion tracks and droppings, as well as the carcass of a zebra that the lion has fed on recently. The lion stashed the carcass in the undergrowth to hide it from scavengers, but several hyenas have discovered it. When they see the hunters approach, they are aroused and make mock charges with raised manes and tails, uttering their devilish giggles.

"Make a big noise and wave your spears," Bari advises, putting his own words into action. Jason follows Bari's example. The hyenas abandon the carcass with yelping objections, tails between their legs. Jason is surprised at the cowardly response of these fierce-looking predators. For a while, they circle around at a safe distance.

"Hyenas play it safe," Bari explains. "When few, they flee. When many, they attack. Then, even lionesses climb trees to get out of their reach. But when the male lion appears, only one roar scatters them in fear. They know he's a hyena-killer."

Bari decides to set the trap near the carcass. They will use part of the carcass as bait in the cage, and hoist the rest into a tree, out of the lion's reach.

First, they have to make the cage. Before they start working on the cage, they rub their hands and feet in dry animal dung to curb human odor.

They use the trunks of two straight young trees to function as a sledge for the bottom of the cage. Once the lion has been caught, it will be hauled in the sledge-cage by oxen to Bari's home. Faki will eventually take it by felucca to Alexandria.

They hack off straight shoots, about two inches thick, to build the cage on top of the sledge. They use the tough ropes the women have rolled from palm tree leaves to hold the poles together, leaving only nine-inch square openings between the crisscross poles. At every crossing point, a piece of the wood is cut out and then tightly secured by cross-ropes, preventing the lion from pulling the bars down with its mighty paws. All corners are strengthened by diagonal trusses to secure a rigid structure. The floor is covered by cross-rafters spaced an inch apart, so urine and droppings can pass through.

When Bari is satisfied that the cage is solid, they set the bait, trap lever, and trapdoor. To camouflage their odor, they crush leaves with a strong smell, mix them with antelope droppings, and scatter the mixture in and around the cage. In the meantime, the hyenas have given up hope and left the area.

A full grown lion is a mighty beast. When the trapdoor falls down, the trappers must act quickly to secure the trapdoor with chains before the lion forces the catch open with its strong forepaws. They wait downwind, nearby.

At daybreak the next morning, they suddenly hear vicious snarls and growling coming from the trap. They approach cautiously from the downwind side. They spot no other lions around. Inside the cage is a large lion in a very bad mood. It is a beautiful animal with a fantastic mane.

They approach with a mixture of excitement and fear, hearts throbbing, spears ready. When the lion sees them, it growls and jabs with its forepaws against the cage. Seeing the mighty beast up close and hearing its rasping snarls fills them with awe and anxiety. Bari knows the tricks of the trade. He asks Jason to distract the lion at the opposite end of the cage while he secures the latch with a chain.

When done, they are relieved. The dangerous part is accomplished. Now, they have to haul the catch home. They fetch the oxen to do the hard work. Eventually, the lion settles down. Faki will not be back with the felucca before three months; therefore, when they reach home, Bari transfers the lion to a larger cage with the help of trapdoors. In the following month, they trap two more lions.

Although Jason realizes that these lions may be used to rip humans apart in the arena, he does not interfere with Bari and Faki's trade. Their income is small, their lifestyle simple. They have families to care for.

To feed the lions for such a long time, Bari and Jason go into the woods once a week with oxen and sledge, spear a zebra, and haul it home, where it is slaughtered. To protect the meat against insects and predators, it hangs with insect-repelling twigs in a cage beneath a tree. Though a lion pride kills a zebra about every third day, they never finish it completely, leaving a lot to hyenas and vultures. By rationing the caged lions, they feed for a week on one zebra. It keeps them in shape without making them fat and lazy.

*

Bari introduces Jason to the traditional festivities of his tribe. He wants Jason to participate, so Bari assists him to get properly dressed in local attire. Then Bari's two teenage daughters help to paint Jason's face, arms, and torso with red and white clay.

He joins the circle of men in colorful dress, holding an ox-hide shield and club in his left hand and a spear in his right. They chant in unison, stamping their feet in tune with the rhythmic drum-beat. Jason soon gets into the dance movements and intermittent war-cries. He reaches out to them by taking part and becoming like one of them.

Despite the brown tan Jason has acquired in the past few months in Africa living with a bare upper-body in the warm climate, Jason's lighter skin color still makes him an obvious outsider among the black warriors.

When the sun sets, a huge campfire is lit, enabling the party to continue into the night. After each dance, a huge calabash with fermented drink is passed around so each warrior can take a few sips. When the talk and laughter become noisier, Bari knows the beer is working. He loudly tells his guests—in somewhat exaggerated terms—about Jason's bravery and hunting skills. Added to Jason's huge stature, this fame evokes the guests' adoration, signaled by slow hand-clapping and exclamations. Women start chanting a song, praising Jason's attributes.

The merry, gregarious occasion is suddenly interrupted by a loud war-cry from the dark forest. A painted warrior-chief and two bodyguards, all armed with shields, clubs, and spears, step out of the dark. The guests fall silent, waiting for the intruder to state his business. All know this means trouble. They are probably surrounded by the enemy.

The intruder is a chief of another tribe. He accuses Bari of trespassing and hunting on his territory. As compensation he demands Bari's two teenage daughters as concubines for two of his sons. If denied, a duel between the champions of both tribes will decide the outcome. He ends his demand with a war-cry, echoed by his warriors hiding in the surrounding forest.

Having heard of Jason's bravery, one of Bari's friends shouts Jason's name. The others agree in chorus. It suits them: While Jason will do the fighting, they can get hold of their weapons and prepare for any further repercussions.

Bari briefs Jason on the situation. Bari is in a tight spot. Having sung Jason's bravery a while ago, he can hardly suggest someone else. It will show non-confidence in his hero. Jason, too, realizes he does not have much of a choice. While he took small sips from the calabash, the other guests helped themselves pretty well. They will be easy victims. Jason feels he can't allow Bari's daughters to be taken as concubines to a hostile tribe. They will surely suffer abuse as sex slaves.

Jason sends up a brief prayer to Tabitha's God. He stands up, holding his spear and shield above his head, and shouting the war-cry they used in the dance. He must look brave, though he does not feel so. His fellow warriors repeat the cry in unison, affirming their full support. The intruding chief is taken aback by the tall warrior with such weird skin color and strange facial features. Obviously, he is a foreigner. He may have superior skills. However, the intruder cannot back down now—he issued the challenge. After a few silent moments, he signals to one of his bodyguards to take on the "foreign devil."

Jason's stab-spear experience is of the essence now. The challenger holds his spear in his right hand and his shield and club in his left. He tries to intimidate Jason by mere showmanship—waving his shield and weapons and making fake moves while uttering scary shouts and hisses. Despite his scare tactics, Jason moves forward and blocks the opponent's blows with his shield.

Then Jason surprises the guy by throwing down his shield and holding the spear with both hands, as he was trained in the desert. Jason attacks by using both ends of the spear in quick succession. His opponent soon suffers shallow cuts to his right arm and leg. As the guy backs off, trying to avoid the superior onslaught, he stumbles. Jason kicks his shield and club from his left hand, stamps his foot on his right arm, and puts his spear-head on the guy's chest. A shout of victory arises from Bari's guests and family. Jason has saved them!

At Bari's command, a dozen of his guests jump to their feet and surround Jason and his opponent. Their outward-facing shields form a protective wall, preventing the enemy from launching an arrow or spear from the dark in an effort to eliminate Jason's victory. When Jason withholds the killing thrust, Bari sees an opportunity to appease his accuser. He enters the ring of shields, telling the intruder he will save his friend's life if he withdraws his claims and leaves in peace. Realizing that Jason's spear is only inches from his friend's heart, the intruder concedes, turns around, and disappears into the jungle, followed by his scared friend, who keeps looking back with fear on his face.

It is now too dangerous for Bari's guests to walk back to their homes in the dark. Bari invites them to stay over. After another few rounds of beer, amid lively discussion of the interruption and the duel, mats are rolled out so they can sleep off the excesses of the party. Jason, Bari, and two of his sons take turns as night watch—just in case the intruders try their luck again. At sunrise, the guests get up, say their goodbyes, and return home. Jason's fame will spread far and wide, preventing attacks on Bari for a long time to come.

Bari thanks his friend from the heart. Jason saved him from the lioness, and now he saved his daughters from the enemy. Bari hopes he can repay Jason's favors someday.

*

Spotty is growing fast in size and in affection for Jason. He has been accompanying Jason and Bari on hunts lately. Jason anticipates a tough goodbye when the time comes to leave. Fortunately, Bari's brother is delayed by floods. The rainy season lasts longer than usual. The sad moment of farewell is postponed for several weeks.

The bond between Jason and Spotty is strengthened by rough-and-tumble play. At the end of the rainy season, Spotty has become quite strong, sometimes going a little too far in the enthusiastic wrestling with Jason. Then, Jason calls him to order with a firm voice: "Back off! Back off! Stop it!" The tone of voice tells Spotty to calm down and give Jason a break. When a truce is established, Jason reinforces the bond by patting Spotty's head, calling his name. Spotty knows his name well now. When Jason calls, he follows right away. Spotty knows Jason's name, too. When Bari calls Jason, Spotty jumps to his feet, eager to see if they're going on a hunt.

By the middle of October, Faki arrives in his felucca. After a good meal, the lions are returned to cage-sledges, which are hauled to the riverbank with oxen, and swung onto the felucca by means of a shaduf. Bari gives them three salted zebra hind legs for the journey. They will be done before they get spoiled.

Jason had a long walk that morning with Spotty, hoping he would be exhausted and sleeping when Jason leaves. The plan works. Jason hugs the whole family one by one before he steps into the felucca. He waves at Bari and his family, with whom he has shared five months of adventure and learning.

He does not know what will happen to Spotty. Maybe Bari will release it into the wild, or maybe it too will one day be sent off on the river in a cage—a thought too ghastly for Jason to contemplate.

They sail off, downstream (north) on the White Nile, covering four times the distance per day than they did with the upstream journey. Though the water of the Nile is subsiding, the cataracts are less of a problem on the downstream journey. Thanks to Faki's skill, they shoot through the narrows. In Egypt, it's plain sailing, without any delays. They have no passengers—nobody will share a felucca with three lions in lattice cages.

Jason has a lot of time to think about his situation. He wonders if Tabitha still waits for him. Maybe she has given up on him and found love with someone else. He has to make a plan to contact her as soon as possible. He must know her feelings.

Without stops, they proceed to Alexandria. From there, Jason goes by fishing vessel back to Apollonia. In Cyrene, Lucius and his family hang on to Jason's words as he tells them about his Nile and African adventures.

Having penetrated Africa by Nile boat up to the jungle of Southern Sudan, and having lived with the locals there for several months, Jason is convinced that life in wild Africa is not what he wants in the long run. At the moment, he cannot see how his African adventure will help him in the future.

Deep inside his heart, he yearns to be back in Corinth with his family and with Tabitha. Sooner or later, he will have to grab the bull by the horns, return to Corinth, and face his adversary. The crucial question is: Has Krato changed? Has he matured and mellowed over time, or will he stubbornly cling to his stupid, unfounded, revengeful obsession? Jason realizes he cannot merely walk up to Krato and ask him about his progress. He will have to find a way to test the water before it gets over his head.

CHAPTER 9

Shortly after Jason's return from Egypt, an opportunity arises to make secret contact with Tabitha and his family. He realizes the plan may backfire and alert Krato to his whereabouts, but his love for Tabitha impels him to make the effort in hope.

One of his friends, Rufus, son of Simon of Cyrene, is going on a business trip to Greece and Asia Minor. He is seeking new export markets for their leather industry. He offered to make casual contact with Jason's family, invite Tabitha over for the occasion, and update them on Jason's circumstances.

Rufus boards a ship to Crete, another one to Athens, and then proceeds with a fishing vessel to the Diolkos. From there, he gets a lift into Corinth. He makes contact with several businesses that trade in leather, he shows his products, and makes deals.

On his rounds, he also meets with Isaac and Tabitha. He has to suppress his thrill to see the girl his friend Jason is yearning for so intensely. He wishes Jason could be in his shoes now.

In the middle of conversation, Rufus whispers to Isaac, "Can we speak privately? I have a message from a friend."

Isaac's eyeballs almost pop out, hoping it is news from Jason.

When they get to the back of the shop, heads together, Isaac whispers, "Jason?"

Rufus nods, adding, "He's okay. He's doing well."

"Thank God!" Isaac sighs with relief. "Wait here. I will call Tabitha."

He casually goes to the front counter and asks Tabitha to help the gentleman in the store with info about stocks.

She finds it a little strange, but goes to the back to find out what the problem is.

"I'm Rufus, a friend of Jason's," he whispers.

Her mouth falls open in surprise and disbelief.

With excited eyes and her hands on her cheeks, she pleads, "Is he well?" Her eyes swim in tears. Just when her hope was fading, fearing Jason may have found love with another girl, her thirsting soul is revived by a dewdrop.

"He's doing well, strong as an ox! He sends his love."

Smiling with joy, wiping off tears, she whispers, "Where is he?"

"First, promise you won't go there."

"No, no, no, I won't. I promise!"

"Cyrene, Africa," Rufus whispers.

"Africa?!" She gasps in disbelief.

"Ssshhh…" Rufus warns, index finger on his lips.

"If you work in Alexandria, he may visit you regularly," Rufus whispers, with a twinkle in his eyes.

Ecstatic, Tabitha grabs Rufus by his upper arms, shakes him, and affirms, "Yes! Yes! Yes!" Then she hugs him, whispering: "Thank you! Thank you! Thank you, Rufus, for this wonderful news!"

"Come over to Helena at sunset. I will share some more news with Jason's family." Rufus ends the short, risky chat. He concludes his business with Isaac.

A platoon with Krato in command marches over the *agora*.

"That's the bastard!" Isaac mumbles.

Rufus can understand why Jason left. It's bad to have a whole regiment against you. To be chased off by such a scoundrel—life is not fair!

That evening, Rufus briefs Philip and his family about Jason's life in Cyrene. Tabitha is present, too. Each bit of information helps her to imagine Jason's present life. They speak in subdued voices and do not mention names. Sometimes, the walls have ears.

They rejoice about Jason's successful enterprise, his mixing with good people, and his sober lifestyle. They are amazed about the Roman layout of Cyrene having all the facilities Corinth has. They decide it will be best not to send letters to Jason. If Rufus is mugged, the letters may fall into the wrong hands.

Rufus returns to the tavern, where he stays. Philip and Helena walk Tabitha home. There is new hope in their hearts, putting jubilation in their minds and smiles on their faces. The contact Rufus established has fed their yearning souls. They feel as if bright sun rays have broken through ominous dark clouds. They can breathe freely again. The heavy burden has been lifted.

Tabitha's mind works overtime, devising plans to go to Alexandria.

After meeting with prospective clients in Athens, Ephesus, and Miletus, Rufus returns to Cyrene three weeks later. Jason hangs on to his lips, taking in every bit of information about Tabitha and his family. Fortunately, Rufus is sensitive and observant. He listened well. He gives Jason a fairly detailed report about what he saw, heard, and sensed. He conveys the greetings and best wishes of Jason's loved ones. Jason is thrilled to hear that Tabitha is still deeply in love with him and yearning to be with him.

Jason feels refreshed. The report feeds his inner soul as he rethinks and enjoys it over and over again. Will Tabitha come to Alexandria? She can be very determined. He hopes he will get word from her out of Alexandria soon.

The sharing of news to both sides was long overdue, and thus welcomed with sincere gratitude. Though it soothed the pain, it also opened old wounds. From both sides, the yearning intensifies. Jason and Tabitha are restless...hoping...waiting. Both pray repeatedly, *please, God, please, help us!*

*

Tabitha gets a lucky break when Abner, a twenty-five-year-old Jew, formerly from Corinth, now working as scroll copier in Alexandria, visits his family in Corinth. When he is welcomed in the synagogue, Tabitha sees her chance. Isaac and his family are still attending both synagogue and church.

Isaac asks Abner's dad to introduce his son to Tabitha. Tabitha and Abner click immediately. Tabitha shows interest in his work, and inquires about Alexandria. She is amazed to hear that the city has a large Jewish and Christian community. She invites Abner to enjoy supper with them.

Abner has visited many historic Egyptian sites, and enjoys sharing his impressions. He mentions that they have a shortage of scroll copiers. The work demands high precision and concentration. For most people, it is too monotonous and painstaking.

"Do they employ women for scroll copying?" Tabitha inquires cautiously.

"Oh yes," responds Abner, sensing he may have a fish on the hook. "Almost half of our staff is female. Actually, I think their writing is more refined than that of the men," he adds with a chuckle.

Tabitha's heart beats faster. A unique opportunity is opening up for her. She is a go-getter. When she identifies a problem, she searches for a solution, and when she finds one, she gets moving towards her goal.

"What do you think, Dad? Don't you think I should give it a try?" She shoots this arrow blindly, hoping it will somehow hit the target.

"Give what a try?" Isaac responds, having lost track of the conversation.

"Working as scroll copier in Alexandria!" Tabitha repeats, biting her fingernail, swinging her foot as she sits cross-legged. Isaac picks up her tension. He knows Tabitha well. He also knows her motive. Love is unstoppable, like a flooding river. He has seen this coming since Rufus' visit.

With a lump in his throat, he stammers, "If you really want to do it, my child...I will not stand in your way. I assume... sooner or later...children leave their parents. If that time has arrived for us now...well, what I mean, you know...we have to face it...hard as it is..."

Abner's excitement overrides his guilt for luring Tabitha to Alexandria. He likes her adventurous spirit. It will be fun to have her in Alexandria. They can explore Egypt together. Maybe their friendship can develop to something deeper.

Tabitha cannot tell Abner the real motive behind her decision. That will put Jason's secret in jeopardy. Two weeks later, she departs with Abner to Egypt. Tabitha bubbles with excitement to see the city she has heard so much about from Apollos and Abner.

She is employed as apprentice scroll copier with Abner in the renowned library of Alexandria. She must go through meticulous training first. This library not only has the most extensive collection of scrolls in the world, they also make copies of scrolls for libraries in other great cities. The Alexandrian Hebrew text of the Bible has become the starting point of a famous text family. The Septuagint, the first Greek translation of Hebrew scripture, was made in Alexandria.

*

Jason is working on a new invention. The axles and bushes of wagon wheels have been causing problems since the wheel's inception three millennia ago. For centuries, the bush and axle were made of wood. The friction between the two caused rapid overheating and scouring—just as fire can be made by rotating a stick quickly on a piece of soft wood.

In the past century, the quality and precision of iron bushes and axles have increased. The iron bush fits like a sleeve around the axle. The immense friction between bush and axle is limited by grease made of animal fat. However, the pressure of the axle on the bush pushes the grease out, increasing friction gradually as the wheel rolls. Therefore, new grease must occasionally be squeezed into the bush from a small skin-bag. On the uphill road from Apollonia, dry axles are taboo, because they make the task of the oxen much tougher. It takes more time and feed to get the job done.

Watching workmen move colossal blocks of stone on wooden rollers gives Jason an idea. If he puts iron rollers in a circle around the axle, they should have the same effect: facilitating movement by reducing friction. Instead of grinding the bush, the axle will glide over rotating cylindrical bearings.

Watching the stone-on-rollers, Jason noticed that the rollers work best if they don't touch each other. While the front side of one roller descends, the rear side of the next one ascends. If they touch each other, the downward movement of one roller impedes the upward movement of the next.

Jason decides to keep the iron rollers apart by putting them in a slotted cylinder, a racer. One third of the rollers protrude above the racer, and two-thirds below, so the weight will be on the rollers, not on the racer.

By trial and error, Jason experiments with various options. He eventually decides to enclose the rollers and racer between an outer and inner bush. The inner bush will fit tightly around the axle and does not turn. When the outer bush turns with the wheel, the inner bush glides on the rolling bearings. Iron washers on either side of the bearings prevent them from falling out. By encapsulating the bearings and racer between the outer and inner bush, he combines all the parts into one unit. It will be easier to carry, demonstrate, and install. These units are only three inches wide, so Jason decides to put one on the inside and one on the outside of the twelve-inch-wide wagon wheel hub.

Before Jason requests that an engineering company manufacture the bearings, he first has to satisfy himself that his theory works in practice. He asks his workers to put a wagon's rear end on blocks so that one rear wheel can spin freely. The men burn with curiosity and wonder if this thing will work. Jason has an old-type wheel greased. He puts a grease mark on the rim, grabs a spoke at that point, and spins the wheel with one heave as hard as he can. The old wheel completes almost five revolutions before it stops.

Jason now widens the old wheel's hub to hold the inner and outer bearing units. He adds grease and tests the new-type wheel on the same axle that he tested the old one. The new wheel completes nine revolutions—adequate proof of less friction. His workers cheer and whistle to express their astonishment, adoration, and joy for Jason's invention.

Now Jason needs an engineer and factory to put his prototype into production. He has to go to Alexandria for that. Their iron works are far more advanced than those in Cyrene. When the wagon drivers tell him of a ship in the harbor of Apollonia that is heading for Alexandria shortly, he grabs the opportunity. Two days later, he arrives in Alexandria, unaware that Tabitha is working in the library.

Jason has grown a black beard. He is dressed in an Egyptian outfit, including a turban, to disguise his identity. If Krato perhaps has a few friends in Alexandria, Jason will not be recognized easily by one of them.

From the harbor, he passes the library of Alexandria. He has a strange feeling that Tabitha is near. Maybe she has followed up on Rufus' suggestion to come to this city. What if she suddenly appears round the next corner?

Searching for her among the thousands of this city would be more daunting than looking for the proverbial needle in a haystack. He dismisses his feelings as unrealistic: *I doubt if Isaac will allow Tabitha to come to such a big city by herself.*

Jason searches for technicians who can manufacture the roller bearing unit according to his specifications. One iron worker refers Jason to the next. Eventually, he tracks down a huge enterprise that manufactures advanced iron tools and steel swords.

The chief engineer, named Akton, looks at Jason's contraption with skeptical interest. Nobody can teach him anything about iron.

The more he looks and thinks, nudged by Jason's explanations, the more he realizes the sense of the simple design. He tells his technicians to widen the hole in a wheel's hub so it can hold the roller bearings. When he tests the new wheel against an old one, he is stunned. He is immediately convinced that this invention will be a giant leap forward in the development of the wheel.

Excited about the potential of the invention, Akton builds on Jason's concept. The massive weight of loaded wagons may grind iron bearings to paste very quickly. When they make the roller bearings from steel (a mixture of iron and carbon) the bearings will last much longer. Akton is an expert in making swords from Damascus steel.

At the end of the day, Akton and Jason strike a deal. For the right to make and sell this invention, Akton's company will manufacture one hundred and sixty bearing units, enough for twenty wagons, for Cyrene Transport at cost price. Jason does not mind that his invention will be used by others—as long as he gets it into production for his business.

On his way to the harbor the next day, he passes the library again and experiences the same strange feeling about Tabitha's closeness. He inquires at the front desk but they don't know a person with that name. Jason is not in the mood to search through the whole enormous place, so he departs, hoping that his gut-feeling will soon come true.

*

Although Alexandria is farther from Cyrene than Corinth is, Tabitha feels closer to Jason in Alexandria. Here they can meet, while in Corinth they could not.

Her problem is how to get word to Jason about a meeting place with the help of a reliable person. She attends synagogue and church in Alexandria, hoping to find the right person to use as messenger. She tries to become better acquainted with people to judge their integrity. When a female friend one day mentions that she knows the son of Simon of Cyrene, the man who carried the cross of Jesus, Tabitha knows she has struck gold. They are pleasantly surprised that they both know Rufus.

Having something in common, they open up more to each other. Learning that Tabitha needs to send a message to someone in Cyrene, her friend recommends her brother James, who goes there by ship occasionally for business purposes. He is also a member of the church. A letter may fall into the wrong hands, so Tabitha sends a verbal message with James: "Library basement, Room 15."

When Jason receives this short message, he tries to get more information from James. He showers James with questions: "How is she? Is she okay? Does she look good? Where does she work? How often do you see her?"

"Wow! Slow down! She's in good health, looks happy, burns with enthusiasm to see you, and she doesn't want to blow your cover," James responds, overwhelmed.

Jason is in seventh heaven. He invites James to dinner at the best tavern in town. They share views on Alexandria and Tabitha. Jason's return message is short: "See you soon."

A few days later, Jason gets a ride with a fishing vessel to Alexandria. It's not the best ride, but the quickest one. When

Jason appears in the doorway of Room 15 in the basement of the library Tabitha glances at him for half a second, without recognizing him in his Egyptian clothes and black beard.

"Can I help you?" she says casually without looking up, thinking he's a customer who has lost his way in the great complex.

"Yes, please. I'm looking for Tabitha."

That voice she would recognize among a crowd. "Jason!" She throws herself into his arms.

He holds her with passion, whispering, "Tabitha, Tabitha, my darling!"

Their hearts burst out in joy. Laughs, exclamations, and questions bubble up like a fountain. The moment they yearned for so passionately has arrived.

Abner is totally dumbfounded. He didn't know about this relationship. His own hopes regarding Tabitha are dashed. She introduces Jason to Abner, who sums up the situation quickly, excuses himself, and leaves the room.

Tabitha closes the door. They surrender themselves to a long and passionate kiss; body and soul have a lot of catch-up to do. They cherish that exciting fizz inside themselves, that insatiable appetite for each other's closeness, experienced by lovers who have been separated for a long time. Both wish that they don't have to go through that love-starvation again.

They realize God often provides for his children by bringing the right people to them. He used Rufus, Abner, and James to bring two yearning young lovers together again.

"Maybe God has a place for other friends in his great plan too," Tabitha guesses.

"Quite possibly," Jason agrees.

Tabitha takes leave for two days. They have to make the best of the available time. They enjoy snacks and drinks, walk in the park, sit and talk on a bench, and share what has happened to them since Jason left Corinth.

By sharing his experiences with Tabitha, Jason relives and reviews them, gaining insight as he proceeds: "I realize a higher power controlled the challenges and provided the victories, helping me to make the right choices. Paul was right when he said that all things work together for good to those who love God."

Tabitha briefs Jason on developments in Corinth since his departure. As Jason has not yet attended a reading of Paul's letter to the church in Corinth, Tabitha conveys to him as much as she can remember of that illuminating epistle. She adds: "In my yearning, the part about love made the deepest impression on me. Although Moses already emphasized love for God and neighbor fifteen hundred years ago, Paul presents the same truth in a fresh and inspiring way."

"How can we reconcile love for neighbor with defense against neighbor?" Jason wonders. "I enjoy it to be friendly and helpful, and I hate harming others, but when the robbers attacked us in the desert, I knew I could not avoid the bloody conflict. I had to fight viciously for my own and my hosts' survival. Did I violate the law of love?"

"No, not at all!" Tabitha reacts. "To the contrary: You practiced the law of love. Moses said, 'You shall love your neighbor as yourself.'[18] That is exactly what you did when you protected yourself and your hosts. We live in a fallen world, Jason. Sometimes we have to protect victims against abusers. The attackers' lack of love sealed their fate."

As they exchange ideas, Jason and Tabitha sit together, holding hands, kissing in between, looking into each other eyes—lost in love. When they sit on a bench she cuddles up to him. She turns her body so that her hip is on the bench, legs pulled up, and knees toward the backrest. Her upper body rests against his chest, enfolded in his strong arms. This position enhances their closeness and kissing. Jason's arm rests on her thigh.

---

18 Lev. 19:18

The two days fly by like a swooping eagle.

When Jason complains about the upcoming long periods of separation, Tabitha tries to comfort him with Psalm 139, which she copied recently:

> [7] Where can I go from Your Spirit?
>   Or where can I flee from Your presence?
> [8] If I ascend into heaven, You *are* there;
>   If I make my bed in hell, behold, You *are there.*
> [9] *If* I take the wings of the morning,
>   *And* dwell in the uttermost parts of the sea,
> [10] Even there Your hand shall lead me,
>   And Your right hand shall hold me.[19]

"Yes, it's true," Jason concurs reluctantly, "God has provided for me wherever I went. Nevertheless, I look forward to the day we can be together continuously."

However, the long silence and separation has been broken. They know they can see each other more often. They feel they must maintain vigilance regarding Krato.

When the fishing boat leaves for Apollonia, they wave to each other until other vessels cut their view off. Jason returns to Cyrene with jubilation in his heart. His cup is running over. He has seen, heard, touched, kissed, and smelled his beloved Tabitha again. His soul is refreshed.

For the next two years, Jason visits Tabitha at the end of every second month. The round trip to Alexandria takes at least four days. With the two or three days there, it adds up to a full week away from his workshop in Cyrene. However, his apprentices have made great progress in building and servicing wagons. They can proceed without him.

In spring and autumn, Jason and Tabitha spend a vacation of two weeks together. Being emotionally famished by their long separations, they need to enjoy each other as much as possible

---

19 Ps. 139:7-10

during the short visits. This exposes them to temptation. Both have conflicts about intimacy.

Though their bodies yearn for sexual completeness, their souls want to respect the boundaries they have accepted for themselves. In line with Jewish tradition, Tabitha wants to present herself as a pure bride to Jason. With his Greek background, he does not have strong feelings about sex before marriage. However, as he respects her values, he will not try to seduce her. After all, it was her strong character and values that made her so attractive to him in the first place when they became friends.

Tabitha allows Jason to caress her thighs, but as his hand gradually creeps up higher to the forbidden zone, she feels they need to discuss the matter.

"Jason, we have to talk."

"Yes, darling, what do you want to talk about?"

"About that naughty hand of yours."

"What's wrong with it? Don't you enjoy it too?" he teases, kissing her neck.

"Yes, I do—too much."

"So?"

"Jason, if we fondle each other intimately, we may not be able to stop the process. Our physical drives may become irresistible. My body craves for unity as much as yours, but we have to decide what we really want."

"What do you want, Tabitha?" He continues to kiss her cheeks, trying to distract her. He senses where she's going.

"I always wanted to be a virgin on my wedding day, Jason. That is in line with the Law of Moses and my tradition. What about the consequences? Do you really want a baby in our present circumstances?"

The thought shocks him back to reality: "A baby? A BABY! Oh my goodness, not now! Tabitha, I yearn for the moment we can become one. I have to admit, though, that a baby at this point will complicate matters immensely. Apart from that, your purity attracted me from the beginning. If I rob you of that, I actually defeat my own ideal. I suppose we have to draw a line and stick to it."

"Okay, Jason, draw the line."

"Right there!" he responds, drawing an imaginary line with his finger on her thigh. They seal their commitment with a laugh and a kiss.

Knowing that human nature likes to push the boundaries, they complement their caresses with other forms of fellowship. They tour Alexandria, take boat trips on Lake Maryut or the Nile, visit ancient sites, and attend sports and cultural events. In this way, they don't get preoccupied with the physical side of their bonding, but give space to the emotional side, too. They build their mutual respect and companionship by getting to know each other better as persons. Being together—that's what really counts.

Tabitha uses Egyptian dress to conceal her identity. Friends of Krato will not easily recognize them as a Corinthian couple. Tabitha visits Cyrene once. Lucius takes Tabitha and Jason on a three-day camel trip to the northern fringes of the Sahara. They marvel at the bright stars and eerie silence at night. Engulfed by the majestic greatness of creation, Tabitha softly sings Psalm 8, which she learned as child in the synagogue, and then explains the Hebrew to Jason.

[3] When I consider Your heavens, the work of Your
fingers,
The moon and the stars, which You have ordained,
[4] What is man that You are mindful of him,
And the son of man that You visit him?
[5] For You have made him a little lower than the angels,[b]
And You have crowned him with glory and honor.
[9] O LORD, our Lord,
How excellent *is* Your name in all the earth![20]

20 Ps.8:3-5, 9. Psalm 8:5 Hebrew Elohim, God; Septuagint, Syriac, Targum, and Jewish tradition translate as angels.

Jason introduces Tabitha to his friends at the Cyrene church, hoping to diminish the attention he gets from other girls. They sense the two are deeply in love.

Although Jason and Tabitha find the seven week stretches between visits long and cumbersome, it is still better than the first two years of emotional famine when they did not have any contact.

Jason cannot help but to feel a little jealous toward Abner, who is with Tabitha every day. She often refers to him. Jason senses Abner and Tabitha have become dear friends.

*

Jason has received his first shipment of the new bearing units. Refurbishing existing wagon wheels with new bushes is time-consuming work; therefore, Jason changes the design of new wheels so that they are ready for the bearings right from the start.

Some of Jason's partners are still skeptical about Jason's invention. Is it really worth the large investment of money, time, and effort? Jason decides to conduct a demonstration. For most people, seeing is believing.

Jason uses two identical new wheels, one with the old type of bush, and one with the new type. He has the rear axle of a wagon put on blocks so that the wheel can spin freely. The workmen grease the axle and put the wheel with the old-type bush on the axle. Jason makes a grease mark on the wheel's rim to help them count the number of revolutions the wheel completes.

Skeptical but curious, his partners watch the whole process. To ensure the two wheels are spun with the same force, Jason uses a bag of sand attached to a rope running over a pulley in the roof. The other end of the rope is hooked to a hole in the wheel's band. When the bag is dropped from a height of ten feet, it pulls the wheel into motion via the rope and pulley.

They count the number of times the grease mark on the wheel reaches the bottom. They all agree: seven times and a bit.

Now the new wheel with roller bearings is installed and marked. The wheel is spun in the same way. It completes almost fifteen revolutions. The new unit is twice as efficient as the old one. A repeat performance shows the same results.

The next question is: How long will it last? Jason knows the answer. Because of less friction, it should last longer. However, only the long-term test in working conditions will convince the hardliners. They will have to wait and see.

Jason anticipates another problem: The bearings may make the uphill journey from Apollonia to Cyrene easier, but it may make the downhill trip riskier. They don't want runaway wagons. Locking the rear wheels will wear the iron band thin at the point that slides over the ground. To increase braking and to decrease wear on the wheel bands, Jason devises five-foot long sledge-like blocks to go beneath the rear wheels on steep downhill stretches. The front ends of the blocks are fastened by chains to the wagon's ribs to keep them aligned to the wheels.

*

Jason and Tabitha realize they cannot proceed with the present circumstances indefinitely. They want to marry and raise a family; that is the logical goal to pursue. They cannot allow Krato to spoil their lives forever. However, they are not quite sure how to proceed. They don't want the feud between Jason and Krato to end in bloodshed.

CHAPTER 10

One of Jason's church friends, Petros, is training for the discus event in the approaching Cyrene Games. Though the competition is much more localized than the Isthmian Games, the athletes and public are quite excited about the peak athletic event of Cyrenaica, also known as the Pentapolis (five-city) region.

When Petros discusses his training with him, Jason offers help. At a practice session, Petros makes a few throws. Jason notices several points that can be improved. Without sounding authoritative, he makes suggestions: "Why don't you try this or that?"

Petros' throws gain from every piece of advice. He senses that Jason has more expertise than he is willing to advertise. He asks Jason to demonstrate some of the intricate combinations of movements. Jason's smooth style impresses him. However, Jason stops power at the last moment. The discus lands only a few paces from him. Petros urges Jason to do a complete throw. He wants to see the whole movement from start to finish. Jason complies, reluctantly. Although he does not use full force, his throw is several paces better than that of Petros.

"I guess you are an Isthmian champion, aren't you?" Petros wagers.

"I did well in the under-twenty division."

"Will you help me with my training?"

"On one condition: You don't tell anybody about my discus background."

"Agreed!" Petros is so glad he has discovered Jason's hidden talent that he will do anything to secure his help.

For the next six months, Petros and Jason practice together every second day. On alternative days, to strengthen their muscles and tendons, they exercise with two stones, as Jason did before the Isthmian Games. One secret Jason does not reveal is the spinning movement he used before the throw.

In this time, Jason is plagued by a recurring nightmare. He dreams he and Krato are in a confined space, like a corral or arena, fenced in by long vertical posts. He cannot get away from his archrival. Both of them are armed with spears. Krato holds his spear at shoulder height, aiming, looking for the right moment to pierce Jason. Jason tries to employ his stab-spear skills, but his movements are slow and clumsy. When Krato eventually throws, the spear approaches Jason in slow motion. He observes the rotating spearhead and wobbling handle coming straight at him. He wants to sidestep the projectile, but feels glued in lameness. His heart beats slowly and loudly like a bass drum. Just before the spear hits his chest, he wakes up in a cold sweat. *Thank God, it's only a dream!* In the subsequent sleepless hour, he worries about Krato's plans.

On the day of the games, Petros amazes his family and friends with his smooth style, powerful throws, and unbeatable distances. He wants to tell them that Jason is to be thanked for his success, but he decides to stick to his promise.

After the athletes have finished, members of the public are invited to try their luck with the discus. It is a fun event. Several former champs in their forties and fifties take part, amid a lot of humorous comments and laughs.

Lucius, Simon, and Rufus dare Jason to join in.

"Please, Jason, please!" urges Mary.

"Only if you guys join me!" Jason hopes they will decline. To his amazement, they all get up.

"Okay, lets go!" they shout in chorus.

A dozen men, one by one, have their shot with the discus. Some do amazingly well. Despite his fifty summers, Simon's big hand and long arm swings the discus to a mark close to that of the young athletes.

"Come on, my son," he tempts Jason, "let's see if you can beat the old guy!"

From the stand, Mary and her friends start chanting: "Jason! Jason! Jason!"

The crowd joins in. The spirit of the moment gets the better of Jason. His memory carries him back to that day at the Isthmian Games when he made his record throw. He wonders if he still can. Practicing with Petros has restored his fitness.

He swings his arm three times, spins around, and puts all his power into the throw. He is amazed at his own effort. The height is good. The discus climbs with speed on the breeze. The crowd roars with applause. They have never seen that style before. Jason's throw is several paces better than Petros' best. Lucius and Simon carry Jason on their shoulders from the field. Mary, Rufus, Petros, and many others join them, chanting, "Jason the Great! Jason Magnus!"

One spectator recognized Jason's style right away. He saw it only once before—at the Isthmian Games several years ago. He shares his suspicion with his friends. Some of them affirm that Jason is from Corinth. Immediately, the rumor spreads: Jason is a champion of the Isthmian Games. Then the questions and speculation arise: Why has he come to Cyrene? Why on earth would anyone from Corinth choose to live in Africa? Has he done something wrong? Is he on the run?

The guy who recognized Jason mentions in his first letter home that Corinth's vanished champion has surfaced in

Cyrene. The rumor spreads in Corinth too, from friend to friend, from tavern to tavern: "Have you heard this: Jason, our missing discus champion, has turned up in Cyrene, in Africa? Yes, in Africa! Can you believe that?"

*

Diana's hostess business has been flourishing in Rome. She feels the need for a break, for a vacation with her family and friends in Corinth. She trains one of her best hostesses to run the business in her absence. Convinced that she has left the business in good hands, she boards a ship to Corinth.

When the ship docks in Lechaion, she bubbles with joy, waves to her excited family on the pier, and takes a deep breath of Corinth's air. *Home again, at last!*

On the two-mile trip into town by horse carriage, she is showered by questions about life in Rome. Her parents and younger sister try to visualize her descriptions of the place that all want to see but only some will reach.

Though many elements of Rome have been duplicated in her colonies—such as the forum, avenues, aqueducts, theaters, baths, temples, shops, chalets, arenas, and hippodromes—those in Rome are so much more colossal and beautiful.

Asked about her business, she vaguely refers to it as a beauty shop where women can buy whatever they need to make themselves more attractive to their lovers. She brought some of her soaps and perfumes as presents for her mom and sister. Her dad gets an expensive ostrich skin wallet he can strap around his waist beneath his clothes.

After two days of sharing with her family, she starts to reach out to former friends. She is shocked to hear about the tragedy regarding Toni and Jason, and even more so about Jason's disappearance. The fact that Krato went on a long leave shortly after the news arrived that Jason now lives in Cyrene worries Diana. She knows Krato; if he swore vengeance about Toni, he will not rest until he has accomplished his self-imposed mission.

Diana also visits the luxurious upper-class pleasure houses, evaluating their styles and methods. She is considering the possibility of opening a branch of her Roman enterprise in Corinth. She hopes it will lure the rich like bees to nectar.

She has a lot of money, but it is in a bank in Rome. She submits proof of that to her dad, and asks him for a substantial loan to buy real estate in Corinth. Knowing how fast her type of business escalates, she is confident that she will be able to repay the loan soon.

As she has done in Rome, she does not want to associate her business with the red-light district of town. In the elite residential area of the city, she finds a large home badly in need of repair, paint, and gardening. The wealthy owner now lives in a chalet on a Greek island, seldom visiting Corinth.

Diana asks her dad about the person and the property. He knows the fellow, named Tertius. Andreo thinks he may get the home for his daughter at a reasonable price. The next day, they depart by yacht to the island.

Tertius is glad to see Andreo, and is impressed by his beautiful daughter, "How time has flown! The last time I saw Diana, she was ten years old!" They talk about the good old days, enjoying wine and cheese.

After an hour or so, Tertius has mellowed quite nicely. He finds it hard to keep his eyes off Diana. She softens him up with sweet smiles and friendly eyes. She leaves the negotiation to her dad.

When Andreo inquires about his property in Corinth, Tertius admits that the house has become a headache to him. He thought he would go there more often, but his plans have not materialized. Now, it will cost him a lot to prepare the place for the market.

"Spare yourself the trouble!" Andreo suggests, "I have a better idea!"

"It sounds good. I'm listening."

Andreo has his offer ready: "My daughter needs a large place to use as a guest-house for people who want to overnight at a quiet place in Corinth. The taverns can be quite rowdy. However, you know how it is with young people—they have the ideas, but lack the money. I'm willing to help her get started. Sell the place as it is to her at a fair price, and we will do the renovations. It saves you the expense and the trouble."

"Make an offer!" Tertius looks more than interested.

Andreo puts the bid in much lower than he expects to pay after bargaining. To his amazement, Tertius accepts his starting bid without any quibbling. Getting most of his money out without any further expenses and effort just looked too attractive.

Andreo takes Tertius' letter to a lawyer in Corinth, ordering him to complete the deal. Within a month, the mansion belongs to Diana. After spending time there, planning alterations and repairs, she gets the artisans in, and three months later, the place looks like new. Diana blooms with pride.

In the meantime she has done some canvassing among her old female friends. She tells them about her business in Rome, explaining the basic philosophy of a hostess business. When the home is finished, she has five girls who are eager to begin. After a few weeks, she has to hire more hostesses. Diana is conquering Corinth with her vices—social and erotic entertainment for bored, wealthy men.

*

A few months after Jason amazed his friends with his discus skills, his Cyrene serenity is rudely shattered.

Once a week, he joins his partners for a beer and a chat at one of the taverns. He is strict with himself. He sticks to one beer, knowing that after the second one, he is caught up by the social spirit of the occasion, losing count of his consumption.

Jason tells his friends about Agizul, the guy he met in the desert, who arrived on a surprise visit to Cyrene this morning. "Agizul is deeply concerned about me. He believes I am in great danger and may be struck by a calamity shortly."

"What makes him think that?" one guy asks.

"He and his daughter had similar nightmares in which I am pursued by a dragon," Jason chuckles. "Being deeply grateful for my help in driving the desert pirates off, his family convinced Agizul to undertake the long journey to help or warn me. He believed that God would delay the peril until he arrived. He was immensely relieved to find me in good health. He is convinced, though, that the danger is still imminent."

"How can he defend you if the threat is unknown?" one of Jason's partners wonders.

"I have no idea what the meaning of his nightmares and concerns may be," Jason remarks, mystified. With a serious frown, he adds, "I've learned, though, not to ignore a strong premonition."

"Well, Jason, we hope you slay the dragon and retrieve the Golden Fleece, whatever it may be," another partner ventures. All enjoy the pun and drink to Jason's health. They continue enjoying the drinks and company at leisure after a long day's work, chatting about recent and upcoming events.

Suddenly, Jason hears behind him a voice he hates: "Well, well, well. How's the champion of Corinth doing in dark Africa?" It's Krato's taunting, unmistakably.

Expecting no answer, Krato continues, "Gentlemen, Jason happens to be an old friend of mine. May I join you?"

Jason's partners look back and forth between him and Krato. They search for a signal of what to say or do. Jason's expression makes him look as if he has smelled something bad. Krato's tone and Jason's face tell them there is trouble in the air.

"Yes, sure, why not?" Jason's invitation does not sound very friendly.

Then he continues with a broad smile, "Friends, may I introduce you to the dragon, my discus arch rival, Krato, a centurion in the army."

Jason introduces his friends by name, not mentioning their business ties. Jason does not want to involve them. By calling Krato "the dragon," Jason indicated that this man is the dragon from Agizul's dream.

The situation and conversation remain stiff. Krato continues with his sarcasm. He wants the party to break up. He wants Jason alone in a dark spot. After a few minutes of failed efforts to get out of the glum conversation, Jason's partners excuse themselves. Satisfied that he has spoiled Jason's social moment, Krato also leaves after a while.

Jason sits by himself, thinking about what Krato's plans may be, and how he can thwart them. Is his nightmare about Krato's spear becoming a reality?

Eventually, he decides to leave. It's dark already. He will have to stay alert to avoid an ambush. Instead of leaving by the main entrance, Jason asks the bartender if he may slip away through a dark hallway and backdoor.

He can't see much. He stands for a while, allowing his eyes to adapt to the darkness. The faint light of an outside torch flickers through a small window.

"I thought you would try to sneak away like a true coward," he hears Krato's voice from the dark hallway ahead of him.

"Tonight's the night, Jason. The night of reckoning," he goes on, hoping to paralyze Jason with fear. "Tonight you will pay for what you did to Toni and Diana."

It suddenly dawns on Jason that Krato thinks he infected Diana. In this situation, though, there is no time to discuss the matter.

Krato moves a little forward. Jason notices the shining blade of the dagger in Krato's raised right hand, reflecting the dim light from the window.

Jason is remarkably calm. *I floored Krato before; I can do it again. Yes, this is the night of reckoning. I'm tired of running from this brute,* Jason reasons in his heart. *It's either him or me; it's either kill or be killed, like that night when the pirates attacked us in the desert. I must not allow him to rob me of my precious life.*

Krato lifts his arm, ready to strike.

"Put it down or you're dead!" It is Agizul's voice from the dark hallway behind Krato. For a moment, Krato hesitates, instinctively turning his head to where the voice came from.

Jason's left arm shoots forward, grabbing Krato's right wrist just below the dagger. A split-second later, Jason's right fist lands with full force on Krato's throat.

There is a soft popping sound as Krato's larynx collapses. He falls to the ground, gasping for air, making hissing sounds. Jason heard that such a blow could be fatal; he hopes it will be. Agizul wants to finish Krato off with Krato's own dagger. Jason removes Agizul with force. He does not want his desert friend involved in murder.

Jason realizes he may be linked to Krato's death. His underdog instincts take over. He decides to flee from Cyrene. He asks Agizul to explain his position to Lucius. His partners have seen Krato. They will understand.

At home, Jason puts some precious golden coins in his coin holder and straps it to his waist underneath his tunic. He wants to travel light. He packs only a few essentials into his backpack. He saddles one of the company's horses. In the light of a half-moon, he rides to Apollonia, hoping to sail by fishing boat to Alexandria.

Determined, he decides: *I want to be soon so far from Cyrene that authorities can't link me to Krato's death.* Once again, he is a refugee. This time, he is fleeing from Roman justice, not from a vengeful opponent.

By midnight, Jason reaches Apollonia. There are three deep-sea fishing boats moored in the harbor; fishing was bad the past few days. Jason inquires of the watchmen if they are going to Alexandria the next day. No luck.

"I'm setting sail for Darna shortly," one guy says reluctantly, looking Jason up and down with suspicion. "Maybe you can get a boat from there to Alexandria," he adds, shrugging his shoulders as if he doesn't care. "But I must warn you: the wind is picking up, and my boat is rather small."

Jason accepts the offer gratefully. He reasons: *It takes me away from Apollonia, in case I'm followed. And I do not have to find another horse to ride all the way to Darna.*

Despite a choppy ride, they make good progress. At sunrise, they can see smoke from the chimneys in Darna. An hour later, they are at the breakwater that shields the fishing boats from the waves.

This time Jason is fortunate to locate a fishing boat that will depart to Alexandria later that morning. The skipper agrees to take him along as deckhand. The boat is larger than the one that brought him here. Though the wind is strong, the ride is not too rough, as they sail in the same direction the waves run. The skipper keeps them busy. There is no time to take a nap. Thanks to a clear sky, they keep on sailing when night falls, navigating by moon and stars. Shortly before daybreak, they see the light of Alexandria's famous Pharos Lighthouse, one of the Seven Wonders of the World.

Jason is exhausted after two sleepless nights. The fishermen share some of their fish and bread with him. At least he will not be famished when he sees Tabitha. He wants to bid her goodbye before he boards a ship to the north.

The library opens an hour after sunrise. Jason tries to spot Tabitha among the many employees arriving at the last minute. Tabitha is a little late. Just when Jason is about to run to her and brief her about his plight, he notices Abner approaching her from the steps of the library. Abner puts his arms on Tabitha's shoulders and says something to her. They hug each other for several seconds. While Tabitha's arms are still around him, Abner kisses her on the forehead, followed by a short kiss on her lips.

Jason stops in his tracks and hides behind a tree. He does not know what to make of the affection he witnessed between Tabitha and Abner. They haven't noticed him. Arms around each other's waists, they turn and proceed up the steps of the building. Part of Jason wants to inquire, make sure what is going on, and give Abner a licking. Part of Jason is so ticked off that he wants to walk away.

He is physically and emotionally drained by the events of the past two days and nights; he can't find the strength to grab the bull by the horns. He shifts to negative thinking and sinks into a pessimistic mood. He concludes: *Tabitha and Abner have moved from friendship to a love affair. I haven't had contact with her for several months. Every time I wanted to come to Alexandria, something forced me to cancel my plans. Day by day, she works with Abner. For ten hours per day they enjoy each other's company. It's only natural that they have developed a close bond over time. Maybe I was too blind in my love to see it before. Now, my eyes have been opened with a shock.*

Jason slowly walks back to the harbor. This knock is much harder than the one Krato dealt him. He has been robbed of both his Cyrene freedom and his Alexandrian love.

The next day, Tabitha receives a letter from her dad. A shipment of goods he ordered for his shop has been seized by pirates; it is a total loss. His creditor is pressing him to pay, and he is flat broke. His business has suffered since he joined the church. The family is about to lose everything, including their house. Tabitha decides to go home and support her family. As a go-getter, she is determined to find the money somewhere, somehow, come what may!

*

Jason had a good income in Cyrene. He can pay for his passage. He inquires at the dock-master's office about ships leaving for the north. He learns that a medium-sized freighter will depart within an hour to Ephesus. The captain accepts him on board as a passenger. Jason is so sleep-deprived that when the ship sails out of the harbor, he is already fast asleep on bales of wool. It is a blissful escape from his troubles.

He wakes up in the late afternoon. The ship makes slow progress with the light breeze. The cirrus cloud sunset paints the sea gold, then red. The shock of the past hectic days makes it impossible for Jason to fully enjoy the peace of the scenery.

He thinks of Tabitha with mixed feelings. Beautiful memories are displaced by what he saw in Alexandria. It causes him too much pain to think of her. Deliberately, he directs his thoughts to Diana. He wonders where she is now, and what she's thinking and doing. *Maybe she also has a new lover. My luck with the girls I cared about has turned terribly sour. I'm a born loser,* he concludes with bitterness.

Shortly after he has supper with the crew, Jason feels sleepy again. He has not yet recovered all his lost sleep. He prepares his den on the wool bales, and settles in for a good night's rest, yawning for sleep, and subconsciously yearning for Tabitha.

This time, his sleep is rudely interrupted by the old Krato nightmare. When he wakes up with a pounding heartbeat, he worries: *Will my altercation with Krato have adverse consequences? Will the Roman authorities link me to Krato's death?* Exhausted and dismayed, he dozes off eventually.

Before sunrise, he wakes up, refreshed in body and clear in mind. He absorbs the colorful sunrise, enjoys the sounds of seabirds, breathes the fresh air, and tastes the salty spray on his lips, wishing his beloved could be with him to enjoy the good and the beautiful. *But now she's in Abner's arms…Life can be so wonderful—why must there always be a fly in the ointment? Why are joy and success often spoiled? Why do nasty things happen to nice people?*

He thinks back. *Just when I emerged from my drinking, found love with Tabitha, and became Isthmian champion, I was suddenly hit by Toni's death and Krato's revenge. I had barely escaped successfully, when I was hit by the storm and shipwrecked. I slowly crawled to success in Cyrene, only to be devastated by Krato's vengeful pursuit. Tabitha and I had found a way to see each other regularly, only to be cruelly ripped apart again.*

However, the sun has repeatedly broken through the dark clouds. In spite of the bad things, the good was never totally defeated. It emerged victoriously time and again.

I survived the bullying, drinking, lusting, competition, fleeing, stranding, desert, jungle, unemployment, and persecution, he recalls. *In fact, I flourished despite the setbacks. It is as if a huge, almighty, loving hand provided, enabling me to turn problems into challenges, and challenges into victories.*

He thinks of the words of Jesus quoted by Paul in the synagogue, "Come to me all who are weary and burdened, and I will give you rest...for my yoke is easy and my burden is light." *Yes, I can see it now; I have triumphed over my burdens with God's grace.* "Thank you, God!" he whispers.

Though he feels positively about the Christian faith, has attended church, and has mixed with Christians, he has not yet committed himself to Christ. He has remained in limbo because the score with Krato had not been settled yet.

*

The harbor of Ephesus is connected by channel to the sea. Only small and medium-sized boats are hauled through the channel into the harbor. The city struggles with the challenge of preventing the harbor from silting up.

Jason explores the city renowned for its magnificent Artemis Temple, another wonder of the ancient world. He walks from the harbor along Arcadian Way, which is paved with huge flat stones. Right in front, against the hill, is the massive, unfinished amphitheater looking out to the sea. On the right is the *agora* with its shops and stalls and the beautiful triple-arched Augustus Gate. Jason proceeds up

Curetes Street, flanked by beautiful public buildings and private mansions.

Jason wanders back, passes the amphitheater again, and proceeds to the temple of Artemis. It is built in the same style as the Parthenon in Athens, but it covers an area almost four times larger. The roof rests on one hundred twenty-seven marble pillars, sixty feet high. Jason is astounded at the beauty and size of the building. No wonder the Ephesians don't allow any negative remarks about this sanctuary, the pride and fame of the city.

The statue of Artemis inside the temple does not impress Jason at all. This Artemis is of Persian origin. She is a goddess of love and fertility, signified by her two dozen breasts. She is obviously not the same as the Greek Artemis, the slim and agile goddess of the hunt.

On his way back to the city center, Jason and other temple visitors are met by men calling them to the amphitheater for a demonstration in support of Artemis against the Christians. When Jason reaches the theater, it is filling up with people coming from all directions, not knowing what is going on, but curious to see what will happen. Piece by piece, Jason learns what caused the uproar.

During Paul's three year ministry in Ephesus, so many people have converted to Christianity that the business of the silversmiths—making and selling Artemis statuettes and replicas of her temple—is suffering. Led by Demetrius, they incite the crowds to support Artemis worship and to reject Christianity.

For two hours, the crowd in the theater chants, "Great is Artemis of the Ephesians!" The hollow shape of the theater amplifies the shouting, making it echo among the hills, drawing more curious crowds.

When the throats get sore and dry, the city clerk calms the multitude by affirming in a short effective speech the famous and untouchable greatness of their goddess and her temple, and reminding them of the legal channels available to lay charges against alleged offenders. Reason prevails, and the crowd disperses.

Paul's friends urge him to leave Ephesus for a while. The atmosphere has become too hostile and unsafe. Paul sends Titus with a letter to Corinth, while he travels via Troas to Macedonia, where he restlessly awaits Titus' return.

Jason is amazed at the growth of Christianity, despite vicious attacks. In Corinth, too, neither Jewish opposition nor internal church problems blocked the steady increase of church membership.

*

Although Jason yearned for the day he could return to Corinth without fear, he feels empty now that the time has arrived. What will happen to Tabitha in Alexandria? Will she come to her senses? What will happen to himself in Corinth? Will he be arrested on arrival? Will he be charged with murder? A nasty feeling of pending doom strangles his soul. He is heading home with a heavy heart.

CHAPTER 11

Jason returns by merchant ship to Corinth. Though he does not have to hide from Krato anymore, he does not want Corinthians to stare at him. He plans to lay low for a while. He is not keen to explain his disappearance and comeback to all his joking friends.

He arrives at Cenchrea after sunset and walks the few miles home. His family is overjoyed to see him. They shower him with questions faster than he can answer.

After he has stuffed himself with the leftover lamb's leg the family had for dinner, he is ready to satisfy their curiosity. First, Jason gives them a general overview of all his adventures. Then he fills in the detail of events, without mentioning the shock that Tabitha gave him. Helena envies her brother's wide variety of thrilling experiences that took him deep into Africa.

His parents can see that by trials and tribulations, their son has become a man. In spite of his yearning for loved ones, the past four years offered a tremendous learning experience. He has become tougher and wiser.

However, they notice some sadness in Jason. He is not as exuberant as they would like him to be. They ascribe it to fatigue, hoping he will be his old self soon.

The family is so excited that they share their joy with their friends. When Diana learns about it, she visits right away.

After they have had a good hug and kiss, her first words are, "You did not answer my letter!"

"It was for security reasons. Krato was serious about his death threat. I did not want to disclose my whereabouts. I could not dare to let anyone know, not even my parents," Jason explains.

"But your girlfriend knew. I've heard about Tabitha."

"She did not either, at least not for the first two years. When she started working in Alexandria, I visited once in two months."

"I suppose...you slept with her..."

"It's none of your business! She's not that type of girl!"

"Gentleman Jason!" Diana teases.

"Our love was on another level."

"Was?" Diana asks with a frown.

"Something happened. I don't know yet where we stand at the moment," Jason confesses, reluctantly.

"Another lover?" Diana fishes.

"I don't want to discuss it now." Jason closes up. He's hurting too much to open up his shell and let others poke their noses into his suffering.

"Well, if your body still yearns for a woman of flesh and blood, Jason, you know where to find one."

Jason does not respond. Something between him and Diana was lost. His former lusting after her has died down.

Sensing that she is not a lure to him anymore, she tries another kind of bait: "If you come to my guest house tomorrow night, you may have something special—a virgin who brings her body as a sacrifice to Aphrodite. At least you can be sure she has not been infected," Diana says, with some self-pity in her tone.

Diana prepares to leave. She knows she can't talk Jason into it. She has planted the thought. Mother Nature will work on his brain and glands.

They say goodbye with a formal hug and kiss on the cheek.

*

Jason does not realize how vulnerable he is right now. His nerve-racking encounter with Krato, his hasty flight, several sleepless nights, his fear of arrest, his shock about Tabitha's relationship with Abner, his pondering about his hardships, his telling and reliving his story with his family—all of it tapped his emotional reserves. On top of it all, there is the nagging uncertainty and ambivalence about Tabitha. *I played true love for four years—all in vain. I should have used my chances with Mary.*

Despondent in his emotional low, deprived of his confidants, he takes his old escape route—drinking. Instead of giving him an artificial high, the wine makes him sad. He pities himself for all the undeserved hardships that have befallen him. He sinks into the drunken blues.

The next day, suffering a severe hangover, he wonders what else can pull him out of the pit, give him a high? In his loneliness, he has a full-blown pity party: *Why can't I be happy too? Why can everybody else be happy? Why do I have to suffer blow after blow?*

With a brain dulled by alcohol, he can think of no other excitement than sex. *Diana, perhaps? Yes, she invited me! Why not?! Tabitha is in Abner's arms; why should I be faithful anymore? Maybe that silly virgin who wants to sacrifice herself to Aphrodite, maybe she can lift my spirit.*

Shortly before sunset he freshens up at the baths, puts on clean clothes, and walks over to Diana's guest house.

Diana is amazed and amused to see him. She didn't think he would take the bait. When she smells wine on his breath, she knows the reason. *He must have been pretty down to relapse so suddenly. Poor guy, he's been through a tough time lately,* she thinks.

Diana pours Jason another drink. She also persuades the virgin in the bedroom to take another drink—to calm the nerves and to dull the pain.

Diana briefs them separately about the rules of the game. When an ordinary woman brings herself as a sacrifice to Aphrodite in her guest house, the woman and the man are masked to protect their identities. They don't want to be recognized on the street after the event. Except for two narrow slits for the eyes, the mask covers the whole upper head, including eyes, ears, and nose, and is fastened by a bow on the back of the neck. They pledge not to remove the masks, neither their own nor their partner's. They have to limit talk to a few whispers.

"Be gentle with her, Jason. Remember, she's a virgin," Diana advises.

"I've never broken in a virgin. Any tips?" Jason wonders, somewhat anxious.

"Prepare her well. Good lubrication makes it easy. Use this on yourself." She hands him a small bottle with special oil. "It will facilitate penetration," she says, winking with a naughty smile.

When they have finished their drinks, Diana helps Jason to put on his mask. She takes him to the bedroom, nudging him to enter.

One small oil lamp spreads a dim light from a dressing table in a corner. Romantic paintings on pastel pink walls, a light blue carpet, white and pink bedcover, and fresh flowers on the dressing table create the subtle atmosphere of a wedding suite. It doesn't look like a brothel.

A delicate perfume hangs in the air. The feminine fragrance entices his senses.

Jason enters apprehensively. For a moment, he considers quitting. He has never done this before. He turns to seek Diana's support, but she has vanished. He enters and closes the door behind him. There is nobody in the room.

Suddenly, his conscience accuses him: *What will Tabitha think of this?* He snuffs out that flame immediately with the excuse that she's probably in bed with Abner. This thought convinces him: *I have good reasons to do what I'm doing.*

A masked girl, clothed in light feminine nightwear, enters from a side door. She approaches, smiles, and temptingly starts to undo his clothes. She rubs her body against his like an affectionate cat. She puts a short silky cloth around his hips. Then she leads him to the bed, folds back the cover and sheet, and invitingly stretches herself out on the bed.

Now Jason begins to lead. He takes his place on her right side, freeing his right hand for exploring. He pulls the sheet over them.

Their nudity accentuates her femininity and his masculinity. They start kissing. Blissful sensations run through them. It feels like the day he and Diana had their first kiss. The intense sensation overrides all complaints of his conscience.

In spite of Jason's dulled brain, he senses something familiar. The girl's perfume does not completely cancel another faint aroma he has smelled before. He cannot identify it. Maybe it's the one that Diana used to wear. *Can it be Diana? She could not have undressed so swiftly...could she?*

Jason can't care a bit. He can't run away now; he doesn't want to. *Whoever this girl is, I'm going to stretch this pleasure out and enjoy her as long as possible. I'm not forcing her into this—we do it with eager mutual consent.*

Ah! It's good to have some joy after all the hardships!

*

After long caressing and a wonderful peak, both are relaxed and satisfied.

"Thank you. You have been great," he whispers, kissing her tenderly. Then he reclines on his elbow alongside her, still enjoying caressing her beautiful body.

She puts the tips of her fingers on the side of his face, softly gliding them to his lips. Jason senses affectionate tenderness in her touch. Is she in love with him?

"It was wonderful," she whispers, "thanks for your gentleness, Jason."

His body jerks upright.

Shocked, he asks, "How do you know my name?"

She removes her mask.

Flabbergasted, he exclaims, "Tabitha! What the hell are you doing here!?"

"Protecting you from prostitutes," she responds, with thrilled giggles, savoring his astonishment and embarrassment. She still feels a little tipsy from Diana's drink.

With wide, serious eyes she then asks, "And what are you doing here, Jason?"

Shocked and self-conscious, Jason removes his mask, too.

"I...I...I don't know. I have no excuse, I'm just a stupid, depressed, and sex-hungry man," he confesses bluntly.

Then he shifts to double standards, "But you, Tabitha, my pure little turtle dove, how could you prostitute yourself like this?"

"At least I have good reasons: saving you from infidelity and my family from bankruptcy," Tabitha tries to justify her actions, silencing the inner voice of shame and guilt, accusing her of sin. She has to convince Jason and herself that she did not have another choice.

"Listen to me, Jason! There was no other way I could earn enough money in one night to bail out my family. When I saw the brokenness of my parents and the panic of my sisters, I knew I had to do something drastic. Diana paid me an unexpected visit. When I told her about my family's crisis, she told me about her business, and how much the girls earn. To help me, she offered to take me in at triple pay. Without our knowledge, she planned the whole thing to bring us together. She caught us for suckers in her trap."

Now Diana is blamed for their sin. Like Adam and Eve, they blame others for their mistakes. Their defenses are going into top speed.

They backtrack to explain how it happened that they are in this room and not in Alexandria or Cyrene.

Tabitha tells Jason about the letter she received from her dad in Alexandria. "I got on a ship the next day and sailed via Athens to Corinth. When I arrived here yesterday, I discovered that Dad will lose everything if he can't pay his creditor by tomorrow. He is too proud to beg. He would rather go under. I had to do something! I could not stand by watching my family being kicked out on the street. Where would they go without money? Accommodations in Corinth are scarce and expensive."

"Why didn't you ask me or my dad? We would have been glad to help! We're friends!" Jason argues.

"I did not know you were in Corinth. My dad's crisis hindered me from contacting your parents. In any case, I didn't want to saddle your family with my family's problems. Your family has enough of their own. And when I decided to sell my body to rescue my family, I knew that I would not be worthy of you anymore. Great was my surprise when I entered this room, saw the birthmark on your arm, and realized my customer was no other than my beloved Jason. Then I knew a mighty hand had intervened."

He pulls her closer, kissing her on the forehead.

"If I identified myself, you would not have proceeded. I wanted you to go ahead. I wanted to become one with you, Jason. I have been waiting for you long enough. The sacrifice became a privilege," Tabitha coos, deeply in love.

"I'm glad you did not tell me," Jason concurs, "I would have walked out in shock!" He thinks for a while, concluding, "However, I must admit: I'm glad I have not missed this. It was fantastic!" He does not want her to feel bad about what happened.

As Tabitha has come up with excuses for her presence in Diana's guest house, Jason feels he, too, must find some good reasons for showing up here.

He explains what happened to him, "Krato showed up in Cyrene. He tried to ambush and kill me in a dark hallway. My friend distracted him for a moment, enabling me to punch him on the throat. We left him for dead. Fearing arrest for murder, I fled under cover of darkness. When I arrived in Alexandria two days later, drained and depressed, I went to the library to brief you about my situation. Then, I saw you and Abner hugging and kissing. I saw you entering the library, arms around each other's waists. In my pessimistic mood, I concluded that you were in love. I turned around and boarded a ship to Ephesus."

"Abner and I in love?! Ha! Are you out of your mind?" Tabitha reacts, indignant. "You still don't know me after all these years, Jason Ben Philip! Let me enlighten you on what happened there that morning. When I arrived at the library, Abner was waiting and told me he had received the sad news of his father's death. I hugged him in sympathy. He misused my sympathy to steal a kiss. Because of his grief, I didn't want to offend him. I put my arm around his waist as a token of moral support, not love. Damn it! Why didn't you come to me and get the true facts?"

Jason senses his distrust has hurt Tabitha deeply.

"I'm sorry, darling, I was wrong. I don't want to use it as an excuse, but I think the events of the preceding days put me in a negative state of mind, interpreting everything in the worst possible way. Please, forgive me."

"Yes, I can understand that. Knowing you and loving you, Jason, make it easy to forgive. Shame! You must have felt terrible to leave in that state of mind." Tabitha puts herself in his shoes and confirms her forgiveness by kissing him all over his face.

When the truth about the circumstances that brought them together today has sunk in, Jason remarks, "It is indeed a strange string of events. If I had not misinterpreted your actions with Abner, I wouldn't have been so depressed to start drinking. And if I hadn't been drinking, I wouldn't have accepted Diana's silly invitation to forget my sorrows in the arms of a virgin sacrificing her virginity to Aphrodite. And if I were not here today...you would have lain with another man!"

"And if I have not stupidly decided to buy my dad free with my own body, you would have lain with another woman today," Tabitha fires back, showing that they are in the same boat. Jason and Tabitha realize that the pot can't blame the kettle. Both of them entered this room tonight expecting to have sex with another person. The only difference was that Tabitha learned who her partner was before their union, while Jason learned it immediately afterwards. However, in their hearts they were both unfaithful to each other when they entered the room. Fortunately, they landed together.

Jason realizes that from the viewpoint of Greek mythology, this could be a typical prank played on them by the manipulative gods. Tabitha knows that Jewish religion would not ascribe such action to a holy God. She has to admit, though, that God's book tells of two similar incidents. In the Genesis scroll, it is recorded that both Jacob and Judah[21] slept with a veiled woman whom they believed to be someone else. God included these two women, Leah and Tamar, in the lineage of the Messiah.[22]

---

21 Gen. 29, 38
22 Matt. 1:1-3

Jason and Tabitha admit their folly and forgive each other for taking such wicked risks. They experience a strange ambivalence: On the one hand, they feel terribly guilty for violating their own values; on the other hand, they feel good about their unity in body and soul. Though their intent was wrong, it turned out for good. They decide to look back on this night as their wedding night.

"Tabitha, will you marry me?"

"Yes, Jason, as soon as possible!"

They want to rectify the wrong immediately. They kiss as bride and groom.

"Thank you, my love," he affirms, "we were meant for each other. Fate intervened. Or maybe it's your God."

"I don't think we should blame God for our sin. Let's thank him for turning our sin into something good."

"Yes, that sounds better," he admits.

As they prepare to leave, they hear a soft knock on the door. Jason opens the door; it's Diana. He lets her in, waves his index finger in her face, and accuses her with an embarrassed smile, "Diana, you are a naughty, naughty, naughty girl! But thanks anyway, it was great!"

"Oh, thank God—you're not mad at me!" she responds, with a sigh of relief. "Jason, when you told me your relationship turned sour, and Tabitha, when you told me about your dad's crisis, I got this plan to solve both problems at the same time."

"Diana, you succeeded wonderfully," Tabitha joins in. "As a matter of fact, it inspired Jason to propose. We are getting married soon."

"Lucky you!" Diana savors their joy—not without envy. At the same time, she cherishes the success of her crazy plan to solve their problems.

During the past years, Diana has come to realize her disease and her lifestyle have caused an unbridgeable gap between her and Jason. Nonetheless, she will always have a special place for him in her heart. Doing this favor for him gives her immense satisfaction—the joy of a friend helping a friend in need.

When Jason and Tabitha walk home, she shows him the little leather bag with coins that Diana gave her.

"I have not paid her yet," Jason wonders.

"Then it must be Diana's own contribution," she concludes.

"I want to double it," he insists.

They pick up five of Jason's expensive gold coins at his parents' home. Without realizing it, they are obeying the Torah regarding premarital sex.[23] When Tabitha presents the money to her dad early the next morning, she says it's a gift from Jason, Diana, and herself. Their jobs provided the dough.

Isaac is speechless at first. In a moment, he is elevated from despair to victory. He praises the God of mercy, unaware of the strange route God allowed them to take this time.

When Jason and Tabitha tell Isaac of their plan to marry, asking his permission and blessing, Isaac is on cloud nine. His hell has been replaced by heaven.

During the next days, Jason and Tabitha savor their new relationship. However, they can't rid themselves of the nagging guilt-feelings deep inside. They become aware of a need in both of them to make peace with God through Christ. They have postponed this surrender long enough. Their moral failure increased their need for salvation tenfold. As thirst makes hikers seek water, so repentance makes sinners seek forgiveness. They have a compelling need to confess their sin and receive God's gracious pardon. They want God to remove the blot from their relationship, turning human error into divine mercy. Jason knows his guilt-feelings do not arise from pagan Greek culture, but from his interaction with Christian communities the past four years. Taking part in church activities prepared him for surrendering to Christ. He belonged before he believed.

Titus is in Corinth now. He can show them the way.

---

23 Ex. 23:16

*

Jason immediately comes to the point: "Titus, we listened to Paul several times, so we know the basics about Jesus. I also learned a lot from Lucius in Cyrene. We attend church and associate with Christians. We go with the flow, but we have not made a commitment to Christ yet. We are sinners, but we can't cleanse ourselves. We want to confess our sin and receive God's forgiveness. We are ready now, but we're not sure how to do it. We want to know Jesus personally as you and Paul do."

"It's so simple that many people think it is too good to be true," Titus responds, chuckling.

"That's good news. Please, go ahead," Tabitha urges.

Titus continues, "I will explain it to you as Paul explained it to me. Jesus said, 'Whoever comes to me, I will never drive away.'[24] That is his word of honor. So when I came to him, he accepted me. I know it's true because HE SAID SO," Titus emphasizes. "His word of honor gives me certainty. That's all you have to do. Come to him and believe he accepts you as his children. He gives you his word of honor."

"How do we come to him? We can't see him," Jason wonders. Tabitha nods.

"God is omnipresent. He is here; you can be sure of that. However, we have to go through God's Mediator, who paid our sin-debt on the cross. Jesus said, 'I am the way, the truth, and the life. No one comes to the Father except through Me.'[25] Do you want to surrender yourselves to him now?"

"With all our hearts!" Tabitha confirms.

"We're ready," Jason adds.

"Before you make the surrender, let me recap what that means," Titus suggests. "The better you understand this act of faith, the less you will struggle with doubts in the future. By accepting Jesus as your Savior, you accept that he paid your sin-debt to the Father in full by his suffering and death. Thus

24 John 6:37 NIV
25 John 14:6

Jesus, the Mediator, reconciles you to the Father. His payment is complete and sufficient; you can't add to it. The new life you live from now on is to thank God for the salvation you received as a free gift. This is the core of the Christian faith," Titus stresses. "Is it clear to you, or shall I elaborate?"

"That's how I've understood it from Paul and Lucius," Jason responds.

"Me too," Tabitha concurs.

Titus continues, "Then pray this simple prayer after me: 'Lord Jesus...I believe your good news...I believe you are the Messiah...the Savior who paid my sin-debt in full on the cross... and who now reconciles me to God. I now surrender my life to you. I know you accept me...because you said whoever comes to you...you will never drive away. Help me to grow in faith, hope, and love. To you be the glory forever. Amen.'"

Jason and Tabitha repeat in unison each short sentence after Titus. He remembers how he felt just after Paul led him to Christ; therefore, he immediately proceeds: "You may not feel very different right now. Remember, your certainty does not rest on your feelings, but on Christ's atoning sacrifice and on his word of honor. When Satan attacks you with doubts because of your imperfections, remind him and yourself that you have not been saved by your own merit, but by God's grace in Christ. I myself have doubted many times, but this is how Paul reassured me that nobody can snatch me from God's hand."

"Thanks, Titus," Tabitha responds, "I feel happy already. I feel as if the adoption papers have been signed. I am a child of God now, but I still have to learn to live like one. I still have to grow in my faith."

"Yes, I feel the same," Jason affirms, "I'm sure we've taken the big step with your help. God has been working in our hearts for a long time to prepare us for this moment. I'm convinced that God used you as his instrument to lead us to salvation."

They hug, their eyes swimming in tears of indescribable joy. They realize, *only those experiencing assurance of faith know this joy.* Titus is grateful he could have assisted them. Jason and Tabitha are relieved and elated. A weight has been lifted from their hearts. This commitment has to be followed by another—their wedding.

Jason accompanies Tabitha to her home. She showers her family with the overwhelming joy she and Jason have discovered. At first, the others are somewhat baffled. They thought they were Christians already. As the two young people share their experience, Tabitha's parents and sisters realize they have not yet made that personal commitment.

"Jason, will you please ask Titus to come and help us right away? Let's not delay this crucial step any longer," Isaac says softly.

Esther nods her head and whispers, "Please, Jason."

Paul brought the gospel like one candle to Corinth. Many people have been lighting their candles at his flame. From them, the light will spread to others. In time, they will find out a flame not only gives light, but can also burn one's hand painfully.

Two Sundays later, Jason, Tabitha, and her family are baptized by Titus into the Christian faith. It symbolizes what happened in them spiritually—their sins have been washed away.

This ceremony is followed by another: Jason and Tabitha are united into holy matrimony. During the preceding week, the news of the coming wedding has spread through the Christian community. As all know of Isaac's financial crisis, members of the congregation worked together to organize a surprise wedding feast for the young couple. Everyone brings something to eat or to drink. Children from Jewish and Greek backgrounds demonstrate their folk dances, then all try them together. Some adults volunteer to sing well-known songs solo or in groups. In between, they feast and chat like crazy.

Titus proposes the toast to the bride and groom: "To Life!"

"To Life! To Life! To Life!" the threefold wish of the crowd resonates in unison, confirming their sincere prayer that the couple will have a long and happy marriage, and that their children and grandchildren will bring them joy.

The church is united in a merry atmosphere, sharing in the exuberance of the newlyweds. Titus can take the good news to Paul, that his wish and prayer have been fulfilled: The Corinth church is one at heart again. Although the wedding has not caused the unity, it gives opportunity to express it.

Philip pays for the couple's week-long honeymoon on Aegina Island. The two young lovers enjoy each other fully. Walking on the beach, sitting on the rocks, watching the sunsets, enjoying special meals, sharing experiences and ideals, they adore one another and feel they are part of each other. Every day they improve on their first union in Diana's room, now without masks and guilt-feelings. They are open books to each other. Tabitha hums a song for Jason:

> One in body, one in soul;
> hearts united to a whole.
> Touching, kissing,
> tasting, wishing
> it will last and last forever,
> never, never, never sever.

"Yes! Yes! Yes!" Jason affirms, holding her firmly.

In their young, sparkling love, they are blissfully unaware of the new burdens coming their way. Occasionally, the Krato nightmare still repeats itself. The spear is still coming at Jason in slow motion, and he can't get out of the way in time.

CHAPTER 12

Though Jason has expected some reprisal from authorities for his self-defense against Krato in Cyrene, he has been so engulfed by the joys of the past weeks that the preceding traumas faded out of his awareness.

Sooner or later, however, Roman justice (or injustice) will find him, wherever he is. The newlyweds decide to stay with Jason's parents for the time being.

A week after their honeymoon, there is a knock at the front door at sunset. Jason answers the door. Four Roman soldiers greet him, "Are you Jason, son of Philip?"

"Yes."

"Did you meet Krato, the centurion, in Cyrene?"

"Why do you ask?"

"You are charged with his murder. You are under arrest!"

One of the soldiers slams a chain on Jason's right wrist, fastening the other end to his own left wrist. A nauseating feeling of pending doom shivers through Jason's body and soul. The bottom of his bucket is dropping out.

"May I tell my family?"

"You may."

They enter the living room together.

"I'm being arrested for Krato's murder," Jason announces softly, his voice breaking.

For a moment, Jason's family and Tabitha are stunned.

Philip rises and approaches.

"What the hell is going on here?" he demands.

Tabitha runs to Jason and throws her arms around his waist, pressing her face and body to him, confirming her solidarity with him. She has immediately grasped what is happening. She wants to stay with Jason through this ordeal.

"No! No!" she cries bitterly, realizing Jason is being taken from her once again. Death casts a dark shadow over life once more.

"We're sorry sir, ma'am. We act on orders from the commander."

They have lived long enough under Roman law to realize any pleading with the soldiers will be useless. They are only doing their job—following orders.

A short preliminary hearing is held in a small courtroom the next morning. The judge (a proconsul) hears the charge and decides that the trial has to take place at Cyrene, where the alleged crime occurred and where the witnesses will be.

Tabitha, family, and friends are allowed to visit Jason. The visits are limited to one person at a time for a few minutes. Jason's wife and parents are allowed double visiting time. They want to share his burden, but don't know how. They feel depressed, angry, and powerless. Their words of encouragement sound empty.

Jason feels like a caged animal, talking to his loved ones through iron bars. He sees the pain in their faces, hears it in their voices, and feels it in their hands.

Krato's spear is again coming at him—a living nightmare!

Jason realizes that this calamity has been spawned by the lifelong feud between him and Krato. He scans the past: *if*

Krato had not teased me as a child; if I had responded differently; if I had not been obsessed with revenge; if I had not tried so hard to beat Krato at the games; if Toni had not run into the path of his javelin; if Krato had not persecuted me for the accident; if I had not knocked Krato down in the tavern; if I had not made that impressive discus throw in Cyrene; if I had handled Krato differently that night in the Cyrene tavern…if, if, if.

Jason knows: *All the "ifs" are now only hypothetical alternatives with no real practical value. The real question is not how I got into the mess, but how to get out of it. It will be hard to get witnesses to testify either for or against me.*

Jason's partners in Cyrene saw Krato's provocative attitude, but that may be used to prove his motive for the murder. Agizul saw what happened, but the prosecutor may paint him as an accomplice. Lucius and his Christian friends can testify to his character, but Christians are not exactly the favorites of Rome.

Just when Jason's negative reasoning has painted him into a corner, Titus pays him a visit. Titus reminds him of what Jesus and Paul have suffered, and yet they did not abandon their missions. He encourages Jason to trust God to turn this problem into a challenge. "Though Jesus' death looked like defeat, it earned eternal life for thousands. The blood of the martyrs has been the seed of the church. Paul's persecution drove him from place to place, spreading the gospel even faster. God can turn trials into triumphs. Don't succumb under Satan's pressure, Jason. Ask Jesus to empower you by his Spirit. Stand fast and prevail for him. He promised rest for the burdened." Titus hugs Jason through the bars.

When Titus has left, Jason looks at his own predicament from a different angle: *My real problem is being falsely accused. The challenge is overcoming the odds against me by prayer, faith, careful planning, and powerful steps to exonerate myself. In the past, I did it in my own power. Now I will do it with faith in God.*

Crispus, the former synagogue ruler who became Christian, is Jason's next visitor. He empowers Jason with King David's twenty-third psalm:

> [4] Yea, though I walk through the valley of
>   the shadow of death,
>   I will fear no evil;
>   For You *are* with me;
>   Your rod and Your staff, they comfort me.[26]

Crispus urges Jason to hold on to the Good Shepherd.

The next day, Jason asks his dad to hire a lawyer who can gather good witnesses about his reputation, about the accident at the games, and about Krato's attitude toward him. In Cyrene, Jason will ask his lawyer to do likewise. They have to use every shred of evidence to defend him against the biased army and judges.

*

When the commander has found a ship that goes straight to Apollonia, he makes a deal with the captain to take Jason, guarded by two soldiers, to that port. The commander sends a soldier to Philip's house, telling them the departure time.

Jason and Tabitha's families go by horse carriage to Cenchrea. Ten mounted soldiers escort Jason to the port. On arrival, he is amazed by the number of people who turned up in support of him and the involved families. During the week he has been held in custody, the news about his arrest has spread through the city. Church members have come to stand by their burdened brother and sister. Other friends have come to support their modest champion who has been persecuted so unfairly after the accident at the games.

---

26 Ps 23:4

As ordered by the commander, the soldiers take their handcuffed prisoner to his wife and family. The soldiers look the other way. They have to fulfill their duty, but they feel for Jason and Tabitha. It's unfair and inhumane to rip a young couple apart like this shortly after their wedding.

Tabitha suppresses her grief. She does not want to make it harder for Jason. He knows her, though. He notices her swollen eyes, her trembling lips, and the tremors in her body when she kisses him goodbye.

All Jason can get out is, "Keep faith, my love! We will prevail. Paul said all things work together for good to those who love God. We now qualify, we love him."

"I love you, Jason! I will keep on praying," she sobs.

He lifts the handcuffs over her head so he can hold her. Family and friends are affected by the sad farewell. Women wipe tears off and turn their heads away. Men shake their heads in disbelief and swear under their breath.

Jason lifts the chain again over Tabitha, nudging her gently into her father's arms. With chained hands, Jason extends handshakes to family and friends. Then the two soldiers who will escort him to Cyrene take him on board.

The sails are hoisted. Slowly, the ship sails out. Jason waves with chained hands above his head. Family and friends wave back. It's not the time to shout goodbyes. Sadness about the injustice has fallen over everybody like a thick fog. Family and friends wonder: *Why is such cruelty dumped on someone who is inherently benevolent?*

The ship has good weather and favorable breezes. Three days later, after a brief stop at Crete, they moor in Apollonia. An escort of four soldiers takes them uphill to Cyrene. Jason remembers the first time he traveled this road after the stranding of the ship. *It was the beginning of four good years in Cyrene. Now, my prospects are bleak. I'm up against the prejudiced Roman army and judiciary system.*

Jason is locked up. On his request, Lucius is informed of his arrival and invited to visit him. Lucius comes immediately. They shake hands through the bars. Lucius wants to hear the whole story from Jason. Agizul was so upset that night that he could not give a good account of what happened in that dark hallway.

Jason briefs Lucius on that night and on subsequent developments, including his conversion and wedding. Lucius is overjoyed about the latter two, and grateful for Jason's survival on that eerie night.

"God protected you, Jason. He used Agizul to distract Krato, so your fast reaction could shield you from death," Lucius concludes.

"I trust God to help me through this trial, too," Jason responds. "I'm faced with a biased prosecutor and judge. We will have to throw in everything we have and trust God will use our efforts and make me a victorious victim."

Jason now knows how Jesus and his followers must have felt when they were innocently charged and dragged before Roman courts of law. *Jesus did not defend himself, because he had to fulfill the Father's plan to die for sinners. I'm convinced that I am not under the same obligation, and am free to defend myself vigorously,* Jason believes.

Lucius is one hundred percent behind him, "I agree we have to do our utter best. A good lawyer and good witnesses are paramount. I will get the wheels rolling right away."

"Most of my savings from Cyrene Transport are still in the bank here. Please, bring me the bank documents to sign so you can draw money from my account to pay the lawyer," Jason suggests.

Lucius secures the services of Cyrene's best advocate (*parakletos*[27] in Greek). He is a Roman named Quintus. Though not a Christian, he is sympathetic towards Christians, having defended several of them successfully. Lucius helps him to list

---

27 1 John 2:1

possible witnesses and the ways to contact them. Lucius sends one of his workers by camel to fetch Agizul. The round trip will take at least two weeks; that is, if Agizul is at home. They have to pray that neither the messenger nor Agizul will fall into the hands of robbers. Quintus hopes the trial can be postponed long enough to enable Agizul and the bartender of Corinth to reach them in time.

In the opening trial, the charge is read, the not-guilty plea registered, the prosecuting and defense lawyers identified, and the lack of concrete evidence recorded. Quintus draws the judge's attention to the general lack of evidence and witnesses on both sides. He suggests that the trial be postponed for three weeks so that both sides can prepare better. He asks the court to grant bail to the accused.

The judge (a proconsul, called *anthupatos*[28] by Greeks) grants most of Quintus' requests. Because of Jason's tendency to flee, the judge orders that he be kept in *free custody*: he can stay with Lucius but will be chained to a soldier day and night. It is a fairly safe way to restrain a prisoner, and the army doesn't have to feed him. Lucius welcomes Jason back in his old room in his backyard. Now they can talk and talk, and the soldier has to listen to the gospel, whether he likes it or not. Soldiers relieve each other every three hours. Eventually, many of the regiment will hear the good news.

*

During the three week delay, the lawyers frantically scrape together all possible evidence and witnesses they can find. When the trial resumes, they are still ill-prepared.

The opening statements at the trial paint a rather vague road ahead. The prosecution intends to prove that the accused had motive, means, and opportunity to commit this heinous crime. The defense will show that there is no hard evidence or

---

28 Acts 19:38

any eyewitnesses to support the charge, that the little evidence they do have is circumstantial, and that such a crime in not in line with the character of the accused.

Both sides list the witnesses they intend to call, and reserve the right to call new ones that may emerge.

The next day the prosecution calls the soldiers to the stand who escorted Jason to Cyrene, one after the other.

Knowing the soldiers have been under Krato's command, Jason put his best foot forward during the trip from Corinth to Apollonia. He gave his full cooperation, even having chats with them to pass the time. *Will their testimony be hostile or fair?*

The first one confirms under oath that a long-lasting rivalry existed between Krato and Jason. When asked, he gives a good description of the arduous preparation the two subjected themselves to, culminating in the nail-biting competition at the games.

The prosecutor (*retoros*[29] in Greek) tries to make hay of it.

"In your opinion, did the deceased and accused make too much of this competition?"

"For top athletes, competing against the best in the country, I don't think it was unusual."

The prosecution searches for any sign of continued antipathy after the games.

"Do you know of any hostility between the deceased and the accused after the games?"

"Yes."

"Please describe what you saw."

"A few weeks after the games, a few of my friends and I went with the deceased to a tavern for drinks. The accused was also there with some company. The accused and the deceased met at the counter. They were talking, but we could not hear them. Suddenly, the accused knocked the deceased unconscious. We intervened to prevent further fighting."

---

29 Acts 24:1

Jason now regrets that flair-up of anger more than ever. It gives the prosecution arrows in their quiver.

"Did the deceased provoke the accused in any physical way, such as pushing?"

"No. They were just talking."

The prosecution concludes, "Let the court note that the accused showed sudden violent behavior, apparently without provocation."

Quintus cross-examines, "Was the deceased a sturdy fellow?"

"Yes, he was tough and muscular."

"Do you think that the accused would dare to strike such a strong fellow without any provocation?"

The prosecutor objects, "The witness is not a mind-reader!"

Quintus rephrases, "Would you strike out at such a strong fellow unless provoked?"

"Definitely not!"

"Apart from talking, can you remember any other behavior, like laughing?"

"Yes. The deceased started giggling. I got the impression he was teasing the accused."

"No further questions."

The witness is dismissed. The next soldier takes the oath. He affirms that he knew the deceased as his centurion, and that he occasionally saw the accused. He knew about their plans to beat each other at the games.

"Did you see how they competed at the games?"

"Yes."

"Describe what you saw."

"It seemed to me that they were both tensed up, and that they put in all their power in their throws."

"How did they fare?"

"The accused won the discus. With the javelin, there were complications."

"What complications?"

"The best throw of the deceased was disqualified because he stepped over the line before the javelin landed. They were equal at that point. The accused then came up with an extraordinary effort, beating the deceased by several paces. Unfortunately, a child ran onto the field and was killed by the javelin of the accused."

"Was the child related to the deceased?"

"Yes. The child was the half-brother of the deceased."

Jason expects: *the prosecution will try to use this fact to frame me as a murderer who tried to hurt my opponent by killing his little brother.*

"Do you think the accused killed the child on purpose?"

"No. The moment the accused performed the throw, the child started running onto the field. I don't think the accused could have planned it that way."

Jason is grateful for that piece of truth.

"What was the reaction of the deceased?"

"He yelled after the child to look out. When the javelin hit the child, the deceased was devastated. It was the first time I saw tears in his eyes."

"What was the reaction of the accused?"

"He looked shocked and emotional."

Jason is relieved: *No vile motive for Toni's death could be established.*

When questioned, soldier number two confirms the testimony of the first one about the altercation in the pub a month after the games.

Under cross-examination, the soldier tells the court that he did not know of a death threat from Krato's side. He affirms that Jason disappeared shortly after Jason knocked Krato out. He admits the two events may be linked. He also affirms that Krato took a long leave shortly after they had heard Jason was spotted in Cyrene; he suspected that Krato went after Jason.

The defense draws the court's attention to the possibility that in the given circumstances, the deceased might have threatened the accused. "The accused tried to avoid confrontation by fleeing, but when the deceased detected his hiding place he went after him, obsessed with revenge," Quintus concludes.

The court is now faced with the possibility that Krato had motive to kill, and that Jason had motive for self-defense, giving a totally different perspective to the scenario.

There is a lot to digest. The judge adjourns the court until the next week. The prosecution has a lot of damage-control to attend to. The defense urgently needs some evidence from Corinth and Cyrene to prove Jason does not have an anger problem.

*

The court resumes the next week, three hours after sunrise. The prosecution calls the bartender of Cyrene who served the night of the alleged murder. The prosecution wants to place Jason at the scene of the murder and to show his motives.

"Did you see the accused in the tavern shortly before the assault on the deceased?"

"Yes. He and his friends were drinking beer."

"Did you notice any contact between the accused and the deceased?"

"Yes. The foreign guy joined them at their table."

"Did you notice any argument between them?"

"No."

"How and when did they disperse?"

"They did not talk for long. Then the friends of the accused left, followed by the other guy a few minutes later."

"When did the accused leave?"

"About ten minutes later."

"Which way did the accused leave?"

"He asked me if he could leave through the back door, using the hallway."

"Where was the deceased found?"

"In that hallway."

"When?"

"A few minutes after the accused left through the hallway."

The prosecution concludes, "The accused had motive and opportunity to commit the crime. Given the sturdy build of the accused, and the fact that he once before knocked the deceased unconscious with his fist, he had the ability to have killed the deceased."

Quintus senses something fishy. The bartender refers to "the guy," not "the deceased." Quintus starts his cross-examination with a shot in the dark. It hits.

"Please tell the court: Did you see the body of the deceased?"

"Yes, I saw a body."

"Did he show any signs of life?"

The bartender shifts uneasily in his chair. He glances helplessly at the prosecutor.

"Yes. He made strange noises, as if he was choking."

"Who discovered him?"

"I did."

"How come?"

"He knocked on the door between the hallway and the bar. When I opened the door he was stretched out on the floor, gasping for air."

"What did you do?"

"I pressed on both sides of his throat and popped his larynx out. I have seen this kind of injury before in bar fights."

"What happened next?"

"He took a few deep breaths, coughed a lot, thanked me, and ordered a beer. He said the accused knocked him on the throat. After he finished the beer, he left."

With a dramatic wave of his hand and sarcasm in his voice, Quintus concludes, "Let the court take note that the so-called 'deceased' walked out of the tavern on his own legs!" The new evidence sets off a stir of whispers in the courtroom.

Jason tries not to show his inner joy at this breakthrough. He himself assumed Krato was dead. *Why would the army arrest me for a murder that did not happen?*

Then it strikes him: *Krato staged a conspiracy with the help of his army pals to frame me as a murderer. This thing may bite Krato from behind.*

The prosecution asks for a delay. The judge refuses. He, too, senses that there is a snake in the grass. He wants any undue process exposed as soon as possible.

The prosecution calls a centurion of the local regiment to the stand. He testifies that they had a funeral the next day. He was told that the deceased was Krato, a centurion on leave from Corinth, and that he was killed by the accused that knocked in his throat.

Quintus proceeds with the cross-examination. "You said the army buried Krato, a centurion from Corinth, that week."

"Yes."

"Did you see the deceased, named Krato, before he was buried?"

"No. It wouldn't make sense. As I didn't see him alive either, I could not confirm his identity."

"Was any other soldier killed that week?"

"Yes."

"How was he killed?"

"We had chariot training. When his chariot's wheel went over a rock, he was jolted out of his chariot and run over by another chariot."

"Was his face recognizable after the accident?"

"No. He was badly injured."

"Do you know if the two bodies were switched?"

"No."

"Were there two funerals that week?"

"Only one, as far as I know. I checked the records again yesterday."

Quintus suggests to the court that there is reasonable doubt about Krato's death, and a reasonable possibility that a story was fabricated to frame Jason as a murderer.

The judge calls the prosecution and defense to a sidebar. Realizing that his case for a conviction on murder charges is crumbling, the prosecutor agrees to change the charge to "premeditated assault to cause serious bodily harm to a Roman officer."

When the judge announces the change of charge, Jason is relieved: *I'm now off the hook for murder. It will not be too hard to prove that I acted in self-defense. Oh, if Agizul can only arrive in time! Please, God, open the way for my Berber friend.*

The bartender of Corinth who overheard Krato's threat to Jason has arrived. Maybe his testimony will convince the court of Krato's ill intent. This barman also brought documents about Jason's character from Jason's lawyer in Corinth.

The court adjourns till the next day.

*

When the court resumes, the prosecutor has lost most of his fire. He knows he has been taken for a ride by a conspiracy among a group of soldiers. He expects that the charge of "premeditated assault to cause serious bodily harm to a Roman officer" will probably also fall flat.

The prosecutor calls the military physician to the stand.

"Did you treat a centurion, named Krato, for an injury to the larynx?"

"Yes."

"How serious was the injury?"

"Though the patient's throat was sensitive inside, and the skin bruised on the outside, I did not think that the injury was life-threatening. However, the patient did speak with a hoarse voice."

The prosecution's own witness has sunk them further.

The defense proceeds.

"Did you follow up on this patient?"

"No."

"Why not?"

"I have to attend to so many real and imaginary ailments among the soldiers that I cannot follow-up on individuals. I assume that they will seek my help if their ailment persists or worsens."

"Have you issued a death certificate for a centurion, named Krato?"

"No."

Quintus suggests to the court that Krato's injury was not so dangerous that he needed follow-up treatment, nor was a death certificate issued for him.

The prosecutor decides to rest his case. The military conspiracy has blown their case with poorly construed evidence. The prosecutor has no leg to stand on anymore.

Quintus wants to prove that Jason acted in self-defense against relentless, baseless persecution. He wants Jason to be fully acquitted and exonerated.

He calls the bartender of Corinth, who overheard Krato threatening Jason. The bartender repeats the threat as he remembers: "The two guys came to the counter for a fill-up. Krato told Jason he intended to kill him in a staged accident. Jason called Krato a 'barbaric brute.' Krato said Jason was a softy who didn't have the guts to stand up for himself. The next moment, Jason knocked Krato out with a powerful right hook."

When cross-examined by the prosecution, the bartender gives information about the ensuing altercation. The prosecution launches a desperate attempt to highlight Jason's temper and power, enabling him to inflict serious harm.

The bartender interrupts, "Jason is a regular customer who has never before hit anybody. I assume he must have been provoked over a long period of time to respond with such a..."

"That will be all!" the prosecutor cuts him short with an angry look.

The prosecutor fails again to prove a point. Desperate, he states, "The accused probably had the same flare-up of anger that night in the tavern's dark hallway."

At that moment, the courtroom's door opens; Agizul enters. Lucius bends over to Quintus and informs him about the arrival of their key witness. Quintus' request for a ten minute recess is granted. They learn from Agizul that he was on a trip deep into the Sahara, so the messenger had to wait two weeks for his return.

When the court resumes, Quintus calls Agizul to the stand. After he is sworn in, Quintus takes him step-by-step through the evening when the alleged assault happened.

"Do you know the accused?" Quintus points to Jason.

"Yes. What is he accused of? He's a good man."

"Just answer my questions. Where and when did you meet him?"

"I met him at my place in the desert, a few years ago."

"You say he's a good man—why?"

"When he and Lucius were at my oasis, we were attacked by raiders. Both of them fought bravely. If they were not there, my whole family would either be killed or enslaved."

"Were you in Cyrene that night Jason was attacked?"

"Yes."

"Why?"

"My daughter and I had the same dream of a dragon attacking Jason. We thought it was an omen. I had other business with Lucius, too. So I decided to come."

"Had you been watching Jason's back that night?"

"Yes, I was."

"How did you discern the men from each other? How did you know who the culprit was?"

"Lucius was with me. He pointed out who Jason's partners were. He didn't know the other fellow. After that, Lucius went home."

"Tell the court what you saw."

"I saw the foreign man at Jason's table. When Jason's partners left, I asked them who the foreign guy was. One of them said he was the dragon I saw in my dream, so I watched him. After a while he left, went to the backyard of the building, and sneaked in by the back door. I decided to follow. Jason and I entered the hallway at the same time from opposite sides. This man was focused on Jason. He did not notice me behind him."

"What happened then?"

"I could see the man against the faint light from the window. I saw him draw his dagger. I heard him utter the threat. 'Tonight is the night of reckoning,' he said."

"And then?"

"When the man raised his dagger, I warned him. In that moment of distraction, Jason acted. Man, was he swift! *Zap*! The next moment the guy was on the floor, choked, fighting for air. I wanted to finish him off, but Jason dragged me out by force. As I said, he's a good man. We left in a hurry."

Quintus states the obvious: "The accused acted in self-defense. He and the witness could have killed the centurion if they wished to, or assaulted him further. He was at their mercy, but they left him, knowing that the resilient centurion could reach the bar and ask for help."

The prosecution tries to frame Agizul as an accomplice, so that his version of events can't be trusted. Quintus attacks this notion immediately.

"Had you made plans with the accused to assault the man you believed to be the dragon in your dream?" he asks Agizul.

"No, definitely not! How could we? I did not know who the dragon was until Jason's friends left the tavern. From that point, until Jason knocked him down, Jason and I had no contact—how could we have conspired to assault the man?" Agizul's logic is self-evident. The prosecution abandons their effort to prove conspiracy. Agizul's testimony is accepted as the observations of a concerned friend who was not an accomplice to crime.

The only real witness to the "crime" has taken the wind from their sails. They have no grounds to prove that Agizul's testimony is unreliable.

Quintus calls Lucius, Jason's partners at Cyrene Transport, and Petros, the discus champion, to attest to Jason's character.

Then, the judge dismisses all charges. He rules that Jason acted in self-defense. He advises Jason, though, that his fleeing made him look guilty. "It is far better to stay on the scene and supply authorities with the needed information." Quintus and his client concur.

Jason is free again. He thanks God for letting truth prevail. He is convinced that the prayers of Tabitha, his family, and the church have carried him through this testing time. The heavy burden of murder charges has been removed. Jason has tasted victim victory once more.

Agizul has gained perspective, too. "Thank you for dragging me out of the hallway that night," he says to Jason. "You prevented me from crossing the thin line between helping a friend and committing a murder."

"That's what friends do, helping each other," Jason responds, hugging his friend from the desert, not knowing if he will ever see him again.

Jason winds up his partnership at Cyrene Transport. By this time, his partners have no doubts anymore about the benefits of the wheel bearings Jason installed on their wagons. The invention has shortened the time of a round trip between Cyrene and its harbor. On his request, the company pays out his share. He deposits the money in his Cyrene bank-account, authorizing the transfer of funds in five equal amounts to his Corinth bank-account.

He learns from his business friends that a freighter at Apollonia will depart for Corinth via Crete within three days. Jason uses the time to visit his Cyrene friends. *Then I will rush back home to my beloved Tabitha. What a relief it will be for her and our families that this burden have been lifted!* However, Jason's repeated bad luck since the Isthmian Games has made him apprehensive. *Will God give me a breather, or will he subject me to even tougher tests?*

CHAPTER 13

Three days later, Jason sails from Apollonia on the *Perseus*, a medium-sized freighter that is northbound for Athens. Its cargo consists of Cyrene's finest wheat and leather. Halfway between Crete and Corinth, they encounter cool, overcast weather. They make slow progress against the breeze. Visibility is poor, due to intermittent showers.

Another ship appears from the rainy haze. The watch on the *Perseus* blows a horn. The foreign ship comes straight at them. The *Perseus* changes course. The other ship turns in the same direction. The distance between the boats shrinks to a few hundred paces.

Suddenly, the other ship raises the flag every seafarer dreads. *Pirates! Oh my God!* A dark feeling of inescapable calamity overwhelms Jason. He realizes they have no chance of escape or victory whatsoever. They are far outnumbered by armed, merciless pirates. The *Perseus* only has fifteen crew members and twelve passengers.

Though the Roman fleet, under command of Pompeii, wiped out pirate activities in the Mediterranean a century ago, pirate gangs gradually have sprung up again. Like weeds, they need to be uprooted constantly. Their main strongholds are in Cilicia, northeast of Cyprus. They are not as strong as a century ago, but they are becoming a nuisance again.

Shocked and worried, Jason sums up his precarious situation: *Fighting in these circumstances will be useless and fatal. I will have to win by the power of wisdom, not by the force of weapons.*

The pirates signal the *Perseus* to lower the sails and throw anchor. To prevent the spillage of blood, the captain of the *Perseus* surrenders. The pirate ship circles them and anchors parallel to the *Perseus*. The pirates hurl a hook tied to a rope over to the *Perseus* and pull the vessels closer together. Wool bales hanging from the side of the pirate ship cushions the impact when the sides of the ships connect.

The pirates jump on board and bind the hands and feet of the crew and passengers. They place them apart from each other so they can't untie each other's ropes. Having seen the valuable cargo of grain and leather, they decide to seize the *Perseus* with all its contents. The pirates leave fifteen of their men on board to handle the *Perseus* and to guard the prisoners.

The two ships sail off. Dusk is falling, and the crime remains hidden to the world.

Occasionally the clouds break, revealing stars to the pirates to guide them under cover of darkness to their hideout on a small Greek island. From there, they will convey their loot by fishing vessels to other islands. The prisoners will disappear one-by-one.

Jason prays for a miracle. He cannot imagine how Paul's motto—that all works out for good to those who love God—will materialize in this dismal situation. He prays that God will grant him an opportunity to turn things around.

As the pirates lose men in battles regularly, they have to recruit substitutes, usually from among the prisoners. Once the recruits have blood on their hands, they fear reprisals by Roman authority. Instead of exposing the pirates, they continue to serve them.

The pirate captain selects a few strong prisoners from the present catch for a softening up process, coercing them to join forces with the pirates. Jason is one of the chosen group. They are taken by dinghy to the pirate ship, treated well, praised, fed, and allowed to take turns to stretch their legs. They never see their fellow prisoners again.

After a few days of humane treatment, the pirate captain puts on his best face and interviews them one-by-one. With a callous smile, the captain makes it clear to Jason that he has only one choice: Join them, or die. They don't take passive hostages. Jason realizes that he has to play the game to survive. Fighting the pirate crew will be futile. He has to turn the other cheek now. His grandpa said that there were times when you have to adopt a submissive role and wait for a better opportunity. This seems to be such a time. In this way, he may win the pirates' trust and find a chance to escape. His sturdy frame will make him a valued addition to the pirate crew. He feigns interest in the captain's proposal.

The second-in-command puts the cooperative prisoners through training and a testing process. The uncooperative ones simply disappear.

The captain wants men who are not talkers but doers. He has instituted a fitness schedule that keeps the men fit, and rates them according to their abilities. They compete in five exercises: pushups, sit-ups, pull-ups, squats (with a sandbag on each shoulder), and climbing up and down the rope ladder to the crow's nest on the main mast. The ranking is determined by the number of repetitions each man completes.

The only way one can move up in the rankings is by outperforming those above you. However, killing competitors is not an option. A murderer is judged by the captain, and if found guilty, he is immediately beheaded and thrown overboard. To demonstrate his point, the captain has kept such a culprit for this occasion, and executes him unceremoniously.

The new recruits get the unambiguous message: Stay in line, or else...

Jason passes the tests easily. With his strong body, he outperforms many of the pirates, except for climbing the rope ladder. He has not done that before, so he is somewhat slow and clumsy in this event. The captain places him fifth on the ranking list. He will have to show his steel to move up in the chain of command.

The most difficult test will come when they conquer their next ship. Jason prays for guidance. He always has been against violence and killing, and as a Christian, he feels even stronger about it. What must he do when they attack another ship? He has no problem defending his God-given life against killers. He feels guilty, though, that he may have to secure his own survival by killing others who are in the same position as he is.

Jason tries to analyze the problem in his quest for a solution: *Do soldiers also experience this moral dilemma I am facing, having only two choices, both unacceptable? Soldiers either survive by killing the enemy, or they succumb and are killed by the enemy. If soldiers hesitate to kill in battle, they put themselves and their comrades at risk.*

Jason reviews his survival strategies of the past: *I fled to survive Krato's persecution; I fought to survive the robber attack in the desert; I thwarted Krato's attack in the Cyrene tavern; and I defended myself in a court of law to prove my innocence. Apparently, now I have to survive by submission.*

Jason realizes that working with the pirates will make him look like an accomplice. In his own mind and heart, he is sure that he does it under duress. There's no way he can reconcile his Christian faith and his cooperation with these terrorists. He sees himself as a victim of abuse. He has to endure the torture, hoping that God will open a door of escape somewhere. Once again, he has to choose the best of various imperfect options.

Oh God, help me to survive this ordeal too, for your sake, and for Tabitha's. Jason sighs. He wonders how God will give rest to his burdened soul in this evil situation.

*

Tabitha anxiously waits for news about the trial in Cyrene. The messenger who delivered the subpoena to the bartender in Corinth also delivered a note from Jason with the news that the trial has been postponed for three weeks to allow the lawyers to prepare. Since then, Tabitha has had no contact with Jason.

Tabitha prays several times a day that God will provide for Jason, and that evil will not prevail over good. Their families give her their genuine support. She still lives with Jason's family, expecting Jason to return soon.

When she skips her monthly period, she waits a week and then discusses it with her mother. When her mom asks her about some other symptoms, they realize she is probably pregnant. She bursts out in joy. She can't wait to share it with Jason! She cherishes the thought that she carries a piece of Jason inside her. They are united in this new life. This closeness with Jason comforts her yearning heart.

Corinth's bartender returns with the news that Jason was acquitted on all charges. Tabitha and the two families are ecstatic. When a week passes without any sign or word of Jason, their joy gradually turns to concern, and the concern to despair.

What happened to him?

Tabitha needs pastoral care that is solidly grounded in God's word and in experience. Titus departed to Macedonia to report to Paul that the problems in the congregation have been solved. The elders are not as experienced as Paul and his helpers are. There are many questions churning in her mind, questions about the trials and tribulations of the believer and how these relate to God's love, will, omniscience, and omnipotence.

She does not want to live in despondency, fearing it may affect her unborn child. She forces herself to think positively, to ban all thoughts about negative possibilities from her mind, and to sing songs of praise. However, sometimes the suppressed worries just boil over into uncontrollable weeping. Then her soul throws up all the "why" questions that drift away like chaff in the wind, unanswered.

After such a catharsis, realizing she has been fretting, she starts fresh with positive thinking, praising God for all his provisions and for all her answered prayers of the past, hoping against hope that she will receive good news soon.

*

Titus arrives in Philippi with the good news that the church in Corinth has accepted Paul's authority and advice for getting their church in order. Paul is overjoyed.

He immediately begins to dictate another letter to that church. He explains why he changed his travel plans. He urges the church to forgive the repenting culprits.

Paul uses the scene of a triumphant general returning from a successful campaign, showered by the crowds with flowers and perfume, to explain the paradox of how the gospel brings life to some and death to others. As the aroma of the flowers symbolizes life to the victors, but doom to their prisoners, so the gospel of Christ is a fragrance of life for those who accept Christ as Savior, and an odor of death for those who reject him.

Paul uses another metaphor. As Moses veiled his shining face after he had spoken with the Lord, so a veil of unbelief causes some Jews not to see the glory of Christ and the truth of scripture.

Paul shares with the church in Corinth all the hardships he already endured for Christ. This part of the letter is an encouragement for Tabitha in her tribulations. She wishes

Jason could have this letter of Paul at his disposal to help him in his situation, whatever and wherever that is.

Paul enlightens the church about the wonderful life after death. The moment believers pass away, their spirits are with Jesus—absent from the body, present with the Lord. Paul depicts the new life in Christ with words that will become famous: "If anyone is in Christ, he is a new creation; the old has gone, the new has come."[30]

He summarizes what Christ did for Christians, and what they should do for Christ: "God reconciled us to himself through Christ and gave us the ministry of reconciliation."[31] Christians must work for reconciliation between people and God, and between people and people. Christians are ambassadors for Christ. They have to implore unbelievers to make peace with God through Christ while they still have the chance. "Behold, now is the accepted time; behold, now is the day of salvation."[32]

Paul gives guidance on how to interact with unbelievers, and how to handle tricky situations such as partaking of a meal that has been offered to idols.

He encourages them to be generous to God and to the needy. Those who work full-time for God's kingdom should receive adequate support to cover their living expenses.

The last part of the letter deals with false apostles who want to make the church part of Judaism. The Jerusalem Decree has already sorted out the matter, and informed all churches accordingly. However, the false prophets have not stopped their vile efforts to smear the gospel of grace with their legalistic heresy.

When Titus returns to Corinth with the letter, the church is empowered by the clear guidance. They are also excited about the prospect that Paul plans to visit them soon. Tabitha is encouraged by Paul's triumphant spirit amid burdening tribulations.

30 2 Cor. 5;17 NIV
31 2 Cor. 5:18 NIV
32 2 Cor. 6:2

When Paul arrives in Corinth a few months later, he receives a warm welcome. He is sad to hear, though, that the false apostles have moved to Galatia, where they stir up the same trouble they incited at Corinth. While staying in Corinth for the three winter months, Paul writes a letter to the churches in Galatia and in Rome to help them understand the essence of the Christian message, and to avoid any teaching that is not in line with the one and only gospel.

During those three months, Paul conveys the same truths to the church in Corinth. He leaves them copies of his letters to the Galatians and the Romans. The church cherishes the eternal truth embodied in Paul's letters. They are read, reread, and discussed.

Tabitha absorbs the messages and grows in faith. Paul's letters enlighten and empower her through the dark times. Paul's teaching about salvation for the Jews reassures Tabitha that she and her family took the right steps by committing themselves to Christ. Regarding salvation, Paul emphasized that there is no difference between Jew and Gentile, as both can only be saved by faith in Christ. She knows by personal experience, "The Spirit Himself bears witness with our spirit that we are children of God."[33] She prays that Jason soon will share in the wisdom of Paul's letters.

*

Jason is fighting the toughest moral and physical battles of his life. He has to survive amid the immoral and brutal lifestyle of the pirates. *Will the thorns of tribulation stifle the wheat of faith in my heart? I hope divine intervention will create a breakthrough, enabling the fruit of the Spirit to vanquish the fruits of the flesh.*

Though Jason is superior in strength and fitness compared to the rest of the pirate crew, he lacks training and experience

---

33 Rom. 8:16

in close combat with sword and dagger. The captain orders two of his best fighters to train Jason in the vile art of dirty fighting. They explain and demonstrate the tricks of the trade, and then let Jason practice these to perfection.

These tricks are aimed at vulnerable body parts that are usually not targeted, such as the face, genitals, arms, and legs. They use blunt wooden swords and daggers for practice. While blocking the opponent's sword with his sword, Jason has to move quickly to the left and try to stab the guy in the arm or ribs with the dagger. When the opponent pulls his sword back after the swords locked, Jason has to slide his sword forward, trying to give the guy a cut on the face or body. When close enough, blows with the knees or elbows may throw the opponent off balance, opening up an opportunity to give a lethal stab with the dagger or sword.

When Jason has mastered the dirty tricks, he introduces his trainers to the stab-spear fighting he learned in Africa. He hopes it will convince the pirates that he has become one of them. They realize that Jason is a formidable foe when armed with a spear. Soon, they all trade the dagger of the left hand for a stab-spear. They keep their daggers sheathed on their belts, to be used when they lose the spear or sword.

After a few weeks, the captain thinks it is time to put Jason and the other recruits to the test in real battle. They sail out in search of a ship to raid. As the strongest pirates have strongholds in Cilicia, Jason's captain has to be cautious not to attack another pirate ship, causing an unnecessary bloody battle. To avoid clashes between pirate ships, they carry a secret sign on their main masts, known only to pirates, telling other pirate ships that they are in the same business. However, the greed of pirates sometimes does incite them to attack their own kind, like wolves in time of scarcity.

Jason's group approaches a ship that lies low in the water as she sails in the direction of Cilicia. The ship carries no pirate sign on the main mast. Jason's captain decides to attack. They signal the other ship to lower their sails and throw anchor. There are only a few of the crew on board. When they anchor alongside the other ship, a horde of pirates suddenly emerges from the lower deck, swinging over with ropes, swords drawn, and daggers held between their teeth.

Jason's crew is prepared for such a scenario. They change tactics fast. They light an oil-soaked rope on the enemy side of their ship. The flames delay the enemy's speed of entry. The overzealous few who make it to Jason's ship are overwhelmed by sheer numbers. Some of those who are halfway try to swing back and land in the water. The attackers have lost the initiative and some of their best fighters.

Now, Jason's crew goes on the attack. With bows and arrows, they eliminate a dozen more on the other ship. Then, all at once, they swing over by ropes. A fierce fight with swords, daggers, and spears ensues. Men on both sides are fatally wounded, but Jason and his javelin-squad have an advantage.

Jason's training in dirty fighting serves him well now. His survival instincts override his moral reservations completely. Either he or his opponent will die—a kill-or-be-killed situation. It is self-defense against imminent, mortal danger. He eliminates his opponents one-by-one with his stab-spear or with a swift slash of his sword. On two occasions, he saves his captain from a rear attack.

Eventually, the few weak ones left on the other ship surrender to the few brave ones left on Jason's side. After binding the prisoners, Jason and his captain calculate the losses. The other ship lost its captain and twenty-three men, compared to ten on Jason's side, including the second-in-command.

In view of Jason's bravery and fighting skills, and the lack of interest among the crew to be second-in-command, the captain promotes Jason to that position, thanking him for saving his life during the battle.

They take the conquered ship, heavily laden with iron strips, to their island hideout. They will have to find and train recruits. Jason also has a few suggestions for improving their weaponry and fighters. He will convey it to the captain gradually.

The captain has enough insight into human nature to realize that Jason is not a typical pirate. As they talk, he tries to fish for information about Jason's background. When he learns that Jason was married recently, the captain's fatherly instincts instill in him some empathy for the young man.

"We'll have to do something about that," he remarks.

Jason prays for the opportunity to contact or see Tabitha. He wants her to know what happened to him. By this time, she must be worried sick.

*

Akton, the Egyptian engineer who manufactured roller bearings for Jason's wagons while he was in Cyrene, has found a new field of application for Jason's invention: chariot races. He devised a smaller bearing for the light chariots used for racing in the hippodromes. These races have become one of the main entertainments of Roman society, attracting thousands every week. The new bearings will make the chariots even faster, and thus the spectacle even greater.

Akton tried it out locally in Alexandria. By comparing the performance of chariots with new bearings to those with old bushes, it was evident that the ones with roller bearings have a great advantage. Such a chariot taps less strength from the horses in the first seven rounds, leaving them with more reserve energy for the two final rounds.

Akton has a bright idea: Instead of selling the bearings, thus revealing the secret, he should rather try to persuade some rich owners to use his "wonder grease," and pay him a percentage of their winning money. He will install the bearings on the owner's chariots secretly. Thus, his product will secure ongoing income, while his secret remains hidden.

He decides to go for the big fish. He goes to Rome and sows the seed in the mind of a senator, one of Caesar's main opponents at the Circus Maximus. The senator is extremely interested. He would relish a win over Nero, who currently dominates the races with his superior horses.

Akton installs the bearings in secrecy on one of the senator's chariots. He tells the senator and his charioteers that he uses wonder grease.

When the horses are gradually exhausted by the long, gruesome race, the diminished friction on the axles shows in the last two rounds. For a few weeks the senator's upgraded chariot not only outperforms his chariot with the old type of bushes, but his new chariot beats Caesar's teams race after race. The senator has his second chariot outfitted with wonder grease too—with the same results.

The senator blooms; the emperor steams. Nero and his advisors can't figure out what is happening. The senator has the same horses and chariots as before; why is he suddenly winning all the races? His second chariot at first has not shown the same improvement, and then suddenly caught up. They cannot believe that a mere change to the chariot can make such a difference. The senator guards his chariots day and night, as if they were made of gold. They have increased his income from the races dramatically, and Akton gets his share.

*

While Akton enjoys the benefits of Jason's invention, Jason remains a hostage of the pirates. A few days after their victory over the other pirates, Jason's captain wants to have a word with him privately.

"I thought about a plan to make it possible for you to see your wife, without giving you the chance to escape."

"That sounds good. May I hear it?" Jason is excited.

"I need information from you about places and people. If we can bring her by fishing boat to a certain spot, you can meet there under guard, and then we take her back. If it works out well, we can try it again from time to time."

Jason is willing to subject himself to the control as long as he can see Tabitha. He gives information about the Diolkos, the distance to town, and the location of his dad's workshop, enabling the messenger to make contact and bring Tabitha to the fishing boat.

Jason writes a short note to his dad, assuring him that he can trust the messenger. It's the only way he and Tabitha can see each other for the time being. He also warns Philip that any attempt to intervene will be fatal.

Against his will and better knowledge, Philip gives in to the urgent pleas of Tabitha, Irene, and Helena. Despite the danger, the women are convinced they have to use this window of opportunity.

Jason waits on a small desolate island, the tip of an undersea mountain. Three men position themselves on rocks on three sides, about thirty yards from Jason. The main ship is anchored half a mile from the rocky island. There is no chance for escape.

When the fishing vessel shows up at long last, Jason is devoured by mixed emotions. He fears his family may have refused to take the risk to let Tabitha come; however, he is excited in the desperate hope that maybe, just maybe...

The guy at the bow blocks his view. *Is she there or not?* The boat turns. *Yes! Yes! There she is! Thank God!*

They row her over in the dinghy. Before the bow plows into the narrow pebble beach, Tabitha jumps into the water, splashing toward Jason, who also rushes in. Knee-deep in the water, they forget about the peering eyes and embrace with passion. The men enjoy Jason's moment with him, expressing their feelings with wolf whistles.

The captain said he'd give them half an hour together. Apart from seeing and touching each other, they have to exchange information quickly and plan ahead.

Jason explains that he was taken hostage by pirates. To stay alive, he plays the game. He is winning the friendship and trust of the captain—the reason for this privilege to see Tabitha. If there is no outside interference, they may meet occasionally.

"Jason, we're going to have a baby!" Tabitha interrupts, her face glowing with joy.

His face lightens up, too. Overjoyed, he shouts, "A baby!"

His shout is overheard by the men.

"Yahoo!" one shouts.

Jason holds her tightly, looking into her proud brown eyes—his expecting wife.

"Mommy and daddy!" he says with exuberant joy, stroking her belly, oblivious to their predicament.

In the light of this precious news, it is all the more important that they stay alive for the sake of their child. It fills them with fresh resolve to beat the odds against them. He will now defend his life with even more resilience and determination. Though burdened, he has to triumph. Jason shares his determination with Tabitha, but adds that he feels guilty about killing others to secure his own survival.

"I can understand that, Jason," Tabitha responds, but then she immediately empowers him from scripture by pointing to men of God who had to take up arms for the Lord: "God is the source of life, Jason; he gives and takes it as he sees fit. He commanded Joshua to conquer the Promised Land by killing the wicked inhabitants. He commanded and empowered the Judges and King David to throw off the yoke of foreign oppressors by waging war against them…"

"Yes, but my situation is different," Jason interrupts.

"Darling, please listen to me. It's of paramount importance for our survival. When the Spirit of the Lord came on Samson, he killed thousand Philistines with the jawbone of a donkey. In his victory psalm, King David praises God for his triumphs, saying, 'You have armed me with strength for battle.'[34] Jason, do you understand?—God empowered them to fight evil. Likewise, you must remain steadfast despite the dismal situation. Don't allow your kindness to make you weak. For the sake of our child, don't give up! Keep fighting for survival."

Tabitha's pleading eyes swim in tears. Jason realizes the truth of her words.

"I will," he agrees, hugging her tenderly, while new determination surges through his body and soul. For Tabitha, he would take on a dragon.

Too soon, the half hour has run out. They embrace and kiss long and passionately. The men give them leeway. When the second bugle sounds, they tear themselves apart. That night, there is a lot of excited talking on the ship as well as in Philip's house. It is a mixture of joy and worry, gratitude about the good, and grief about the bad.

*

From Jason's viewpoint, life at a pirates' den is not much different from the nightlife of Corinth. Man's sinful nature craves pleasures like eating, drinking, sex, and sleep. Ego satisfaction is derived from power, conquest, honor, achievement, and possessions.

The pirate community swings to and fro between raids, enjoying the loot. After a successful raid, they first have to sell the loot to buy what they need. Then they ship in lots of liquor, food, and blindfolded prostitutes from Athens and Corinth. They party until they drop into sleep. This goes on for days.

Jason does not participate in the orgies of gluttony, inebriety, and harlotry. He testifies to them by example. The others are too busy with their own pleasures to worry about him. In any case, they need a sober watchman to look out for attacks from other pirates or from the Roman fleet.

---

34 Psalm 18:39

After a few weeks, the captain prepares them for the next raid by restoring their fitness, developing their fighting skills, repairing and improving the ship, and practicing their strategies. After the crew has abused their bodies by overindulgence, they can see that Jason's fitness is now far superior to theirs. When the captain thinks his crew and ship is ready for another adventure, they sail out, determined not to attack another pirate ship, which may cost them dearly.

This time they hold up a merchant vessel, unaware that the ship also carries a platoon of Roman soldiers on their way to a new assignment. When most of the pirates are already on the freighter, dozens of soldiers suddenly pop up from the lower deck. The pirates are outnumbered, but they have no other choice than to fight for their lives. The young inexperienced soldiers suffer heavy losses against the unflinching pirates armed with swords and spears, stabbing and slashing mercilessly.

Three soldiers isolate and attack Jason's captain. Jason, also attacked by three soldiers, sees from the corner of his eye how the captain is pierced by a sword and shoved overboard. Jason eliminates two soldiers, but the three who prevailed against the captain now converge on him. He fights like a desperate wild beast against four over-confident attackers. He uses his stab-spear and the dirty tricks he was taught, wounding two soldiers in the stomach. The other two realize they are facing a superior fighter with unusual weaponry. They try to back off, stumble over rigging on the deck, and are heavily wounded in the ribs. They pay a high price for underestimating their enemy.

After an exhausting twenty minutes, Jason and his crew prevail. They lost their captain and half of their men. The crew and soldiers of the merchant ship were totally eliminated. As the second-in-command, Jason takes charge of both vessels. His men accept him as the new captain. They make their way back to their hideout.

Jason finds himself in an awkward position. *Good heavens! I'm a pirate captain now—what an appalling thought! I am also now virtually my own hostage.* He cannot help to smile about the tragic humor of the situation.

What are they to do next? He does not want to be a pirate, and he will certainly not attack other ships. However, he cannot just walk out of the dilemma. Most of his crew are outlaws. If they get the impression he is going to drop them, they will force him to comply.

He now realizes that the pirates and their captain are each other's prisoners. Neither the captain nor the crew can dare to abandon each other. Jason has to plan cautiously to throw off the unwanted burden. He wonders: *Why has God placed me in this situation? Can he use me to win some of these men for him? Though it's highly unlikely, I will try.*

First, he persuades his officers to feast moderately, because overindulgence makes it so much harder to regain fitness afterwards. They see the logic, try it out, reap the fruit, and gradually, it rubs off on the other men. The second-in-command asks Jason privately what the secret of his success is. It gives Jason an opportunity to sow a seed about Jesus.

*

While the crew feasts more moderately, Jason comes upon a bright idea: *What if I change the pirate ship into a security guard? Instead of robbing freighters, I can offer these ships protection against pirates at a reasonable fee. In this way, I can secure income for my crew, keep their loyalty, and turn the pirate ship I inherited into something good.*

Jason does not want to risk the lives of his crew in bloody battles with other pirates. He wants to eliminate other pirate ships without bloodshed on his side. Sinking pirate ships with a ram looks like a promising idea.

He starts planning on an adjustable ramming device. Roman warships have a huge wooden beam protruding from the bow. In a sea battle, Romans try to ram as many of the enemy's ships as possible. Punching a giant hole into another ship's hull usually results in panic on that sinking ship. However, the ram of a Roman galley sits above the waterline, so it can strip off the oars of enemy galleys. When the ram hits the hull of the enemy ship above the water line, it causes that ship to sink slowly.

Instead of a permanent ram above the waterline, Jason plans a ram that will operate under water, in order to drive a hole in the enemy ship below the waterline, causing it to sink fast. This ram will be fastened to a hinge on the keel. When not in use, its other point will be swung upward and fastened to the bowsprit.

Jason decides to use part of the main mast of the conquered ship for the ram, and the iron they robbed on a previous raid for making the heavy duty hinge. With the help of a drawing on the ground, Jason explains the concept to four of his officers, telling them how they are going to eliminate the competition. Though they are not quite sure what Jason is up to, they know he is smart. They trust his better judgment.

First, they have to forge the hinge. He shows his men how to build a charcoal fire and flare it up with bellows. They heat two strips of iron to red-hot condition. Three guys forge the two pieces into one by hammering it in succession. The guys take turns at the hammers. They add new strips, forging them again, until they have one big piece of iron.

By heating and hammering, they thin out the forged iron, fold it onto itself, and forge it into one again. They hammer it into the shape Jason wants, and cool it quickly in water to harden the iron. It takes a week to forge two eight-foot strips of iron, nine inches wide and one inch thick. These strips will form the upper part of the hinge that will be attached to the ram. They follow the same arduous procedure to forge the lower part of the hinge that will be attached to the keel.

To protect the point of the ram, they cover it with a sharp-pointed thimble, construed from two iron strips forged together at one end. It forms a massive spearhead that can easily pierce the wooden hull of a pirate ship.

Now they have to get the front end of the ship out of the water to attach the hinge to the keel. Jason directs them to strip wood from one of the confiscated ships and build a sledge with a cradle on which their ship can rest. In high tide, they pull the ship close to shore, slide the sledge in beneath the ship, and pull the ship and sledge onto shore as far as possible. At low tide, the ship's front end is exposed, resting on the cradle. They fasten the hinge with bolts to the keel. The hinge enables the ram to swivel up and down. When not in use, the front tip of the ram is tied to the bowsprit. When lowered, it becomes a massive spear that can pierce pirate ships in seconds. It is held in place by ropes running over the right and left side of the bow, limiting the sideways movement of the ram.

Jason names his altered ship *The Spear*.

In another high tide, they maneuver the ship and sledge back into water. Jason has the crew practice how to lower and raise the ram. They look forward to the first clash with a pirate ship. They try to imagine what their secret weapon will do to the enemy.

They sail to Miletus, where Jason offers his security services to captains who plan to sail south to Israel or Egypt, facing the possibility of pirate attacks. The third captain he approaches accepts his offer. He does not know exactly how Jason will defend his ship, but just having another ship nearby may deter most pirates.

The Spear stays within one mile from the ship it protects. On the second day, they are approached by a pirate ship. Now *The Spear* can be tested in a real-life situation.

When the pirate ship positions itself parallel to the freighter, Jason moves in from the other side with *The Spear*. Keeping the ram beneath the waterline while approaching at a slow speed, they punch a hole in the side of the pirate ship. The wooden hull cracks with a bang. Water rushes in through the gash. The pirates relinquish their efforts to board the freighter.

The bewildered pirates disappear into the deep, ship and all, within ten minutes.

The Spear and its crew have passed the test with flying colors. They vanquished a pirate ship and its entire crew without any injuries or casualties on their side.

The captain of the freighter is immensely grateful for the quick rescue in perilous conditions. He knows he and his crew would have been killed and his cargo lost if he did not have Jason's protection. He calls Jason "Angel of the Sea," a reputation that will spread quickly.

Jason's crew is at first uncertain of how to think of themselves now. They have suddenly changed from cruel abusers to benevolent helpers. No exhausting, bloody battles—and they still get paid! They see the wisdom of Jason's invention, praising his brilliant leadership. Their adoration makes them interested in his faith and lifestyle.

Jason smiles with satisfaction and amazement—a few months ago, he would not have believed it was possible to turn a pirate ship into a security guard. God used him again to accomplish a Joseph's deed, changing a destructive operation into a constructive one. He relishes the bittersweet sensation of victim victory.

As the pirate ships disappear with their crews, there are no survivors to warn other pirates about *The Spear*. The captains and crews, who benefit from Jason's protection, know their lives depend on the secret.

Jason does not want to stay in this business long; therefore, he does not acquire more ships. As soon as he gets a good second-in-command, he will retire, hand over *The Spear,* and hurry home.

*

After six months, Diana's hostess business in Corinth has shown rapid growth, establishing itself with good profits and faithful clientele. She figures it's time to leave this business in the hands of her best hostess and pay a visit to her Roman enterprise.

In Rome, she is not disappointed. Her manager has kept the place in tip-top shape, and reservations are made more than a month in advance. Occasionally, they lose a girl due to pregnancy, but there is no shortage of girls who want to join the club.

The number of senators has doubled. Diana hopes that eventually she may win over the emperor himself. It happens sooner than she has expected. One of the senators, wishing to win the favor of the Caesar, told him confidentially about the fantastic hostess facility where romanticism and eroticism are blended in a new splendid way. The emperor sends a few of his advisors to test out this facility and rapport to him personally. They like what they see and experience. They report to Caesar that the head lady is fabulous, but she never entertains customers herself. "A jewel suited for an emperor!" they conclude their investigation.

Diana is invited to a small private party of the emperor. She uses her tricks wisely and sparingly. Her green eyes and moist lips are directed more at the few other guests than the Caesar. He falls for the trick. If she tries to evade him, he will hunt her down. Gradually, her tempting eye-contact becomes longer. Eventually, the most powerful man in the world is in her web. He comes and sits with her, starting a personal chat.

A walk in the garden is next, followed by an invitation to his personal quarters. Only after another two hours of playing the hunting game, Nero gets Diana of Corinth into his bed. She makes it so fantastic for him that he is immediately addicted to her and to her method of luring while eluding. Diana has won the big prize.

To prevent him from getting bored with her, she often travels to Pompeii, where she has started another branch of her lucrative business. She has the walls of the mansion decorated with erotic frescoes of nude men and women. When Diana returns to Rome after a month in Pompeii, Nero is starved for her superior entertainment. By keeping the wolf hungry, she assures his return.

Nero loves Diana and her style. She begins to influence him in a subtle ways. He discovers that she has a shrewd political mind. She gives him good tips on how to handle people and problems to his best advantage. When he rehearses his plans with her, she asks questions that make him see dangers and solutions he has not thought of. He sometimes invites her to watch arena entertainment from his booth.

*

Jason and his crew have successfully changed their methods and image from robbers to helpers. They escort many ships with *The Spear* through the treacherous East Mediterranean waters. In the process, they have destroyed a dozen pirate ships. The second-in-command and another officer have asked Jason for more information about the Christian faith, a request he eagerly grants.

Having won the crew's trust with the new approach, Jason decides to make contact with Tabitha again. To eliminate any suspicion of abandoning his crew, he decides to throw anchor near the Diolkos, stay on the ship, and send men to fetch Tabitha. This time, Philip is more helpful.

Jason tenderly embraces his beloved Tabitha, now five months pregnant. They go into the captain's cabin to talk privately. Jason briefs her about the turn of events. His enterprise, providing security for commercial ships, is doing well. However, it is not where he wants to stay. As soon as he has trained his second-in-command, he will hand the ship over to him and return home.

Tabitha is glad he no longer collaborates with pirates, and that he has turned the ship into something positive. However, she is still worried that the encounters with pirates may turn ugly. She pleads with Jason to get out of this business as soon as possible.

When the sun approaches the horizon, they say goodbye, glad to have seen, heard, and touched each other, but sad to part again.

*

Jason's soft spot for people in need becomes his downfall. Instead of mercilessly sending pirates with their ships to the bottom of the sea, he starts to rescue those who desperately sprawl to keep head above water. They are taken prisoner and handed over to Roman authorities.

Some of these rescued pirates, in an effort to save their own skins, testify that Jason is actually a pirate posing as a security guard. When the Roman navy hears this allegation repeatedly, they decide to investigate.

If the *Spear* would be followed by a Roman warship, Jason and his crew would be on their guard. Therefore, the Romans use an ordinary freighter and hide a hundred soldiers on the second deck. The captain is ordered to follow *The Spear* and the ship in its protection from afar, keeping them just in sight on the horizon.

On the second day, Jason's customer is attacked by pirates. As usual, *The Spear* deals quickly with them. The Roman ship is just in time to see the pirate ship disappear underwater. The Roman soldiers emerge on deck, and the centurion informs Jason that they have to search his ship.

The centurion and fifty men row over in life boats and board *The Spear*. The centurion inquires about Jason's methods. Sinking the pirate ship so quickly intrigues him. Jason shows him the adjustable ram and demonstrates its operation. The officer is impressed. He wonders: *Is this deadly weapon only used against pirates?*

He observes the faces and clothing of Jason's crew and their prisoners. To the centurion, they all look like a bunch of cutthroats. He orders the soldiers to search *The Spear* thoroughly. Unfortunately, packed away in an old wooden box in a little storage cabin on the bottom deck, they find a pirate flag and a few pirate sabres.

Jason's excuse that they confiscated the stuff from pirates is not accepted by the centurion. Half an hour ago, he saw how Jason sank the pirate ship. There was definitely no time to confiscate anything from that ship.

Jason, his crew, and his prisoners are taken into custody and transferred to the Caesarea Praetorium. *The Spear* is seized, pending the outcome of the trial.

Jason is accused of piracy. He pleads not guilty. He is allowed access to a lawyer. He made enough money with *The Spear* to pay the legal fees.

*

Jason is put in a cell with several other prisoners awaiting trial.

His imprisonment in Cyrene taught him that prisoners hate to be stared at, so he unobtrusively glances at the faces for a moment, one at a time. An elderly man sitting on the floor with his back against the wall looks familiar. *Where did I see him?* When the man talks to the guy next to him, Jason recognizes the voice. *Why on Earth is Paul in prison?*

Jason slowly moves in Paul's direction, leans against the wall for a while, and then sits down an arm's length from the famous missionary.

Paul has watched the movements of the newcomer, turns his head slightly toward Jason and whispers, "I wonder why our paths cross here and now."

After a few seconds, Jason softly replies, "I heard you in Corinth a few years ago, with your first two messages."

With a frown between his eyes, Paul tries to recall that day in the synagogue. The memory of a tall, dark, and handsome young man slowly emerges from the past.

"Oh yes, now I remember! You stood out above them all. I wondered if God had a plan for this sturdy young man. I said a quick prayer for you."

In silence, they relive that day.

The other prisoners gather around a dice game. Amid the talk and laughter, Paul and Jason can chat softly without being overheard.

"Do you know this?" Paul draws with his finger the sign of the fish on the dusty prison floor and wipes it out immediately.

"Yes, but..." Jason hesitates, looks down to the floor, embarrassed, and confesses: "I did not accept him then. I had to flee for my life."

"Are you perhaps the vanished lover of a beautiful Jewish girl?" Paul tries to connect the dots. When Jason nods, Paul adds, "I know the family. I supped with them often. They were gravely concerned about you. We prayed together for your safety."

"I lived with Lucius in Cyrene," Jason continues. "He said he worked with you in Antioch."

"Yes, we did! How is he now?" Paul responds, excited.

"He's doing well. He's a leader in the local church. I accompanied him on a mission into the Sahara. I listened to his teachings to a Berber family at an oasis. It gave me more information and insight regarding the gospel. When we returned to Cyrene, I attended the meetings, but kept on postponing the decision. When I returned to Corinth, Titus helped Tabitha and me to make the commitment."

Paul smiles with inner joy, affirming reassuringly: "God leads each person along a different way. Every journey of faith is unique. Getting into God's fold at long last—that is what really matters." Paul realizes with profound gratification: *I sowed the first seeds in Jason's heart. Although it took a long time for the seeds to germinate, I can see and enjoy the fruit of my work today.*

"You bring good news to every place. Why have they locked you up?" Jason wonders.

"I can assure you it is not the first time I've been imprisoned for the good news I bring," Paul responds. "After my last visit to Corinth, I attended Pentecost in Jerusalem. Some of the enemies of the church were there, too. With false accusations, they tried to get me killed by inciting a riot. God used the Romans to save me from the mob's wrath. When the commander learned of a plot to kill me, he sent me with a strong escort to Caesarea. Though the governor is interested in my teaching, he wants to please the Jews, too. My case has been postponed time and again."

Why do people who have been reconciled to God through Christ have to suffer one tribulation after the other? Jason wonders. However, he refrains from discussing his doubts with the revered missionary.

Paul shifts the focus to Jason, "What brought you to this place?"

"When I returned from Cyrene, I was taken hostage by pirates. To survive, I submitted to their demands. I became a pirate against my will. Hoping for a chance to escape, I worked my way up through the ranks. When the captain was killed in a raid, I took charge of the ship. I refurbished it to be used as a security guard for freighters. We sank a dozen pirate ships."

"Incredibly fantastic!" Paul interrupts, amazed and amused.

"Unfortunately, things turned ugly," Jason adds. "When the Romans acted on a rumor that I was a pirate in disguise, they found some old pirate gear on the bottom deck. I'm now accused of piracy."

There is silence while Paul weighs the extraordinary sequence of events. In amazement he wonders, "Well, well, well...the ways of the Lord are indeed above our understanding. He must have a special plan for you, my friend, to stitch a plan together in such an extraordinary way."

*

The guard calls Jason's number. His lawyer wants to speak with him.

As Jason tells his story, the lawyer watches him with suspicion. Jason's kidnapping by the pirates, his progress in their ranks, having been promoted to captain after a few months, and then turning the illegal, destructive enterprise around to a legal, constructive security business—it all sounded just too farfetched to the critical mind of the law expert.

"My friend, if your story sounds fishy to me, it will be even more so to a Roman court. We must get solid evidence from trustworthy witnesses to support your claims."

The more they search for possible witnesses, the more Jason realizes how hopeless his case really is.

"It is true that I have been a pirate for a time, but I did it under duress to save my life."

"That's important. That scenario justifies a not-guilty plea. Can you prove it?" the lawyer responds.

"Only a few of the original crew who know I was taken hostage by the pirates are still alive," Jason remarks.

The lawyer weighs this option for a few moments and replies, "As accomplices, their testimony will not carry much weight with the judge."

"The captains of the trade ships I protected can affirm my role as security guard," Jason shoots back.

"Yes, but they are ignorant about your activities between these good-guy periods. Can you prove that you have not played double agent? We have to anticipate the questions of the prosecutor so that we can prepare good responses," the lawyer explains his critical approach.

It dawns on Jason: *No lawyer can save me this time. I can only trust in God's mercy.* When he returns to the cell, Paul agrees and says a prayer for him.

Sensing which way both of them are heading, Paul adds, "Man proposes; God disposes. When God sends us to Rome,

we have to assume that he has important work for us there—
right under Caesar's nose."

They ponder the possibility.

"My friend, if God could use you to turn a pirate ship into
a vessel of security, then he can use you to turn the arena into
a church," Paul concludes with a chuckle.

In serious tone, he adds, "Don't be discouraged by the
devil; look out for God's opportunities. Despite dismal
circumstances, cling to God's promise about the Messiah,

> [3] A bruised reed He will not break,
> And smoking flax He will not quench.[35]

God's mercy through Jesus is limitless."

*

At Jason's preliminary hearing in Caesarea, the judge
decides that in view of the severity of the allegation, Jason
must go to Rome and be tried by Caesar himself.

Jason gets permission to send a letter to Tabitha. It is
taken by a Roman courier carrying other correspondence to
the commander in Corinth.

The news brings Tabitha and the two families to their
knees. They realize that, from the practical viewpoint, Jason
does not have a chance. If he is found guilty of piracy, he will
be executed or—even worse—condemned to the death-facing
life of a gladiator. They expect Jason's huge frame will most
likely land him in a gladiator school.

Their burden has been increased immensely. Some church
members join them for a regular prayer meeting. They lift
Jason up daily at the throne of grace.

On the last night Jason and Paul spend together in the
Praetorium of Caesarea, they are the only prisoners in the
grim Roman cell.

---

35 Is. 42:3

Jason wrestles with a problem regarding God's will: "Paul, how can it be God's will that you are prevented from spreading the good news, and that I may be forced to fight in the arena to survive?"

"We must discern between what God wants and what he allows," Paul says confidently, having tread this path before. "God does not want man to sin, but if man wants to sin, God allows him to bump his head. Unfortunately, innocent victims may get hurt, too. In our case, Rome is the culprit and we are the victims. However, God uses both man's sin and hurt to achieve his long-term goals."

Silently, Jason links Paul's words to the sin Jason and Tabitha committed: *Yes, God used our sin to lead us to the joy of salvation and marriage.*

"Can anything good comes from killing in the arena?" he wonders.

"Even that God weaves into his large tapestry," Paul retorts. "God did not keep Daniel outside the lion's den, but he cared for him *in* the lion's den. Rome's injustice may throw you into the arena, but God can use you in that situation to do something good to others who have lost hope and are about to succumb to despair. We must trust God's guidance, even when we can't see the road ahead. He sees the big picture and provides for situations we can't foresee yet. We can't cover all future situations with our prayers; God covers them with his love."

After some moments of pondering, Paul continues, "Regarding you fighting for physical survival, God may allow that to teach you truths about spiritual warfare. We have to put on the full armor of God to prevail against Satan's relentless attacks."

"What does that armor consist of?" Jason asks, not sure he has it.

"Think of a soldier's armor," Paul responds. "Gird yourself with the truth of the gospel. Protect your heart with the breastplate of righteousness, your mind with the helmet of salvation, and your feet with the shoes of service to the gospel. Ward off evil attacks with the shield of faith, and attack Satan with the sword of God's word. The final part of the armor is invisible but crucial: remaining watchful through prayer.[36]

"Jason, you must endure hardship like a good soldier of Christ Jesus. Keep fighting the good fight; keep running the good race; keep faith in God Almighty. The tougher the battle becomes, the stronger we must trust in the Lord. However, we must pray for and look forward to the day when the spears will be broken, the war will end, and lasting peace will arrive. In Psalm 46, a broken spear symbolizes peace."

After a few moments of silence, Paul proceeds to equip Jason for the tough times that may lie ahead: "In Psalm 27, David shares with us his attitude in the battles of his life."

[1] The LORD *is* my light and my salvation;
>> Whom shall I fear?
>> The LORD *is* the strength of my life;
>> Of whom shall I be afraid?
[2] When the wicked came against me
>> To eat up my flesh,
>> My enemies and foes,
>> They stumbled and fell.
[3] Though an army may encamp against me,
>> My heart shall not fear;
>> Though war may rise against me,
>> In this I *will be* confident.[37]

Jason wants to learn the words by heart. Phrase by phrase, he and Paul repeat the words several times.

The next day, the guards come to take Jason to the ship that will carry him to Rome. Paul says goodbye with a powerful promise from Psalm 37:

36 Eph. 6:13-18
37 Ps. 27:1-3

⁵ Commit your way to the LORD;
    trust in him and he will do this:
⁶ He will make your righteousness shine like the dawn,
    the justice of your cause like the noonday sun.[38]

Jason is empowered by the salted words of wisdom coming from God's aging messenger. He is ready for whatever Rome throws at him. He is confident that as long as he stands with God, he is on the winning side. Even when he cannot understand God's goals, he will trust and obey.

Paul has helped Jason to put his faith into practice. He has been prepared and equipped for the next severe test of his life.

---

38 Ps. 37:5-6 NIV

CHAPTER 14

Tabitha carries Jason's child. She is now in the seventh month, deeply concerned about Jason's trial by Caesar. While the young Christian mother suffers, the pagan prostitute basks in the ideal circumstances she created for herself.

Diana entertains Caesar in the private quarters of the imperial palace. Sometimes Nero wants to get away from the glamorous high-society parties, saturated by the phony, artificial, and hypocritical interaction of wealthy social climbers trying to impress those higher up. With Diana, he can be his natural self. She treats him as a human being.

Nibbling on exotic foods and drinks, chatting about the events of the day, Nero mentions that he sentenced a Corinthian today to his gladiator school. He knows Diana is from Corinth, so he watches her reaction furtively.

"What was the crime?" she inquires casually, as if she doesn't really care, picking a grape from a bunch.

"Piracy," Nero retorts, glancing at Diana's face. He relishes the opportunity to tease her curiosity.

"Piracy? Come on! Corinth doesn't have pirates!" she responds with giggles.

Nero munches on a bunch of Tuscany grapes.

"Strange case, I must say," he muses.

He continues, "Can you believe it? This pirate presumed to protect merchant ships against other pirates. To protect his real identity, he actually sank a number of pirate ships. However, eventually his fellow pirates blew his cover. Unfortunately for him, typical pirate gear was found on his ship."

"Maybe he had been a pirate before and decided to change his ways," Diana says, playing devil's advocate.

Nero bursts into laughter, "Have you ever heard of a rehabilitated pirate? No, the evidence against him was quite convincing, and he failed to submit any evidence or witnesses to the contrary. Actually, he didn't look like a bad guy to me—sturdy, tall fellow with an open face. So, I gave him a chance by sentencing him to my elite gladiator school. If he proves himself, he may earn his freedom. A former pirate should do well in the arena, don't you think so?"

"You say he's from Corinth? Do you remember his name?" Diana prompts, now more interested. Nero chews on a piece of succulent duck. He frowns as he tries to remember; there were quite a few cases.

"Yes, his name was interesting. Let me think, what was it?—Something from Greek mythology. Oh, yes, Jason. He reminded me of Jason and the Golden Fleece."

Nero enjoys his own joke. A terrible feeling of pending doom rushes through Diana. *It can't be! My beloved Jason sentenced to a living death?*

"Maybe I know him," she whispers. "I know a tall, sturdy Corinthian with that name. He's a dear friend."

"Oh no! Come on! There are many men with that name. It is probably a mere coincidence," Nero tries to comfort her. He doesn't want his evening spoiled.

"May I see him?"

"Sure! You can accompany me to the gladiator school tomorrow. Come now, don't spoil our night because of an extremely remote possibility that a condemned pirate may be your old-time friend."

"You're right. It is impossible that my friend can be a pirate."

She pushes the matter out of her mind as totally unrealistic. As usual, she offers her best to the emperor. After all, he pays extremely well.

*

Despondent, Jason ponders his predicament in a cell of Nero's gladiator quarters. He is unable to comprehend the bad luck that has befallen him since he became a Christian. It went from bad to worse.

First, he had to face the false murder charges and the trial in Cyrene. By God's grace, he was exonerated. Then, he was taken hostage by pirates. God helped him to survive the moral dilemma; he ended up in control of the pirate ship, and turned their vile operation around to something good. Then came the final blow—charged and sentenced for piracy. This time, there's no light in the tunnel; it caved in around him.

Here I now sit, in a living hell. To stay alive, I will have to kill others every week. The arena is not different from the jungle—some die so that others may live. How can God weave this mess into his big tapestry? Does God want me to give up my life by refusing to fight? Or does God want me to fight for survival and perform another Joseph's deed? How will Christ give me rest with this burden?

He feels his prayers bounce back from the walls of his cell. He feels abandoned by God. Paul's words of encouragement seem irrelevant in this gruesome reality.

In view of his previous victories over tribulations, Jason knows he should have faith. Like Joseph, he made positive contributions wherever he went. He helped to turn the assault in the desert to victory. He saved Bari and his daughters in the jungle. He upgraded the transport system of Cyrene. He transformed a pirate ship to a security guard.

However, with the best will in the world, he cannot envisage how God can use him now to turn this misery around. He has lost hope that God will provide again as He has in the past. The future seems pitch-dark for his downcast spirit.

Then, some obstinate anger stirs up in him. *I'm not going to give up my life without a fight. My grandpa planted this seed in my soul at age nine. It has become part of my bone and marrow.* He knows deep inside that he has to survive this ordeal, too, for the sake of his beloved Tabitha and their child. *I must prevail, even if I have to kill all the gladiators in Rome! That means I have to train hard and put in my very best all the time.* Though his faith is wavering and his insight limited, his will is still as hard as steel. The instinct to fight for survival—imprinted on the human psyche for millennia—is superseding Jason's depressed mood and morbid circumstances.

*

The trainer determines training schedules. Newcomers start at the bottom. They have to earn their promotions.

Jason starts with basic training: pulling himself up on a horizontal bar, picking up a heavy stone and placing it on a six-foot high platform, doing squats with another gladiator on his shoulders, and carrying two buckets of sand up and down stairs. He has to repeat every exercise ten times. Then, he must chop wood with a heavy ax for half an hour. After a short rest, he has to repeat all the exercises. The schedule goes on for three hours in the morning and for three hours in the afternoon.

Despite his pirate training, he is completely exhausted by the end of the day. Fortunately, in Caesar's elite school, they receive enough good food to build muscle and accumulate energy. Some of the animals killed in the arena end up in their stew.

Jason is relieved to hear from fellow inmates that Nero's elite gladiators never fight against each other in the arena. The emperor has several gladiator schools. The schools fight against each other, but the members of each school don't. They fence with one another to fine-tune their skills, but they never have to kill each other, a policy that ensures a strong team spirit. This *esprit de corps* is crucial for group fighting in the arena.

The next day, Jason's muscles are stiff and sore. The pain diminishes as he warms up. He is working with the ax on a block of wood when Caesar enters, protected by twenty soldiers of the Praetorian Guard. The gladiators are told to continue with their training.

With the emperor are a few veiled visitors, including Diana. When she recognizes Jason, she gasps with shock. Jason continues chopping wood without glancing at the visitors. He hates to be put on display like an animal.

Back in the palace, Diana confirms to Nero that Jason is indeed her old-time friend. She pleads with Caesar to grant him clemency. Nero sees an opportunity to gain more control over Diana. Thus far, she choreographed their togetherness. By going to Pompeii often, she even rationed his sex life. Now, he can get her to dance to his beat in order to secure the well-being of her friend Jason. This gladiator has become a useful tool.

"It's not easy to revoke a sentence issued by Caesar," he informs her, enjoying torturing her troubled soul.

"Why? You are Caesar, you can do anything!"

"My dear, we are not barbarians, we are a civilized state," Nero elaborates. "We do not make or revoke laws and sentences whimsically. The right procedure must be followed, securing that all citizens and subjects of the empire are treated fairly."

"What is needed to overturn Jason's sentence?" she inquires, in desperate hope.

"Well, when new evidence comes to light, proving a prisoner's innocence, the Caesar or the senate may overturn a sentence. However, we don't have such new evidence for your friend. I can't go to the senate and plead for mercy on the grounds that the prisoner is a friend of my mistress." Nero laughs from his stomach, imagining himself in such a ridiculous situation.

"Is there any other way?" Diana is desperate.

"The only way a gladiator who is a condemned prisoner can free himself is by staying alive, fighting well, and killing his opponents. After a few dozen extraordinary impressive fights, he may be granted his freedom if the Caesar so wishes."

"So my friend just has to go through this horrible process of mortal danger and senseless killing, and maybe one day he will be set free?" Diana is disgusted with Roman justice.

"Yes, that seems to be the case, if no new evidence turns up. But remember, even when he fights well and survive, it is I who will decide if he goes free. By serving me well, you may persuade me to treat your friend well..."

Diana realizes Nero has her cornered: *This is extortion! I'm no longer in control of his sensual appetite; he will call me whenever he wants. Denying Nero in any subtle way may be bad for Jason. Oh Jason! Why have you landed yourself and me in this horrible situation? How will we ever get out of it? God help us!*

*

Diana knows it will devastate Tabitha and both families to hear of Jason's fate, but not knowing may be even worse. She feels obligated to inform them. At the least, they can pray that their God will somehow work a miracle.

When Jason goes into the arena for the first time for team combat, fighting for his life against well-trained, brutal men, Tabitha receives Diana's letter.

She has begun the ninth month of her pregnancy. The shock is too much for her. She goes into early labor. The physician and midwives are urgently called. They try their best to handle the abnormal birth. Tabitha's life is in danger.

Tabitha and Jason fight simultaneously for survival, Tabitha in childbirth, Jason in the arena. Her pushing and his stabbing are intertwined. She pushes bravely to live and give life; he fights valiantly to live by taking life. The battle for each of them is intense. Never before has death been so close and real to them. No one can help them; they have to win this battle by God's grace and their own exertion. They fear they may not make it. Determined, they put in every bit of strength they can muster and pray for mercy.

After an hour of draining strain, the life-and-death struggle is over.

"It's a boy!" one midwife shouts.

She holds the baby by his feet with her one hand, and gives him a slap on the butt with the other. The shock makes his rib cage contract, forcing the air from his lungs. With a mighty cry, he announces the beginning of his life outside the womb.

With a mighty stab and cry, Jason ends his opponent's life.

Tabitha's body lies motionless and pale. She has lost too much blood. The second midwife wipes Tabitha's lifeless brow with a cool, damp cloth.

"Come on, girl! Don't give up! You have done well! You have a beautiful son to care for! Keep fighting!"

Tabitha opens her eyes weakly and turns her head slowly toward the midwife, whispering, "A boy? Jason will be so proud." Then she lapses back into a coma.

The midwife keeps on wiping Tabitha's face, tapping her on the cheeks, encouraging her to prevail against the fog of death encroaching on her.

After the baby's umbilical cord has been attended to, the midwife covers him in a soft sheet and lays him in Tabitha's arm. They open her breast and position the baby to enable suckling. Tabitha opens her eyes again, glances at the cute little face in her arm, and smiles. She's back! She has won the battle.

Tabitha and Jason both survive, trusting in their God. However, they are drained and exhausted. They looked death in the eye. Too tired to think, they don't grasp the meaning of their suffering.

Tabitha triumphs by giving birth to a healthy eight-pound son. Jason and four of his teammates survive and stand as victors—fatigued and bruised—before Caesar's arena booth. Jason sustained several bruises on his torso and a shallow cut on his thigh. His body aches for a bath and rest. Worn out, he doesn't look for faces, so he doesn't see Diana in the emperor's pavilion. In powerless empathy, her eyes swim in tears.

Tabitha is tired, but restful. Her faith has been vindicated. Indeed, all things work together for good to those who love God. She looks at their son in her arm. She feels his soft lips instinctively sucking her teat. She wishes Jason could be here to enjoy this little bundle of love and life with her. She can imagine the pride and joy on his face.

*

After two months of futile efforts by the emperor's charioteers to end the senator's winning streak, Nero is desperate and grumpy. Now, Akton moves in for his big deal. He informs the emperor that he has a solution for his problem. Modestly, he presents his conditions. Nero is so desperate to win again that he endures the insult of being extorted by a foreigner.

Akton secretly removes the bearings from the senator's chariots and terminates his contract with him. Then, Akton installs the bearings on only one of Nero's chariots. He has to prove to Caesar that it is not a fluke. Not even the charioteers know what Akton has done to the chariot. The secret is hidden in the hub of the wheel.

To Nero's utter amazement and excitement, his altered chariot wins the next race by two lengths. Elated, he gives Akton a hard slap on the back: "Akton, you've done it!" For the next two weeks, the altered chariot keeps winning. Totally convinced, Nero commands Akton to alter the other chariot as well, promising Akton his share of the prize money.

Sure enough, Nero's second chariot moves into second place and stays there. For the time being, Akton's secret remains undetected. He alone greases the wheels. He proceeds with the misinformation that he is using wonder grease. They don't expect a mechanical alteration, so they don't investigate.

Nero is so pleased with Akton's miracle that he sometimes invites the engineer to sit with him in the imperial pavilion at the circus or arena. They cheer together when Nero's chariots take the lead; they agonize together when the emperor's team is cut off and falls behind. In the end, Akton's secret secures Nero's win, and when Nero wins, Akton is generously rewarded.

*

In the Circus Maximus, Jason's invention brings glory to the Caesar. In the arena, Jason repeatedly faces death, fighting for his life. Nero is unaware of the irony that he is torturing the man whom he should be awarding.

Having survived his first day in the arena makes Jason grateful, but not joyful. The fight in the arena was tougher than he expected. His opponent delivered his utter best to stay alive. Jason knocked the man's helmet off and inflicted several light wounds to his torso. As the guy realized he was losing the fight, Jason saw the raw fear in his eyes. For his own survival, though, Jason had to finish the job. Like a hunter facing a charging lion, he had to kill to save his own life. He will have to face death again and again, and overcome his opponents one by one. He has to keep fighting tenaciously against this relentless cancer of the Roman world that tries to devour him.

One of the gladiators, a Nigerian, who fought and prevailed with Jason the previous day, starts a conversation with him. He is of the same stature as Jason.

"You're new here. I'm Hercules."

"Hi, I'm Jason."

"Have you fought before?" Hercules inquires.

"Not against gladiators."

"I'm here for five months now. It's my first time, too. I can still remember those first weeks. Terrible!" Hercules shakes his head in disgust.

"You may give me some advice, if you will?" Jason suggests, hoping he can pick up some tips from Hercules' experience.

"No problem! Someone gave me good advice when I was a novice. It saved my life and my sanity. I've passed it on to a few guys. It helped them, too."

"I'm listening."

"Of primary importance is state of mind—whether exercising, fighting, or resting. Without that, you can't do anything properly, and will soon be a corpse."

"What is the right state of mind for this dirty job?"

"Concentrate on NOW. Forget about past or future. Yesterday's fight is gone; tomorrow's fight is not yet. When you focus on the here and now, it takes your mind from family and friends, from what you had and lost, and from what you hope to gain. A gladiator who grieves and yearns…fights poorly and dies."

"It will be difficult, but it makes sense."

"The second thing is to stay determined to win and to live. You can only keep on living if you keep on winning. Any slack in resolve will be fatal. Tough challenges demand resilient responses. Don't think you're the best; such a big ego will make you complacent. You have to prove you're the best in every new fight. Remember, your opponent will do his utter best to save his life by killing you. If you keep that first and foremost in your mind, you will do your exercises well, fight with all your might, and afterwards, rest well to recuperate. That will give you the edge in the arena."

"That makes sense, too. I'll work on that."

"The third thing is to cut out any thinking about morals and guilt. There is no right or wrong, meaning or purpose, for a gladiator. There is only ONE REASON for doing what you do: to live. Like street children, we have to do whatever it takes to stay alive. You have to value your life above everything else. Life itself is our only moral and motive."

"That one, I have already started. I have decided that I will prevail, even if I have to kill all the gladiators in Rome."

"Good! Work on the other two as well."

"Thanks! I will."

The pep talk Jason received from Hercules relieves him from debilitating worries about Tabitha, his fruitless planning for escape, useless memories about the good old days, or the deceiving dreams about a better future.

He keeps his focus on what he does, his resolve to prevail, and the only moral behind it—to stay alive. He and Hercules now exercise together. They develop new exercises to strengthen muscle groups that have been neglected. They compete with each other, spurring each other on. There is no letting up.

In his misery, Jason has found a true friend. He shows Hercules the advantages of a stab-spear as well as the dirty tricks he learned as a pirate. They practice these moves over and over until they become second nature. Their efforts pay off. In the arena, their power, speed, and tricks overwhelm their opponents within minutes.

Despite the kill-or-be-killed situation, they prefer not to kill, but to disable their opponents with a severe stab in the shoulder, cutting muscles and tendons, rendering the man's fighting arm useless. They send these men to early retirement, instead of death. However, when the Caesar gives the thumbs-down signal, they have to obey.

After three months, only the guys who have been following Hercules' rules and Jason's tricks are still alive. They instill the same state of mind in all newcomers. Caesar's elite gladiator school becomes invincible. They become known as the Javelins. However, they need some flair to dramatize their efficiency.

"Hercules, how do you feel about a war cry?" Jason wonders, thinking of his experience with Bari in the Sudan. "If we begin and end our group fighting with a war cry—maybe one right out of Africa—it may boost our spirits and demoralize opponents."

"Wow! That will be cool!" Hercules responds. "What about this one?"

> Vrrroooomm! Vrrroooomm! Vrrroooomm!
> Ha-ta-ka! Ha-ta-ka! ... Ha-ta-ka! Ha-ta-ka!
> Wham! Wham! Wham! Victory!"

"Brilliant!" Jason reacts. "Maybe we should repeat it three times before we end with 'Victory.' A nice big drum will make it even more impressive. But what's the meaning of the war cry?"

"My people in Africa use it before a lion hunt. The 'Vrrroooomm' mimics the roar of a lion," Hercules explains, "so we should try to bring forth those deep bass tones of a roaring lion: 'Vrrroooomm! Vrrroooomm! Vrrroooomm!' The next part, 'Ha-ta-ka! Ha-ta-ka!' resembles the beating of spears on the hard ox-hide shields of the hunters. The last part, 'Wham! Wham! Wham!' portrays the spears hitting their target."

"Fantastic!" Jason rejoices, "Let's introduce it to the others."

The other gladiators in the elite group like the idea. The group practices the war cry together. It lifts their spirit. In unison, they mobilize quite a loud, awe-inspiring rallying cry. Their supervisors agree that a big drum will enhance the performance.

With their next performance in Nero's small private arena, they surprise the emperor and unnerve their opponents with the loud rhythmic dance. With slightly bent knees, they stamp their feet, and beat their chests with their fists, while thundering in tune with the drum:

"Vrrroooomm! Vrrroooomm! Vrrroooomm!
Ha-ta-ka! Ha-ta-ka! ... Ha-ta-ka! Ha-ta-ka!
Wham! Wham! Wham! Victory!!!"

The spectators love it and cheer. Nero is amused. With a wave, he signals his approval. He likes seeing his gladiators in good spirit. The war cry fills them with courage and pride, and instills fear in their adversaries. After the fight, they repeat the cry before leaving the arena victoriously.

Without realizing the full extent of their influence, Jason and Hercules have facilitated major changes in the quarters of the elite gladiators. Although the situation is the same, their attitude toward the situation has changed dramatically. The morbid, death-focused mentality has been replaced by a hopeful, life-focused approach. The team's improved skills and attitudes increase their chances for survival considerably. Another form of compassion has materialized in the most unexpected place. Life is not perfect; helping one's neighbor sometimes compels people to confront another.

Jason knows he has an additional secret, but he is reluctant to share it with Hercules. Jason is convinced that he would not be able to keep up the strenuous schedule without his faith in God.

No matter how well he prepares and fights, there are those moments when a part of his body is exposed to deadly attacks. He prays for God's protection before he enters the arena, because he is absolutely sure that God has saved him from mortal wounds many times so far. When he leaves the arena, he thanks God for his mercy.

Jason's philosophy of life has changed a lot since he came in contact with the gospel of Christ. The motto for success he inherited from his grandfather (smart planning and hard work) contributed nothing from his side to the salvation Christ earned for him. Salvation is a gift from God. He accepted this gift in faith.

Furthermore, the good works he does after receiving the gift of salvation have been prepared by God for him so that he can practice them. Therefore, good works are also gifts of God. Jason has to acknowledge in humility that his planning and work only succeed when blessed by God.

One evening, while sitting on his mattress in the gladiator cells, his back resting against the wall, his eyes closed, praying, Hercules asks him about his religion.

"Christian," Jason says, without hesitation.

"How come you don't turn the other cheek?"

"The three rules of Hercules."

They chuckle, realizing the strange paradox.

"I'm Christian, too," professes Hercules, adding, "That's why I thought you needed the three rules. You looked like a nice guy to me. Maybe he's a Christian, like me, I thought. He needs the three rules. So I gave them to you."

"Believe me, Hercules, I really needed them. I'm soft-hearted by nature. I have a soft spot for underdogs. This attitude would have killed me if you had not put my head straight. Your three rules saved my life. Thanks."

"Now we are really blood brothers. We are brothers in the blood of Christ—our destiny. We are also brothers in the blood of the arena—our misery," Hercules concludes.

They shake hands. They are closer than ever.

"Hercules, I can see why the three rules are crucial for survival. However, how do we reconcile them with the rule of Jesus, loving one another as he loved us?"

"Yes, it is a paradox, an apparent contradiction," Hercules admits, and continues, "For me, the difference is in the situation. When I'm forced into a kill-or-be-killed situation, I should defend my God-given life with all my might, killing my adversary if necessary. The arena situation is not my choice; fighting to survive *is* my choice. I'm a victim of Roman injustice, and I have to endure this abuse in the hope of regaining my freedom in future. It's not a perfect choice, but it's the best

I have. Soldiers face the same choice in battle. Like us, they are also forced into kill-or-be-killed situations by the Roman authorities."

"I see what you're driving at," Jason concurs. He tries to digest what Hercules said by putting his thoughts in words: "Twice I ran away from my problems, but it did not work. I was repeatedly forced to defend myself in kill-or-be-killed situations: in the desert, jungle, court of law, on a pirate ship, and in the arena. I hate to kill, but when it's forced on me, I have to defend my life. Being a gladiator is not my choice, but I can choose to stay alive. Yes, I choose to be a victorious victim. We are not murderers going after other gladiators because we like killing, but like soldiers, we fight for our survival and freedom."

"Correct!" Hercules affirms. "Yes, that's about it."

After a few seconds of weighing the evidence, Jason wonders, "The logic seems convincing, but are we not just soothing our consciences, using excuses to justify our actions of surviving by killing? Some Christians refuse to serve as soldiers or to defend themselves against attacks. They choose martyrdom above self-defense. Are they not more Christ-like than us?" Jason still needs some convincing.

"I don't think so," Hercules responds. "Simon Peter visited me once in this place. I asked him similar questions, and he shared valuable insights with me. As Christians, we must follow Christ—right? With his first coming he was humble and meek, especially during his trial and crucifixion. However, his power sometimes did emerge: He forcefully cleansed the temple, and he scolded the Pharisees. With his return, he will destroy all his enemies. I think we must follow him not only in humility, but also in victory. Both should be given their appropriate place. The wise King Solomon said there is a time for war and a time for peace. Turning the other cheek means to ignore an insult. However, it does not mean Christians should be doormats to be walked over. We have the right to self-defense, like the Jews in the time of Esther," Hercules concludes his argument.

"Yes, that makes sense to me," Jason admits. "You know what? When I was still a kid, my grandfather said something similar to me. He said I must never question my right to defend my one precious life. He planted the seed, not knowing how it would sustain me in this horrible time."

"There you have it," Hercules concurs, adding, "Let's not forget that as a shepherd, David killed lions and bears so he and his flock may live; and as king, David subdued neighbor countries by war, securing peace for his people. Likewise, we have to prevail against our adversaries so we and our comrades may survive and regain our freedom."

"Yes, I suppose our trying ordeals serve the same purpose as our strenuous training: increasing our spiritual strength and stamina," Jason adds.

They discuss their strange predicament. They feel compelled to place high value on their God-given lives. To be is better than not to be. They have to fight to survive. In so doing, they keep the only escape route open: the possibility to be set free someday. Yes, like soldiers, they also fight for freedom. Refusing to fight in the arena would end in death, ending their options to life, freedom, and testifying for Christ. They are serving God's purpose for their lives to the best of their abilities in the most gruesome of circumstances.

Jason and Hercules are respected by the group for their skills, attitudes, and wise leadership. Though the two leaders don't advertise their Christian faith, it has become known to the rest of the group. Several men have asked them for guidance about Christianity. Without Nero's knowledge, the yeast of the gospel spreads slowly but surely among the Javelins. The Caesar still believes that Christians refuse to fight in the arena.

*

Nero informs Diana about the inter-dependent structure and functioning of the entertainment industry. It plays a major part in the empire's economy. In Rome and its colonies, the main entertainment for rich and poor is derived from the tavern, brothel, arena, circus, and theater. For unknown reasons, the Romans have not become addicted to the athletic games of Greece.

The word gladiator comes from the Roman word for sword, *gladius*, indicating the important role this weapon plays in the hand-to-hand combat performed in the arena to entertain the bored, bloodthirsty population. The word arena is derived from the Roman word for sand, *harena*, because the arenas are covered in a layer of sand that makes the removal of spilled blood easier.

The size of arenas varies from the small private arenas of the rich to those for the general public that can seat thousands. In the time of Nero, the Circus Maximus can hold 150,000 spectators. Though mass gladiator shows are occasionally presented there, this circus is actually famous for its chariot races.

The rich prefer small arenas for gladiator fights because it brings the spectators closer to the action. They can see up close the faces and muscles, the sweat and blood, and hear the breathing, grunts, and shouts of the gladiators, and the clatter of their weapons. In the arenas, people can watch state-sponsored violence without guilty feelings. The gladiators are either criminals who deserve the death sentence anyway, or they are professional fighters who chose this career voluntarily.

The Roman armies fight their battles far from Rome. Ordinary Romans don't see these spectacles. Gladiator fights give them a peek into real battles. The armor and weapons of some gladiators depict the fierce enemies of Rome while others represent the valiant soldiers of the empire. The crowd identifies with their heroes—their skills, their exertion, their determination, their injuries, and their victories.

The people in Rome and other cities have become soft, lazy, bored, spoiled, and demanding. There are more slaves than citizens. The state has to provide jobs, income, food, drinks, and entertainment.

The self-sustaining entertainment business is one of the major engines of the economy. It creates jobs for many people all over the empire. The trapping, transport, and feeding of wild animals for the arenas keep many busy. Elephant, rhino, buffalo, and lion are caught in Central Africa and transported via the Nile and Mediterranean to Roman arenas. Tigers come from eastern countries and brown bears from northern regions. These animals, brought from afar, highlight the vastness and power of the Roman Empire and enhance the pride of a conceited nation. Sometimes hundreds of animals are killed on a single day in a large arena.

Slaves and prisoners-of-war have to be captured, fed, transported, and trained to perform as gladiators. Charioteers and horses need continuous training to outsmart the competition. Actors in the theaters have to be trained and paid.

The industry takes money, but also generates money. It provides income for the people, and in turn, they spend much of their income on entertainment. Thus, the economic cycle is self-perpetuating: workers sustain the entertainment industry, and this industry sustains the workers. Whenever the economy slows down, the Caesar organizes massive shows in the arenas to give a boost to the cycle of entertainment.

Diana realizes that Jason is just one bee in a hive, one grain of sand on the beach. His life means nothing to the Caesar or the spectators.

*

Jason's life and love are precious for Tabitha. Her heart goes out to him all the time, lifting him up to God's throne of mercy. She strengthens herself from the scripture passages she has been hearing since childhood. She repeats the line from

Psalm 23 often: "Even though I walk through the valley of the shadow of death, I will fear no evil, for you are with me; your rod and your staff, they comfort me."

Tabitha beseeches God to make these words a reality for Jason, too.

The days become weeks, and the weeks become months. Sometimes her faith fails her, exasperated by unanswered prayers. In despair, she wonders if Jason will survive, and if so, when he will be released. She knows that from the human perspective, her hope is unfounded. However, she refuses to adopt this approach. She steadfastly sticks to the divine viewpoint—for God, nothing is impossible.

When despair pushes her down, she recites Paul's words that everything works out for good to those who love God. She embraces Jesus' words that He gives rest to those who are weary and burdened.

She asks the rabbi for passages from scripture that can sustain her with new power when her faith fails her. Because she was a scroll copier in Alexandria, the rabbi allows her to copy several passages from the synagogue scrolls onto paper so that she can read them over and over at home. Two of her favorites are Psalms 40 and 91:

[1] I waited patiently for the LORD;
    he turned to me and heard my cry.
[2] He lifted me out of the slimy pit,
    out of the mud and mire;
he set my feet on a rock
    and gave me a firm place to stand.
[3] He put a new song in my mouth,
    a hymn of praise to our God.
    Many will see and fear
    and put their trust in the LORD.[39]

---

39 Ps. 40:1-3 NIV

¹¹ For He shall give His angels charge over you,
To keep you in all your ways.
¹² In *their* hands they shall bear you up,
Lest you dash your foot against a stone.
¹³ You shall tread upon the lion and the cobra,
The young lion and the serpent you shall
trample underfoot.
¹⁴ "Because he has set his love upon Me, therefore I
will deliver him;
I will set him on high, because he has known My
name.[40]

Tabitha fights against the evil spirits who try to wear her down. Jason has his physical battles in the arena and his emotional and spiritual struggles in the gladiator quarters. Occasionally, the Krato nightmare still pops up—mixed up with Jason's arena struggles. Often the opponent in his dream turns out to be Krato.

By faith in God, they tackle every day on its own, trusting that his grace will be sufficient for that day.

---

40 Ps. 91:11-14

CHAPTER 15

The group spirit of Nero's elite group is excellent until a bad apple is thrown into their midst. He is soon nicknamed Golla (a merge of Goliath and gorilla), a fitting description of his stature, strength, and attitude.

This guy is a seven-foot giant. He has a heavy bone structure—every part of his body is massive. His big head rests on a thick neck, sloping onto broad shoulders. He could probably lift an ox with his broad back and huge hairy chest. Though his arms do not show individual muscles, his massive arms with colossal hands and fingers—looking like banana bunches—can squash one's head as if it were a ripe peach. His pillar-like legs don't show definition, but no one would like to be kicked by his foot, nor bumped by his knee. His long untidy black hair and beard make him look like a man of the wild.

He has the attitude of an alpha male, intimidating everybody. From the start, his domineering attitude is obvious, "Give me that! Stand aside! Move over, this is my place! What are you staring at? I'm strong; don't mess with me!"

Nobody dares to oppose the arrogant bastard. His heavy frame and thick arms will crush anybody's ribs. He is disliked, feared, and avoided.

Jason and Hercules occasionally glance at each other, trying to show no emotion. Deep inside, they fear that sooner or later this guy will force a confrontation on them. Though they are also tall, sturdy fellows, none of them would like to take on this grumpy buffalo. It will take a team effort to subdue him, and even then, many will get hurt.

"Maybe we should first try to befriend him," Jason whispers to Hercules, "then we can see what is behind that fierce facade."

Hercules nods, "Yes, let's try."

When the elite group works out the next day, Golla slowly paces through the place as if it belongs to him. He does not train; he feels he doesn't need it. He can finish off any opponent without any exercises. Golla approaches Jason and Hercules, where they are lifting heavy stones onto a six-foot high wooden platform.

With a knowing smile, Golla mumbles, "Let me show you." He picks up the stone from the ground with his massive hands, straightens up quickly, and with a mighty heave, he hurls the stone several feet into the air. When it comes down, it crushes the wooden scaffold to pieces.

"So much for your stupid little pebble game," Golla grumbles, dusting off his hands, and walking off as if nothing happened.

Jason and Hercules go down on their haunches, look in disbelief at each other with widened eyes, and then burst into laughter. Golla really made them look feeble.

"What the hell are you laughing at?" growls the brute, towering above them like a grizzly bear on his hind legs.

"Man, you are phenomenal," Hercules remarks. "Here we struggle and sweat to put that darn stone on the platform, and you hurled it into the air like a sponge."

Golla enjoys the admiration, "Ah, that's nothing!"

"You will be a great help to our group in the arena," Jason tries to get in on the conversation.

"Every man for himself," Golla responds bluntly. "Don't expect me to cover your backs."

Hercules tries some flattering again: "You are fantastic! You should be a general in the army. Why did they put you in this joint?"

"None of your business!" growls the big man, walking off slowly with a swaggering gait.

Jason and Hercules decide that being grumpy is probably Golla's natural state of mind. It is better to leave him in peace. Hopefully, he will leave them in peace, too.

In the arena the next day, Golla plays around with his opponent for a while, finishes him off, and then watches at leisure how the other gladiators struggle against their opponents. He does not know Nero.

Suddenly, four stalwart gladiators enter the arena and attack Golla from all sides with their swords. They make fake moves at him to wear him down. He has to dance around to ward off rear attacks. Jason sees Golla is in trouble. He is too slow to get to his attackers. Before he can get to one, the others move in from the rear, like a clan of hyenas attacking a lone lioness.

Jason swiftly finishes off his opponent and runs to Golla. "I'll cover your back!" Jason shouts.

Jason and Golla stand back-to-back. Now they each have only two opponents. With his stab-spear, Jason soon eliminates one of his attackers. The other one fights viciously for his life. Once Golla fatally wounds one of his opponents, he quickly overcomes the second one. When he turns around to help Jason, he is just in time to see how Jason slashes his opponent's arm, ending the fight with a debilitating stab to the right shoulder.

That evening at supper, Golla comes and sits near Jason and Hercules. He doesn't talk, but smiles when they enjoy a joke. He is a silent partner to their conversation.

"What crime landed you here, Hercules?" Jason inquires.

"A Roman officer forced himself onto my sister. I knocked him down. He fell with his head against a stone wall and died of a head injury. Nero found me guilty of murder. Because of my size, he sent me to this gladiator school. What was your crime?" Hercules asks Jason.

"I was kidnapped by pirates. To survive, I played the game and became one of them. I worked my way up through the ranks and became second-in-command. When the captain was killed, I took his place."

"You, a pirate captain? Jason, I can't believe you!"

Hercules is stunned. Golla smiles and shakes his head.

Jason continues: "I refurbished the ship with a ram, and became a security guard for freighters. We sank a dozen pirate ships with the giant spear. Some of the pirates we handed over to Roman authorities told the Romans I was a pirate posing as a security guard. When the Romans searched my ship, they found an old pirate flag in a box on the bottom deck. They accused me of piracy. Nero found me guilty and sent me here."

"Incredible!" Hercules exclaims.

"I killed two Roman soldiers who were sent to arrest me," Golla suddenly chimes in. "I took them by the necks and smashed their heads against each other. I didn't think soldiers died that easily."

All three start giggling. They imagine the mighty Golla with the two soldiers dangling in his big hands.

"How did they arrest you in the end?" asks Hercules.

"They send a whole platoon with spears, bows, and arrows; I surrendered. I didn't want them to poke me full of holes," Golla dryly comments.

Loosened up a little, he suddenly turns to Jason, "Thanks for covering my back today, man. I just couldn't fend off so many attacks all at once. I became tired. I must increase my fitness. I said I wouldn't cover your back, but you covered mine. I now realize we are all vulnerable. We need each other. Thanks again. I hope I can repay you someday."

Golla's big-ego defense system soon fades away, revealing an amicable person with dry humor. Jason and Hercules have won over a strong and loyal ally.

*

When Caesar's elite group under Hercules' leadership excels, Nero thinks up new ways to display their strength, speed, and stamina—humiliating other gladiator schools in the process. In this way, he exposes them to escalating dangers.

Today, Nero has invited his friends and their families to a special showdown between his elite gladiators, the Javelins, and a rival school, the Assassins, that aspires to replace the Javelins as the champion team of Rome. The emperor has invited Diana and Akton to sit with him in his booth and share in the excitement.

The event takes place in Caesar's small private arena, oval in shape, about thirty paces long, and enclosed by a fifteen-foot wall. Above the wall, on the west side of the arena, there is an amphitheater with five rows of seats. During afternoon performances, the spectators do not face the sun. In the small arena they can see, hear, and feel the aggression, exertion, pain, and triumph of the fighters, becoming one with them.

About two hundred spectators wait excitedly for the brutal showdown to get going. They will watch the two best teams of Rome competing for dominance.

Thirty Javelins enter the arena, delivering their bone-chilling war cry before the show starts. They repeat it twice with gusto.

To increase the tension, five Javelins are equipped with stab-spears only, while five Assassins are armed with shields and swords. Not weaponry, but skill will determine the outcome. The other gladiators are locked up in cells from where they can watch the fighting through barred windows in the arena wall.

It thrills Nero's private audience to see how the Javelins overpower the Assassins with sheer speed and power, dexterity, and ingenuity. The stab-spears of the Javelins clatter against the swords and shields of the Assassins. By moving their arms back and forth in quick succession, the Javelins hit the Assassins from top to bottom. A hit to the chest with the spearhead is immediately followed by a hit on the shin with the spear handle. In the next moment, the handle hits the head, and the blade, the leg. The movements of the Javelins are so swift that their opponents retreat and fight defensively. However, it is not only the Assassins who shed blood. The elite group leaves the arena with some nasty wounds and bruises, too. When the best gladiators of Rome compete, no one gets an easy ride. As a gesture of sportsmanship, Nero grants mercy to the wounded. They may live to fight another day.

In the next event, Nero and his challenger put their gladiators two-by-two up against brown bears or African buffalos. The crowd decides which team thrills them the most. The teams want to make a good impression without losing their best gladiators; therefore, they put two men against one of these dangerous animals.

Though the men do not escape unscathed, they manage to kill the animals with cooperated attacks. While a buffalo hurls an Assassin into the air, his mate attacks from the side, driving his sword through the animal's heart. While a huge brown bear slams a Javelin to the ground and pounces on him, his comrade rushes forward and pierces the bear's heart with a spear.

It thrills the spectators to watch how these colossal beasts are overpowered by mere men—tiny in comparison. The crowd identifies with the victorious gladiators, boosting their egos, and reinforcing in their minds the myth of Roman invincibility. Conveniently, they ignore the fact that most of the gladiators are not Roman. In this event, the crowd favors the Assassins.

Nero now calls three Javelins—Jason, Hercules, and Golla—into the arena, and challenges the Assassins to put six of their men against them. The three Javelins, armed with spears and swords, stand in a triangle, backs together, facing outward. They know they must keep this formation to protect themselves. If one of them is overcome, the chances of two against six will be extremely slim.

The six Assassins attack cautiously at first, but with increasing fervor as the fight becomes more intense. Jason and his two friends fend off the attackers without exerting themselves too much, allowing the Assassins to do most of the work, exhausting themselves in their zeal. Fast spear-stabs to the heads and legs of the attackers make them cautious and keep them at bay.

Suddenly, Hercules shouts, "Now!"

All three Javelins jump forward, each stabbing an opponent with the spear. Now, they can concentrate on one opponent each. They break up their triangular formation, each pursuing his quarry. They play around with their opponents for a while, entertaining the crowd. After another "Now!" from Hercules, they finish the fight quickly. Four of the victims are not dead, but seriously wounded in the hip or shoulder. Nero gives the thumbs-up signal of mercy, sparing their lives. Most likely, they will never fight again, but take early retirement. Being gracious toward the rival club may pay off later.

The spectators cheer. Nero waves at the victors. The three walk out of the arena, Golla in the middle, his huge arms resting on the shoulders of his two "brothers." The trio prevailed once more. In this event, the Javelins are the undisputed winners.

*

There is an intermission, and refreshments are served to the emperor's guests. The owner of the Assassins challenges Nero to a duel between their champions. The challenger specifically asks for Jason.

Caesar is in a tight spot. If he backs down to save Jason for Diana's sake, he gives his rival an emotional victory. He knows Jason is excellent. He accepts the challenge, hoping that Jason will not disappoint him.

After the intermission, a fight between two champions is announced.

Jason enters from one side of the small arena, and his opponent from the other side. They have the same armor, so no one will have an advantage. Their tanned upper bodies are naked, protected only by two crossed leather bands running from hips over opposite shoulders. The visors of their helmets are down. Both are armed with a javelin.

Two paces from each other, they halt and lift their visors as a courtesy gesture toward one another in the arena of death. One of them could die shortly.

A cold chill runs down Jason's spine. He looks into the face of his archenemy.

"Krato?" Jason exclaims in disbelief.

With a hoarse voice, Krato taunts, "Yes, Jason, we meet again! The last time we met, you busted my throat and destroyed my career. Today, you will pay for that. Today it is man-to-man, slave boy. Dirty tricks won't save you now."

"You have only yourself to blame. Why has the valiant centurion fallen so low?" Jason teases, smiling.

"When the army realized I faked my death in Cyrene, they fired me. When I learned from my friends in Corinth you had been condemned to Caesar's elite gladiator school, I joined a rival group as professional gladiator. I proved myself, and then suggested to my owner that I should have a duel with you. I once said that the arena is the only place where I can kill you legally. Finally, that day has come."

"Don't sell the skin before you've killed the lion," Jason remarks dryly.

They turn toward Caesar's pavilion, march closer, halt, salute the emperor, and remove their helmets to identify themselves, showing no secret switches were made.

Akton and Diana sit behind Nero. Up till now, they could not identify individual gladiators because of the helmets they wear. Akton is shocked when he recognizes Jason. Leaning forward, Akton whispers to Nero:

"Sire, your gladiator, the taller one, is the guy who invented the wonder grease I use on your chariots, securing your victories in the Circus Maximus."

Hoping Caesar will call off the confrontation, Akton adds enthusiastically, "Sire, he's a brilliant inventor. Just think what he can do for your navy and army!"

Nero weighs the information for a few seconds.

"I can't stop the fight now. It will be a victory for the opposition," Nero decides, intensifying Akton's concern.

Diana, too, has recognized Jason and Krato.

"Sire, I know both men. They are my friends," she says with a squeaking voice, near crying. Desperate, she tries to buy time for her friends, "They were champions in the javelin event at the Isthmian Games. Please, let them compete and show off their spear-throwing skills. They are excellent; the spectators will be thrilled."

Nero's cruel and crooked mind immediately thinks of a gruesome way to thrill the bloodthirsty crowd. He commands the centurion to bring the Christian condemned for treason against Caesar, and to crucify him right there in the arena. The crime and sentence of the man are announced.

A lone, slow-rhythm kettledrum accentuates the gravity of the sentence. The small military band has played at many arena shows—they match their music to the action.

The spectators heckle the poor victim, squirming as the nails are driven through his hands and feet, suffering the worst form of execution Rome ever devised.

With the cross erected, Nero tells the centurion, "Introduce Jason and Krato by name as the javelin champions of the Isthmian Games. They will now show their skill by throwing their spears from fifteen paces at the heart of the crucified man. The one hitting the target will be the winner of this event."

The centurion makes the announcement.

"Lunatic!" Jason hisses. Fortunately, Caesar does not hear him.

Jason can't throw a spear at a crucified man—it would be like throwing a spear at Christ, his Savior.

"Come on, Jason!" Krato taunts. "Relieve the poor guy of his misery. You are a fellow Christian, aren't you?"

A little plank with the man's sentence written on it hangs above his head on the cross. It gives Jason an idea. The cross is short; the man's feet are only a few inches above ground.

While the kettledrums roll, Jason lifts his spear. He aims, pulls his arm back, and hurls the spear with power and anger. Accompanied by one loud cymbal, the spear hits the charge-plank right in the center, splitting it into pieces. The javelin missed the man's head with a few inches. The spear sticks to the cross, its rear end swinging up and down. Unaware of Jason's motives, the crowd boos him for missing the target Nero specified.

"Shame! You missed, Jason!" Krato jokes.

Now it is Krato's turn. He has no sympathy for Christians. Against the same musical backdrop, Krato pulls his arm back and hurls the spear with deadly force and accuracy, hitting the crucified man in the center of his chest. For a moment, the victim pushes up on the spikes in his dying convulsion, and then his body collapses. His head falls forward on his chest. He's dead. His suffering is over.

The spectators cheer and start chanting, "Krato! Krato! Krato!"

He is now the crowd's favorite.

Jason's contempt for Caesar's charge against Christians has not gone unnoticed by the shrewd eyes of the emperor. He is going to tighten the vice. He will not protect them against each other any longer for Diana's sake.

The centurion announces Caesar's next command: "A swordfight between the champions—without shields."

Each of the gladiators receives a sword. Jason realizes, *God has prepared me over several years for this fight. My pirate training may now fall into place. That dirty fighting may help me survive Krato's assault. He is a well-trained Roman warrior, for whom the sword is bread and butter. I cannot flee from him now. I must subdue the brute—or get killed myself. Will the underdog at long last become the top dog?*

Jason's strong hand clamps the sword handle with determination.

A fanfare signals the start of the duel.

Jason does not engage in a sword clattering display. He fakes moves, following them up quickly by real jabs or slashes. Krato has a problem with Jason's unorthodox style. Sudden attacks to his head or legs make him feel vulnerable. When protecting his legs, his body is open for a sudden upward slash of Jason's sword.

However, Krato is a seasoned Roman soldier. He has fought in several battles and prevailed over many enemies. He, too, has some tricks up his sleeve. His reflexes are agile. With swift-footed moves, he evades Jason's slashes. His blocking movements are quick and precise. By not attacking at first, he makes Jason think he is gaining the upper hand. Then, Krato delivers a combination of fast offensive maneuvers. His sword gives Jason a shallow cut on the left chest muscle. It draws blood.

Jason realizes he won't win a fair sword fight with Krato. Jason resolves to fight this battle on his terms, not Krato's. He has to use his pirate tricks to the full and end this duel as soon as possible.

They both move forward, their swords lock, and their faces are close for a few moments as they try to push each other back. Each feels the other's breath, smells his sweat, and senses his tension.

"I'm going to kill you!" Krato hisses in Jason's face.

Jason lifts his right knee fast, hitting Krato in his testes. Krato folds with a groan. The next moment, Jason's knee hits the side of Krato's face with force. Jason could have stabbed him, but refrained from killing his rival. He wants to overcome Krato in a different way, either disabling him for good by a shoulder-stab, or by facilitating a change of heart.

Jason's knee-blow makes Krato stagger backwards, dizzy and bewildered by Jason's weird methods. His defense is inadequate, leaving him open for attack.

Jason attacks viciously. His sword cuts a shallow flesh wound in Krato's left shoulder. Blood trickles down. Krato realizes the softy he has teased and humiliated all his life has developed into a superior and hardened, fearless gladiator. Krato's fear makes him retreat, trying to get away from this fighting machine.

They pass the cross with the dead body still hanging on it. Unexpectedly, Jason moves toward the crucified man and plucks the spears from the cross and the body. He passes one spear to Krato, and takes the other one in his left hand. Now Jason feels more at home. He can give Krato a lesson in stab-spear fighting.

Krato grabs the spear Jason supplied. Krato holds his spear in his right hand at shoulder height, ready to throw. Jason holds his javelin at hip level, ready to stab.

The scene of Jason's recurring nightmare is now being played out in reality. *In the dream, I could not sidestep Krato's approaching spear. Will I succeed now?*

They are only a few paces from each other. They move around in a circle, seeking an opening for an attack, making fake moves, and trying to catch the opponent on the wrong foot.

Jason must come close to stab, which makes him vulnerable to Krato's throw. At such a short distance, Jason may not be able to sidestep Krato's javelin.

Krato's throw is swift. Jason ducks to avoid it. The spear lands ten paces behind Jason—he has not fallen prey to the lameness of the nightmare. Before Jason can get up, Krato storms forward, dives on Jason, and pins him to the ground by forcing the handle of Jason's spear on his neck. The obsession to subdue Jason with brutal force drives Krato to use this method instead of his sword. Krato applies all his power and weight onto the spear in a vicious effort to throttle his opponent. Jason is pinned down on his back. He is literally the underdog again. He grabs the spear with both hands and tries to push the spear, with Krato on top, away from his air pipe.

For a minute or two, their efforts are equal. The two muscular young men strain against each other. The veins on their necks and arms swell. Their faces turn red. Their muscles bulge. Their tanned bodies shine with sweat. Not one of them makes any progress. Who will crack first?

Diana knows what will happen if Krato wins this pushing match—he will not stop before he has squeezed all life out of Jason. She prays that Jason's God will empower him to get Krato off his chest.

As fatigue sets in, Jason's superior fitness prevails. His relentless training with Hercules over the past months pays off. Slowly, he pushes Krato and the spear away from his throat. He lifts Krato up, swiftly pulls up his legs, and kicks Krato with both feet in the tummy. Krato lands on his back several paces away. Both get back on their feet as fast as possible, resuming their duel. Krato is now without his spear, and Jason without his sword.

Once again, Jason is the terrifying pirate. His muscular torso leans forward. With knees slightly bent, his leg muscles play beneath his tanned skin with every step. Holding the javelin with both hands for stab-spear fighting, his strong arms are ready for attack. Krato notices Jason has put on a lot of muscle since he last saw him in Cyrene.

Jason drives Krato back with dexterous combinations of spear jabs to Krato's head and legs. Krato exhausted himself when he tried to throttle Jason. He is out of breath. His lungs burn, and he gasps for air. He does not have the strength to attack. He fights defensively, trying to shield off Jason's blows, now coming to his head and legs in quick succession. Krato begins to realize he will not win this fight.

As he retreats, he stumbles. His sword falls. In the next moment, Jason towers over him, the tip of his spear on Krato's chest. Jason's black eyes stare mercilessly into Krato's yellow ones, which are wide with fear. Now Krato is the underdog. Jason's desire to overpower Krato eventually has come true, in an unexpected place.

However, Jason cannot help to pity the brute.

Having overstressed their bodies, both breathe heavily.

"Why are your eyes so wide, Krato? Is the Roman centurion…afraid to die?" Jason taunts his powerless opponent, pricking Krato's chest with the spearhead.

"The slave boy you despised…is now on top of you, merciless bully!" Jason rubs it in, "If Caesar gives the thumbs-down signal…I have to drive this spear through your evil heart. How does that grab you, mister invincible?" Krato gets another prick.

Deep inside, Jason hopes Nero will spare Krato's life. Jason glances towards Nero's seat, waiting for the Caesar's signal. If the emperor gives the opposite signal, will he be able to thrust the javelin into Krato's heart? Is this how his nightmare will end—with a gesture from a callous emperor?

Diana pleads with Nero to spare her friend's life. The crowd likes Krato and gives the thumbs-up signal, calling for mercy. Nero does not want to finish this interesting duel so soon. He has some other mean plans in mind. He decides to please Diana and the crowd, and grants mercy.

Jason maintains his threatening posture, lifting his spear with both hands above Krato's chest, ready to strike.

"No, Jason, no!" Diana yells.

Jason drives his spear down with full force. The crowd responds with a collective groan. Has Jason misread Nero's signal? The spear sticks into the ground, only three inches from Krato's chest. When Krato stands up unharmed, the spectators cheer the emperor's decision long and loudly—glad their hero has been spared.

Now they are even. Krato won the first event, Jason the second. Nero's wicked mind devises a new perilous test. Instead of having them fight against each other, he decides to let them fight with each other against a common foe. Will these rivals help or betray one another when both are threatened by the same danger? Nero has a bright idea. He whispers his orders to the centurion.

The swords and spears are removed from the arena.

*

Amid the usual introduction of sounding drums and trumpets, a huge black bull with formidable crescent horns is released into the arena. Agitated, it moves around, kicking up sand with its front hooves, searching for the enemy it has been trained to demolish. Jason and Krato have only their bare hands to defend themselves. There are no handy steps by which they can exit the ring when the beast is on their heels.

Krato's steer-wrestling experience may be of value now. However, he has never faced a bull of this size or with such dangerous horns and such a thick neck.

Jason sends up a quick prayer for courage and power.

"When it storms, I will take it by the horns," Krato insists. "Then, you must help me to break its neck."

"Break its neck?" Jason reacts in disbelief. "Krato, that's a full grown bull, not a steer!" Jason warns.

"Nevermind! We have no other choice!" Krato shouts, ready to tackle the devil himself. The strategy looks crazy, but it is all they have. Krato has been invigorated by the crowd's support. He has caught his second breath. The adrenaline is pumping.

The bull has worked up enough courage and anger. It is ready to charge. Krato slowly approaches the agitated animal, taunting him with jerky forward movements.

The bull storms forward with lowered head, horns pointing forward like lances, ready to gore Krato and hurl him into the air.

When the bull is five paces from him, Krato moves backwards while facing the bull, limiting the impact of the bull's head on his body. Krato folds over the bull's head, his chest on the bull's neck, his hands grabbing the horns, and his legs crossed underneath the bull's jaw. The beast swings him up and down, left and right, unable to rid himself of the thing that has fixed itself on his head, blocking his vision. Krato clings to the bull's head like an octopus.

Jason moves in quickly, positions himself against the bull's neck, grabs the horns, and together they twist the bull's head sideways...farther...farther...until the animal loses its balance and falls over on its side.

Using the massive horns as levers, they now turn the bull's head in the opposite direction, preventing the animal from rolling over. Relentlessly, the two sturdy men keep on turning the bull's head, but they just cannot break its neck. Their brown muscular bodies glisten with sweat. Their energy is tapped.

The bull kicks wildly, trying to get up. If they lose control, they will be in trouble.

"Let me help you!" It is Golla's voice. He knocked the gatekeeper down and rushed into the arena to help his friends. With Golla's mighty arms, they turn the bull's head until the neck snaps. The beast has a few convulsions, and then lies still. Soon, it will be dragged out by horses and slaughtered for Caesar's palace. Arenas are extensions of abattoirs; the meat of the killed animals is not wasted.

Jason and Krato rise as exhausted victors. They give Golla the Roman handshake and pat him gratefully on the back. Both of them are winners in this event, thanks to their cooperation and the intervention of their colossal friend. The spectators have enjoyed the brutal test of strength between man and beast.

Although Jason and Krato are still equal, the crowd favors Krato—he had the guts to grab the bull by the horns. They show who their hero is by chanting, "Krato! Krato!"

Golla leaves the arena. From now on, the barred iron gate will be locked. Golla will see them, but he will be unable to help them again.

What will the merciless Nero think up next?

*

Officials throw two spears into the arena. Jason and Krato each take one. Will the next test be against...?

The rasping growls of lions answer their question.

The kettledrums roll, the trumpets sound.

"Oh, my God, have mercy!" Jason sighs.

Two lions are released into the arena. One is a lioness, the other a young male with small mane. Nero wants to see how far the two opponents will go in cooperating against a common foe. Instead of one bull, there are now two lions. What can two spears do against ferocious, hungry lions? If one of the two men survives the lion attack, he may or may not help the other. Will hate or compassion dictate their behavior?

Diana, consumed by fear and stress, bites her nails and prays for God's mercy.

Although her friends are so close that she can discern their facial expressions, she is powerless to end the insane power-game of the cold-blooded Caesar.

Nero smiles with delight, intrigued by human and animal nature, and relishing the mounting tension in the arena and on the stands. The emperor is giving his guests a memorable afternoon. Many couples hold hands. Their grips are tight, their knuckles white, their hearts galloping in excited anticipation of the inevitable.

After pacing to and fro for a while, summing up the situation, the two lions approach their prey. The lioness stalks Jason, the lion chooses Krato.

Each man has worked out a strategy against the enemy. Jason decides to throw his spear form about eight paces. Krato decides to wait for the moment the lion raises up against him, planning to stab him from below.

Jason can now use the advice he received from Bari in the Sudan: *When a lion comes straight at you, go for the soft spot at the bottom of its neck.*

To improve the angle of his throw, Jason kneels on his right knee. His right arm, holding the spear, is already stretched backwards for the throw.

The lioness slowly approaches Jason, her head low, ears flattened. If Jason were to run away, her instincts would make her chase the prey. However, this motionless prey, staring fearlessly at her, makes the lioness hesitate.

Jason prays in his heart that God will guide his javelin to the right spot.

The soft spot below the lioness' neck is shielded by her lowered head. Jason's spear can't reach it. When the lioness is about eight paces from him, Jason waves his left arm and shouts, "Ya! Ya!"

The lioness stops, surprised, uncertain, lifting her head, and exposing her chest. At that moment, the lion pounces with a snarl on Krato. Distracted, the lioness glances for a moment in that direction.

Jason throws his spear with full force at the soft spot where her air pipe enters her body. The movement is so swift that some spectators miss it. The spear glides right through her heart. Her legs collapse under her body; she falls down with a grunt. After a few convulsions, she's dead.

"Thank God!" Jason sighs. If the spearhead has hit the lioness only three inches to the left or right, Jason would have faced a wounded lioness.

He glances in Krato's direction. The lion is on top of him. Krato misjudged the power of a lion. Before he could use his spear, he was slammed down by the lion's big paw. His spear was broken like a twig.

Jason quickly pulls his spear from the dead lioness, and without any hesitation, rushes toward the lion mauling Krato. While running, Jason hurls the javelin as hard as he can, hitting the lion in the ribs behind the shoulder blade. The beast rears up, striking with its forepaws at an invisible foe, while the terrible pain grips his mighty body.

Jason has no weapon now. If the lion turns on him, he will be history.

Then the lion sees him, and pounces in his direction with a fierce growl, the spear stuck in the lion's ribcage.

Its second pounce throws Jason to the ground. The wounded lion lands on top of him. For a moment, Jason thinks he will be mauled. When the lion does not move, he realizes the javelin has done its work. The lion is dead, the spear shaft is broken in two.

Jason rushes to Krato. He is still conscious. He has protected his neck and face with his arms. His left forearm has been crushed and lacerated by the lion's mighty jaws. His right forearm has deep wounds, too. His face is covered with blood. He suffered a heavy blow to his head by the lion's forepaw, its nails leaving bloody stripes on his brow.

Before the cruel Nero can come up with another mean trick, Diana climbs over the rails, down into the arena. She hangs by her hands, and then jumps down to the ground, determined to help Jason with Krato's wounds. Her concern for her friend has superseded her fear of the emperor.

Krato is in shock. Tremors run through him from head to toe. He shivers like a poisoned dog. Diana rips her dress into strips and makes pressure dressings to stop the bleeding from Krato's arms.

The mood of the spectators shifts. By risking their lives for Krato, Jason and Diana's compassion kindled the crowd's empathy and goodwill. They appreciate the help extended to their hero. Instead of calling for blood, the crowd cheers them on and calls for mercy. Fortunately for Krato, Jason was swift enough to spear the lion before it could do more damage to Krato.

Shivering in shock and pain, his teeth clattering, Krato mumbles, "Thanks, Jason...you saved...my life...I release you... from the curse...you're free...forgiven."

While helping Diana to nurse Krato's wounds, Jason— still breathing heavily—responds, "I forgive you too, Krato. You messed up my life...but God brought us together today... in an awesome manner...fighting for each other. Someday...we may understand it better."

Jason experiences a wonderful, inner sense of relief and freedom.

He is still a prisoner, condemned to a gladiator life, but he feels free. Instead of killing Krato, he saved his life. Their bitter rivalry did not end in murder, but in compassion. Light has triumphed over darkness, forgiveness over bitterness.

The Krato nightmare has ended, the burden is gone. Victim victory is sweet.

*

Jason has only a minute to savor his relief. A door in the arena wall opens. A guard enters, holding a handcuffed young woman by her arm. Jason's face turns white with shock—it's Tabitha! What sinister plan has Nero's sadistic mind in store for them? What wrong could she have done to deserve this torture? What a terrible place to be reunited after a year of painful separation!

Jason runs to Tabitha, embraces her, and whispers, "Darling, what happened?"

The guard does not try to push the tall, muscular gladiator aside. He wouldn't dare. He was ordered to allow the doomed husband and wife a minute together, giving the crowd the opportunity to take in the gravity of the situation. Nero's evil mind wants to increase the agony in the arena and on the stand. He has corralled the four Corinthian friends into his arena. The mighty emperor thinks he has full control.

The spectators are curious onlookers, wondering what the relationship between Jason and the two women may be. Then the announcer's voice rings through the arena, "Gladiator Jason will now defend his pretty young wife, Tabitha, and his friends, Diana and Krato, against a lion and two spotted hyenas."

"Oh no!" the crowd groans when the cruelty of the evil moment grabs them.

Drums, cymbals, and trumpets work up a crescendo.

The guard ties Tabitha to a post near the arena wall. Amid the slow, ominous beats of a bass drum, another guard approaches with a bucket filled with blood, collected from the bull Jason and his friends killed a while ago. The guard dips a brush into the blood and paints two vertical dark-red stripes on Tabitha's dress, from her shoulders to her knees. Then he splashes blood drops on the ground with the brush, dipping it occasionally in the blood as he walks in a half-circle to the opening where the hyenas will be released. Obviously, they want the hyenas to attack Tabitha while Jason faces the lion.

"May God protect us against this evildoer," Jason whispers to Tabitha.

Tabitha briefs Jason about her presence in the arena: "Nero sent a senator to Corinth a month ago. He lured me to Rome with the promise that my personal plea may convince the emperor to release you. I grabbed the straw, no matter how small the chances were. Since my arrival in Rome, I've been kept in custody, pending an audience with Caesar. Now he has brought me into the arena for his perverse entertainment."

Nero secretly plans to release Jason and Tabitha as a surprise birthday gift to Diana. He wants to do it in style, though, at the pinnacle of agony. If they are killed, well, then it's just too bad, pure bad luck dealt to them by fate. Most likely, their demise will give him even more pleasure than their freedom. Not knowing which way the gods will make the ax fall excites the shallow emotions of the callous emperor.

Nero gives the order to release the hyenas. The two disgusting, black-faced creatures burst into the arena—aroused, manes and tails raised, uttering their unnerving, devilish giggles as they rush back and forth, trying to sum up the situation. They stop at the carcass of the lioness Jason killed, nervously sniffing at the lifeless body of their archenemy. Their sensitive nostrils soon pick up the blood trail. They start sniffing the ground, moving in Tabitha's direction. A kettledrum-roll reflects the rising tension.

Jason is still at her side. He remembers how Bari scared off these fierce-looking but cowardly creatures in Africa. Jason plucks his broken spear from the dead lion. Jason jumps forward, stamps his feet, and waves his arms, yelling, "Wha! Wha! Wha!" The hyenas see several humans and hear the crowd shouting. They feel outnumbered, turn tail with moaning howls, and seek refuge at the far end of the arena wall.

Nero gives the signal to release the lion. He hopes that will distract Jason's attention from the hyenas. Nero does not know the ways of the wild.

A kettledrum-roll, ended with a few strokes on the bass drum and cymbals, announces the entrance of the king of beasts. A majestic lion enters slowly and confidently. It is a big male with beautiful mane. It utters a few snarls and growls, telling everybody who's the boss. The hyenas crouch down submissively, anxiously dripping urine as they see their fiercest enemy so close by while they are hemmed in by the wall.

"Oh, my God!" Diana gasps. Now she also knows how it feels to be in the arena with a vicious lion. Tabitha prays in her heart that God will work a miracle to thwart the plans of the mean emperor.

The crisis turns everything upside down. The mighty Krato is now just a pathetic, pitiful pile of misery. Blood loss, pain, and shock make him slip in and out of coma. Diana, the pagan prostitute, prays to the unknown God for help against the Caesar she serves with her body. Tabitha, the resilient Christian wife and mother, is horrified by the hideous cruelty meted out to her and her beloved. The underdog, Jason, has become the top dog, guarding his wife and friends against deadly predators.

The perception, attitude, and behavior of the spectators have been changing, too. They hate Nero's meanness towards the young couple. The valiance and friendship of the four young people have conquered their hearts. They no longer view them as condemned criminals who forfeited their right to live, but as fellow human beings, young people with names and families.

Jason is as tensed as the string of a bow. This is really bad! The spears are broken. He can use a broken spear as a dagger, but what will such a puny weapon achieve against a full-grown lion? What can Diana and the tied-up Tabitha do to keep the hyenas at bay? These animals are notorious for ripping living prey apart by their powerful jaws that can crush the thigh bones of antelope.

The lion scans the arena. He sees the two dead lions. Then he sees and smells his archrivals, the hyenas. Maybe they killed the lions. Male lions have zero tolerance for this kind of competition that gangs up against lionesses and kills lion cubs in the wild. The lion pounces on them with a snarl. With one swift bite, he crushes the neck of the first hyena.

The second one tries to escape with anguished yelps, but is locked in by the arena. The lion hunts it down and demolishes it with a crushing neck bite, shaking it viciously, as if it were a rat. It drops the dead hyena with a grimace of disgust, lifting its upper lips as if it finds the scavenger's taste appalling.

The lion's power fills everyone with awe. As it grimaces, the beast's massive canines are clearly visible to the spectators and to Jason. The lion killed the hyenas in seconds—what resistance can Jason offer to such a powerful predator?

The lion now identifies its human quarry. It starts walking slowly toward the four friends, stopping to sniff the footprints in the sand and the place where Jason was pinned down by Krato half an hour ago. The self-confident king of the jungle shows no signs of agitation or anger. Calmly, he sums up the situation with nose, eyes, and ears.

Then the lion looks up, its gaze fixed on Jason, who is nearest to him.

Jason's gladiator friends shout their encouragement and objections from the barred windows of their cells. They can see the whole drama, but can't do anything to help. Hercules prays out loud for God's mercy.

The locked iron gates rattle as Golla shakes them in frustrated anger, unable to help his friend. With his big, bass voice, Golla roars, "Kill him! Kill him! You can do it, Jason! Stab him! Kill the bloody beast!"

The lion turns his gaze in the direction of the noise, distracted for a while.

The crowd is furious. Women yell in rage. Men shout obscenities at the heartless emperor. Many spectators wave their fists at Nero, shouting on top of their voices.

Nero has overplayed his hand. He misjudged the compassion of his guests.

For the first time, Jason has the nauseating feeling that he will not survive. He will do his utmost to protect Tabitha, but his strength has been drained by Nero's relentless tests. Jason's determination to survive flickers like a dying candle. He swings between surrender and fighting to death. In desperation, he considers offering himself up to the lion, enabling the others to escape while the lion feeds on him.

He places himself into the hands of the Almighty: *Not my will, but your will be done, O God.* New power flows into his exhausted body and soul.

He decides to risk his life for Tabitha and his friends, putting up a brave fight with his last bit of energy. He stands his ground between them and the lion. He holds the broken spear firmly in his right hand. He will try to stab the beast in the ribcage when it is on top of him.

It strikes Jason—he, too, is a broken spear, powerless against the mighty lion. Broken spear? Bruised reed? What did Paul say? "...a bruised reed he will not break..."

For a moment, he glances back at Tabitha. He reads the pain of helpless agony and concern on her face. He lifts his hand to her in one last wave.

"Goodbye, my love ..." he whispers.

All his efforts to survive now hang on a spider's thread. Jason wonders, *Is this it? Is this my end? Have I prevailed over all the challenges for nothing?*

With an ominous growl, the lion makes a mock charge, stopping only a few paces from Jason. They stare into each other's eyes.

"Back off! Back off! Stop it!" Jason shouts in commanding voice, pointing the broken spear in the lion's direction with every command. The lion backs off a few paces while uttering short deep-throated grunts, the sound by which returning lions identify themselves to the pride.

Jason is surprised by the lion's reaction. However, he does not think the reprieve will last long. The next charge may be for real.

In awe, Jason observes the colossal head and mane of the magnificent animal, its massive paws, its penetrating yellow eyes…

Then, a tiny detail strikes him like a bolt from the blue.

Impossible! It can't be!

The lion has a black spot above its right eye.

Can it be Spotty?

If so, will the lion remember him after four years?

He has to try…

Jason goes down on his haunches, calling as he did long ago: "Hi, Spotty! How is my big boy? I'm Jason! Do you remember me, Spotty? Yes, Jason, Jason, Jason. Come, Spotty! Come! Come! Come!"

The lion hesitates. He has already sniffed Jason's footprints and sweat in the sand, detecting a scent he has smelled before. Deep inside his brain, a memory awakens. He lifts his head, sniffing the air for a clue. A light breeze swirls Jason's odor toward him. His sensitive nostrils detect the familiar scent of his beloved playmate. As Jason keeps calling, the lion's ears confirm the well-known voice. He gazes intensely at Jason. The tip of his tale swishes to and fro.

Then he clicks. With playful movements, he trots toward his friend. Jason stands up, ready for the worst. Instead of mauling Jason, the lion puts his large forepaws on Jason's shoulders and rubs his massive head against Jason's—as lions do when they greet each other. It looks as if the huge lion is hugging an old friend. Indeed, Jason is the best friend Spotty ever had. He has been longing for his human companion since Jason left so suddenly.

The crowd is stunned into silent awe. What is this? They can't believe their eyes. Lions don't behave like this in the arena! Usually, the starving animals kill and devour their victims in seconds. This lion's behavior is totally inexplicable and bizarre.

Then Spotty goes down on his side and allows Jason to rub his tummy and ears. Jason reassures him with the tone of voice he used when they played together in the Sudan. For a while, they are back in the jungle.

"Thank you, Jesus, for bringing Spotty to this place at this moment," Jason whispers. By God's grace, Jason's prayer turns arena into church, as Paul prophesized.

"Thanks, Spotty, for recognizing me," Jason adds, realizing God has been planning this moment since his journey to Sudan. God used Bari to send Spotty to Rome on time, and so Bari has unknowingly paid his debt to Jason for saving him and his daughters.

"Thank you, dear Jesus!" Tabitha sobs in relief and gratitude. She senses that Jason and the lion must know each other. Diana's mouth falls open in amazement. With hands on her cheeks she stares in disbelief at the incredible scene.

The spectators hold their breath, puzzled by the surprising behavior of the lion.

When they get over their amazement, they start cheering. Nero is completely at a loss, watching the new development with a sheepish grin. It turned out quite differently from what he had in mind. He had ten soldiers ready to storm into the arena and save Jason's life at the last moment. Nero realizes he could not have staged a greater surprise.

Jason and Spotty come and stand in front of Caesar's pavilion. With his left hand on Spotty's head, Jason raises his right arm in salute and bows to the emperor. Maybe his submissive posture will help Nero to do the right thing. Indeed, Jason is turning the other cheek to the man who condemned him to the hell of the arena.

Nero has one of his better moments. The cheers of his guests inspire him to be gracious—he craves adoration. He stands up with a smile of satisfaction, gestures for a fanfare of trumpets, and lifts his imperial baton in Jason's direction.

The crowd expects an important announcement. The cheering dies down.

Then, Nero says loud and clear: "Jason, on the grounds of your extraordinary performance, I declare you a free man!" The arena amplifies the emperor's voice.

The crowd burst out into jubilant cheering, showing their approval by throwing flowers into the arena. Nero got his wish, too: Diana receives her gift at the pinnacle of agony—in the arena, with a lion, and surrounded by her friends.

Nero is thrilled. He could not have orchestrated a grand finale that would bring him more spontaneous adoration. The emperor himself has been stunned by the unexpected turn of events and by the surprising reaction of the crowd. The callous crowd, who has become desensitized to cruelty and suffering, has suddenly been touched and inspired by the compassion among friends and the affection between man and lion.

Mercy has descended on the arena-church. Nero and Krato have granted Jason his freedom, and he has received the grace to forgive them for the wrongs of the past.

"Sire, what about him?" Jason asks, pointing to Spotty.

"He's yours!" Nero answers, adding softly, "He's no good for the arena."

Seeing the three friends helping each other touched a cord even in Nero's heart. He commands the physician and his helpers to carry Krato out on a stretcher and attend to his wounds.

Now, Jason and Diana have a chance to talk.

"From where did you come so quickly?" Jason wonders.

Knowing they have only a few minutes, Diana summarizes, "Nero uses my hostess business. Sometimes he invites me to sit with him at the arena. I urged him to test your spearing skills, instead of engaging you in close combat. I didn't want to see my friends kill each other." She starts sobbing. "Then he suddenly brought in his wicked ideas to give you hell!"

Together, they walk to Tabitha. Jason unties her hands, informing her about his friendship with the lion. When her hands are free, Tabitha throws her arms around Jason's neck.

They embrace and kiss with zeal. They have prevailed; they are free to go home.

Spotty senses he is among friends of Jason, and allows them to stroke his head. Without realizing it, Spotty is the hero of the day. When he recognized Jason and showed his affection, he prevented a grisly tragedy.

Whether Nero's heart of stone was softened by the brave fight Jason and Krato put up, or by Nero's affection for Diana, or by Akton's advice about his inventor, or by the unexpected affection between man and beast, or by the attitude of his guests, or maybe by all together, they will never know.

The fact is: Jason is a free man; he can go home!

Diana invites Tabitha and Jason to stay with her.

Jason walks Spotty back to the cells. He picks up the broken spear and stares at it for a moment. *With this spear, I subdued Krato and overcame two lions. I will keep the broken spear as a souvenir of my great victim victory—the day my war ended.* Paul said that a broken spear signals the war is over and peace has arrived. "Amen!" Jason whispers.

His fellow gladiators come out of their quarters and conclude the show with the usual war cry. Shaking his head in disbelief, Jason greets them jubilantly, laughing with joy. They cluster at Jason's right side, avoiding the lion on his left, congratulating him excitedly on his freedom.

Jason is overwhelmed by the sudden change of his circumstances: *One moment I was a doomed prisoner, the next a free, exuberant person! God is good, indeed!*

Another promise quoted by Paul springs to Jason's mind: *Commit your way to the LORD; trust in him and he will do this: He will make your righteousness shine like the dawn, the justice of your cause like the noonday sun.*[41]

---

41 Ps. 37:5-6 NIV

CHAPTER 16

Diana invites Jason and Tabitha to her apartment to have a refreshing bath and put on the clean clothes Tabitha brought with her from Corinth.

They relive and discuss their nerve-racking experience in the arena. They are amazed to hear how diverse their focal points, perceptions, and emotions were. Tabitha was appalled by the blood, and terrified of the hyenas. When Diana saw how easily the lion demolished the hyenas, she was paralyzed with fear. They cannot imagine how Jason survived that death-defying place, fighting for his life several times a week for the past eight months. Jason shares with them his hopelessness when he faced the lion and his immense relief when he and Spotty recognized each other. One thing the three friends had in common: the awareness of their togetherness and solidarity.

However, Jason is fed up with the arena. He is more interested to hear news from Corinth. It is the first news Jason has had since he saw Tabitha on the pirate ship. He is excited to hear about their son Victor, now eight months old and crawling all over the place. Tabitha left him in the excellent care of the two grandmothers.

She shares her love and concern with Jason, and her continuous prayer that God would work a miracle, freeing him from the arena. She kept on hoping that God, in his omnipotence, would open a way so the three of them may be together. Her prayer has been answered with a resounding *Yes*.

Diana does not mention her brush with royalty while Jason and Tabitha suffered one severe test after the other. Looking at Jason and Tabitha's happiness now makes Diana realize that despite their ordeals, they are better off than she is.

*

The next day, Diana and Jason visit Krato in hospital. Tabitha is not ready yet to face the man who brought so much trouble and suffering to her, Jason, and their families. For her, it will not be quick forgiveness but rather slow, gradual healing.

Krato's broken arm has been set and put in splints. His wounds have been disinfected and stitched. He receives medication for pain. Cleansed of blood splashes, he looks much better. He greets them gladly, though it's painful to move.

He describes his brush with death, "When that beast knocked me over like a feather, and I saw that colossal head, those large, penetrating, yellow eyes, and those massive canines in my face, hearing my bones being crushed, I knew I was looking at death…I knew it was over…I closed my eyes for the end. Then a miracle happened! When I opened my eyes I saw Jason's face—the person I believed to be my demon, changed into my angel. Thank you, Jason, thanks for saving my life, thanks for your forgiveness."

Jason explains, "Jesus forgave his executioners from the cross. It urges us to forgive others. Love achieves more than hate; forgiveness more than revenge."

"You must tell me about this Jesus someday. He must be a terrific guy," Krato says with a weak smile.

"He is indeed!" Jason confirms.

"Yes, I want to know more about him too," Diana interrupts.

"When you're ready," Jason promises, hoping that day will come soon.

He urges them to visit Corinth, "Though it will never be the same as in the old days, we can enjoy those times with new perspective."

*

When they have left Krato, Jason shares with Diana something that weighs heavily on his heart. He can't leave and just forget about the predicament of Hercules and Golla. He has to do something to secure their release.

Diana is his only link with the emperor. She tells him about Akton, and how Jason's invention helps Nero to win in the chariot races. Jason is amazed by the cruel irony—while Nero has been profiting from his invention in the Circus Maximus, he has been exposed to death repeatedly in Nero's arena. Maybe the moment of truth has come for the mighty emperor.

Diana contacts Akton, asking his advice. They decide to arrange a meeting between Nero, Diana, Akton, and Jason. It's a gamble, but if Nero is in a good mood, then something good may happen. Tabitha does not want to meet Nero, the man who condemned Jason to the arena, forcing him to face mortal danger repeatedly, and letting her suffer in agony for so long.

When Diana submits the request to the emperor, he is more than willing. Nero is curious to meet Jason. He is intrigued by his resilient survival skills. He also wants to hear how Jason got to know the lion, and how he got hold of the pirate ship. He grants Diana's request eagerly.

Nero gets more surprises than he hoped.

Jason tells about his visit to Africa where he cared for a lion cub that now saved his life. He summarizes the story about his kidnapping by the pirates, how he became the captain, and how he refurbished the ship into a security guard for freighters.

Nero is quite interested in the ramming device with which Jason and his crew sank a dozen pirate ships. He gives orders to release Jason's crew and *The Spear* in Caesarea so that they can continue with their good work. He hopes more entrepreneurs will follow Jason's example by equipping ships with the same ramming device so that they can act as security guards against the pirates.

"Sire, I have a confession to make. I lied to you to protect your interests," Akton suddenly chimes in. He hopes: *If I confess before Nero finds out for himself, I may be forgiven for protecting the secret.*

"That may cost you your life!" Nero reacts, lifting an eyebrow.

"Sire, I hope you will find my motive acceptable."

"It depends...go ahead."

"Sire, the reason for your winning in the circus is not due to wonder grease, but to the wonder bearings Jason invented. I have been using his invention with his consent. I lied to protect the secret."

"What are wonder bearings?" Nero asks, frowning with curiosity.

Jason explains how the rollers used to move heavy stones gave him the idea to place rollers around a wagon's axle to reduce friction.

"Jason, did you give Akton permission to use your invention?" Nero inquires.

"Yes, Sire. I gave Akton permission to produce the bearings for his own profit on the condition that he manufactures the bearings at cost price for my business in Cyrene. He fulfilled his part of the contract. I did not know about his deal with you, Sire, or about the false information."

"Interesting…" Nero wonders what to do.

He thinks aloud, "Akton, you did help me to regain my winning streak at the Circus Maximus. I can understand your motive for fabricating the lie about the grease. Jason, your invention has been the real secret of my success. Both of you should be rewarded."

Nero has made up his mind.

"Jason, on the grounds of insufficient evidence, I wrongly sent you to my gladiator school. You helped to make it a great success. In the mean time, your invention has secured my winning at the races. How can I compensate you for my unwitting mistake and for your brilliant response?" Nero asks, in a rare moment of honesty and realism.

"Sire, nothing will please me more than the release of my two friends, Hercules and Golla."

"Is there nothing you want for yourself?"

"Sire, I have already received what I desired: my freedom."

"Those two are my best gladiators. My school may lose its fame if I let them go!" Nero objects with a frown, searching for a solution.

"Sire, may I suggest a plan?" Jason wagers.

"Go ahead."

"Sire, I suggest you exempt Hercules from further fighting in the arena. Let him train someone for two months to take his place as leader. The elite group already knows the principles of success. It will be easy to drill newcomers into the team. For the tradition to live on, the success formula should be passed on continuously. When Hercules and Golla are released, the elite group will continue prospering."

"That's an excellent plan, Jason. You are an inventor indeed. I concur. Your request is granted." Nero sounds genuine, but who can trust such a wicked mind?

Before they go, Nero commands, "Akton, from now on you have to share your winnings from the races with Jason.

To ensure there's no cheating, I will tell my treasurer to send Jason's winnings by the same courier who delivers the army's monthly pay to Corinth. Of course, if any one of you lets out the secret, you will forfeit your winning money immediately. Understood?"

"Yes, Sire," both agree. The secret will go with them to the grave.

They leave the emperor with broad smiles and genuine gratitude. They have scored a great victory. The burdened have triumphed. However, Jason can't get rid of a lingering feeling of gloom. Though the marathon is over, he is too drained to celebrate.

*

Within a few days, Jason and Tabitha go by ship to Corinth. They take Spotty along in a cage. She is curious about Jason's plans for the lion.

"What are you going to do with a lion in Corinth—start a zoo?" Tabitha jokes.

"I want to return him to his native land," Jason responds. "I plan to rest and recover for a few months. The bruised reed has to heal. My ordeals probably have hurt my soul more than my body. To survive, I had to kill and wound many opponents. I have to make peace with God and myself about that. I feel like a war-weary soldier going home. I have seen too much blood, suffering, and death."

"He leads me beside quite waters, he restores my soul," Tabitha plants a seed.

"Yes, that's what I need—God's healing. When I have recovered, I will sail with Spotty to Alexandria where I will leave him in Faki's care. I will pay Faki and Bari to release him into the jungle, where he can be free. When I tell them what the fate of lions and victims in the arena is, they may reconsider their trade. I know Bari will respect my request. I saved him from death and his daughters from slavery."

"Shouldn't you do it immediately? I suppose a lion devours a lot of meat every day—with what are you going to feed him?" Tabitha tries to bring Jason back to reality.

"Lions are social cats. I can see Spotty yearns for my attention. I want to spend some time with him. Besides, he saved my life. I want to spoil him a little. I am going to build him a larger cage. He will feed on the carcasses of retired mules and oxen that I will buy from Corinth's transporters," Jason replies. "The winning money from Nero will help a lot. It's a windfall of the roller bearings I invented."

Tabitha rests her case. She expects that the public reaction to lion roars in Corinth will persuade Jason to advance the date of Spotty's return to Africa.

On their home voyage, they have intermittent rain, gusty wind, and choppy sea, but—thank God! —there are no gales, no shipwrecks, no pirates, no warships, and no Krato to mess up their lives. They are filled with immense gratitude and relief. Though emotionally drained, they feel empowered in their faith and companionship. They praise God over and over for the mercy bestowed on them amid their tribulations.

"If we could survive all these ordeals with God's grace, there is nothing we cannot handle with God's help," Jason concludes. "The trials have made us salted veterans." In silent reminiscence, scenes from the past few years flash through their memories.

"On my journey of faith, I think I have completed my twelve labors. I hope I can have a normal life from now on," Jason ponders.

When the rain stops for a while, they gaze over the gloomy scene, from the white-crested waves to the blue-grey clouds rolling by.

"A picture of our stormy lives," Tabitha remarks sourly.

"Maybe we will discover the purpose of it all later in life with the advantage of hindsight," Jason remarks. "At the moment, a few insights already come to mind."

"Such as…?" she probes.

"Realizing how precious life is," Jason says softly, but intensely. "Though I hate fights, I had to learn to survive in violent circumstances. Over time, the truth of my grandpa's words has become a practical reality: 'Don't allow anybody to rob you of your one precious life.' I now know what it really means."

"Yes, I suppose you do," Tabitha concurs, thinking of Jason's fight for survival on sea and in desert, jungle, and arena. "Anything else?" she inquires.

"Our commitment to Christ," Jason fills in. "In our struggles, we have made peace with God through Christ. Even if there were no other gains, this one is incomparable and will last for ever. Without Christ, I would have given up all hope."

"Absolutely!" Tabitha concurs, cuddling against Jason to avoid the breeze.

"Though the flame of my faith often flickered, I know today that my faith enabled me to persevere. Paul urged me to keep fighting for the good, to keep running the race of life, and to hold on to my faith in God. Sustained by God's love, I did!"

"His mercy *endures* forever!" [42]Tabitha quotes a well-known passage from the psalms. They hug, filled with thanksgiving in their hearts. By reviewing lessons learned, their views and mood start changing to the positive side.

"And you, sweetheart, what have you learned from our ordeals?" Jason asks, enfolding Tabitha in his arms and coat.

"The one lesson I have learned repeatedly is to wait on the Lord without fretting," Tabitha confesses with a sigh. "When the weeks and months rolled by without answers, I got impatient and rebellious. After each outburst, I had to ask forgiveness and surrender myself again to God's will at the foot of the cross."

---

42 Ps. 136:1

"It seems to me that while I fought against man and beast, you fought the devil himself," Jason concludes, hugging her with caring love.

After a while, Jason proceeds, "Another thing I noticed is that one phase prepared me for the next. If I had not gone through the African and pirate experiences, I would not have survived the brutal life of a gladiator. I had to learn the difference between turning the other cheek, and defending my precious, God-given life."

"Yes, I felt that too," Tabitha agrees. "I had to learn to take the tribulations one step at a time, and be grateful that God had not dumped them on me all at once."

"Something else that amazed me repeatedly is God's timing and planning," Jason continues. "You know, without any help from my side, God had the right things happen on the right time. At the right night, he brought us to Agizul's oasis so that we could help them survive the robber attack. God brought you and me back to Corinth at the right time for our commitment to Christ and to each other. He brought Paul and me to the same prison cell at the same time so that he could prepare me for the challenging life as a gladiator. God led Bari to send Spotty at the right time to Rome to save me in the arena. If it were another lion, I would have been killed."

"It is indeed amazing," Tabitha concurs, encouraged by Jason's insights. "What about the root problem that caused all the others: the rivalry between you and Krato?" Tabitha asks, knowing too well what fanned the flames.

"I have also learned a lot about the handling of injustice. The rivalry between Krato and me spawned many problems. Bullying, as well as revenge for it, bred nothing but problems. Helpful service, though, and nurtured friendships turned bad situations around to good ones. By God's grace, I could do a Joseph's deed wherever I went, even on a pirate ship and in a gladiator school. Despite the hardships, God made me a blessing to others."

"I admire you for that, Jason. God heard our prayers for you."

Jason takes Tabitha in his arms, looks into her eyes, and admits, "I also know our mutual love sustained me—even when everything looked hopeless. I cannot wait to see and hold our son, born from our love."

They kiss long and tenderly, relishing the touch of lips, the pulsing bodies, and the familiar fragrance—just as much as the first time it happened in Apollo Temple.

"I love you, Tabitha," Jason whispers with sincerity.

"Oh Jason, I'm so glad God spared your life. I love you!" Tabitha affirms.

Jason's thoughts wander off to his family. He wonders: *Has Tabitha talked about Christ to my parents? I hope they will become Christians too—if Isaac could, why not Dad?* Jason does not inquire. He will see for himself.

He remembers the chat with Isaac about circumcision: *Thankfully, that will not be necessary any more. Isaac was badly hurt financially when he chose Christ. Yet, he stayed the course. I hope his business has recovered.*

*

Jason and Tabitha could not send a message ahead. Letters go by ship, too, so they and the letter would have arrived at the same time.

Some people of Corinth have come by horse carriages to Lechaion to pick up passengers from the ship. Jason and Tabitha get a ride into town. He will ask Diana's dad to bring the caged Spotty home with one of his wagons.

They walk along Lechaion Road and over the *agora* to Isaac's shop. They take in the well-known scene with Acrocorinth towering to the south.

"Ah! This is home," Jason sighs with satisfaction.

Seeing Tabitha and Jason, overjoys Isaac. He throws his arms in the air, amazement and jubilation on his face.

"Is it true? Are you really home? Esther! Come! Look who's here!"

To keep herself occupied instead of brooding on their problems, Esther often helps Isaac in the shop. Irene and Esther take turns looking after Victor.

Esther comes from the back of the shop.

"Yes, Isaac, what's the matter?"

Then she sees Jason and Tabitha.

For a moment she freezes. Is this an omen? Is Jason dead? They have had so many disappointments, she doesn't want another.

Tabitha runs to her, arms stretched out, laughing, calling to her, "Mama, Mama!" Only when they embrace, the truth sinks in. It's not a dream or a vision.

Jason and Isaac join in. The four put their arms around one another. Jason jubilates: *Together at last—heaven on Earth! Thank God from whom all blessings flow!*

Tabitha cannot wait to show Jason their son.

They hurry to Jason's home. He gives his mother and sister a minute of hugging, while Tabitha enjoys her reunion with her baby. Proudly, she brings Victor to Jason.

"Look, Victor! Daddy has come home!"

Smiling, Victor waves his little hand at Jason and says, "Dada!"

Jason blooms with pride. He takes Victor from Tabitha, and rocks him gently on his arm, cooing, "My son! My son! Victor is a big boy!" Jason looked death in the face many times in order to relish this moment. Victor immediately takes to Jason, as if his daddy has been there all the time. Jason's natural feeling for children makes bonding with the bundle of love easy. Tabitha relishes the moment, seeing Jason play with their son. She has hoped and prayed for this day ever since she got pregnant. Now it is happening.

However, it feels unreal. Are the nasty times of murder charges, kidnapping by the pirates, and a brutal gladiator life really over? Is another calamity just around the corner?

Shivering, she sighs, *Please, dear Jesus, give us a break!*

When Philip comes home from work, he is stunned to see his son. They hug. Both are choked up, overwhelmed. They will talk later. The emotions are too near the surface now. They grew up with the Spartan philosophy that men don't cry.

Irene invites Tabitha's family over for supper. During the meal, they just enjoy each other's company. To be together, to experience the closeness, that is worth more than all the riches of the world.

Isaac lifts his chalice. With a broad smile, tears of gratitude twinkling in his eyes, he proposes a toast: "Jason, it's good to have you back. To life!"

"To life!" the others exuberantly affirm, lifting their chalices in victory.

Jason knows he could have been killed many times. The fact that he is alive, enjoying the company of loved ones again, is nothing less than a miracle.

"To a new life, for all of us!" He utters his deepest wish with a lump in his throat. He values his own life and the lives of those he loves more than ever. Facing death repeatedly has given him a new appreciation of life.

After supper, they start with the healing process, talking about what happened, step-by-step, from the day Toni was killed. They share their feelings—the whole mixed bag of shock, anger, fear, despair, yearning, disbelief, faith, hope, and love. Tears, laughs, and a somber replay of events in their imagination alternate as the sharing takes place.

They end the evening with thanksgiving. One by one, they thank God for his loving-kindness that led them to victory against the odds. Most of them can utter only a short sentence before choking up.

Tabitha volunteers to lead them in song. She chooses Psalm 23, which sustained her during the long months of yearning when Jason was gone.

¹ The LORD *is* my shepherd;
  I shall not want.
² He makes me to lie down in green pastures;
  He leads me beside the still waters.
³ He restores my soul.[43]

Right now, the turn of events feel unreal, too good to be true, as they are haunted by the fear that another catastrophe may strike soon. Despite the anxiety, they savor the joy of the moment and praise God from the heart.

*

On the first Sunday, all three families are at church in the theater. Yes, Tabitha has conquered Jason's family for Christ, first by her example, then by telling them what she knew about Jesus.

It's a great day. Philip, Irene, and Helena are baptized as mature members of the church. As a child of the Covenant, Victor receives the sign of God's grace. Jason and Tabitha partake with immense joy and gratitude. Their cups overflow indeed. On their request the congregation professes the first part of Psalm 103 in unison, saying each line after the leader:

¹ Bless the LORD, O my soul;
  And all that is within me, *bless* His holy name!
² Bless the LORD, O my soul,
  And forget not all His benefits:
³ Who forgives all your iniquities,
  Who heals all your diseases,
⁴ Who redeems your life from destruction,
  Who crowns you with lovingkindness
  and tender mercies,
⁵ Who satisfies your mouth with good *things,*
  So that your youth is renewed like the eagle's.[44]

43 Ps. 23:1-3
44 Ps. 103:1-5

By hard experience, Jason has learned: *The impossible is possible with God. All things work together for good to those who love God. My faith has been empowered by trials and tribulations, just as kneading and baking turn dough into bread, and pruning makes the tree lush and fruitful. However, surviving my ordeals should inspire thanksgiving, not incite bragging rights.*

*

Time flies. After a few months, Spotty has been returned to the wild in Africa. Being in his prime, he may become king of a pride and father many cubs. Maybe one of them will have a black spot on its face.

Jason persuaded Tabitha to pray for the ability to forgive Krato for the suffering he brought on them. As she asks for the grace to forgive, her bitterness is slowly fading.

Several months later, Diana and Krato visit Corinth.

The first day they spent with family. However, they can't wait to chat with Tabitha and Jason. When they do, they admire their joy, and adore Victor, who now runs around on wobbly legs. Tabitha realizes her attitude toward Krato has improved.

Diana shares with them her growing guilty feelings about her business: "All too often, some of the girls get unwanted pregnancies or contract venereal diseases. I feel that I get rich from their misery," she confesses, with a deep sigh. Gazing down on her restless hands, she admits, "My business is nothing but prostitution in disguise."

Krato nods, clears his throat, and adds, "I realize my tough pose was just a smokescreen to hide my true feelings. I'm sorry, Jason and Tabitha, for all the misery I caused you. For me it was a game—a stupid, cruel power-game. I just could not allow Jason to overtake me. When it happened, my humiliation turned into rage. However, it all changed in a moment when that lion mauled me in the arena. He scared all the bravado out of me. He changed my life. He ripped the façade away and revealed my real self."

"Jason was also saved by lions," Tabitha muses. "Your lion freed him from the stupid rivalry; the lion of Sudan saved him from a hopeless situation in the arena; and the Lion of Judah saved us from hell."

Diana grabs the opportunity, "That's what we want to discuss with you—salvation. We visited a church in Rome and liked what we saw. However, we feel the need to be introduced to Christ by people we know and trust."

Making eye contact with Jason and Tabitha, Diana asks, "Please tell us more about Jesus. How did you come to know him, how did your faith survive during those testing times, and how have you become victorious victims?"

"Well, it's a long story," Jason responds, taking a deep breath. He knows the pain of revisiting his experiences. However, as he has learned in his family, sharing his story brings recovery to himself and salvation to others.

The spear of animosity is broken. The healing of reconciliation has begun.

***

~ ~ ~ ~ ~ ~ ~ ~ ~ ~

[17] Therefore, if anyone is in Christ, he is a new creation;
the old has gone, the new has come!
[18] All this is from God,
who reconciled us to himself through Christ
and gave us the ministry of reconciliation.[45]

~ ~ ~ ~ ~ ~ ~ ~ ~ ~

---

45 2 Cor. 5:17-18 NIV

APPENDIX

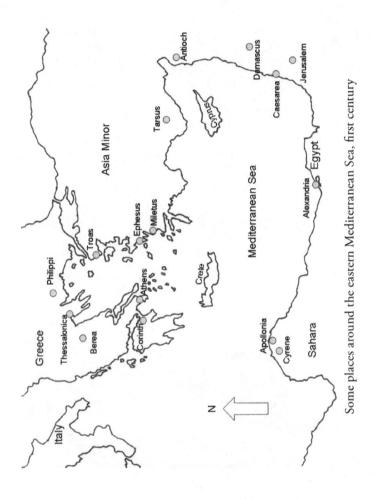

Some places around the eastern Mediterranean Sea, first century

Greece Mainland and Peloponnesus.
NASA Photo, Public Domain.
(Markers and names inserted by author).

Isthmus of Corinth. Public Domain. Suggested Credit: NASA/GSFC/METI/ ERSDAC/JAROS, and U.S./Japan ASTER Science Team. (Diolkos line, markers, and names inserted by author).

Jacob M. Van Zyl

Ancient Corinth. Remains of Apollo Temple against Acrocorinth background. (Photo by author). For more photos of Corinth go to www.messiahstudy.net

Ancient Corinth: Remains of shops, Apollo Temple in background. (Photo by author).

Jacob M. Van Zyl

Remains of the Bema (Judgment Seat) in ancient Corinth, against Acrocorinth background. Acts 18 describes how the Apostle Paul was dragged by the Jews to this very place and accused of inciting unrest. (Photo by author).

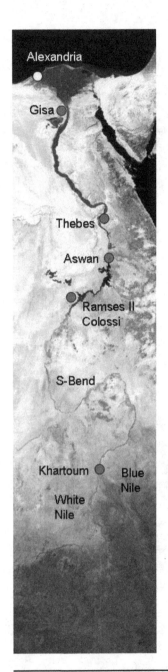

The River Nile
in Sudan and Egypt.
NASA composite photo.
Public domain.
(Markers and names
inserted by author).

Jacob M. Van Zyl